DOLPHIN SUNRISE

Also by Elizabeth Webster:

DOLPHIN SUNRISE

Elizabeth Webster

St. Martin's Press
New York

For Neil
who knows eternity's sunrise

Library of Congress Cataloging-in-Publication Data

Webster, Elizabeth.
     Dolphin sunrise / Elizabeth Webster.
         p.   cm.
     ISBN 0-312-09276-8
     I. Title.
PR6073.E2312D65   1993
823'.914—dc20   93-21744
                                                                              CIP

First published in Great Britain by Souvenir Press Ltd.

First U.S. Edition: June 1993
10 9 8 7 6 5 4 3 2 1

CONTENTS

He who binds to himself a joy
Does the wingéd life destroy,
But he who kisses the joy as it flies
Lives in eternity's sunrise.
William Blake

PART I

JOY AS IT FLIES

It was the smell of smoke that woke him. He sat for a moment where he was, head on arms, slumped across the table where he had been working. Fallen asleep again, he thought. So much for revision . . . His books made hard lumps under his arms, and he felt stiff and bleary. To hell with exams . . . What time was it? How long had he been asleep? . . . And had the Farleys come in yet, or was he still supposed to be listening out for the kids upstairs?

He had heard his mother and Len slam out of the house earlier on, after the usual shouting and smashing match. They'd have gone down to The Green Man, he supposed. They usually did, after a row. But the Farleys? . . . They were quieter than his Mum or Len. And much more reliable. They had said they'd be in by eleven. What time was it now?

He looked at his watch. Half ten. So they wouldn't be back yet. Maybe he'd better check on the kids. And that smoke. He knew his Mum and Len smoked like chimneys — always had. But if they were out, where was it coming from? Surely the kids upstairs wouldn't be trying anything funny? . . . Come to think of it, the smell wasn't exactly like tobacco — or pot either . . . More like . . . What was it like?

He sprang to his feet. What was the matter with him? His brain seemed to be functioning at half speed. He knew quite well what that smoke smelled like . . . It smelled like burning foam cushions . . . It smelled like fire.

He went to the door and opened it cautiously. At once a billowing cloud of acrid smoke began to pour into the room, curling up the stairs from below. He couldn't see any flames anywhere, but the lower floor was thick with dense black smoke and the fumes were rising towards him in a choking pall. The living room door was shut, but he could see the dark fingers of lethal vapour creeping out from underneath it in ever-increasing volume.

'Mum?' he shouted. 'Len? . . . You in there?'

There was no answer. But now he could hear an ominous

3

crackling sound from within that closed door, as if wood was alight somewhere and flames were already beginning to take hold.

'Mum?' he shouted again. But it was obvious they weren't there. They must have gone off to the pub, as he thought, and left a cigarette burning somewhere. The idiots.

Then he thought of the kids upstairs. I'm the idiot, he said. Must get them out. Of course. Now. Before that thing down there takes hold. How long have I got, I wonder? And what am I doing here, standing gawping and wasting time?

He raced up the stairs to the flat above. Then raced down again, cursing his stupidity, to fetch the key that the Farleys had left with him.

The smoke was getting thicker and making him choke. He seized a towel and wrapped it round his nose and mouth, and charged up the stairs again.

The kids were all asleep. He had a job to rouse them. Danny, the oldest, lay sprawled in a tangled heap with Jampy, the two-year old, curled up in a ball inside the shelter of one outflung arm. Donna, who was seven and sensible, had the baby, Kirsty, cradled in a careful embrace.

'Wake up!' hissed Matthew, shaking them. 'Come on. Wake up! You've got to get out of here. *Wake up!*'

Drowsily, they climbed out of the abyss of sleep and looked at him with round, startled eyes.

'Come on!' he said again. 'Danny, get all the towels you can. Dowse them in the sink. Donna, get some nappies and wet those . . .'

Scolding and pushing, he got them up, draped them in wet towels and dragged them out of the bedroom on to the stairs.

When they saw the smoke Danny and Donna looked at Matthew with a flick of fear, but they did not scream. They were much too disciplined for that. The Farleys were fairly tough parents, Matthew knew. Tough but kind. And not totally feckless and violent like his Mum and Len. They would never leave a lighted cigarette burning in a room full of foam-filled furniture . . .

'Come *on*,' he urged, repeating it yet again. 'Never mind the smoke. We'll get down somehow.'

But as he spoke there was a whoosh of hot air from below, and his mother's living room door fell outwards in a spurt of flame.

He looked down in horror. He could never get the kids

4

through that. They'd fry. 'Into my room!' he shouted. 'You'll have to go out of the window. Like Batman. It'll be fun.'

The children obeyed him instinctively. Matthew knew what he was doing. But *fun*?

'We'll tie the sheets together,' he said, pushing them into his room and as far from the smoke as possible. 'We're only two storeys up. You'll manage easily.'

He seized his bottom sheet, realizing as he did so that the duvet on top was a dead loss. Have to get some more sheets off the kids' beds. Fool. Why didn't he think of it before?

'Tie this end to the leg of my bed,' he told Danny. 'Won't be long.'

He dashed upstairs, fighting now through even denser smoke and a rising heat from the flames below, seized some more sheets, and plunged recklessly down the stairs again, eyes streaming and breath coming in painful gasps in spite of the wet cloth round his mouth.

He saw, glancing down, that the flames were already reaching the bottom stairs. Once they took hold, the stairwell would act like a funnel. They'd never get out.

'Quick!' he said, and began knotting the sheets together with clumsy hands. 'Donna, you go first with Kirsty.'

Donna looked at the sheet-rope doubtfully and clutched the baby more tightly in her arms. Matthew saw her hesitate, and knew why.

'I'll tie her on, then she can't fall, and you'll have your hands free. Hold the sheet and slide down. Understand?'

Donna simply nodded and waited while Matthew tied the baby on to her back with another bit of sheet. Kirsty wasn't yelling yet. She seemed to think the excitement was all a big game, and gave Matthew a dewy, toothless smile as he strapped her into place like a papoose. Then he shoved the bed leg hard against the wall below the window and hoped desperately that the sheets would hold. He checked Danny's knots again. They seemed firm enough.

'Go on,' he urged, and leaned out of the window to look at the dangling sheet-rope before helping Donna to clamber over the sill. It was dark outside, but to his surprise he could see heads craning upwards from the pavement below. The neighbours had come out. That must mean the fire had really taken hold — it must be visible outside. The flats were part of the terrace anyway. The other houses would be at risk.

'Help her down!' he yelled. 'Someone ring the brigade!'

5

He watched Donna and the smiling baby disappear down the dark house wall. Were the sheets long enough? . . . There weren't any more up here. Danny was more agile. He could probably jump the last few feet. But Jampy? He was only two and his legs were very short. On a sudden impulse, he seized the thick duvet off his bed and flung it out of the window. It might be something to land on. Softer than the pavement anyway.

'Quick!' he said to Danny. 'Now you and Jampy!'

Behind him there was another ominous whoosh of hot air, and he saw the flare of flames rushing up the stairs outside his door. Fool! he thought. First rule of a fire. Shut the doors! And he rushed over, almost as fast as the flames came towards him, and tried frantically to slam his door against them. But he was too late. A wall of fire seemed to belly out at him through the doorway, and the wooden door simply blackened and buckled before his eyes and then suddenly crackled into edges of flame as well.

No good wasting time on that. He ran back to Danny and Jampy by the window. At least he could get them out. But the smoke was now appallingly thick and acrid, and he found the two-year-old slumped in a heap on the bed, with Danny furiously shaking him and crying: 'Jampy! Wake up!' He looked up in terror as Matthew bent over them. 'Is he dead?'

'Of course not. It's the smoke. We've got to get him out to the air fast, that's all. I'll —' He glanced round in despair. Nothing left to tie him on with. But wait. He could tie the small boy's hands together with his own shirtsleeves and then sling him round Danny's neck like a sack. Wildly, he flung off his own shirt and knotted the sleeves round the two-year-old's thin wrists.

'Put him round your neck. Fireman's lift,' he instructed. 'That's it. Very professional. *Quick!*' He didn't say "the fire's coming." He didn't need to. Already the doorway was alight, and he suddenly noticed that the floorboards were getting too hot to stand on.

'Hold on tight!' he said, and heaved Danny out of the window, with Jampy hanging round his neck like a limp rag doll. He hoped he wouldn't be too heavy for Danny — but there was nothing else he could do.

As Danny's head disappeared from view, the floor beneath Matthew's feet suddenly exploded in a roar of falling ceiling and splintering boards, and a whole new line of flames began

6

springing upwards through the cracks. The knotted sheet on the bed-leg began to smoulder before his eyes.

'Oh my God,' he muttered, and rushed back to the window, grabbing the sheet in his hands to stop it giving way before Danny got down. The thing seemed to be holding so far. But the flames were getting closer, and the heat was getting unbearable. Suddenly he felt the thin sheet give behind him and begin to run through his hands. He tried to brace himself against the window frame and hold on, but he only succeeded in slowing its progress a little, and the cloth was already burning as it reached his hands. He clung on, eyes shut and streaming, until he heard a shout from below. He supposed they were down safely. It was just as well, for by now the sheet-rope was a charred ruin his end and had slipped through his burnt hands out of the window. His feet were burning too now. Got to get out fast.

But how? The rope — such as it was — had gone. There was nothing left to hang on to now. His bed was alight. Even his hair felt scorched, and the bottoms of his jeans were smouldering. Also, the smoke was making him stupid.

He climbed out on to the window ledge and sat there, looking down. The ring of faces was still there, and a torch or two glimmered palely up at him, while a bit further away under a streetlight he could see two men struggling with a ladder. No time for that. No time at all.

'Jump!' shouted a voice. 'Jump, son! We've got a sheet. We'll catch you.'

Jump, he thought. Yes, that's it. Jump. Maybe if I hang on to the window ledge and slide down it won't seem so far . . . But the window ledge was now too hot to hold on to, and he could see flames below him even outside the house, spurting out through the downstairs windows.

No, I'll have to jump, he told himself. No time for anything else. No time to be frightened. Jump!

He jumped.

There was a rush of air on his face. His hair seemed to stand on end. Then there was a sickening teeth-jarring thud and a white flash of pain.

His last thought was: The fools! They didn't hold the sheet tight enough! Then the world seemed to turn in a shower of sparks and clanging bells and go suddenly dark.

7

★ ★ ★

There were voices somewhere in the dark. Only, it wasn't dark any more. It was unbearably light. So light that it hurt his eyes even though they were closed, and it hurt his eyelids too. They felt stiff and naked under the light and he wanted to cover them with his hands. Only, he found that he couldn't move his hands. They seemed to be strung up in some sort of cage . . . The voices hovered over him, rising and falling, sometimes near and sometimes far. He could only catch snatches of words but they didn't make sense.

' . . . some shock as well.'

Shock? As well as what?

'No need . . . yet.'

Yet?

'Not extensive, no . . . Hands . . . '

Hands? He couldn't move his hands. He tried, and fierce sharp agonies seemed to shoot through them. Why?

' . . . and feet. But the fractures will give them time . . . '

Time. For what? He tried to move his feet. Nothing happened. They seemed to be held in some sort of heavy vice. He tried again, but the effort made his face hurt. It seemed just as stiff and unworkable as his eyelids. Stiff and fiery.

Fiery? Suddenly, he remembered. He knew what had happened — and this was the result. Well, he was alive, wasn't he? Just.

He struggled to open his eyes, and a sort of croak came out of his mouth. It was supposed to be words, but he found that words were extraordinarily difficult to catch somehow. He tried again.

'Kids . . . ?'

'They're safe, Matthew. All safe. Thanks to you.'

His eyelids would not open. They seemed to be stuck. He sighed. 'Oh . . . good.'

'Coming round . . . another shot,' murmured a voice — a rather commanding voice.

'Just a little prick,' said someone else — a gentler voice this time. 'Don't try to move yet. It will hurt.'

He had discovered that already. So he lay still, and presently he floated off again into the merciful dark.

The next time, he did manage to get his eyes open a crack, and he found himself looking at his own legs strung up on a pulley in front of him. He seemed to be in a sort of open sideward on his own, but he could just see the ordinary long hospital ward stretching away beyond him.

He turned his head a little, and met the eyes of a young and friendly nurse who was bending over him. They were blue eyes, concerned and kind, and they posed no threat.

'Feeling better?'

'Yes.'

'Up to visitors?'

His heart gave a curious lurch of fear. What visitors? He didn't want his mother and Len arguing the toss all round his bed. Or coming here drunk or something. They'd be sure to make some kind of scene. They always did.

'What visitors?'

The blue eyes seemed to grow a little wary. 'There are plenty of people who want to see you. Bit of a hero, you know.' She saw his reluctance and added gently: 'We'll have to ration you.'

The first to come were the Farleys. Not his mother and Len. He breathed a silent sigh of relief, and tried to make his stiff face smile.

Madge Farley cried all over him and called him 'You poor boy', and gasped out halting words of undying gratitude. It was unlike her to be gushing. She never was under normal circumstances. Jim Farley just stood there, looking red in the face, and growling: 'Good lad . . . good lad, Matt . . . ' from time to time between Madge's outbursts.

Matthew was vaguely surprised at all this, but at last he managed to get a word in edgeways and asked: 'What about Jampy?'

He was fond of Jampy, somehow. He didn't know quite why. The two-year-old was a menace, really — tough and independent, usually in some scrape or other, and always asking questions, particularly about knobs and buttons. He adored Matthew's computer . . . Well, that was gone now, he supposed, like everything else . . . A melted heap.

'Jampy's fine.' It was Jim Farley speaking. 'A bit smoked, mind. Makes a good kipper.' He grinned at Matthew's anxious face.

'Oh good.' It seemed inadequate for what he felt, but there it was. Words seemed altogether too difficult to manage.

Matthew supposed it was the painkillers, but he kept seeing the faces before him in flashes of startling clarity. Madge's was usually tight and scraped-looking, what with the four kids to look after and a part-time cleaning job in the evenings when

9

Jim got home. Her brown eyes usually looked flat and sharpish, and her nose got thin and sharp too, as she got more overworked and tired. So did her chin, while her pale mouth got clamped tight and looked grimmer and grimmer . . . But now the pebble eyes were bright with tears, the pulled-back hair had escaped in straggling wisps round her face and her mouth was actually trembling. Her whole face looked softer, somehow, and more vulnerable — almost naked, and it shocked him.

As for Jim — he was always big and silent, and often red in the face with the effort of trying to communicate. He was not a talkative man at the best of times. Now, his faded blue eyes seemed almost puzzled by something — as if they could not think how to express what he felt, and the wide, generous mouth was slightly open, as if it didn't know whether to laugh or cry.

'It was nice of you to come,' said Matthew politely, trying to dispel Jim's look of silent stress.

This innocent remark produced another tide of tears in Madge, and she began to babble something about 'when we've got everything, and you —'

But here Jim cut in sharply with one warning word: 'Madge!' — and to Matthew's surprise, the two of them looked at each other in distress and then hurried away, promising to come again tomorrow.

'Bring the kids,' called Matthew, after Madge's retreating back. 'I'd like to see they're all in one piece.'

She nodded, and gulped a little, and fled.

Matthew was mystified. But he was tired now, so he forgot Madge's gulps and Jim's anguished blue stare, and drifted into a doze.

The next thing that happened was a kind of commotion outside in the corridor, with a lot of people jostling and pushing, and then a camera crew burst in backwards, and a foxy face was thrust close to his.

'How did you feel, Matthew,' said the face, 'when you saw the house going up in flames?'

'Hot,' said Matthew.

The gimlet eyes seemed to blink.

'And how does it feel —' began the persistent voice again, 'to be on your own . . . ?'

But before Matthew could even think of replying, Sister came up to his bed and crisply ordered foxy-face out of the room. He went, protesting volubly, and his camera crew went with him — still backwards.

Matthew dozed again. But something was bugging him. *On your own . . . How does it feel to be on your own? . . .* And come to think of it, why had it been the Farleys who came first? . . .

He opened his eyes and called the little nurse. 'I want to see Sister.'

He thought the concerned blue eyes looked scared for a moment, but then they cleared and she smiled at him and hurried away.

'Why hasn't my mother been to see me?' he asked, wasting no time.

The question seemed to hover in the air between them. Then Sister spoke hesitantly: 'I'm afraid she can't.' She moved starched skirts, as if to hurry away. 'I'll get the doctor to explain.'

'They're dead, aren't they?' he said dully. 'That's why. They're dead.'

Sister did not answer. But presently a grave young doctor came and sat down by his bed.

'I thought they were out,' said Matthew, in a voice of growing horror. 'I *heard* them go out.'

'They were asleep, Matthew.'

'But I called — I called and called.'

'I'm sure you did.' The serious, assessing eyes were kind. 'It was much too late then, you see. They'd have been unconscious by then — or even dead. The smoke would have killed them.' He leaned forward and laid a friendly hand on Matthew's shoulder. 'They wouldn't have felt a thing, you know. They just — never woke up.'

'I thought they were out . . . ' Matthew repeated, like a sleep-walker.

'You did everything you could,' said the young doctor, suddenly filled with sympathy for this shock-ridden fifteen-year-old. 'More than most people would dare to do. You saved four young lives, after all.'

'You don't understand,' said Matthew. But it was hopeless to explain. How could he say: I didn't like them. Not either of them. They were always drunk and always fighting. They were a dead loss as parents. *But I never wished them dead.* 'You don't understand,' he repeated, and slow, shameful tears began to drip out of his eyes.

11

* * *

After that, a whole lot more people came to see him. There was a friendly young policewoman who was quiet and patient and took down a careful statement. There was a woman from the Welfare who tried to ask questions in a soothing voice that put his teeth on edge. There was someone from the Insurance who didn't make any sense at all and got shooed away by Sister, and there was Foxy-Face who tried to get in again. And someone else from Pimlico Council, but Sister shut him up, too.

But one day the Farley kids came on their own after school — Donna carrying the baby who was still smiling, and Danny holding firmly on to Jampy who wanted to know why Matthew's legs were strung up to the ceiling, and what all the knobs and bells and radio-headphones were behind his bed. He was glad to see the kids. Somehow, their sturdy unconcern made him feel better. He was sick of all those hushed voices and sympathetic glances. He was dying for some practical common sense.

'Where are you all living?' he asked suddenly, realizing all at once that they had lost their home too, and all their possessions.

'Bed and breakfast,' said Donna, in a matter-of-fact and absurdly adult tone. She made a face at Matthew and added: 'Till the Council gets us a new flat.'

Matthew nodded. 'Is it OK?'

'Not bad.' She still sounded flat and off-hand. 'But Mum hates it.'

'Can't swing a cat in it, she says,' agreed Danny.

'Swing a cat!' echoed Jampy, running round in circles by Matthew's bed.

Danny grabbed him, and turned back to Matthew with a hard and challenging stare. 'When you comin' out then?'

Matthew tried to shrug, but it was a mistake. 'When I can walk, I s'pose.'

'Better getta move on, then.'

Jampy was still jumping up and down. 'Getta move on!' he chanted. 'Getta move on!'

Donna was looking at Matthew as if weighing up something in her mind. 'Mum says we're all going to the sea,' she announced. 'Soon as you're ready.'

Matthew stared at her. 'The sea?'

'Getta move on!' chanted Jampy.

12

And Kirsty, the baby, smiled and smiled.

* * *

It took him all of six weeks to escape from the hospital. During that time, they took the cages off his burnt hands and the traction pulleys off his broken legs and taught him to walk again. It was a slow and somewhat painful process, and he got very cross with his own clumsiness. They gave him a walking iron on one leg and a pair of crutches, and told him he must keep the other leg off the ground for longer because it was a multiple fracture and his burnt foot was still not quite healed. So he learnt to swing himself along in a lopsided fashion, and tried not to fall over too often.

They might have let him go at this stage, but they didn't, and Matthew wondered vaguely if they kept him longer than necessary because they didn't know what to do with him. In truth, the doctors were worried about the boy — the effects of the fire seemed to have left him curiously flat and weary. Since the news of those two unnecessary deaths in the house blaze, he had been very quiet — very silent and withdrawn, Sister told them. He only seemed to light up when the four rescued kids came to see him — and that not for long.

Then there was the problem of the boy's future. He was, it seemed, now an orphan, and totally alone in the world, unless the Welfare people could come up with a distant relation somewhere. In the meantime, where was he to go? And was he fit to go anywhere?

The doctors talked of delayed shock and a natural exhaustion, but they did not like Matthew's closed white face, his docile acceptance of idleness, and his silence. So they did not let him go. Not yet.

At last, however, Madge Farley announced that the neighbours had all clubbed together, and someone had offered them all a free caravan on a site in Cornwall, and she was only waiting for the doctors to release Matthew. So what were they going to do about it?

They debated among themselves, admitted that some sea air might do him good, and swimming would be ideal for his legs. They thought they might let him go if he would report to the local hospital for physiotherapy once a week. But then one of the doctors remembered that there was an Aqua-Surf Club in that area, and it would have its own physiotherapist and swim-

13

ming instructor to give Matthew all the right exercises on the spot, so he agreed to write a letter and fix it up.

At this point, Madge Farley lost patience, and put her hands on her hips and looked the doctors up and down with a stern and beady eye.

'Satisfied?'

They nodded, though somewhat doubtfully.

'Well then, what are we waiting for?'

★ ★ ★

So there they all were, at the sea. It was early autumn by now, and the days were mild and sunny. The sea, they told him, was as warm as it would ever get round these rugged Cornish shores. The caravan was set a little apart from some others on a site among grassy dunes above the sea, but they could walk down from it across a sloping sandy cliff to the beach. Matthew found the caravan steps a bit tricky at first, but they gave him a tent of his own and he only had to negotiate the steps for meals. At first the walk to the sea seemed over long, especially over the shifting dunes, but he soon got used to it.

The beach itself was a long, curved stretch of flawless sand, and the surf pounding on it was simply beautiful. But Matthew knew, sadly, that he couldn't hope to stand up in those magnificent waves, let alone ride them like the surfers. He could only stumble along on his stiff, ungainly legs, and look at the sea from a safe but craven distance.

The kids scampered and shouted in front of him, and Madge and Jim Farley plodded on behind with rugs and towels and orange squash and piles of sandwiches. For them it was the holiday of a lifetime — they had never been able to afford one before — and they were determined to enjoy every minute of it, sunburn and sandflies and all.

But for Matthew it was all strange and dream-like, and he seemed to see the world through glass, as if he was on the other side and could not reach it.

The sea seemed real, though. Deep and dark, heaving and churning, blue-black and glass-green . . . But you could penetrate *that* glass, you could swim in it and be part of it . . . He longed to swim. To escape the heavy drag of his legs, the gritty sand that was too soft to walk in, the bright day, the heedless, smiling world that went on turning, when he had sent two equally heedless people to a fiery death and made no move to help them . . . It would be cool in the water, he could sink under the waves and lie floating in the arms of the wide sea swell, he could swim and swim until he was tired, and forget his own clumsy limbs, his heavy body, and his guilt.

'Are you Matthew?' said a voice, breaking into his dream.

He looked up. The man standing before him was young and smiling, with tawny gold hair that clung in wet tongues round his head, and very blue, far-seeing eyes in a tanned, wind-scoured face. He was carrying a surf-board under one arm, and rivulets of sea-water were running down his gleaming wet-suit on to the sand.

'I'm Skip,' he told him, holding out his other hand in friendly welcome. 'At least, they call me that because I run the Club. I've been looking out for you.'

'Have you?' Matthew took the proffered hand. It was cool and firm, and seemed to generate strength and confidence.

'Come along, I'll introduce you to the others.' He was leading Matthew across the wet sand towards a dark line of rocks at one end of the bay.

'Now, just listen to me before we meet the boys,' ordered Skip, suddenly sounding serious. 'No surfing for you — not yet. It's much too dangerous for damaged legs.' His smile was warm and encouraging as he turned his head to glance at Matthew. 'But swimming off the rocks is OK. If you *can* swim, that is?'

'Oh yes,' assured Matthew. 'I was fairly good — before.'

Skip nodded, not wasting time on commiseration. Matthew was grateful for that. 'You can slip into fairly deep water from the rocks. None of that staggering about in the shallows with the surf knocking you down.' He cocked an observant eye in Matthew's direction. 'Round the point, it's a bit more sheltered. Keep to calm water until you're stronger. Understand?'

'Yes,' agreed Matthew humbly. It made sense, after all.

'There's a heated pool at the Club where you'll do your physio exercises. I'll see you through those.' Once more he paused, assessing Matthew's confidence with a practised eye. 'And I'll swim with you the first couple of times in the sea, just to make sure you don't get cramp or something.' He added, to Matthew's protesting face: 'These are dangerous waters. Mustn't be stupid. It puts other people's lives at risk.'

Matthew nodded, chastened.

But then Skip's extraordinarily sweet smile came out like the

15

sun. 'Right. Lecture over. Come and meet the boys, and we'll fix you up with a wet suit.'

The boys — who seemed to be mostly young men of about Skip's age, with a couple of younger ones who were called First-timers — greeted Matthew cheerfully. They didn't comment on his legs, or seem to know anything about the fire and his subsequent media notoriety, and for this he was thankful. He had got very wary of people's approaches and their motives since the persistent persecution of Foxy-face. Here, it seemed, he was unknown and would be accepted for what he was — a boy who wanted to swim. This they understood, and made room for him with instant friendliness.

'Seals come in sometimes,' volunteered one.

'Seals?' Matthew looked startled.

'Grey seals — out there.' A brown hand pointed towards the distant line of rocks round the point.

'You can get quite close,' agreed someone else. 'They're quite happy unless you splash too much.'

'And unless the virus gets to them,' growled Skip, shading those sea-blue eyes with a salty hand. His voice sounded curiously proprietorial and anxious. Clearly, the little seal colony was yet another of his responsibilities.

Matthew looked out to sea. He thought there were small heads bobbing about among the waves close to the rocks, but he couldn't be sure.

'Here,' said Skip, holding out a limp rubber wet-suit. 'Try this for size.'

★ ★ ★

There began for Matthew a time of painful enchantment. The sea was always there, beckoning and calling — and he was always trying to keep up with Skip or one of the other Aqua-club members who had been appointed to watch over him. His legs hurt and his back ached, and tears of frustration mingled with the salt sea spray, but he loved every moment of it — even the pain — and he couldn't keep away.

Sometimes he just idled, floating and drifting, gazing up at the sky, watching the sea birds wheel and glide above him, feeling the lift and fall of the ocean like a gentle supporting hand under his tired limbs. Sometimes Skip gave him a snorkel and he turned on his face and lay looking down through trans-lucent depths of green and gold to fronds of floating weed, the

16

waving fronds of anemones, small darting fish and pale shells lying on the silvery sands washed by a thousand tides . . .

Once or twice the dark bobbing head of a seal came up through a wave to have a look at him, and then disappeared again under the next sea swell. None of them came very near, but he caught occasional glimpses of a dark, lissom shape turning and diving in the emerald water of the little bay beyond the rocks.

One day there was a storm, the seals retreated to their own sheltered rocks, and Matthew was not allowed to swim. Instead, he took the four kids along to the beach shop for ice-creams (feeling a little guilty about neglecting them), and then settled down to help them build an elaborate fort with a moat in the wet sand just above the tide-line.

'Where's your shiny suit, then?' asked Donna, who clearly thought Matthew was rather splendid in his borrowed gear.

He grinned at her. 'Wouldn't give it me today. Too rough.'

'Shiny suit,' said Jampy, jumping up and down and ruining his own sand castle.

'Look out, you clot,' yelled Danny, saving his battlements from imminent disaster. 'Now look what you've done!'

'Shiny suit!' repeated Jampy, still dancing in the sun and paying no heed at all to the ruin beneath his small brown feet.

Madge looked across at them from the safety of her deck chair and wind-breaker, and then turned to smile at Jim. They seemed happy enough, the kids — and Matthew was already beginning to look better. But she could not help noticing that the closed look of shuttered sadness was still on his face when the kids failed to distract him. So far, she had not tried to talk to him about anything serious. It wasn't really her business, anyway — but still, she felt responsible. His future, for instance. What was he going to do? Where was he going to live? Who was going to look after him? It was the Welfare people's job, of course, and they would probably want to put him into care. But she didn't much like that idea. And after all, she and Jim and the kids were the only friends he'd got really, and considering everything, they owed him, and she ought to try to do something . . . But, looking at that remote and brooding stare, she could not bring herself to say anything . . . Better wait a while — till he felt a bit easier about things. There was plenty of time.

'Jim,' she said doubtfully, 'oughtn't we to—?'

'No.' Jim shook his head in slow reproof. 'Leave 'im be.'

He seemed to consider the whole difficult matter with ponderous caution, his kind, wind-reddened face screwed up with concentration. 'A breather,' he said at last. 'That's what he needs. A breather.'

Madge nodded and said no more. Instead, she gathered her things together and plodded off through the blowing sand to the caravan, where she began to cut an enormous pile of sandwiches. When you didn't know what to do for someone, you could always feed them.

★ ★ ★

The old man sat in the sun and watched the sea. It was sheltered down by the deserted lifeboat station, and the bench was set into the harbour wall with its back to the wind. Only, of course, there wasn't a harbour any more. Just the small, derelict quay where the fishing fleet used to come in, and the slipway for the lifeboat below the flaking life-station doors that were permanently closed now. Beyond that, up the hill a little and leaning into the headland, there were still some cottages occupied by the same old fisher-folk families. But for the most part, nowadays, it was holiday flats and caravan sites and bungalows, and the four-square hotel at the other end of the sea wall, looking out into the bay.

It wasn't a bad hotel, as hotels go, and the villagers still liked to use the smoky old bar with its low ceiling and polished brass ship's bell. It had its own deep-set windows embracing the view of the sea, but he liked to get out into the air and look at the passing world by himself. He was there every day on that bench, if the weather was fine. And if it rained, he climbed a little higher and went into the shelter outside the old seamen's union building next to the chapel.

Today, it was fine and glittering after the storm, and he sat in the splintered sunlight admiring the surf.

The boy with the limp was there again. Not swimming today, of course — even the experienced surfers were being cautious in those seas, and the red flag was up over the bay. But the boy was there on the beach, playing with the rest of his young family. Doing his best to be playful, thought the old Captain, watching him — for he seemed to be a grave, somewhat shadowed boy who rarely smiled. A bit awkward too, on land — his leg clearly hurt him still when he walked. But

18

in the sea he looked entirely different — almost happy, and much more graceful.

At this point in his thoughts, the old man on the bench heard a sudden spurt of laughter from the beach below him as the tide came in behind the group of children and quietly demolished the fortress they had so carefully built on the sand. The boy picked up the youngest child — that smiling baby — and whirled it above his head, and then deposited it safely beside its mother, who seemed to be busy handing out sandwiches to everyone. But the boy did not seem to want a sandwich. He left the children in a cheerful munching group, and wandered off by himself. In fact, he was coming up the beach towards the harbour wall.

Matthew came up the steps from the beach and saw the old man sitting there in the sun. He had noticed him before, several times, and now — for some reason that he could not quite understand — he smiled at him as he passed.

'Hallo,' said Captain St George, smiling back. 'Too rough for swimming today?'

''Fraid so.' Matthew hesitated for a moment, and then sat down on the bench beside him. 'It's nice here in the sun.'

The old man nodded. 'I come here most days.' He let the silence flow between them, looking out at the sea with faded, tranquil eyes. 'Cuts you down to size, doesn't it?'

Matthew grinned. 'A pinhead in all that ocean.'

'You swim very well.'

'Not as well as the seals.'

'True.'

They were silent again for a while; and then, greatly daring, Verney St George asked: 'What happened to your leg?'

'Legs.' Matthew shot him a half-smiling glance. 'Fell out of a window.'

'Oh. Awkward.'

'Very.' And then, in case he sounded self-pitying, he added swiftly: 'But they're improving.'

'I can see that.'

Matthew looked pleased. 'Can you really?'

'Oh yes. Definitely more mobile. Don't your family think so?'

'Who?'

Verney St George waved an expressive hand at the cheerful little party on the beach below them. 'Your family.'

'Oh.' For a moment the boy seemed embarrassed. Then he

said in a carefully careless tone: 'They're not my family. Just —
friends who brought me along.'

The Captain regarded him with puzzled attention, but he did
not enquire further. Instead, he said neutrally enough: 'They
seem a nice bunch of kids.'

'Yes,' agreed Matthew, sudden warmth in his voice. 'They
are. Especially Jampy.'

'Instant joy,' murmured the old man, watching the antics of
Jampy, who was running round in circles, trailing a long crimson ribbon of seaweed in swirling patterns on the new-washed
sand. 'Wish I had it.'

'So do I,' admitted Matthew.

The two of them — the old man and the boy — looked at
one another in perfect understanding. They did not say any
more.

★ ★ ★

Several times after that Matthew climbed up the steps to talk
to the old man. They didn't say very much — old Captain St
George and young Matthew — but a curious, unspoken bond
seemed to be growing between them. The Captain was content
just to have his company, and Matthew was content because
the old man was peaceful and undemanding.

They looked at the surf together, and watched the antics of
the surfers (with Matthew hiding his private aching desire to
be agile and balanced enough to join them), and they smiled
indulgently at Jampy and Donna chasing Danny across the sand.
Sometimes Matthew felt as old as Captain St George, watching
the kids playing down below — so heedless and carefree, but
old Verney St George never felt as young as Matthew, though
sometimes he badly wanted to understand why anyone so
young could be so sad.

But he did not ask — not then — and Matthew did not
tell him. They just talked idly of neutral things and let the
unacknowledged sympathy between them grow quietly on its
own.

One day there was another storm, and most people stayed
at home. Captain St George did not come out to his usual
bench, and Matthew missed him — especially as he wasn't
allowed in the sea that day either. So he spent extra time in the
Aqua-club pool, teaching his legs to behave themselves, and
then went for a long, aching walk along the sandy cliff path.

He was tired at the end of it, but he surprised himself by calling back at the square old hotel on the cliff-top to ask after the Captain. Something about the old man's fragility troubled him.

They told him that the Captain was all right but he was resting today. Sometimes, they said, he was not well enough to go out, but felt sure he would be sitting on his favourite bench in the sun again soon. Only half satisfied, Matthew turned away. He was much too shy to ask to see him. Instead, he went back to the beach and helped the kids to make a driftwood fire.

The next day was calmer. The wind dropped, the seas died down, and Matthew was given permission to swim again.

'Be careful, though,' warned Skip sternly. 'There's still a bit of a swell. Don't go too far out.'

Matthew heeded the warning. Skip knew what he was talking about. So he climbed round to the little deserted bay beyond the main beach, and slipped into the water on the sheltered side of the rocks. It was quiet there — deep and quiet. There was no one to barrack him, or interrupt his thoughts . . . and even his thoughts seemed to die down and unchurn themselves like the subsiding seas . . .

He was idling on his back when he suddenly became aware that he was being watched. He couldn't quite understand the sensation, it was so powerful and so unexpected, but he was quite sure about it. Someone — or something — was watching him as he lay surrendered to the gentle lifting arms of the sea. He turned over and righted himself, treading water in the rocking sea swell.

A huge, dark face was looking at him. Two bright, intelligent eyes were fixed on his face — and a wide, welcoming smile was spread across the grey massive head beneath the thrusting nose.

For a moment, Matthew was terrified. A flash of unreasoning fear seemed to paralyse his limbs. But then a curious sense of relief and reassurance seemed to wash over him. It came, he felt sure, from the creature in front of him — the beautiful, gleaming creature that was regarding him with such intense interest.

A dolphin, he thought. It's a dolphin! What am I afraid of? It's come to have a look at me. And why not? I must look a clumsy sort of object to him.

The dolphin seemed to be laughing at him, almost agreeing with him. It dived under a wave, moved in a swift streak of glinting darkness round him, and then leapt out of the water in a graceful curve, not six feet away from him, its pale underbelly gleaming in the sun.

'Oh!' said Matthew, smiling. 'Aren't you beautiful. I wish I could leap like that.'

The dolphin seemed to hear him. It turned in a wide arc and came swimming towards him. Matthew put out a hand, greatly daring, and touched the black-and-silver wet flank as it sailed past him. Somehow, it didn't feel like he expected. It was smooth and firm, and almost familiar — like someone he already knew . . .

The great sea creature turned again in the translucent water, weaving patterns of liquid grace all round him, approaching and retreating, teasing and inviting, innocently playful and friendly, showing no trace of fear.

Matthew was utterly captivated. He swam close and tried to imitate the dolphin's effortless movements in the water — but of course he couldn't. He still seemed hopelessly clumsy beside that wonderful, easy skill. It seemed to wait for him, and to moderate its own flashing speed to suit his slow progress — and its smile when it looked at him seemed to be tolerant and almost affectionate. '*You aren't very quick,*' it seemed to be saying to him. '*But as humans go, you're not too bad.*' And, as if to confirm its opinion of him, it dived again and came up so close that its silken body brushed alongside his own. Matthew laughed and clasped his arms round it in a sudden upsurge of delight. For a moment they swam together, as one, and then, with a flick of its tail-fluke, it shook itself free and leapt in the air again. Matthew heard the sharp hiss of air as it sounded and breathed in again before diving deep below his own trailing feet.

Instant joy, thought Matthew, remembering the old man on the bench, and Jampy dancing on the sands. Yes, instant joy!

The dolphin was laughing at him again, and this time it swam round him in a wide circle and then came up beside him to blow again, resting tranquilly in the water and eyeing him with the same, intelligent, seeking gaze, as if full of questions it needed to ask.

'I would tell you if I could,' said Matthew aloud, 'but I don't know any of the answers either. What can I do? You'll have to take me on trust.'

The dolphin seemed to agree with that. It leapt in the air

22

once more, dived deep and came up close, nuzzling against his body with its thrusting bottle nose.

'I shall call you Flite,' said Matthew. 'Because you can almost fly. Lord Flite a-Leaping. You must be an aristocrat, with a nose like that.'

He put his arms round the dolphin's sinuous body again and hugged it close. 'Flite?' he crooned.

The dolphin smiled and flicked its tail at him.

For nearly an hour they swam and played together, growing in some strange way ever closer in communication as they circled and dived in the clear green depths. But at last, Matthew's damaged legs began to tire, and he knew he would have to go in and leave the dolphin to swim alone.

But the clever eyes seemed to know his reluctance — to recognize his unwillingness to bring their joyous companionship to an end. For suddenly, the powerful body came close again, nudging him gently towards the shore, pushing him forward in the friendliest way towards the shallower water near the rocks.

'All right,' said Matthew. 'I've got the message. It's time I went in. But I don't want to leave you.'

He stroked the smooth, gleaming head with one cold wet hand, and turned away to swim back to the rocks, alone. But every instinct within him screamed to him to stay.

Then Flite gave him one final, cheerful thrust with his beak, leapt high into the sunlight in a bright flash of ecstasy, and headed away out to sea.

'Well, he's gone,' said Matthew sadly, looking back at a sea that was suddenly grey and very empty.

It seemed to him, as he clambered out on to the slippery black rocks, that a brightness had gone from the day.

★   ★   ★

'You stayed in too long,' said Skip severely, rubbing Matthew down with a rough but kindly hand. 'That's counter-productive.'

'I know.' Matthew gave him a lop-sided grin. 'But — I was enjoying myself.' He didn't know quite why he was being secretive about the dolphin. In any case, wouldn't Skip have seen that beautiful shape leaping in and out of the water? But something made him keep quiet. What he and Flite had shared was a private, special joy, not to be told. Not to be exclaimed

23

over, trampled on and spoilt. He knew about that. He knew about private dreams being trampled on and spoilt. Oh yes, he knew. His mother had been a master of destruction. Or should he have said a mistress? He shivered a little, for those were the kind of thoughts he simply must not have — not any more — not after everything that had happened . . . But he sometimes felt that by dying in the fire, his mother and her latest awful boyfriend had somehow put the final seal of destruction on his life — on all his dreams and visions. On all his hopes, his inmost springs of joy . . . Just for a little while, out there with Flite the dolphin, he thought he had found them again, those springs of joy, in the deep translucent spaces of the wild Atlantic.

But it was gone now — that sense of wonder and unthinking happiness. Flite, his gentle playmate, had gone back to the wide, unfettered pathways of the seas he loved. And he might never come again.

Just for a moment he had known it — that pure, ecstatic physical delight, that perfect communion with another sentient being — the whole of tingling life alight between them. He thought of that wide, innocent smile and that splendid, leaping body in the sunlight. And now it was gone — and he felt like a dead thing in a world grown suddenly colourless and chill.

He shivered again, and found Skip watching him with his absurdly blue sailor's eyes.

'You OK?'

'Yes. Of course.'

'Legs aching?'

'No.'

The clear, assessing gaze raked Matthew's thin, tired body to the bone. 'Better get changed before you turn entirely blue.'

'I — I'm not cold,' chattered Matthew, trying in vain to explain.

'No?' Skip's razor-sharp glance seemed to soften a little. 'It's a bleak old world sometimes, isn't it?' His hand came down hard and firm on Matthew's shoulder, propelling him forward. 'No exercises today. You've done enough. Go and sit in the sun.'

Matthew went.

★   ★   ★

The old man was there again when he climbed up the steps to

the harbour wall. He was sitting in the sun, his ruff of white hair sticking out under his seaman's cap, and his watery blue eyes fixed on the restless sea. His knotted hands were resting on the white bone handle of a thin black walking stick with a gold-coloured ferrule, and his head was tilted a little as if he were always listening to the voices of the gulls and the sound of the surf below.

Matthew stopped. He wondered if the old man would have noticed the dolphin. Probably not. The little bay was round the corner, almost out of sight. Probably he would not have been able to see so far. Better keep quiet.

For some reason, he did not like keeping things from him — or from Skip either, come to that. But he had to. Yes, he told himself fiercely, he had to. He had learnt in a hard, bitter school to keep the things he cared about hidden. Hidden deep down where no one could touch them.

'Good swim?' The calm voice did not sound inquisitive — merely friendly. Blessedly neutral.

'Yes, thanks.'

'Sea's gone down a lot.'

'Mm. Just about right for me.' He sounded faintly contemptuous of himself, and the old man laughed.

'Most people wouldn't go in off the rocks at all in this swell.'

So he had seen him go in. What else had he seen? Matthew felt a cold flick of reluctance, almost fear. He didn't want to talk about Flite. Not to anyone.

But the Captain made no further comment. He went on staring at the sea, and then said abruptly: 'You lonely?'

Matthew started. 'Lonely?'

'Yes. Lonely. I'm lonely. Are you?'

Matthew considered it. 'I don't know,' he said at last. 'I suppose . . . I've always been a bit — er — on my own . . . But *lonely*? I don't think so . . . '

'Other company?'

'There's the kids —' He waved a hand at the little party on the beach.

'Boys your own age? Girls?' The smile was faintly roguish, and one bushy eyebrow lifted in enquiry.

Matthew shrugged. 'Ball-games and barbecues? . . . And squeals in the dunes? . . . Or discos in the town? . . . ' He grinned. 'Not my scene — with my legs like this.'

'What about Skip's surfers?'

Matthew's eyes opened wide. 'You know Skip?'

25

'Everyone knows Skip. He does a good job down here.'

Matthew nodded. 'Yes. Especially with me.' He sighed. 'But the surfers are —'

'A bit of a gang?'

Matthew laughed. 'They are a club, after all . . . But they've asked me over for the evening a couple of times.'

'Did you go?'

'No.'

Verney St George glared at him. 'You should. No good mopin' about.'

Matthew opened his mouth to protest and then shut it again. At last he said mildly: 'You've been checking up on me.'

'Fraid so.'

'Why?'

The Captain's glare was still belligerent. 'Not curiosity. Not exactly. Wanted to know what's bitin' you.'

'Oh.' He looked a little embarrassed. 'Well. Now you know.'

The Captain grunted. 'It's a waste of time.'

'What is?'

'Guilt.'

Matthew stared. He was so startled he almost got up and ran. But he couldn't run. Not yet. So he sat there, going slowly pale with shock. 'Guilt?'

Captain St George turned his head and looked straight at Matthew. 'What you did for those kids was only right and proper. Young lives are important. From all accounts, you couldn't have saved those other two. It's sad, but there it is. No point brooding about it. Does no one any good.'

Matthew blinked. 'It's — not as simple as that . . . '

'Why not?' The Captain's voice was crisp.

'I —' he hesitated, looking helplessly at the fierce old man beside him, knowing it was hopeless to expect him to understand.

'Try me,' said the Captain, as if Matthew had spoken aloud.

Matthew shook his head. 'It's difficult —' He drew in a painful breath. 'You see, I — I didn't like them much.'

'What's that got to do with it?'

The boy looked at him, amazed. 'I thought —'

'You thought because you didn't like them, you must have left them to die on purpose?'

The blunt words were meant to shock, and they did.

He put up his hand, as if warding off a blow. 'I didn't mean —'

'Of course you didn't. You'd have got your worst enemy out of there if you could. Anybody would.' The old man leant forward and tapped him on the arm with an emphatic finger. 'Get the facts straight, boy. You thought they were out. They weren't. They were in there, in all that smoke and fire, and they were dead. Long before you called out, long before you even noticed the smoke. There was nothing you could have done. You were not responsible.'

Matthew's eyes were dark with memory. 'I still feel responsible.'

Captain St George sighed with exasperation. 'No sense in that at all.' He paused, and then said in a somewhat casual tone: 'Tell me about her. Why didn't you like her?'

Matthew sighed again. 'What can I say? My mother was a tramp?'

The Captain gave a brief bark of laughter. 'Lots of 'em are.'

A tired grin touched Matthew's face. 'I suppose so . . . With her, there was always someone new — right back from the start. And I was always in the way — cramping her style. She liked a good time, that's all.'

'At your expense?'

'Oh well — I got on OK on my own, most of the time.'

'What about your father?'

He looked blank for a moment. 'Died in a car crash, so she told me. I don't know if it was true. I never really knew him.'

'And — this latest one — did you know him?'

'Not really. They used to drink a lot, and shout and throw things.' The faint, sardonic grin was back again. 'And then they'd go down to the pub and start all over again.' He paused. 'I thought that's what they'd done that night.'

The Captain nodded. 'Natural assumption.'

'No, it wasn't.' Matthew's voice was suddenly brittle. 'I'd forgotten . . . '

'Forgotten what?'

'The other thing they did when they'd had a row.'

The old man looked at him grimly. 'So . . . You couldn't have known.'

'I could've guessed.'

But the Captain was not to be deflected. 'And what then? You called them. Called and shouted, they tell me. If you'd gone down those stairs to have a look, you'd be dead too — and so would all those young kids.'

27

Matthew was silent. He saw the logic of that. 'It's all such a mess,' he said, in a sick and weary voice.

'It's over,' stated the Captain. 'It's *over*, boy. No more looking back. Only a fool spends his life looking backwards. I should know.'

Matthew heard the fleck of bitterness in the incisive voice and wondered at it, but he was suddenly too tired to pursue his thoughts further. An overwhelming sense of exhaustion seemed to descend on him, weighing him down like a heavy pall.

'Here,' said the Captain. 'Have a swig of this.'

'What is it?' Matthew looked doubtfully at the silver flask held out to him.

'Bless the boy — rum. What d'you expect from an old seafarer? Drink up.'

Matthew drank, and choked a little. But the world tilted back into its proper focus.

'That's better. No more talk. I've bullied you enough.' The rheumy blue eyes were regarding him with what looked almost like affection. 'No pillars of salt round here, boy. Understand?'

Matthew managed a pale, accepting grin. 'Only sticks of rock?'

'Exactly. Go get some for those kids, and stop moochin' around.'

Obediently, Matthew stopped mooching around. It was as simple as that.

★ ★ ★

He was almost afraid to go into the sea next day, in case it remained empty and cold. But the dolphin came again. He had not been swimming more than a few minutes, it seemed, before the blue-grey shadow cut through the water towards him, greeting him joyfully.

'Flite!' he called, and held his arms out in welcome. 'You came.'

Flite's response was a series of clicks and squeaks, and a couple of spectacular leaps in the air. *'Come on,'* he seemed to be saying. *'Stop being so earth-bound and slow. Follow me. Look how high I can jump! Isn't life glorious? Look!'*

Matthew looked — and marvelled — and followed as best he could. And, yes! he thought: *Isn't life glorious?*

For a long time they played together, turning and diving,

gliding down into green depths and swimming up again into sunlight, to swirling bubbles and dazzling cascades of upflung water. Sometimes the dolphin made circles round him, but sometimes it came close and allowed him to hold on to its strong dorsal fin and swim beside it, or even to put his arms round it and stroke its supple body as it rode the buoyant sea swell. Once, it brought him a pebble from the sea floor and offered it to him as a gift, and once or twice the great head came close and looked at him eye to eye, as if to say: 'I know you now. Do you know me?'

Matthew began to think he almost did, and wondered if he would ever dare to ride on the friendly sea creature's back as men were supposed to have done in the legends. It would be wonderful to try, but somehow he knew he must let Flite the dolphin make all the overtures. He could not impose his will on this free, magnificent animal. He could only rejoice that it chose to be with him and to introduce him to its own joyous, fun-loving world. So he swam peacefully beside it in a state of happy enchantment, joining in its games and leaps and lightning turns with all the skill he could muster. It seemed as if their loving companionship could never end, and he was almost drunk with a mixture of sea-dazzle and mutual joy. But then, all at once, a terrifying cramp assailed him in his damaged legs, and he curled up in a tight ball of pain and began to sink like a stone.

For a moment, the dolphin seemed to be puzzled by his withdrawal, but then some echo of his pain seemed to reach it — some strange telepathy was clearly at work between them — for the long, fluid body suddenly shot down below his helpless, stiff legs and began to nudge him upwards. He had been under water so long by now that he was almost unconscious, but dimly he felt the smooth, arching curve of the dolphin's back pushing up beneath him, forcing his legs apart until he was in truth riding on the powerful, silken body just behind its head as it knifed its way upwards through the surge and pull of the sea. The thrusting nose broke surface very swiftly, and air rushed into Matthew's lungs, bringing him back to astonished consciousness, but the dolphin did not immediately shrug him off its back. It went on, cutting through the water, entirely sure of its direction and of Matthew's need, until it reached the shelter of the rocks where it had left Matthew before. Then, and only then, did it turn and roll gently in the breaking surf, depositing Matthew safely within reach of land.

The cramp was gone now, but he felt limp and very tired. Even so, he turned in the water and hugged the dolphin hard before he tried to climb up on to the wet rocks. 'Thank you, Flite,' he murmured, close to the dolphin's head. 'I was almost a goner there!'

But Flite merely smiled at him with enormous kindness and leapt in the air once more to show that life was still good. Then it dived deep and shot away out to sea.

Matthew lay on the rocks and gasped a bit until he felt stronger. And even after that he still lay there, thinking of the wonderful, tingling sense of power that had surged through that fluid body as it swam beneath him through the green-dark reaches of the sea.

★ ★ ★

'Did you talk to him?' asked Skip, looking at the old man with challenging blue eyes.

'Yes.' Captain St George nodded, and pushed Skip's drink towards him.

They were sitting in the bar of the hotel, with its big curved windows looking over the sunlit bay.

'Any — result?'

'Some.' The seamed, brown face grew thoughtful. 'It's a difficult thing to dispel — a sense of guilt.' There seemed to be rings of unexplained meaning behind the old man's voice, and Skip glanced at him sharply.

'Sense of guilt?'

'Oh — never mind. I think he's coming out of shock a bit, at least.'

Skip nodded, and took a slow swig of beer. 'He came down to the Club last night.'

'Good.' The Captain did not say that he had told Matthew to do so. 'How did he get on with the boys?'

'Fine. Especially when he got hold of a guitar.'

The old man started. 'Guitar? Can he play?'

'Like an angel. Or no, like a real pro.'

'Pop music and such?' The Captain was a bit vague about such things. Out of date, he told himself. Didn't understand all that racket, not one bit.

'Oh no,' said Skip, shaking his head. 'Not pop at all. Classical stuff — the real McCoy.'

'*Classical*?' He sounded totally mystified.

30

'Yes. Well — he did play a couple of songs for the boys to sing along. Didn't seem to mind what they asked for. But for the rest, he simply sat down with the thing on his knee and forgot we were there. I've never heard anything like it.'

The Captain stared at him in astonishment. That might account for some of the curious distance in those eyes, thought the Captain. Then he said slowly: 'Well — one hidden talent uncovered. What else is he good at?'

'Computers.'

'What?'

'Computers. Mary's got one in the office. She's trying to keep tabs on the seal population, among other things. Got in an awful mess. He put her right in no time.'

The old Captain whistled. 'That's a useful skill today . . . Any idea about his schooling?'

Skip sighed. 'He says he was taking GCSEs this summer. Did most of them, but missed a couple at the end. I don't know how bright he is —'

'Very, I should think.'

The two pairs of eyes met in a curious, bleak concern.

'Skip — what's to become of him?'

The younger man rubbed a salt-stained brown hand through his hair. 'I wish I knew.'

'What did the Welfare people say?'

'They simply told me what to do for his physical recovery — you know, physio and so on — and asked me to keep a general eye on him.' He paused and then added soberly. 'I don't think they know what to do with him, really . . . They're trying to trace a relative, I think. And meantime, they said, the Farleys would look after him.'

'Haven't met them,' growled the Captain. 'But they look a nice enough bunch.'

'They are. The woman — Madge Farley — will do her best for him, I'm sure.'

'Maybe,' said Captain St George, with doubt in his voice, 'we ought to go and talk to her?'

'Maybe we should,' agreed Skip.

★ ★ ★

Madge Farley, when they found her, was almost as blunt as old Captain St George, and quite as concerned.

'Bloody Council put us in B and B.'

31

'What?'

'See, I'd have Matt like a shot. He's a good boy — always was, and my kids adore him. But what can I do? Two rooms they've give us. Two bloody rooms for four kids and Jim and me. No bathroom. No kitchen. Just rooms. I suppose Matt could sleep on the floor . . . but it wouldn't be good for him.'

'No,' said the Captain, with feeling. 'It wouldn't.'

Madge turned to include Skip in the conversation, her scraped, anxious face full of helpless rage. 'They're so flippin' *stupid*,' she said. 'If they'd give us a new flat, it'd be all right for everyone. But they'll dither about until it's too late, and then put the boy into care because he's got nowhere to go.'

Skip exploded. 'They can't do that.'

'Oh yes, they can. He's got no relatives, see — no home — no possessions, neither. Nothing but the things he stands up in — and most of those was donated by neighbours.'

'Is there any money?' asked the Captain.

Madge snorted. 'Money? When did them two ever save anything? It all went on the booze. I don't think they even fed Matthew properly unless they remembered. It used to bother me. I asked him up to mind the kids sometimes just to get a meal inside him.' She screwed up her face in a scowl of disapproval, and then added as an afterthought: 'The Insurance man did come round to have a look, though . . . and he came to the hospital, too . . . There might be something there — if she hadn't already flogged it.'

'Always on his own, was he?' asked St George, picturing that lonely, joyless life in the flat downstairs.

'Oh yes — as long as I've known him, and that's ten years . . . He used to stay in his own room mostly, and study. He was clever, see? I think he took to his books sort of early, to shut things out, if you know what I mean?'

'I know what you mean,' agreed the Captain.

'The school said he was bright. It's a shame about them exams.'

'He can take them again,' said Skip.

'In a Council Home? He'll be lucky.' Her voice was sharp.

'What about his guitar?' asked Skip, remembering that rapt face in the clubroom the night before.

Madge brightened a little. 'Oh yes, he was always strumming something.'

'*Strumming*?' Skip sounded appalled.

'Well — practising he called it. On and on, he'd go, till he got it right. Except when his mother yelled at him to stop. She couldn't stand it.' Madge's face was grimmer than ever. 'But he played a real treat when he liked . . . We used to listen to him upstairs, the kids and all. I swear he used to play 'em to sleep most nights.'

'Did he — did anyone teach him?' asked the Captain, wondering how a self-taught guitar player could manage what Skip called "classical stuff".

Madge nodded vigorously. 'Someone at school. One of the masters, I think.' She paused, considering the matter. 'I remember Matt telling me his Mum wouldn't pay for lessons, so he took on an extra paper round. It would just about cover, he said.' She sighed. 'Of course, that's gone up in smoke as well, poor kid, and his computer. Months of saving, that cost him. I know, because he told Danny when he'd got enough, and he took all the kids downstairs to have a look at it.'

She suddenly stopped and looked at the two men with renewed distress. 'But what I don't understand is, what's to become of 'im? Who's going to pay for a new guitar? Or new clothes, come to that? . . . And where's he going to live?' She was standing in the cramped little caravan, while the two men sat at the small yellow table in the corner, but now she leaned forward and put her hands down on the table, and looked earnestly into their faces. 'I haven't dared talk to Matt about it yet. He seems so — so shut inside himself, somehow. And Jim said to leave 'im be . . . But we're going home in a couple of days — and I don't know what to do for the best . . . '

Skip said suddenly: 'He could stay on with us for a bit — if he wants to.' He glanced at Madge's doubtful expression. 'Just till things are sorted out, I mean.'

'Could he?' The look of doubt dissolved and became one of guarded hope. 'Would they let him?'

'We'll see,' said the Captain. 'Leave it to us. We'll find out.'

Madge began to look a shade less pinched and anxious. 'I'd — we'd be ever so grateful.'

'But,' said Skip firmly, 'we must find out what Matthew wants first.' He seemed to be glaring at the Captain with some sort of challenge.

'Yes, of course,' agreed Captain St George. 'That must come first.'

★ ★ ★

33

Matthew knew what he wanted. That was quite clear. He wanted to stay within reach of the sea, where he could play with Flite the dolphin all day long.

Nothing else seemed to matter. Nothing else even seemed real any more. Except, of course, the feel of a guitar under his hands, and the magic that music could weave on the air.

Music and the sea. The dolphin's dance was like music — those intricate patterns of grace and beauty; and the sound of the surf was like music — a music he could not quite reach with the guitar, it was too delicate a sound for those pouring chunks of mighty power coming in from the mighty Atlantic. But they were all one, somehow, in his mind — all part of the dream, and he did not want to do without them, he did not think he *could* do without them, now.

'Would you like to stay on a bit?' asked Skip, fixing those vivid sea-blue eyes on Matthew's dreaming face.

'Yes,' said Matthew. 'Please.'

He looked at Skip with a wild hope leaping like a dolphin inside him, and then added in sudden shyness: 'I — I could — aren't there some chores I could do?'

Skip grinned. 'Plenty of those.'

'But will they let me?'

'I don't know. The Captain's going to find out.'

Matthew looked puzzled for a moment. 'The Captain? Is he — is that the one I've been talking to?'

'That's the one.'

'Who is he, Skip?'

'Captain St George? . . . ' Skip seemed to hesitate for a moment, and a strange expression crossed his face before he answered. 'Don't you know? . . . No, I suppose you wouldn't, not being a regular down here . . . ' He paused again so long that Matthew had to prompt him.

'Is he really a sea captain?'

'No. Not now. Though I think he was once — when he was young. That's how he began. Master of one small ship. Now, he's just the head of one of the biggest shipping lines in Europe.'

'*What?*'

Skip was smiling again at Matthew's astonishment. 'A real tycoon — and very rich, they say. Though he lives quietly enough down here.'

'But he —'

'Oh, I know. He wears a shabby seaman's jacket and a battered old cap on his head, and he sits on a bench in the sun with an old walking stick in his hand. But if you look closely, that stick is made of ebony with a carved ivory handle and a gold ferrule — and although he pretends to be just an old man idling the day away, he knows precisely where all his ships are, and keeps in touch with his London office every day with his own small computer.'

Matthew whistled. 'What kind of ships?'

'Not the big liners any more — that trade is mostly dead, except for the cruise ships. He has some of those, of course. But mostly tankers, freighters, ferries, tourist boats, caiques — you name it, he's got them all.'

'Does he live down here all the time?'

'No. But he comes to stay at the hotel every summer. Sometimes he stays on through the autumn — he has this year. But he usually goes before the winter.'

'Where to?'

'I don't know. Somewhere south where it's warm, I should think. He's been very ill, they say, though he never talks about it.'

Matthew was silent for a moment, and then he said slowly: 'He's been good to me.'

'So I gather. You're honoured.' His voice was faintly dry, faintly edged with some hidden tension. 'He's not always good to people.'

Matthew still spoke slowly, almost in a dream. 'He said he was lonely.'

Skip's eyes narrowed, and he seemed to go very still. 'Did he? You *are* honoured. He's never confessed that to anyone else, I'm sure.'

Matthew turned his head and looked at Skip thoughtfully. 'Hasn't he? . . . It must be awful to grow old . . . '

To him, at fifteen, it seemed a remote and faintly terrifying process — but he was not too young to recognize how painful it might be, how an old man might long to run about the beach like Jampy the two-year-old, and ride the rough Cornish seas like the surfers . . . or like a wild dolphin?

'Instant joy . . . ' he murmured. 'That's what he said.'

Skip was silent. He was silent so long that Matthew glanced at him again in surprise, and caught a glimpse of some unknown anguish in his face which made him look quite different for a moment. Different and vulnerable — with a curious sheen in his eyes almost like tears.

'Skip?' he said, alarmed.

35

The stillness receded, and Skip's face took on its normal, friendly contours. 'Well, we'll leave the Captain to sort out your problems. In the meantime, the boys want you to play for them again. Will you come?'

'All right,' agreed Matthew, secretly rejoicing at the thought of getting his hands on a guitar again. 'Why not?'

★　★　★

That night the Surf Club greeted Matthew like an old friend. 'Look who's here!' they cried. 'Old Limpy-Legs himself!' and 'Fingers Ferguson in person!'

He had long since given up being touchy about his legs, and he found himself grinning back and accepting a lime shandy and a Cornish pasty before he settled down to play. He almost felt part of a gang again, and the strange wall of glass that had cut him off from people seemed to be dissolving.

He played everything they asked for — as far as he could. Pop songs, folk songs, old sea shanties, and all the past sentimental favourites they could remember. He had a good ear, and didn't find picking up a tune at all difficult. So they yelled out all the old hits and what they called 'soupers', and when they forgot the words they yelled even louder. He didn't mind. He had a guitar in his hands, and his fingers were happy, in spite of the scars.

At least, they were almost happy. They had been stiff at first, and a bit painful on the strings — the fire had left them rather tender. And he was woefully out of practice. (Tudor Davies would be furious with him!) But it came back, and the more he played, the better they felt. So he played on, finding his way through every half-remembered tune and every shouted chorus . . .

But at last there came a small lull, and one of them said: 'Well, come on, Fingers. What about the real stuff? Let's have some class around here.'

Matthew smiled and sat idly stroking a thumb across the strings while he considered. I wonder if they could take Bach, he thought . . . Tudor Davies always said: 'Always start with something calm and disciplined. You can show off later when you've played yourself in . . .' Well, maybe he'd already played himself in . . . All the same, they'd asked for class — well, they could have it.

He began with Bach. But by the time the neat, ordered

36

pattern of notes came to an end, he had forgotten his audience. So he went on to Albeniz — something sad and savage, like the Spanish people, and then on to Granados and those fierce, spiky chords. Yes, sad and dark and savage — and then leaping into those relentless dance rhythms that could not be denied.

Those leaping, upward phrases reminded him of Flite. He wished he could play something like the sea . . . But there was nothing like the sea — that churning, chunky, endlessly-moving weight of water, those clear, green-dark depths, the power and grandeur of the pounding surf . . . No, there was no guitar music like it. An orchestra, perhaps — full of rich symphonic sound, but the single, delicate voice of a guitar? No. Still, it could leap and fly . . . The lilt of the dance, the lift and fall, the soaring ecstasy — they were like a dancing dolphin. Yes, he could conjure up Flite and his instant joy with his two hands . . .

When it was over, and the cheerful applause had broken into the little astonished silence that preceded it, he saw that there was someone new in the clubroom.

It was a girl with short blonde hair that swung in a gleaming cap round her head, and she was staring at him out of strange, tawny eyes that were a curious mixture of brown and gold.

'Where did you learn to play like that?' she asked.

Matthew smiled. 'I had a smashing teacher.'

'You must have.'

Skip strolled up and stood beside her, laying a friendly hand on her shoulder. She looked up, and a gleam like summer lightning seemed to spark between them. 'I see you two have met.'

Matthew waited. He thought more was coming. He hadn't missed that brief glint of light — or Skip's hand so carelessly lying on her shoulder.

'Not really.' She smiled back at Matthew. 'Introduce me to the maestro.'

'Oh, honestly!' protested Matthew, annoyed. 'Give me a break!'

She laughed, and Skip grinned down at him. 'This is Dr Petra Davison — from the Sea Mammal Research Unit. Anything you want to know about seals, or whales, she'll tell you.'

Matthew looked impressed.

'You ought to play to them,' she remarked.

'Who?'

'The seals. You ought to play to them.'

37

'Why?'

'They love music. They come quite close in to listen — especially if you sing to them. I've often done it.'

Matthew had a sudden picture of this vivid blonde girl standing on a rock and singing wildly into the wind — and a whole lot of bobbing heads listening in the water . . . 'Magic!' he exclaimed softly. 'Do they — do other creatures like it too?'

'Porpoises, you mean?'

He had a suspicion she was teasing him, somehow. 'Yes. Or — or dolphins?'

The two of them seemed to be smiling at him, and he suddenly became aware that they knew all about Flite — all about his marvellous, secret friendship with the wild sea dolphin — and had carefully not said anything about it to anyone.

An enormous sense of relief came over him. He didn't have to hide it any longer. He hated deceiving Skip — even in the mildest way. Those far-seeing sailor's eyes deserved the truth.

'You know about Flite,' he said.

'Is that what you call him?'

'Lord a-Leaping Flite,' pronounced Matthew, smiling. 'I mean — the way he flies through the air, and that noble head . . . What else?'

They were laughing again, but he added with sudden, awkward honesty: 'I ought to have told you before, but I —'

'But you wanted to keep him to yourself. I don't blame you,' Skip finished for him.

'D-didn't you—?' He turned to the blonde girl beside him shyly: 'D-don't you want to come out and meet him?'

She seemed to hesitate. 'Not really. I'm only here to monitor the seal colony at the moment.'

'Monitor?'

'Take a count — if I can. And see if any of them show any signs of the North Sea virus.'

'Do they?' He sounded suddenly scared.

'Not so far.' She turned to look up at Skip enquiringly. 'You've had no casualties here, have you?'

'No. But someone reported a dead porpoise washed up on a beach further north.'

A cold fear clutched at Matthew. 'A *porpoise*? Could dolphins catch it?'

Petra sighed. 'We don't know yet. I hope not. There have been reports of dolphins dying from a mysterious virus off the east coast of America. But we haven't seen it here.' She paused, and then added, almost to herself: 'Though pollution can start off all sorts of trouble.' She looked at Matthew with compassion, seeing his anxiety. 'That's only half the story, though. Other terrible things are happening to the dolphins, you know.'

'Such as?'

'Well, for a start, there's the purse-seine nets. They get caught in them — hundreds of them — along with the enormous fish catch of tuna — and they can't get out, or come to the surface to breathe, so they drown.'

'*Drown!*' He thought of Flite — that beautiful, sinuous body leaping out of the water into the sun — and the way he dived and raced through the water, with all the freedom of the wide seas to play in . . . And then he thought of him trapped in the nets, unable to escape, twisting and turning, desperate to get out, entangling himself more and more, and finally drowning — drowning in despair, till he lay limp and lifeless under the sea.

He shivered. 'He saved my life yesterday, I think.'

'How come?' asked Skip — and when Matthew told him, he did not immediately scold him for swimming too long and getting cramp. Instead, he said slowly: 'You know what they say around here? "*Dolphins only come to them as needs 'em!*"'

'Do they?' Matthew was absurdly pleased. Yes, Flite, he thought, I need you all right. You are the only one — the only one in the world who is truly glad to see me!

'They cry in the nets,' said Petra suddenly, in a bleak, strange voice. 'You can hear them through the water.'

'That's terrible.'

She turned on him, almost in anger. 'You don't know the half of it! They wait for the dolphins to find the tuna shoals — the big, factory ships with their lethal nets — and then they go out in little boats and drive the dolphins till they are tired, until they and the tuna are close enough to encircle with the nets.' Her face was grim now with outrage. 'And then they pull the nets in, and sometimes the dolphins escape, and sometimes they don't, and sometimes they even get crushed in the machinery, or hung out in the nets with their dorsal fins torn off . . . '

Matthew gulped. ' . . . awful!'

'It's nothing to what the Japanese do,' she told him, still in that strange, cold voice of impotent anger. 'You know about that?'

'No.'

She looked at him with those extraordinary gold-flecked eyes.

39

'They drive them into the bay with their boats — they block the way out to sea with nets, and then they slaughter the lot. Club and knife them to death, till the sea is red with blood.'

He was appalled. 'Why?'

Petra shrugged slim brown shoulders. 'Tradition, they call it. They always have. The dolphins eat their fish.'

'*Their* fish?'

She gave him a brief, acknowledging smile. 'That's the big question, isn't it? Who owns the seas?'

Matthew nodded. They belong to Flite, he thought. To Flite and his kind — the seals and porpoises, and the great whales, swimming free in the vast oceans of the world . . . and the fish themselves. All part of the same living, breathing pattern.

'I'm sure Flite only eats what he needs,' he said aloud.

'Yes.' She sighed. 'It's only man that is greedy . . . Before we started grabbing the balance was perfect.'

Perfect balance, thought Matthew. That beautiful, joyous creature. How could we be so stupid? So senselessly destructive? How could anyone want to kill a gentle, unaggressive creature like Flite? . . . A creature who came to meet him in love and friendship day after day? . . . Who even knew when he was in trouble, and offered immediate help? . . .

'They eat them, too, of course, now — in Japan,' added Petra, seeming to be driven to lay on the agony.

Matthew just gazed at her, speechless, feeling too sick to do more than look his disbelief.

'Since the whale quota,' she explained remorselessly, 'though they take little enough notice of that — there's still whale meat in the shops. But they make it their excuse for slaughtering thousands of dolphins a year. It's a delicacy, you see.'

Skip laid a hand on her arm. 'You don't need to convince Matthew. He's on your side already.'

The fierce light of anger seemed to die in her eyes, and she smiled. 'Sorry. I get carried away. It's a pet warhorse of mine.'

'So it should be!' agreed Matthew staunchly. Then, seeing that the tension was lessening, he added shyly: 'Why didn't you tell me you knew about Flite?'

Skip glanced again at Petra, and again light-glancing messages seemed to pass between them. 'To begin with, I didn't want to disturb you. The two of you seemed happy enough.' He grinned cheerfully at Matthew. 'And secondly, though it's the end of the season and there aren't a lot of visitors left, I didn't want them all plunging into the sea and splashing about and frightening your dolphin away.'

Matthew nodded. 'Though he doesn't seem in the least afraid of me. I was afraid of *him* at first.'

'They are very powerful creatures,' agreed Petra. 'They can easily kill a shark.'

'But he's so friendly.'

'Exactly.' Petra nodded. 'And we'd rather he stayed that way. People — even well-intentioned ones — can be incredibly stupid, you know — shouting and pushing, harassing innocent creatures to death with the best possible motives.' Her face was quite stern. 'We both thought you were best left alone.'

Matthew looked from one to the other of them. He didn't suppose for one moment that they understood what a marvellous gift they had given him — that careful silence that left him and Flite free to meet and play together in the empty sea . . .

'Thank you,' he said humbly, and was surprised when they both smiled at him as if they knew his thoughts.

★　★　★

There was a tree outside the old man's window, and he lay looking at it, marvelling at its burning brilliance. It was a cherry tree, very old and gnarled, with wide-spread branches, and just now, in the morning sun, every leaf seemed abrim with crimson light. There weren't many trees down here, where the sea winds swept and scoured, twisting them into bent, starved shapes that crouched against the skyline. But the cherry tree stood in the back of the hotel garden, sheltered from the sea on one side, and by the tall flanks of the rising cliff road on the other. So it flourished and grew old and strong, and each year it produced a snow of blossom in the spring, and this miracle of incandescent colour in the late autumn. It was so bright that it cast a rosy glow on the white walls of his room, so bright that it almost hurt his eyes and made them blink with tears . . .

But then he was old — old and susceptible now. Beauty seemed so perilous, so fragile these days, it often moved him to tears.

That boy, for instance. He had a kind of beauty — though he did not know it. The strange grey-green eyes that reflected long loneliness and the secret dreams of adolescence — the sea-wet, half-curling hair that dried in the sun to the colour of the hillside bracken after rain . . . the thin, long limbs, so awkward

41

on land, and so fluid in the water — and that saddened, cautious smile that suddenly broke out and changed the whole contour of his face . . . Lightening the grief, the obstinate, solitary pride . . .

It reminded Verney St George of many things – of other days and other griefs that were best forgotten now. There was nothing he could do to put them right. It was too late for that.

But it was not too late for that boy. He had a whole life to lead — a whole potential to fulfil; and maybe, with a little help from others (if he would accept it), he would succeed and be happy.

Be happy. That, of course, was the point. He must remember that, and go carefully. Too often before, he had forgotten that happiness mattered as much as success. Perhaps more . . . Too often, he had ordered this and managed that, and fixed someone else's life into a pattern which was all wrong. He must not do that now. It was all too easy to be autocratic — especially when you had money. But this time he must remember that everyone has a right to choose his own path — his own griefs and joys, whatever they might be . . . Never again must he lay a contriving hand on someone else's future. The future was their own.

All the same, there were things he could do, and he did them. After a morning on the telephone, he strolled down to see Skip, who was briefing his surfers about the state of the tide.

'Some people are coming down,' said the Captain briefly. 'In a day or two. Let you know when.'

'Good,' nodded Skip. 'Have you told Madge? She'll be glad to know something's happening.'

'I'll go there now,' offered St George. 'Where's the boy?'

'In the sea,' said Skip, smiling, and waved a vague hand at the wide expanse of ocean. 'Well out of the way.'

The Captain grunted, and turned back up the beach, leaning on his white-handled ebony stick.

★　★　★

Matthew was indeed in the sea, and so was Flite. They met as joyously as before, but this time Matthew sensed that there was a certain protective watchfulness about the dolphin's attitude — almost as if he were making sure that his clumsy two-legged friend didn't get into trouble again . . . The gentle smile was as wide and welcoming as ever, and the long, graceful body

42

leapt in the air with the same ecstatic freedom, but in between — while they played and dived and circled round each other — the bright, intelligent eyes regarded him gravely, as if assessing with patient care how much his companion could do.

It was an extraordinary feeling. Matthew had never felt so safe — or so cared for — and he found himself having a playful conversation with the dolphin as they swam together in the green, sun-laced waters of the little bay.

'You see,' he said to Flite, putting an arm round the shining flanks as they swam, 'I've always had to fend for myself before. I'm not used to being looked after.'

Flite rolled lazily in the swell and smiled. *'The seas are wide,'* he seemed to say, *'and very deep. But I won't let you fall. I am strong — stronger than any wave or pulling tide . . . I ride the ocean like a king, and you are safe with me. Come.'*

Matthew came. But the dolphin did not go very far out into the dark Atlantic. He stayed near the sheltering rocks and played in the sun. Once he spotted a small boat putting out from the jetty, and knifed away to have a look at it, surfacing just ahead of it and laughing at the young fisherman at its helm. But he soon returned to Matthew, who was following much more slowly behind, and made another joyous circle round him and another spectacular leap in the air just to show he was glad to see him.

Presently, as Matthew surfaced to draw breath, he became aware that someone was sitting on the rocks and watching him. He swam a little closer in and saw that it was the girl, Petra. She was wearing a wet-suit like his, and dangling her legs in the water, but she made no move to leave the rocks and follow him. Her bright hair hung straight and glinting in the sun, and she sat very still and quiet, but she was smiling.

'Don't you want to come in?' he asked, treading water not far away.

She seemed to hesitate, and then said softly: 'Not if it will worry him.'

Matthew turned to look for the dolphin, and saw him leaping through a wave only a few yards out.

'Nothing worries Flite,' he said, and found himself answering Petra's smile with a cautious one of his own, and holding out his hand to her.

She slipped in off the rocks without a splash and swam quietly towards him. 'I'll stay here,' she murmured. 'Give him a chance to have a look at me. You go and talk to him.'

43

'He won't need an introduction!' He was laughing, like Flite, in the sun.

Petra thought in surprise: He looks a different boy when he laughs. But aloud she only said in the same soft voice: 'Better wait and see.'

Matthew leaned into a wave and dived, gliding down to look for that smooth grey-blue shadow. But he hadn't gone very far down when the dolphin's great head came towards him, thrusting joyfully through the clear water with his powerful beak. '*Oh, there you are,*' he seemed to say. '*Where've you been? You missed my best jump. Look, I'll do another one to show you!*' And he did.

'Flite,' said Matthew, coming up beside him into filtered sunlight and flung spray, 'stop showing off. There's someone here I want you to meet. She's all right. You needn't be afraid.'

'*Afraid?*' The clever eyes looked at him and seemed to dance with reflected light. '*Who's afraid? Look at me leaping! In the ocean, I am a king. Why should I be afraid?*'

With a flash of silver, he leapt high in the air, the wide, innocent smile lifting the corners of his mouth as he looked down at Matthew. Then he submerged, sank out of view, and came up suddenly very close to Petra, regarding her with the same, questioning, searching attention that he sometimes turned on Matthew.

'*And who are you?*' he seemed to ask.

Petra stayed very still in the water and let him circle round her. Then she began to talk to him, still in the same quiet, softened tone. 'You see,' she told the dolphin seriously, 'I am trying to protect you — you and your kind.'

Flite seemed to agree with that. He did a couple of swirls and pirouettes to register approval and came back to hear some more.

'I wish you could tell me where you've come from,' she sighed, and stretched out her arms to their full length either side of her in an attempt to guess at the dolphin's size and weight. 'Or where you're going to . . . ' Greatly daring, she touched the gleaming flanks with one gentle hand. 'For I suppose you'll be going somewhere warmer soon . . . '

Flite did not flinch at her touch, but he turned his great body round in an effortless half-circle to look for Matthew, as if seeking reassurance, and — seeing him there beside him — gave a slow roll over and curved himself round his friend in a fluid, protective arch.

44

Petra smiled. The dolphin had made himself clear. 'It's you he trusts,' she said to Matthew gently.

Matthew had been almost jealous of Petra's ease with the dolphin. Flite was *his* friend — his own private joy — and the strange, unspoken communion between them was something rare and precious. She had no right to come barging in and spoiling things.

But Flite had changed all that. With one smooth curl of his fluke, he had declared his allegiance. He would tolerate this new stranger. He would listen to her quiet voice, and watch her antics with friendly interest. But Matthew was the one he cared about — the one he turned to in the water with fearless trust — the one whose stream of consciousness seemed to flow with his in a tide of innocent delight, in perfect understanding. Yes, Matthew was the one.

The bright intelligent eyes were watching him now, sending all sorts of messages — the sleek head still in the water, the loving smile unshadowed by any doubt.

Silently, Matthew came close and laid his arms round the resting body, letting the lift and fall of the ocean rock them together, surrendered to its thrall. Then, ashamed of his ungenerous thoughts, he turned to smile at Petra.

She was not far away from them — but she made no attempt to come closer. 'That's all I need to know,' she said, smiling back at the two of them. There was respect in the gold-flecked eyes. 'Goodbye, Flite. Thank you for talking to me.'

Flite gave a lazy flick of his tail, but he did not immediately move out of Matthew's embrace. Quietly, Petra turned in the water and swam away.

The dolphin watched her go, and then turned smoothly into the next wave, leaping with joyous abandon into the sun and sparkle as Matthew released his hold. '*Life is for living!*' said Flite, in a cascade of foam, squeaks and clicks and effortless communication. '*Dive deep! Leap high! Swim and fly! The world is all blue and gold! Rejoice, rejoice!*'

Matthew rejoiced.

★　★　★

When at last he came out, tired and happy, and the long silver-grey shadow that was Flite had headed out to sea, he found Petra waiting for him on the rocks.

'I hope I didn't disturb him too much,' she said.

Matthew shook sea-water out of his hair. 'I don't think so. He seemed as happy as ever.' He turned his head to look at her curiously. 'What made you change your mind?'

She sighed. 'I thought I ought to. We're supposed to report sightings — now that they are getting so scarce. And any details we can get help our research . . . We don't know enough about them really — what their life-span is — where they breed — where they go . . . Every little helps.'

Matthew agreed. 'Yes, I can see that.' He smiled at her serious face. She was really devastatingly pretty, and he was more than a little dazzled. 'So what can you tell me about him?'

She sighed. 'Not a lot. A bottle-nose dolphin, in prime condition. But you knew that, anyway. He is a male, by the way, though I don't know how you knew.'

'Nor do I . . . How do you tell?'

'They keep their sexual organs hidden — more streamlined, you see . . . But the male has a slit in his abdomen. You can see it if you swim close under him.'

'Yes, I did notice.'

'And the male is bigger than the female — though we've no way of comparing that here.'

'How big is he, do you think?'

'About . . . two lengths of my arms . . . That's over ten feet, I should think. And he's young.'

'How do you know?'

'Oh — the look of him, somehow. And his teeth are all bright and sharp.'

Matthew laughed. 'A toothpaste smile?'

'It's a lovely smile,' she protested.

You don't have to tell me that, thought Matthew. It's the most loving, welcoming smile in the world. But aloud he only said: 'He's very friendly.'

'Too friendly, perhaps,' mused Petra, sighing again a little. She glanced at him, sadness growing in her face as she thought of Flite's trusting, fearless approach, and remembered the terrible hazards these beautiful creatures met at the hands of men . . .

'It's all very well to get fond of *one* dolphin,' she burst out, suddenly angry. 'What are we going to do about all the others?'

Matthew looked at her. 'You're doing something.'

'Not enough,' snapped Petra. Then she softened a little, remembering the extraordinary closeness between those two in the water . . . It could only lead to heartbreak of one kind or another — this perilous, ecstatic friendship between Matthew and Flite — and she felt compelled to warn him.

'He will go soon, you know — when the weather gets colder.'

Matthew nodded. 'I know.' There was sadness in his face, too — but he resolutely shook it from him, together with another shower of sea-spray as he stripped off his wet-suit and lay back in the sun to dry off. 'I know it can't last,' he murmured, staring straight up at the limitless sky above him. 'But I'm going to enjoy it while I can.'

'*Rejoice, rejoice!*' called Flite's fading shadow in his mind.

★   ★   ★

No one was in when the Captain arrived. The caravan door stood open, and various mats and sleeping bags were put out in the sun to air, but there was no sound from within.

While he was standing there wondering what to do, the children came up in a scatter of laughter, and stopped in front of him. The baby in Donna's arms smiled at him cheerfully, but the others looked at him with suspicion, wide-eyed and doubtful.

'Mum's out,' said Danny helpfully.

'So I see.' There was a spark of amusement in the old Captain's stern glance.

'Shopping,' added Donna, being equally helpful.

'Shopping, shopping,' agreed Jampy, hopping up and down on one leg. He saw someone else's dog sneaking under the caravan, and made a dive for it, trying to crawl under the chassis through the sandy grass. Danny hauled him back.

'Behave yourself!' he hissed.

Jampy laughed, did a pirouette that would have been a credit to Flite himself, and dodged under Danny's arm. 'Behave!' he chanted, dancing. 'Behave!'

Donna looked at the Captain with pained apology. This was not how you were supposed to treat visitors, she knew. 'He's a bit of a handful,' she explained, sounding absurdly like her mother.

'You can say that again,' growled Danny.

Then Donna remembered her manners. She shifted Kirsty to her other arm, and held out her hand politely to the Captain. 'It was nice of you to come,' she said politely.

The baby also held out her hand and tried to grab one of the shiny brass buttons on his coat. 'OOk!' she said.

Verney St George didn't know whether to laugh or cry.

'Dad's gone for some water,' Donna went on. 'He'll be back in a minute.' She put on her best manner again. 'Won't you come inside?'

'Don't mind if I do,' smiled the Captain, and followed them into the yellow caravan. It was swept and clean — neat as a new pin.

'All shipshape and Bristol fashion,' he approved. 'Where do you all sleep?'

'Me and Danny has the top bunks — Jampy and Kirsty are in the bottom one, in case they fall out. Mum-and-Dad's bed folds up into this table, see?'

The Captain examined it with interest. 'And what about Matthew?'

'Oh, he has the tent. But he comes in for breakfast.'

'I wanted to sleep in the tent, too,' volunteered Danny. 'But Mum says Matt needs peace-and-quiet.'

'Peace-and-quiet, peace-and-quiet,' chanted Jampy, not giving anybody any.

'Shut up!' countered Danny automatically — but he didn't sound really cross so Jampy didn't.

At this point, Jim Farley's heavy tread sounded on the caravan steps, and a shadow fell on the doorway. The big man took in the situation at a glance, and set the two brimming buckets of water down on the floor.

'Hop it, kids,' he said.

Donna looked disappointed. 'Can't I make him some tea — now that the water's come?'

'Later,' pronounced Jim, and jerked at the door with his thumb.

They took one look at his face and scattered like dew on the grass.

'Sorry,' said Jim, apologizing for the general state of affairs and Madge's absence all in one.

Captain St George reached out and patted his arm. 'It's all right, Jim. I came to tell you I've fixed up a sort of meeting. Some people are coming down to talk about Matthew's future.'

Jim nodded. 'Madge'll be pleased.' He stared out of the caravan window, frowning with the effort of coherent speech. 'Fair out of her mind with worry, she's been.'

The Captain grunted in sympathy. 'It's a difficult situation.'

Jim was silent. It was certainly that, and he didn't know how to resolve it. All these people, with their cleverness and concern — they were kind enough. But they missed the point, really. 'We're fond of Matt,' he said suddenly. 'All on us.' He looked at Captain St George with painful honesty. 'Not just — er — grateful, if you understand me?'

The old man understood him.

'It's not right — him being on his own.' He shook his head, still seeking for words. 'No way to live.'

The Captain agreed.

'That Evie Ferguson — she never gave Matt nothing. *Nothing!*' he repeated fiercely. Then, with a sudden burst of courage he dared to put his thoughts into words. 'A boy needs affection, Captain. Like any animal. He starves, else.'

Captain St George nodded. But he found himself almost too choked to speak. 'Don't we all?' he said.

★　★　★

That night, when Matthew started playing what he privately called the Yelling Songs, he saw the old Captain slip in at the back of the long clubroom. He did not try to come forward, but stayed there in the shadows, so that he wouldn't be noticed. Uh-hu, thought Matthew. Checking up on me again! . . . I'll show him.

He also noticed that Skip and Petra were sitting close together in another shadowy corner, heads bent in earnest conversation. Skip seemed to be trying to persuade her about something, and she kept shaking her head so that her hair sparked with muted gold. When they glanced up, the lights from the long bar counter fell on their faces, making them look blanched and strange. But then Petra bent her head again and looked down at her hands, almost as if she wanted to keep her face hidden from that blaze of light.

Then one of the surfers noticed the Captain and called for sea-shanties. Oh, really! thought Matthew, exasperated. He's not a rusty old salt with a peg leg. He's a clever old city tycoon. I'd be better playing 'Money, money, money!'

But the demands increased, and soon they were all yelling about Drunken Sailors and Yard-arms and Mizzens. He didn't quite know how he got into the Rio Grande, but all at once the sadness of that old, old song of departure seemed to get into his fingers, and into all those young, careless voices.

'Then away, boys, away —' they sang.
''Way down Rio —
And fare you well, my pretty young gel,
For we're bound for the Rio Grande.'

And then as he came to an end, he saw Skip's and Petra's faces under the light again. They looked riven, frozen into some kind of inarticulate anguish as they looked at one another across the small space of the shabby table. There seemed to be a glitter of tears about them, and Matthew saw Skip lean forward and lay a gentle, entreating hand on Petra's arm. But she still shook her head, still turned it away from the light to keep it hidden.

'Away, boys, away —' repeated the cheerful young voices, not knowing or caring about the long, long history of voyages and partings in that ancient song.

But Matthew knew. And he cared. His hands faltered on the strings, and, to cover the silence, to change the mood of the evening, he plunged into his own limited repertoire — the Spanish songs, the dances — de Falla, and Granados again, and of course 'The Maiden and the Nightingale' . . . But that was sad, too, even sadder than Rio Grande — only it was a sadness compounded of moonlight and dark cypresses, and the romantic dreams of young love, and his fingers could not help making that famous tune sing with sorrow.

He drew back then, and leapt into a lively Jota to cheer everyone up — and then finally slowed down into a calm, rocking Berceuse.

Got to bring them back, he thought, letting the quiet lilt rise and fall under his fingers. Can't leave them shaken like that, with their faces all naked and open to any hurt . . . Got to bring them down, bring them down . . . What about ending with Bach? That slow Eb minor Prelude? . . . Sad still, but steady. Yes, steady. Like Skip. Like Petra. That'll do for them . . . It's like them, really. Sad but steady.

So he ended with Bach.

When he looked up, the old Captain was still sitting there at the back. But Skip and Petra had gone.

★　★　★

The moonlight beat down on the shore as they came walking together across the sand. It cast deep shadows behind them,

50

and sudden gleams and glints on the wave crests — and laid a long, silver pathway on the sea.

'You could stay a bit longer?' begged Skip.

'I have to be in the Pacific next week,' Petra answered, sounding sad but resolute.

Skip sighed. 'It never seems long enough!'

'I know.' Laughter caught at the sadness between them for a moment. Then she said slowly: 'Of course — you could come too?'

There was a faint question in her voice, just as there had been in Skip's. But his answer was just as resolute. 'You know I can't. There's this place to run. And the seal watch . . . And then there's young Matthew. It looks as if he might be staying on for a bit.' He paused, glancing at her in the bright moonlight. 'I can't just walk out on everything.'

'Neither can I.' Her voice was bleak.

They walked on for a while in silence. At last he said, as if at the end of an argument with himself: 'Maybe — in the winter — the surf club closes down then. And perhaps Matthew will be fixed up . . . Maybe I could follow you out — for a holiday?'

She laughed. 'Monitoring the whalers? . . . Some holiday!'

He grinned back, and flung an arm round her shoulders, hugging her close. 'I'd be with you.'

'There's that, certainly!' They were both laughing now, and Skip suddenly paused in his stride and drew her even closer, looking intently into her face under the white moon. Silver touched her eyelids and lay in a bright swathe on her hair.

'Petra?'

'Yes.' Her answer was quiet. 'Yes, Skip . . . It's all right.'

They kissed then, quietly and deeply, with the sound of the sea in their ears, and the moonlight dazzling their eyes. But presently they were walking again beside the sea, and Skip was saying: 'I still think you should have told him.'

'I can't, Skip. I promised.'

Skip swore mildly under his breath. 'That was an old promise — about an old story. Isn't it time it was forgotten?'

She sighed. 'Maybe . . . But I gave my word. I can't take the risk.'

'I think you're wrong.'

She gave another long, shaky sigh, and laid a consoling hand on his arm. 'I know you do . . . But now is not the time. It doesn't seem right, somehow.'

51

'If you leave it much longer, it may be too late.'

'I realize that . . . ' She looked at him, almost shyly now, and added in a hesitant voice: 'But if I did — it would make things more difficult for us, wouldn't it?'

Skip nodded briefly. 'Yes. It would.'

'So —' she tucked her arm through his, drawing him close again. On the sand, their two shadows merged and joined as one. 'When I warned Matthew about the dolphin going south, he said: "I know it can't last. But I'm going to enjoy it while I can."'

They looked at each other in the moonlight and smiled.

'Why not?' said Skip.

★ ★ ★

Matthew saw them down there, walking close together on the shore. But he did not follow them. How could you walk head-long into that blazing closeness? It would be like breaking into a church. Instead, he went along the beach to the rocks and stood looking out to sea across the path of moonlight, and wondered what Flite was doing. He hoped he was still playing out there, somewhere in those limitless blue-dark spaces, leaping up into moonlit waves and flung spray glittering with diamond sparks — a-gleam with silver himself in that pure, white-hot radiance . . .

He could not see any thrusting head or leaping body — but the sea was there, and it calmed him. He needed to empty his mind after all that music. He had been a long way, and he ached with the journey — especially the journey back. Even his fingers ached.

But the moonlight poured down on to the silver sea, and he felt the wheels and patterns in his head subside and grow still. It was peaceful there. Nothing disturbed the stillness — not even a sea-bird cried in the quiet night. Nothing stirred — except the sea itself. The sea was never still, never entirely quiet. Its endlessly whispering voice was in his ears, and he felt the pull of its great tides and mighty surges under his feet, even under the solid rocks he stood on, while he watched the thin line of silver curl over and shatter as each wave broke against the shore . . .

There was no laughing dolphin to greet him in the silver night. Flite was far out — far out in the great deeps he loved,

52

and would not come looking for his friend until bright morning broke on a sunlit sea.

Sighing, Matthew turned away and wandered back through moonlight and shadow to his small tent by the yellow caravan in the dunes.

He did not see the old Captain standing on the sea-wall steps, also watching the moonlight on the sea before he went in to sleep. There was music in his head, too — and thoughts that had been stirred up, memories that he had long since forgotten. That dratted boy and his music — he little knew what deeps and fastnesses of grief and pride he had probed with his magic fingers . . . And this blazing moonlight didn't help at all . . . It reminded him of too much — too many things that still hurt and quivered with unwanted life when he thought them long since dead and buried . . .

But it was beautiful — he couldn't deny that — this amazing wash of silver laid over land and sea. It never ceased to enthrall him, old as he was, and somehow he knew he must not reject it, however much it pierced and haunted him.

Like Matthew, he sighed, saluting its glory, and turned away to his rest. Maybe he would sleep now. The ghosts could walk their moonlit way across this haunted shore. Let them wander in peace.

The passionless moon burned on in a flawless sky.

★　★　★

The Captain called his meeting at the Clubhouse — with Skip's permission. There was a reason for this — which soon became apparent. At the meeting was Margaret Wilson, the social worker who had visited Matthew in hospital; a solicitor called Harvey who apparently was representing Matthew and dealing with Insurance; and — to Matthew's astonishment and pleasure — Tudor Davies, his old friend and teacher from school who had taught him all he knew about the guitar, as well as a fair amount about maths and computer science.

Also present were Madge and Jim Farley, Skip and the Captain. Jim had tried to opt out, saying he was no good at meetings, and anyway someone ought to keep an eye on the kids — but the Captain had been adamant. He knew Jim's worth. He might be a shade inarticulate, but when he did speak, it counted.

Tudor Davies was a small, wiry Welshman with a shock of wild brown hair growing grey at the edges, a wide, flexible sort of grin, and very bright brown eyes that missed nothing. He also had the most beautiful hands, long and strong and sensitive. But only the Captain and Skip noticed that. Matthew knew anyway. He had watched those hands coaxing miracles of sound out of squeaky guitars for clumsy young hopefuls through long years of painful struggle. He knew the patience of those hands, the strength of those fingers, their anger on those fierce Spanish chords, their infinite gentleness on a whisper of melody . . .

'Matthew,' Tudor said, in his absurdly deep, lilting voice. 'Good to see you, boyo. How's tricks?'

'Pretty good,' said Matthew, smiling, and was surprised when the little Welshman put an arm round his shoulders and hugged him.

'Everyone's sent messages,' rumbled Tudor into his ear. 'Hope you're coming back to us — when you're fit.'

'I'm fit now,' protested Matthew.

But Skip intervened here, laughing a little. 'Not yet, Matthew. Got to get full mobility back — doctor's orders.'

Matthew agreed with that when he thought about it. Yes, it would be nice to run and jump and climb again — like Jampy dancing about on the sands . . . And it would be wonderful to know he could dive and swim with Flite without getting tired, or ever getting cramp . . . But then, of course, if he was entirely well, he wouldn't be able to stay here any longer — he wouldn't be able to swim with Flite at all . . . And at the thought he shivered, and decided to stay silent.

The Captain was an old hand at meetings. He knew how to get things done, and he wasted no time. But he spoke to Matthew first.

'Since it's your future we're discussing, I think we'd better put all our suggestions forward, and leave you and Mrs Wilson to decide what's best.'

Matthew nodded. Mrs Wilson? He wasn't in the least sure that this wispy grey woman would know what was best, but he supposed she had the right to decide. That was what social workers did. Decide. But he wished they would leave him alone and let him decide for himself.

Margaret Wilson looked at Matthew with doubt in her eye. How was she to know what was best for the boy? People always expected her to be decisive — to sort things out neatly and work miracles. But she couldn't. She was tied by all sorts of regulations — care orders and court restrictions . . . She could only listen and advise . . . And report back to her superiors in the vain hope that they would listen to her recommendations. They never did.

'Mrs Wilson,' said the Captain, with bluff courtesy, 'is that all right by you?'

Mrs Wilson attempted to smile. 'Of course.' The smile almost reached her eyes which were permanently cautious — and Captain St George was almost inclined to revise his first opinion of her. But he reserved judgement. See how she reacts later, he thought. Still looks a bit hidebound to me.

Aloud he said: 'Skip — maybe you'd better give your Physio report first.'

Skip winked at Matthew and held up a sheet of paper from which he read in a crisp, clear voice. Blind them with science, the Captain had said, and he did. By the time he had finished, they were all looking at him with awe.

'So,' he concluded, 'the visiting hospital doctor suggests another three to four weeks at least to complete the treatment.' He glanced at Margaret Wilson, and added in a casual tone: 'He can, of course, stay here at the club if he likes.'

There was a silence while everyone waited for everyone else to speak. At last Margaret Wilson said in a dry, unconvinced voice: 'I'm sure it's all *technically* correct.'

Skip looked about to explode, but a warning glance from the Captain stopped him.

'If he stayed on here,' the social worker went on, 'what *domestic* arrangements do you have?'

I wish she wouldn't talk in italics, thought Skip, exasperated. 'Domestic?' He sounded totally uncomprehending. 'Oh, you mean food and so on?' His blue eyes met Matthew's in secret amusement. 'We have a resident cook, and a cleaner who comes in from the village. And a couple of bar staff in the evenings.'

'Ah. The *bar*.' Another set of italics, and an even drier voice. 'Do I understand that the bar is open *every* evening?'

Skip's wide blue gaze was level and calm. 'In summer, yes. In winter, no. But in any case, we do not serve alcohol to anyone under age.'

'I *see*,' said Margaret, in the kind of tone that saw nothing.

Matthew spoke suddenly, as if driven to protest at the stupidity of the interrogation. 'I couldn't stay here, Skip, unless I could do some kind of work to pay my way.'

Skip grinned his relief at the diversion. 'That could be arranged.' He leaned back in his chair and looked at the ceiling with an assessing stare. It was already grimy with a season's smoke, and steam from the coffee machine. 'We always redecorate in winter.'

Matthew grinned back. 'Oh, that's OK, then.'

'Speaking of *winter*,' pursued Mrs Wilson, italicizing again, 'what about the swimming?'

Matthew's heart gave a lurch of terror, thinking of those winter-dark seas.

'What about it?' Skip's voice was bland.

'Well, you say a lot about the necessity for continuing Matthew's swimming practice — but won't it be too cold in the sea?'

Oh Flite! Too cold in the sea for you, as well as for me. You'll have gone by then . . .

'We have a heated pool here,' said Skip patiently, as if speaking to a rather dim-witted child. 'Matthew often uses it when the sea is too rough — and he always does his exercises there every day. That is how I can check his progress.'

'I *see*,' said Margaret again, in the same unseeing manner — and Skip suppressed a desire to laugh. He caught Matthew's eye, and noted with satisfaction that he also was having a job not to giggle.

Before Margaret Wilson could raise any more objections — in italics or not — the Captain turned to Madge with an ill-suppressed twinkle. 'Mrs Farley, tell us what you would like to do.'

Madge's pebble-bright glance flashed with scorn. She had taken the measure of this welfare woman, and what she saw she didn't much like. But Jim shot her a warning glance, and she drew a long breath before she spoke. Jim didn't need to say anything, he only had to look. Be careful, she told herself. Put it sensibly, so that it seems right.

'I'd like Matt to live with us — if he's willing. We're all fond of him, especially the kids, and we'd try to give him a good home.'

I sound like a lost dog, thought Matthew, and then was ashamed of being so prickly.

'That is,' Madge pursued with intent, 'if the Council will give us a new flat.' She looked at Margaret Wilson squarely. 'Can't do it, else. No room, see? Not in bed-and-breakfast.'

Margaret Wilson nodded slowly. 'That sounds reasonable.'

'Can you give 'em a push?'

She hesitated. 'I could try. It would be a case of *fostering*,

56

then.' (Those italics again.) Then the light, dry voice went back into the attack. 'But, of course, I would have to report back to the authorities as to your *suitability*.'

'Suitability?' Madge looked bewildered.

There was a moment's stunned silence, and then Jim suddenly spoke. 'Good with kids, Madge is.'

'I'm sure, Mr Farley. I'm *sure*.'

'Works hard. Not much time for fun and games,' he added, with sturdy loyalty. 'But she cares about 'em, see?'

If she says, 'I'm sure' again, thought Matthew, I shall scream.

But she didn't say 'I'm sure'. She said something much worse. 'Can you tell me, Mrs Farley, exactly *why* you were out on the night of the fire?'

Madge went white — and Jim looked at Margaret Wilson dumbfounded, too shocked to speak. Didn't the stupid woman know that was what had been bugging Madge for weeks of undeserved guilt?

But Matthew spoke — in a clipped, brittle voice of anger that nobody recognized. 'I can tell you, Mrs Wilson. I will repeat my police statement, if you like.' His glare was icy. 'Mr Farley works as caretaker in a big office block, and Mrs Farley also works there in the evenings as an office cleaner. Normally, Jim comes home for his tea at six, and Madge — Mrs Farley — goes out at seven. She puts the small kids to bed before she goes, and Jim sees to Danny and Donna.' He glanced coldly at the flustered social worker. 'But that night there happened to be an office party, and Jim Farley had to stay on till the last guest had gone. Mrs Farley had to start her cleaning two hours late, so Jim decided to wait for her and see her home. It's a bad part of town to walk in alone at night.' He paused. Everyone was listening intently. 'Madge put all the kids to bed that night, and came down to ask me to keep an eye on them. They were all asleep before she left — at about nine. I went up to check once — but there was no sound, so I went back to my homework. Just as well I did, really, instead of sitting in their lounge watching telly. I mightn't have smelt the smoke soon enough.'

There was a tingling silence. The silly cow, thought Matthew. No judgement at all. There was my tramp of a mother, as feckless as they come, not caring a damn for me or anyone else — who set the whole bloody house alight with one of her dangling cigarettes . . . and there's Madge — as good a mother as anyone could want — and this stupid woman has the nerve to suggest —

'I can't think of anyone I'd trust sooner than the Farleys,' he said in the same bleak, adult voice, 'and their kids are smashing.' For a second his eyes met Jim's, and something like reassurance seemed to pass between them. 'If I had a chance to live with them, I'd think myself dead lucky.'

'Bravo,' said the Captain, not too inaudibly. Margaret Wilson blinked. 'Now, what about school?' pursued the Captain, covering everyone's embarrassment with brisk good sense. 'Mr Davies — perhaps you'd better explain the position?'

Tudor Davies joined battle with alacrity. 'Taking nine subjects for his GCSE's, Matt was. Promising, look you, and expected to get the lot.' He winked at Matthew cheerfully. 'Took seven of 'em — before the fire. Missed two.' His peat-brown eyes glinted with amusement. 'Never thought to ask about results, did you, boyo?'

Matthew looked confused. 'Er — how did I do?'

'One A. Three B's and three C's. Not bad, considering.'

'Considering what?' said Matthew, suddenly belligerent.

'Considering the stupidity of the questions, and your obstinate mind.' He gave Matthew a mischievous grin. 'Bright the boy is, see? Can't waste talent, can we? Ought to go on, look you. A-levels and university. That's what we think.' His cheerful gaze sparked with challenge.

Matthew was staring beyond Tudor Davies, not seeming to pay much attention.

'What do you think, Matthew?' the Captain asked.

'Oh — er —' His eyes came back from their distance and settled on the little Welshman's face. 'He's probably right.' But he sounded unconvinced.

'What would you read?' barked Captain St George, swiftly following up the advantage.

Matthew hesitated, but Tudor did not. 'Maths and Computer Science,' he interposed swiftly. 'They're his best subjects. I teach 'em. I should know.'

'Not music?'

This time even Tudor paused, and messages seemed to go to and fro between him and his pupil while he waited for him to answer.

'No,' Matthew said at last. 'I'd like to — to go on playing. And learn as much as I can. But —'

'You don't fancy a career as a concert guitarist?' The Captain sounded almost disappointed.

'Not really,' said Matthew. And then, looking at his old

58

teacher, he added lamely: 'You see, music is —' But he could not tell them.

'A kind of journey,' said the Welshman softly, the lilt in his voice more pronounced than ever. 'And you go on it alone, boyo, isn't it?'

Matthew nodded. Alone, he thought. A deep, private aloneness which no one can penetrate — no one can spoil . . . But he felt compelled to explain it a bit to these well-meaning people. 'I don't mind playing for people — sort of casually.' He glanced fleetingly at Skip. 'But concerts — no. I'd never be good enough . . . And if I was — I'd hate it.'

The others looked confused, but Tudor's gaze met his in complete understanding. 'We'd like you back,' said the little Welshman gently, trying to bring things down to normal. 'And I'd like to go on teaching you — till you outgrow me!' His impish smile rested on Matthew, reducing the tension.

'That'll be the day!' murmured Matthew.

'Well then,' concluded the Captain cheerfully. 'Now we come to Mr Harvey. I'd better let him speak for himself.'

John Harvey was quiet and a little prim, as solicitors are apt to be, but he was no fool. He had said nothing so far, but he had followed the proceedings with discreet interest and not a little secret amusement. Now he spoke in a voice that was almost as neutral and colourless as his long, pale face.

'Since you left hospital, Matthew, we have been in touch with the insurance company and have discovered that there was a life insurance policy in your mother's name.'

Matthew looked astounded. 'Are you sure?' There can't have been, he thought. She'd have cashed it. And where would she get the money in the first place?

'. . . taken out for her, presumably by your father,' the solicitor was saying. 'She had cashed all of it she could, of course.'

Ah! thought Matthew. That's more like it.

'. . . but there was a small sum — about £300 — left in trust for you, which she could not touch. With interest, that has increased in value, though it is not a spectacular sum.'

I don't believe it, Matthew thought, and felt suddenly rather sick.

'As to the fire insurance, I'm afraid the premiums weren't paid up. But in view of the circumstances, and the fact that there had been a long-held policy, the insurance company have made a small ex gratia payment of £100.'

59

There was a pause, while Matthew seemed to grow stern and pinched before their eyes. 'Blood money?' he said at last, in the odd, cold tone he had used before.

'Matthew!' protested the Captain.

'I can't take it, of course.' He looked almost contemptuously at the solicitor. 'Can you give it away?'

'Not until you are eighteen. You can give it away then yourself. If you still want to.' He was not smiling. He had the good sense to take Matthew seriously. He realized that the fire had done more damage to Matthew than mere external injuries.

The Captain looked about to explode, but all at once a strange expression crossed his face — a long, long memory of another time and another anger — and he seemed to change his mind and sigh. Oh, the impractical idealism of youth! he thought, staring back down the years.

The social worker, however, had no such qualms. She was just beginning to say: 'But that's ridiculous!' when there was a rush of feet up the steps of the verandah outside the clubroom, and Donna's frightened face came round the door.

'Jampy's gone out to sea.'

'What?' They all leapt to their feet.

'On the lilo,' she added. 'Quick!'

Skip was the first to grasp what had happened. He was already stripping off to his bathing trunks which he always wore by day in case of emergencies. He often did duty as a lifeguard on the beach, as well as his surfing activities. 'Come on,' he said to Matthew, and started running down the beach.

Matthew could not run that fast. Not yet. But he too had stripped off and started to move. He saw Skip reach the water and give one swift glance round till he spotted the tiny figure of Jampy adrift on the floating lilo. It was already a long way out, beyond the line of surf which, miraculously, had not capsized it. Jampy didn't seem to be panicking — or even paddling with his hands. He was just sitting there, enjoying his adventure, totally unaware of the danger.

The tide's going out, thought Matthew. He'll be swept round the point.

He saw Skip plunge in and start swimming fast in Jampy's direction. He'll never catch him, he thought. However fast he is, the tide race is faster.

Then he knew what he must do. He went running with his uneven, lurching stride, to the line of rocks, clambered over them and slipped quietly into the water on the far side. It was

60

at an angle to Jampy's careening progress, and it might — just *might* — cut across it.

Flite! he called in his mind. Flite! If ever you loved me, even a little, help me now!

He began to swim — and in his mind he kept calling the dolphin to him. He didn't know quite how he called, but he was sure he would be heard, if Flite was anywhere within range in those vast Atlantic spaces.

And he was heard. Before long, the great blue-grey shadow was beside him — the smile of welcome gleaming at him through the water, the lively intelligence shining out of those clear, bright eyes.

'Jampy needs you,' explained Matthew, breathless with exertion. 'Over there!' And he raised himself up in the water and pointed. The little speck that was Jampy seemed further away than ever.

The dolphin also reared up in the water, turning himself with a flick of his tail-fluke, and seemed to look where Matthew was pointing. Whether he saw the tiny oblong afloat in the swell or not, or whether he picked up some strange vibration of distress, Matthew never knew — but the great, powerful back suddenly arched into a perfect dive, and he was gone like a blue streak through the water.

Matthew went on swimming towards them, but he was quite confident now that Flite had understood him. If only Jampy doesn't panic, he thought. If he loses his balance and falls off, we may all be too late.

But Jampy didn't panic. He rode his little craft with serene confidence, admiring the waves. He did not even notice how far away the land looked.

Skip, still swimming strongly, but aware now that he was scarcely gaining on the receding tide, suddenly saw an extraordinary thing. The large, dark head of a dolphin came up out of the water not two yards from the perilous little craft with its sublimely untroubled burden, and gently nudged it round so that it swung towards the shore. Patiently, repeatedly, the pointed bottle nose coaxed it forward, urging it through the swell with infinite care, correcting every swirl and sway of the fragile craft.

Matthew saw him too, and a great wave of love and thankfulness swept through him as he swam. Flite would do it. He had come when he called. He knew exactly what was required of him. He would bring Jampy safely back to shore . . . That

61

wonderful, smiling creature only needed a breath of thought to reach him through the wild deeps of the ocean — and he would come joyously to his aid.

Presently, the lilo came within reach of both swimmers, for Skip had also cut across at an angle when he saw where the dolphin was heading. But neither of them spoke or scolded Jampy, or did anything to distract him. They simply swam beside the dolphin until he had finished his careful steering and pushed the lilo close to the shallows in the little bay. There, they took over, and brought the small inflatable in to the shore, and Skip scooped Jampy off it into his arms.

But Matthew turned back in the water for a moment, now that the danger was over, and put out his arms to embrace the dolphin's smooth flanks in a loving hug. 'Thank you!' he whispered. Though there was no need to say it aloud at all. His heart said it — and Flite knew. The long body responded with a shiver of delight and leant against him for a moment in the lift and fall of a wave. Then he gave one slow flip of his tail and shot away into deep water, where he gave one joyous leap of triumph before he swam out to sea, leaving no trace of his coming on the untroubled surface of the little bay.

'A big fish pushed me,' announced Jampy.

'That wasn't a fish,' reported Matthew. 'That was a dolphin — and he probably saved your life.'

'Dolphin?' repeated Jampy doubtfully. Then he began to wriggle and laugh in Skip's strong brown arms. 'Dol-pin,' he crowed. 'Dol-pin save-your-life.'

He didn't understand the danger, even now. And they were thankful he didn't. They looked at each other and grinned their relief.

But people were coming now. Madge, running, tearful and exasperated — wanting to smack Jampy and hug him both at once. Jim, slower and redder of face, but equally thankful and almost as tearful.

And all the others, exclaiming and chattering, bringing towels, and robes, and anything else they could think of that might be useful. Last of all, slowly, came Captain St George, leaning on his stick. He looked at Matthew and Skip — both tired now and beginning to chill — and said simply: 'Well done.'

'Dol-pin, dol-pin,' chanted Jampy. 'Dol-pin save-your-life.'

'Well, boyo, aren't you the lucky one?' remarked Tudor Davies in his deep Welsh rumble.

But Matthew's heart sank a little. Now everyone would know about Flite. Already a little crowd of curious onlookers had gathered round them. They would ask questions, and insist on coming into the sea in gormless, splashing groups, and peer and gawp and shout, turning Flite into some kind of holiday stunt. And he wasn't. He was a great, majestic sea creature, with a secret life of his own — a king in the wide wilderness of the ocean — who came when he wished to come, and went when the whim took him, and dwelt in solitary deeps of green-dark magnitude where the idiot squawkings of men could not penetrate.

He hoped, for one frantic moment of fear, that Flite would never come again — never allow those mindless, squawking, two-legged flounderers to spoil and cheapen his innocent, joyous life.

'Coffee all round,' barked the Captain. 'Pronto. And —' with a glance at poor, startled Mrs Wilson, 'a good dash of rum!'

* * *

The meeting became a lot less formal after that. In fact, it became a sort of celebration. Jampy's escapade had not ended in tragedy after all. He had been rescued in a strange and marvellous way, and they were all relieved and a bit shaken. There was a lot to rejoice about. Even Mrs Wilson thawed — especially after the Captain insisted on a very generous dollop of rum in her coffee.

She agreed to let Matthew stay on with Skip *'pending consultation'*. She agreed to press the Council for a new flat for the Farleys *'pending future arrangements'*. She explained to the solicitor, John Harvey, that fortunately for Matthew, the amount of insurance money was below the limit allowed for savings, (whether he would use it or not) and would not prevent him from receiving social security benefit. She also added, somewhat primly, that Social Services could not administer Matthew's private money, however little it might be, and maybe he ought to appoint someone as trustee, since Matthew himself was only fifteen.

'Sixteen, actually,' said Matthew.

They all looked at him in surprise. 'When did that happen?' asked Skip, smiling.

'The other day.' He spoke carelessly.

'You didn't tell us!' cried Madge.

'Didn't seem important — then.' He looked round at them warily. 'But now — all these arrangements you're trying to make for me — it's very good of you, but . . . ' He hesitated, suddenly embarrassed and shy.

'But what?' demanded the Captain.

'I think I'd better leave school altogether and get a job.'

'What as?' snapped St George, ever practical.

'Oh no, boyo!' protested Tudor Davies, in the same breath.

'I'm quite good at computers.' He sounded undismayed by their doubts. 'Someone would probably have me.'

'But what about your A-levels?' Tudor was always a teacher first.

Matthew looked at him sadly. How could he explain to his old friend? How could he tell him that since the fire, somehow, all his values had changed, and the usual preoccupations of life like ambition and success no longer seemed important? . . . If they ever had. And the thought of going back to school with a lot of mindless kids seemed totally irrelevant. He had long since outgrown all that . . . Nowadays, he felt twice as old as his contemporaries, old and sad and somehow much too aware of the perilous fragility of life . . .

'I'm sorry,' he said, with a small helpless shrug. 'You see . . . since the fire, I've — things are different.'

Tudor nodded. He understood better than Matthew supposed. But at least, he told himself cheerfully, I have some consolation to offer. 'Welcome to the club,' he said, with his wry, lopsided grin. 'Not a particularly pleasing prospect, the adult world, is it? But maybe this will help.' And he brought out from under the table where he had carefully hidden it under a pile of coats and bathing towels, a brand-new shiny guitar case. Smiling, he held it out to Matthew.

Matthew stared at it, growing slowly pale. 'For me?'

'For you.' His eyes slid for a moment to the Captain's, and a brief, private exchange seemed to take place. 'We had a whip round, see — your old mates — and this is the result.' He did not add that the Captain was one of the old mates involved — a very substantial one, what's more. But that was all part of the deal he had made, and his eyes signalled their secret thanks and reassurance. He would keep the Captain's secret, never fear. 'Happy birthday, boyo,' he added, and gave Matthew one of his famous winks.

Matthew opened the case and lifted out the new guitar, still shaken and pale. He smoothed the gleaming wood with his hand, and turned it this way and that to look at the fine fretwork round the sound hole and the decoration on the finger-board. At last, unable to help himself, he curled his hand round the strings and struck one deep singing chord. And then he fell in love.

They all watched him, in a kind of breathless silence, not daring to break into his dream, while he tuned it and laid his ear to the soundbox to hear those rich, vibrating overtones, and stroked it and fingered it in awestruck delight.

But at last Tudor Davies could bear it no longer. 'Play it, boyo,' he said softly. 'It's got a voice, look you. Let it sing!'

So Matthew let it sing.

He only played one piece — the deepest and saddest of the Goyescas, to let that wonderful dark bass loose on the listening air. That was enough for the first time. In any case, he felt absurdly near to tears, and that would never do. But then, after that, he thought of Jampy bobbing about on that flimsy lilo, and he began to play the Skye Boat Song for them all to sing. Better to turn the whole incident into something cheerful.

Oh Flite, he thought. You are like a bird on the wing — leaping and flying in the sun . . . Stay safe — stay far — stay deep in your glass-green spaces, your sea-bed mountains and valleys, your wide, uncharted kingdom beyond our reach. Stay wild and free . . .

Under cover of the final chorus, Margaret Wilson suddenly turned to Jim Farley and said: 'What do *you* think would be best for Matthew?'

Jim looked astonished to be asked, but he pondered the question very carefully in his patient way, watching Matthew's hands on the guitar as he considered. At last, after long and painful thought, he came up with an answer.

'Roots.'

'What?' She sounded totally uncomprehending.

'Roots,' Jim repeated firmly. 'That's what he needs.' He looked at her gravely. 'He'll founder, else.'

★   ★   ★

The weather broke the next day, and Matthew could not swim in the sea. In a way, he was rather glad, for it meant that he couldn't look for Flite, and nor could any of the inquisitive crowd who had gathered round at Jampy's spectacular rescue. But in any case it was the end of the holiday season now, and people were packing up to go home. Farewells seemed to hang in the air, and a kind of rain-washed sadness lay on the empty beach. Everyone was going home.

Madge and her family were packing up too — going back with reluctance to their cramped bed-and-breakfast accommodation, with no more substantial promise of better things than Margaret Wilson's cautious support *'pending future arrangements'*. Madge privately didn't think much of that, but Jim said he thought the Captain was still working on her — and when Captain St George was in on it, things got done. So she got the family and their few possessions together as cheerfully as possible, putting a brave face on it, as usual — and kept her misgivings to herself.

She did not have many doubts about leaving Matthew with Skip at the Aqua Club — but Jampy did. He made an enormous scene, and stamped and roared and clung to Matthew like a small limpet on a sea-dried rock, crying fiercely: 'I want Matt. Gotta come too. Matt come too!'

But Matthew couldn't come too — not yet; and he did his best to explain it to Jampy between the small boy's roars of rage.

'I'll come soon,' he promised consolingly, as the sobs subsided.

Jampy looked at him sideways out of one tearful eye, while keeping his fist in the other. 'Soon?'

The other two children were watching Matthew with the same doubtful mistrust as Jampy, though they did not put their anxiety into words. Nor did Madge or Jim. But the same look of unwilling anguish was in their glance, too.

'Soon,' repeated Matthew firmly, trying to sound convincing. 'Before you can say — er — Floppy Disc.'

'Floppy disc, floppy disc,' said Jampy promptly, confounding them all.

But the laughter relieved the tension, and Matthew hugged them all in turn, wondering in a bewildered fashion why he felt so torn in two at their going.

'I'll be in touch,' said Madge, sounding fierce and upset both at once. 'Soon as ever there's somewhere for you to come to — you just come, see?'

'I'll come,' agreed Matthew, and watched them all pile into the campsite minibus that was taking them to the coach station.

Hands waved — Jampy's lower lip threatened huge disaster any minute — and the shabby bus moved off in a swirl of rain

66

and blowing sand from the dunes. Matthew watched it go and then turned away with a curious lump in his throat. He was surprised how much that little family had got under his skin. He must be getting soft.

★ ★ ★

The parting with Tudor Davies was less emotional but in some ways sadder — for he felt sure now that he would never go back to school, and probably never have another guitar lesson from this friendly, generous-hearted teacher.

Tudor had stayed on after the meeting, ostensibly 'for a breath of sea air, look you,' but in fact, Matthew suspected, to give what useful instruction he could in the time — especially on how to get the most out of his new guitar.

They had spent a couple of rainy days happily trying out everything they knew and all the pieces that Matthew remembered, plus a few more because that blessed man (as Matthew called him) had brought some new music down with him.

'It's a good instrument, mind,' he said, nodding at the rich chords coming out from under Matthew's fingers. 'Lot of heart, isn't it? . . . Give you all you want, it will.'

'I know.' Matthew was smiling, head still bent over the strings. 'All I could possibly want . . . It's a fabulous sound.'

'That's the ticket,' grinned Tudor. 'Keep the fables going, boyo. All of 'em under your hand.'

They looked at one another with understanding. All the fables? thought Matthew. All that magic waiting for me? What a marvellous thing I've been given — if I can only use it. '*If I can only use it,*' he repeated, aloud. And it came out like a prayer.

Tudor gave him a brief, admonitory tap on the arm. 'That's it, boyo. Use it. God-given, music is. Must be used, or it withers.'

He got up to go then. He did not say: You are my most gifted pupil, and you are throwing away a whole future by refusing to come back to me . . . He knew quite well that Matthew understood this anyway — but was somehow driven by a stubborn independence which he could not deny. It was the way of things when boys grew up, and there was nothing he could do about it.

So he only patted his shoulder and murmured: 'Matthew the music, isn't it?' and stumped off to get into his battered little car and take the long road home.

But Matthew laid down his guitar and went swiftly after him. 'I can't begin to —' he stammered through the car window.

'Don't try, boyo,' grinned Tudor. 'Just keep on playing.' He gave Matthew one fierce, challenging glance and added: 'Know where to find me if you need me.' Then he let in the gear and drove away.

'Music —' His deep voice floated out through the window. 'Always the music — remember!'

★ ★ ★

That evening, the sky cleared and the wind dropped, so Matthew went down on the rocks to play to the seals. Petra had said they would like it, and he was curious to see what would happen. Besides, he hadn't seen Flite for two days — not since Jampy's escapade — and he missed the dolphin's joyful company. Missed it badly, especially now when he was a bit blue after all those partings. Petra was going soon, too, and that would be another sadness, but much worse for Skip, he fancied . . . The world seemed full of autumnal melancholy — golden days retreating, the end of carefree enjoyment, with all sorts of sorrowful decisions and finalities in the air; and he needed Flite with his innocent delight, his rapturous celebration of life which seemed to shine through him from the tip of his tail to his inquisitive bottle nose.

So he would play to the seals, and maybe they would come — and maybe Flite would hear him too, in the far-off deeps of the sea, and maybe he would come . . .

He clambered round the rocks a little further this time, so that he was almost opposite the low offshore island that housed the seal colony, and sat down out of reach of the rising spray and began to play.

He played anything he could think of, and occasionally hummed and sang along with his own accompaniment to keep himself company, and to make the sound carry further. At first nothing happened at all, except that an occasional gull stooped down the wind to have a look at him, and flew away again, screeching a protest.

Perhaps they don't like my music, he thought wryly, and tried something else. He got so absorbed in the sound that he forgot to look up for a while, and when he did, he was surrounded by curious heads looking at him with alert attention from the water.

'Well, hello,' he said, rounding off a phrase, and adding a final throbbing chord. 'How nice of you to come. I'm glad someone appreciates me.'

The heads came a little nearer. The beautiful, liquid eyes regarded him in wonder. Where is it coming from? they questioned. Out of that little box? And when Matthew failed to continue, the eyes seemed to implore him to go on. We are listening, said those alert, questing heads. Make those interesting sounds again.

'All right,' said Matthew, smiling. 'How about this?'

He went on playing till it was almost dark, and the seals went on listening, fascinated, their round mottled heads thrusting out of the water and turning to him in enraptured stillness. He never had so attentive an audience.

But Flite did not come.

At last he had played them everything he knew twice over, with a bit of improvisation thrown in for good measure, and he thought again of Jampy drifting out to sea on that dangerous little lilo, so he played them 'Sailing', and began to sing it to them too, in his uncertain new adult tenor. 'Sailing, I am sailing . . . ' he sang, and the gleaming heads still listened, the great eyes still watched him from the darkening sea.

But still Flite did not come.

It's no good, he thought. He won't come now. I shall have to go in before it gets too dark to see. I mustn't stumble on the rocks with this marvellous instrument in my hands.

'Goodnight,' he said. 'Thanks for listening. Come again, won't you?'

The heads remained upright, the eyes watched him go. They were still there, rocked by the deep sea swell, as he walked away up the beach.

But Flite had not come.

*　*　*

There was no one in the kitchen next morning when Matthew came to look for some breakfast, so he helped himself to coffee and a hunk of bread. He had packed up his small tent, and moved into the Club the night before, sleeping in one of the empty bunk beds in the long dormitory. Most of the Aqua Club had gone home now, and the few who were left would be leaving at the weekend. He wondered vaguely where they had gone this morning, but since it was fine and sunny again, he supposed they were already in the surf, making the most of their last day.

He had just decided to cut breakfast after all and go in himself to search for Flite, when Petra came in rather swiftly and stood looking down at him. Her expression was curiously anxious and hesitant, as if she was not quite sure what to say to him.

'Matthew?' She paused, and then went on in a taut, somewhat driven manner. 'Would you know Flite —? Could you distinguish him from any other dolphin?'

Matthew stared at her. 'I — I think so, yes.'

'How?' Her voice was sharp and insistent.

'Well — his colouring — where the pale under-belly joins the grey — and the shape of the markings. And his smile.' He almost smiled himself, remembering it. 'Aren't they all different? He's quite a character.'

'Any special identification marks?' She still sounded sharply anxious, and Matthew began to feel worried.

'Um — yes. He has a kind of knotted scar under his jaw, on the white underside — as if he got caught on a hook once, or got bitten by a shark or something — it's a bit like a raised cross, in a sort of palish lump.' He looked at her now, with the beginnings of fear stirring inside him. 'Why?'

She returned his look with a grim one of her own. 'There's a dead dolphin washed up on the beach, a few miles up the coast.'

Matthew's heart seemed to give a great lurch of terror. 'Oh, my God.'

'One of the local fishermen reported it. I'm going up to have a look. Are you coming?'

'Yes. Yes, of course.' He stumbled to his feet.

But at the look on his face, Petra laid a kind hand on his arm. 'It may not be your friend, Flite, you know. Don't let's jump to conclusions.'

He gave her a stricken smile. 'No. You're right.'

'Skip will take us up there in the jeep. It's quite a climb down to the beach, I'm afraid. Will you be all right?'

'I can manage,' he said, annoyed that his legs were still in question.

Skip was waiting for them with the jeep already turned round to climb the steep cinder track to the coast road at the top of the cliff. Once there, he drove fast in the direction of St Just and then turned off down another steep, narrow lane that wound down towards a thin headland thrusting out between two rocky inlets half-hidden beneath the overhang of the cliff. The lane finally petered out on a bit of rough, sandy turf, and here they all got out and began to climb down a narrow, shaly track that threaded its way between rock and stunted furze to the small cove below.

At last they reached the line of slippery rocks at the edge of the shore, and stood looking down. There was a tiny, flaking jetty and one half-derelict wooden hut at the far end, and a single boat drawn up on the tiny strip of silver sand. And lying not far away, half in and half out of the gently lapping waves, was the long, beautiful body of a full-grown dolphin. The great, smooth head with its thrusting bottle nose lay still, the eyes stared sightlessly at nothing. The slender, elegant tail-fluke that could turn that massive body with the merest flick of movement no longer held any grace or power. Even the strong dorsal fin already looked thin and sharp, like the bones of a man's face in death, suddenly gaunt and stark, with the softness of living flesh withdrawn from it. All that majestic beauty and strength — that joyous, leaping energy — the wild, ecstatic rapture of exuberant life — was quenched and gone. There was nothing there now, no spark, no flicker. Only an empty shell lay on the silver sand.

Petra and Skip had been in front of Matthew, both turning to offer him a hand as he jumped down the last few feet of rock on to the shore. But now he gave a strange, gasping cry and went running past them across the sand to where the dead dolphin lay. He knelt down beside it, struggling frantically to move the huge, heavy head so that he could look under its throat for that tell-tale scar. But out of the water, the dolphin's body seemed enormously heavy, lying limp and flaccid under his hands, and he could not lift it.

'Let me,' said Skip's voice close to him, sounding warm and steadying, and two strong brown hands took hold of the dorsal fin and began to roll the body a little sideways so that the pinkish-white under-belly and long line of throat became visible. Together, he and Petra held on, while Matthew leant down and ran his hands along the smooth, still-gleaming surface of the dolphin's under-jaw and throat down to the limp front flippers.

He was almost sure without what his fingers told him. It was a beautiful, strong young dolphin all right, and very like Flite. But somehow the face was different. Even the shape of the body was different. Though, he supposed, death could change

71

everything. Death could make even Flite's smile look different. There was no smile now, of course. Only this empty stillness — this quiet, patient acceptance of death that all animals seemed to have, and that only man could not find . . . Death? This lovely, innocent creature lying in silent reproach surrendered under his hands? . . . His fingers explored again, felt, smoothed, brushed downwards, confirmed. There was no mark on the skin. No scar. No lumpy raised cross. No blemish at all.

It was not Flite.

Tears stung his eyes as he looked up at Skip and Petra. 'It's not — not Flite,' he said, in a tight, choked voice. 'But —'

'Are you sure?'

'Yes.' He laid his hand back again softly on the quiet head. 'But it's terrible all the same . . . ' *Terrible that anything so beautiful should be dead.*

'Yes,' sighed Petra, knowing his mind, and thinking of all the other dolphins that were dying throughout the oceans of the world. 'And this is only one.'

'What do you think killed it?'

Petra shook her head. 'I don't know.'

'Could it be the seal virus?'

She hesitated. 'It could. Or some other virus. Or simply pollution. Sometimes they swallow oil — or plastic bags — metal rings off beer cans. You'd be surprised what we've found in their stomachs . . . And swimming in polluted waters can simply lower their resistance — to whatever nasty bug is about at the time.'

Matthew looked anxious. 'How will you find out?'

'We'll have to take samples — do a few tests . . . '

'Where?'

She looked round at the tiny, enclosed bay and the steep cliff path to the top where they had left the jeep. 'Not here, obviously.' She paused and considered. 'I think the best thing would be to get it towed round to an easier landing place where a lorry can get down.'

'That can be arranged,' said Skip. 'And then you can take it to the dolphin centre.'

Petra nodded. She stood looking down at the dolphin sadly, seeming almost reluctant to disturb the silent dignity of death.

Matthew felt her reluctance, too. It seemed all wrong to have to drag the helpless body about with ropes and haul it out to sea and then back again to land and on to a lorry . . . And then subject it to all manner of tests and probings by the dolphin research team . . . But he knew it was necessary if they were to save other dolphins — even Flite, perhaps — who might be threatened already by the same unknown peril.

Looking at the long, perfectly proportioned body, he felt ashamed of the sudden surge of joy within him that it was not Flite lying there at his feet. Flite was alive, and he could rejoice for that, but this one was dead and deserved more than a moment of passing sorrow.

He felt he ought to salute it with honour — to cast a wreath of flowers for it into the sea — to pour a libation to Poseidon — Father Poseidon, mighty god of the oceans — and commend to his keeping the joyous spirit of his own wild dolphin . . .

But death was not romantic. Not here. Not anywhere, really. One had to be practical and think of the future. No time for legends and dreams.

Bleakly, he turned away.

'I'll see to it,' said Skip, speaking gently to them both. 'You go back with Petra, Matthew. I'll come round with the boat.'

They climbed the cliff path together silently. At the top, they both paused to look down. Already Skip and the owner of the boat were busy with ropes and nets. The dolphin lay still, uncaring.

Tudor Davies told me to keep the fables going, thought Matthew. I know what I'll do. I'll play for the dolphin tonight. I'll play it to rest in the sea . . . If a dolphin has a spirit, surely it will hear me . . . And the seals will take it home . . .

But Petra said with sudden roughness: 'It's no good being sentimental about *one* dolphin. It's all the others we've got to think about.'

Matthew nodded. He knew this to be true — though he didn't know what to do about it. Not yet. But one day he would have to, wouldn't he? And not leave it all to Petra. He sighed, but even as he did so he could not altogether quench that small flick of joy inside him because Flite, his loving companion, was still alive.

★ ★ ★

That afternoon, after the dead dolphin had been brought to shore by the boat, hoisted on to a lorry and driven away to the dolphin centre, Matthew went away by himself across the rocks and slipped unnoticed into the sea to look for Flite.

73

He had to know. He simply had to know. There was no way he could have been mistaken, he felt sure — but all the same, he had to know. Later, in the quiet evening, he would play for the dead dolphin. He would play all the music he knew to honour that gentle spirit — to give it rest and remembrance in the great deeps where it belonged. But now, in this solitude and space, he was waiting for a living dolphin. This was Flite's country, and all his wide domain of sunflecked water must surely echo with the sound of Matthew's voice calling to him. Surely he must hear?

Flite, he called. If you are alive, please come and tell me so. Please come. I need to know.

For a long time he swam alone, and nothing answered his call. At last, almost in despair, he turned back towards the shore, convinced now that Flite would not come — could not hear him calling through the sounding depths of the sea. He had gone — his friendly companion, gone far away, and was lost to him — lost or dead — and the world would never be the same again.

But as he straightened out from his turn and let the sea-swell lift his body and carry it forward, a dark grey shadow knifed through the water and leapt into an arc of gleaming splendour over his head.

What do you mean, I've gone? said Flite, diving deep and coming up close beside him in a shower of bubbles. What do you mean, I'm lost or dead? I'm alive! Can't you see I'm alive? Look at me leaping! Look at me playing leap-frog with my shadow! Isn't that alive enough? Look at me laughing in the sun. Why aren't you laughing too?

So Matthew laughed — or maybe he cried. He wasn't quite sure which — but who could resist that smile? And he clasped the dolphin in his arms and said in a watery voice: 'You see, it might've been you.'

Flite seemed to understand this. He nudged Matthew confidingly with his beak, as if to say: Well, it wasn't. Here I am, so stop brooding and rejoice! And the great, powerful body curved into another silvery arch and soared upwards into the sunlight.

Rejoice, rejoice, he said.

Matthew rejoiced. But at the back of his mind lay the shadow of another dolphin, and it troubled him. What did it die of? Was it the seal virus? And, if so, would Flite too be in danger? . . . Or was it the sea itself that was the menace? Were even these clear, translucent waters polluted? Was it safe for

Flite and his companions (for there must be others out there with him)? Was it fit to swim in? . . . Wasn't it time the dolphins went south to deeper, less populated waters — less crowded shores? To swim and dive and leap in a sea that posed no threat?

But it did, said his mind. Petra told me. There are the purse-seine nets of the big factory ships. There are the clubs and knives of the Japanese islanders. There are the whalers, now deprived of their illegal catches, turning to dolphin meat for the gourmet Japanese food market. There is nowhere safe for the dolphins. Where can they go?

Beside him, the thrusting head nudged him again, the large jaws opened and deposited a little stone in Matthew's hand as a present, and the supple body turned and curved in the water so that Flite's wide and innocent smile encompassed him. Come on, he seemed to be saying. Life is for living. Today! Dolphins don't think of tomorrow. Today, today!

But Matthew thought of tomorrow — and he could not shake off his sorrow, or his dread.

He decided to tell Flite about it as they swam together, recounting the whole sad tale about the other dolphin and his own secret terror. His voice rippled and swirled with the moving water, but Flite seemed to hear him. Maybe he just liked the sound of Matthew's voice, but he seemed to listen attentively — head tilted towards him — just like the seals to his music.

It seemed to him when he thought about it that this time Flite had come from a long way off to answer his call. It had taken him a long time to return, as if he had been far out in the deep waters of the Atlantic when Matthew's voice reached him. Where had he been? Was he already gathering with the other dolphins to make the journey southwards? . . . Like the swallows on the telegraph wires? . . . And ought he, Matthew, to have called him back at all?

'You see,' he said to Flite, 'it may not be safe for you here any longer. It may be time to go. What do you think?'

But Flite would not tell him what he thought — if he thought at all. He only curved his long body round Matthew, brushing close against him as he came out of another dive, and then rose out of the water in a joyous flash of silver above his head.

Alive! he said, in a cascade of clicks and whistles, gusts of blown air and showers of diamond spray. I am alive. Today! And so are you. Isn't that enough?

Then Matthew was ashamed of his fears and doubts. Only man, he thought, man with his burden of bitter darkness, had the ability to cloud the bright present with shadows of the future. The creatures of the earth — of the deep seas of the world — did not have it. Like Flite, they lived in the un-shadowed ecstasy of the moment, rejoicing all the way . . . And, like Flite, he must do the same — and cast no shade on that boundless, unclouded joy.

That's it, said Flite, turning a somersault. Like me. Dive deep. Dance and dive. Leap in the air and smile. Today! Today!

Matthew could not leap. But he could smile.

★ ★ ★

All the same, when he thought about the other dolphin, he was still worried, and with this in mind he went in search of Petra.

He had not really admitted it to himself yet, but he was more than a little attracted to this golden, friendly girl. To begin with, she was quite extraordinarily good to look at with that gleaming cap of blonde hair and those strange, tawny eyes, and the light dusting of freckles on her small, straight nose. And then she was strong and graceful, both in the sea and out of it — sure-footed and fearless on the rocks when they clambered down to look at the dead dolphin, calm and steady in an emergency — almost as calm and steady as Skip.

Skip. That was it, of course. No good having idiotic ideas about Petra. Skip was the one. And in any case, she wouldn't look at a boy his age — however old and worldly-wise he felt, though she did at least talk to him seriously about her work and treat him like an adult . . . But even so, it was no good making too much of it. She was kind to him, that was all. And when he saw her looking at Skip, he saw how it was. Yes, Skip was the one.

So it was no surprise when he found her talking to Skip on the clubhouse verandah, brown limbs spread out in the sun, gold heads close together in earnest discussion — so earnest that he wondered if he ought to disturb them at all.

'— until the results come through,' she was saying. 'I'll need to report on them anyway . . .'

'Gives us a little longer,' murmured Skip, a strange thrill of longing in his voice.

Matthew hesitated and almost decided to go away and leave

76

them in peace, but at that moment Petra looked up and saw him standing there.

Neither she nor Skip moved, but they both smiled and included Matthew in their closeness.

'Suntrap here,' said Skip lazily. 'Not bad for the time of year. Come and spread out. You're still a bit underdone!'

Petra laughed. 'English summer — what can you expect?'

'It's all very well for you,' growled Skip. 'Swanning off to the Caribbean and Mexico every five minutes.' He stretched out an arm that was every bit as brown as hers and gave her a playful push.

Petra clasped his hand and tucked it comfortably under her head before replying: 'Who's talking? Sunkissed macho beefcake.' Then she turned her head and added in a gentler voice: 'What's on your mind, Matthew?'

He sat down beside them awkwardly and tried not to feel superfluous. 'It's — Flite. I suppose you haven't had any results on the other dolphin yet?'

'Not yet, no.' She looked at him kindly. 'It's early days.'

'How — how long do you think they'll be?'

She considered, while two little lines of concentration appeared above the freckles on her nose. 'Only a day or two. We should know by the weekend.'

Matthew nodded, but he was clearly still troubled.

'What's worrying you?' It was Skip who spoke this time.

'I — if it's the virus — or these waters are polluted, or something — ought I to encourage Flite to come here?' His voice sounded rough with anxiety. 'Oughtn't I to — *send him away*?'

There was a pause. Then Skip said slowly: 'I doubt if you could. A dolphin is a law unto himself. He decides whether he comes or goes.'

Matthew agreed, sighing a little. 'Yes, I know that. But —'

'You think your friendship might be putting him at risk?' Petra spelt it out for him.

'I don't know,' said Matthew miserably. 'I just d-don't want to add to the dangers he has to face — they're bad enough already.'

Petra smiled at him with sudden warmth. 'He'd probably consider it worth it, if you asked him.'

Matthew's answering smile was less certain. 'Yes, but — have I the right to? I mean, he can't know about pollution — or the virus. How can he decide what is safe?'

77

'You can't decide for him,' stated Skip.

'No-o.' Matthew still sounded unconvinced.

'Wait and see,' murmured Petra, laying a consoling hand on his arm. 'We'll know soon enough.' She paused and then added softly: 'In any case, I expect he'll be heading south soon. The seas will be getting colder now.'

They all gazed out across the bay, watching the grey-green rollers pile and climb and surge inwards to break on the shore.

Colder, thought Matthew. Colder and lonelier — when Flite goes. When that wide and welcoming smile is no longer there to greet me. What shall I do without him? And in spite of the warmth of the golden autumn day, he shivered.

'They don't always go,' drowsed Skip, still spread out, with his eyes closed against the sun. 'There was one round here some years ago who stayed all winter . . . ' His voice was slow and seemed to have a smile in it somewhere.

'Was it warm enough?' Matthew sounded absurdly anxious.

'He seemed to think so . . . He found a sheltered spot round Falmouth way.'

If only Flite — began Matthew's treacherous thoughts. But he told himself sternly not to think such things. Not to hope. It might not be safe. It might not be good for his gentle, fun-loving dolphin to brave the cold dark seas and fierce winter storms around this rugged coast. He needed somewhere warm and peaceful — where he need not be afraid.

Afraid? said Flite in his mind. I am a king in the oceans of the world. Why should I be afraid?

Matthew sighed. I suppose he will go when he chooses, he thought. And where he chooses. I cannot alter it . . . I must be content that he was here with me — today.

That's it, said Flite, leaping in his mind like an irrepressible shadow. Today, Today!

★   ★   ★

It was evening, and one of those spectacular autumn sunsets across the western sea, when he went down to play for the other dolphin.

There was a crimson pathway across the bay, and the water round the rocks looked like molten gold — Inca gold, stained with blood . . . It seemed appropriate somehow, but he wasn't sure he wanted to see the seals swimming in it — let alone Flite. There was a threat somewhere in this beguiling ocean,

78

and the bright fingers of fire burning away in the west were a mockery . . .

I'm being morbid, he told himself. Shut up and get on with it. He struck a chord and listened to the overtones throbbing and dying in the quiet air . . . Music, he thought hazily, music solves everything really . . . I only have to play. And listen. And play. Granados, now — or should it be de Falla? . . . That sad one — yes, that will do.

He forgot everything then except the vibrating strings under his fingers and those singing chords . . . He didn't even remember where he was until much later — and then it was a distinct splash that woke him out of dream.

He lifted his head and stared out at the darkening water. There were heads in the bay again, not far away. The seals had come back to listen to his music. But it was not the seals that had made the splash. It was something much larger and much closer, something that now came right up to the rocks and tried to nudge the curved wood of the guitar with his long bottle nose. Flite had come to listen too — but he was not content with listening. He wanted to know what this thing was that made these delectable sounds, and why it would only sing when Matthew stroked it with his hands.

'Take care!' said Matthew, laughing. 'You can't have it to play with. It's much too valuable.'

Flite bobbed up again on the next wave, still trying to nudge it with his inquisitive nose. ('They identify things with their noses,' said Petra's voice in his mind.)

'Sorry,' said Matthew, backing away a little to keep the spray off the shining wood. 'But I'll play you one more piece, if you like, to make up for it. Listen.'

He played one more piece – a small, haunting folk song with an underlying dance rhythm that had something of Flite's leaps and dives in it, and Flite listened. So did the seals. The whole quiet corner of the little bay and its protecting spur of rocks seemed to be listening. Even the waves slapped against the shore with a gentle, muted whisper, and the seabirds rested on the swell and forgot to cry against the small night wind.

At last Matthew drew his fingers across one final deep bass chord, listened to its overtones fade and die on the soft night air, and laid his guitar down carefully on his coat spread out on the rocks.

'That's all now,' he said to the seals. 'You'd better go home to bed.' But to Flite he said softly: 'It was for the other dolphin really, you know. Not for you at all. You don't need singing to your rest, do you? But I'm glad you came.'

And he leaned down over the edge of the rocks and stretched out his hand. A long, thrusting nose came up and nudged confidently against his outstretched palm — and the great domed head rose out of the water for a moment, the wide smile resting on his tranquilly in perfect trust.

Well, since you won't give me that music-box to play with, said the clever, observant gaze, I'll just show you I can dance without any help from you. And he sank under the next wave, and came up in a beautiful flying curve, leaping high in the air against the fading fire of the sunset sky.

'Good night,' said Matthew softly. 'Sleep well in your deep ocean bed.'

Flite did not answer. He blew a small breath of air out of his blow-hole, and sucked in another. Then he turned in a swirl of bubbles and headed out to sea.

★   ★   ★

A fierce and persistent hammering got Matthew out of his bunk next morning, and he stumbled out into the sunlight to find Skip furiously banging nails into one of the rickety posts on the verandah. He seemed to be driving them in with unnecessary force, and Matthew wondered if the whole verandah roof might come down any minute. But — looking at Skip's grim face — he decided to say nothing.

However, Skip saw him there, and after one more vicious swipe with the hammer, gave up his attack on the offending post, and attempted a crooked smile.

'Petra's going today.'

Matthew's inside seemed to churn with terror. 'Does that mean she's heard from the dolphin centre?'

'Yes.'

'What was it?'

Skip sighed. 'A virus, they think . . . But she wants to tell you herself.'

'Where is she?'

'Down on the shore.' He didn't explain why he wasn't down there with her, but Matthew was too anxious to notice.

'Don't you want any breakfast?' Skip called after him.

'No,' said Matthew. 'Thanks.'

'Nor do I,' muttered Skip, and watched him go running down across the dunes to the wide expanse of wet sand below.

Petra was sitting curled up on a rock, looking small and sad. She was staring out to sea, and she didn't turn round as Matthew approached. Her sadness hurt him somehow — like Skip's furious hammering — and he had an irrational desire to shake her and say: 'What is it with you two? Why can't you get together?' But of course he couldn't. He could only talk of the dolphin.

'Skip says you've got news.'

'Yes, Matthew, I have.' She turned her head a little, and he caught the sheen of tears in her eyes. 'It was certainly a virus — the same as they found in the dead porpoise earlier. Similar symptoms — breathing difficulties — a sort of pneumonia —'

'Like the North Sea virus?'

'Yes. But not necessarily the same one.'

'Infectious?'

'Probably.'

'Where does it come from?'

She shrugged slim brown shoulders. 'Who knows?'

'The sea itself?'

'No, not primarily. Other infected animals, of course . . . Though pollution may well weaken their resistance.'

'Could — could other dolphins get it?'

She looked at him unhappily. 'Possibly. If they get together in a school . . . We don't know, really.' She paused, and then added: 'Maybe a solitary one — like your Flite — would be safe enough.'

'What about the seals?'

She shook her head. 'The grey seals don't seem to have it. Though tests done on one earlier showed antibodies.'

'What does that mean?'

'They may be resistant to this particular virus — or they might be carriers.'

'*Carriers*?' He thought of those round, attentive heads listening in the water — those liquid eyes fixed on his face in wonder — and Flite swimming close to nudge at the guitar in his hands . . . What have I done? he thought.

'We can't be sure,' Petra was saying. 'That's the trouble. We can't be sure about anything.' She looked at Matthew's stricken face and added gently: 'But I don't think you need worry about Flite. He's strong and healthy by the look of him, and he seems to prefer to be on his own.'

81

Matthew sighed. 'I hope to God you're right.'

But all the same, he was afraid. And he knew now, painfully, what he ought to do. Only he didn't want to — not now — not ever.

He began to turn away from Petra, from the rocks, from the sea itself, pursued by anguished thoughts and indecision. But then something in Petra's face — a hint of lonely desolation — made him turn back and look at her. The swinging cap of hair seemed to lie flatly against her head, and there was an air of defeat about the set of her shoulders. Even her mouth, which was usually gentle and much given to smiling, seemed to have a downward curve that was almost stern, and those strange tawny eyes were dark with unspoken conflict.

'By the way,' he said, lying cheerfully through his teeth, 'Skip's making coffee. He told me to tell you.'

Petra stared at him for a moment in silence. Then a slow smile began in the gold-flecked eyes, and she suddenly reached out both arms and gave Matthew a swift, affectionate hug. 'You're a good boy, Matthew,' she said, laughing a little. 'But you're a damn bad liar!' And then she went off up the beach towards the clubhouse and Skip.

He watched her go, and then began to walk very fast by himself in the opposite direction.

★   ★   ★

'It's no good,' said Petra, 'I can't stay angry any longer.'

'Nor can I,' admitted Skip, with relief. He dropped the hammer on the floor, and put his arms round Petra instead.

Without hesitation, her arms came up and held him just as hard.

'That's better,' he said.

Petra laughed, though a little shakily. 'Matthew said you were making coffee.'

'Oh, did he.' Skip was laughing too now, but he made no attempt to move.

'Well — aren't you going to?'

'No, I don't think so. I'm much happier like this.'

'I see.'

'Do you?' He framed her face with his two hands and looked at it long and lovingly — as if fixing it in his memory for ever.

'All the same,' he murmured, 'perhaps we should go in . . .?'

'Maybe we should.' She was looking at him with the same loving intensity — held in the same unspoken thrall.

The silence continued between them, their gaze locked in startled recognition, and then Skip slowly bent his head and kissed her.

'We won't lose it, you know,' she said, reaching up to clasp the curve of his head beneath the glinting tongues of hair.

'No,' he agreed, kissing her again. 'I know.'

★   ★   ★

It was much later when Matthew came back and found them — he thought he had given them a decent interval. He hoped it was long enough — but he needed to go in the sea and find Flite, and he had to come back for his gear.

They were sitting quite peacefully on the verandah steps, but Petra's bags were packed and lying beside her on the flaky wooden boards.

'Are you going right now?' Matthew asked, dismayed.

'In a few minutes.' Petra smiled at his anxious face. 'I'm glad you turned up in time.'

'In time for what?'

'To say goodbye, of course.'

'Oh.' Matthew knew quite well that he didn't want to say goodbye at all.

Nor did Skip, by the look of him. He wasn't smiling, but he didn't look angry any more.

'Where will you be going next?'

Petra's brown shoulders moved in a fluid shrug. 'Not sure. Somewhere in the Pacific. Wherever the Marine Institute sends me.'

Both Matthew and Skip looked glum.

'All I know is, I'll be at the whale watch in the Laguna Scammon in January, when the grey whales come down.'

'Where's that?'

Petra and Skip glanced at one another, and strange, swift messages seemed to pass between them.

'In Baja California . . . '

'Mexico —' explained Skip. 'That long thin bit.'

Matthew looked totally bewildered.

'They come over 4,000 miles,' Petra told him. 'All the way from the Bering Sea.'

'To breed?'

83

'Yes. Warm and sheltered. You can see them coming all down the coast of California . . . ' She looked at Skip again. 'It's a wonderful sight.'

But somehow, Matthew felt, they seemed to be saying quite different things to each other behind the words.

'Will you come back?' he blurted out suddenly.

The two of them seemed to look at him in surprise.

'Yes,' said Petra, as if it was a foregone conclusion. 'Of course.'

Skip got to his feet then and picked up her bags. 'We'd better go. You'll miss your train.'

Petra got up too, and folded Matthew in a warm-hearted embrace. 'Give my love to Flite,' she murmured. 'And be happy.'

Skip said nothing more, and together they climbed into the jeep and drove away.

Matthew watched them go — feeling surprised at his own sense of loss. But that was nothing to what he was going to face now. It was almost too difficult to contemplate, and he wasn't in the least sure he could do it. But he knew he had to try.

Sighing, he went in to fetch his wet suit and snorkel mask, and then set off for the beach and his meeting with Flite.

★　★　★

The sea was calm that day, and blue as lapis beneath a clear, windswept sky. A molten glitter of autumn sunshine lay on the water and cast strange shafts and glimmers of light below the surface, reaching down to the pale sea-floor. For a while Matthew swam alone, gazing down at fronds of weed lit into sudden brilliance of green and garnet red and the darting shadows of small-fry between the rocks agleam with instant silver. He did not want to call Flite yet. He did not want to do anything. He wanted to drift in the swell, surrendered to its limitless power, and not think.

Action and inaction were both impossible — and whatever decision he took would be wrong . . . Meanwhile the sea was tranquil and empty, and he could float in its arms suspended in time.

But not for long. He did not need to call Flite. Without any summons from him, the dolphin came. The beautiful, sinuous body appeared silently beside him, weaving effortless circles round him in the translucent water. There was so much light in the sea that day, that the dolphin's long underside seemed almost luminous as it turned and rolled and poured itself lazily in and out of the swell.

Matthew watched it, enthralled, and his heart seemed to leap with the dolphin in a great surge of joy at its coming. He ought not to be glad, he knew. He ought to be stern and decisive. He ought to — but he could not. He could only rejoice and greet his smiling companion with open arms.

'Oh Flite,' he said, as the great domed head came near and the powerful beak nudged him with playful insistence. 'Oh Flite — what am I to do with you?'

Do with me? said those bright, intelligent eyes. Play with me, what else? I've come to play. Aren't you glad to see me?

And the smooth curve of his back arched through another wave, sank deep in the undertow, and then rose in a joyous leap and a swirl of bubbles high over the next wave-crest swelling in from the dark Atlantic.

When Matthew moved rather blindly to follow him, he found that Flite had made a fast turn and come up behind him. The silken flank pushed against him confidingly in the water, close and affectionate.

Matthew put his arms round him, laid his head against the dolphin's warm, pulsing side, and wept.

'It's not safe for you here,' he told him. 'It's not safe any more. These waters are death to you — don't you understand?'

Flite leaned against him, motionless in the quiet sea-swell, with one consoling flipper laid across his back. But in a little while the powerful body turned with a slow flick of his tail-fluke and the inquisitive head came round to look at Matthew in wonder.

Why are you crying? he seemed to ask. I have heard my friends cry in the deep. Their voices follow me through the mighty echoing spaces of the ocean. I know their sorrow. But yours I do not understand. Tell me what it is . . . And the great head came close and nudged him again.

So Matthew told him.

He told him all of it — about the virus and the polluted coastal waters, and the threat that hung over him. As before, his own voice floated and bubbled round him in the water, and as before Flite seemed to listen attentively, lying close beside him and resting his long, powerful body in the gentle lift and fall of the ocean swell.

85

'So you see,' said Matthew at last, 'I think it is time for you to go . . . To warmer and clearer seas . . . Do you understand? It is time to go.'

Whether Flite understood or not, he was not going to let Matthew be sad any longer. He suddenly left his side and went into a series of marvellous convolutions and spectacular leaps and dives, as if trying to distract Matthew from his fears and forebodings.

Look at me! he said, clicking and whistling and blowing bubbles. See how high I can fly! Aren't I clever? Watch me dive! Watch me leap! Isn't life glorious? Now!

It was glorious, now. Matthew had to admit it. And as Flite leapt and dived and swerved through the shimmers of sunlight and cascades of upflung spray, Matthew felt his own spirits rise to meet the dolphin's instant joy.

He had done his best. He had tried to warn him. How much Flite understood, he could not know. And he could not order his going — the going and coming of a great, magnificent sea creature who had all the wide oceans of the world to play in. He could only hope that he would be safe — and meanwhile rejoice in his presence.

And meanwhile, rejoice. For ecstasy was not far off that day. He had never known Flite quite so playful before — so affectionate, so full of unquenchable delight in the blue and gold world around him. He leapt through the waves, he chased his own tail, he skimmed over the water one minute and dived deep the next to chivvy the shoals of small fish that swam in the shadows. He chased the seals, and raced after a fishing boat crossing the bay, and returned like a swift black arrow to Matthew's side. He rolled on his back, and turned somersaults in shafts of deep-sea sunlight, and came back to Matthew again, smiling, after each sparkling display. And last of all, as if offering Matthew a final gift, he came up between his legs and nudged him on to his back again, and set off in a breath-taking burst of speed across the bay, with Matthew riding like a charioteer just below the powerful, thrusting head.

They came to rest again close to the rocks at the end of the bay, and here the dolphin gently rolled Matthew off his back and deposited him in the water. They lay together tranquilly for a few moments, the dolphin's body comforting and close so that Matthew's arm could rest across it in loving response. They were very quiet, very tender with one another, and did not try to break the spell of peace that had fallen on them.

Matthew did not know what strange communication there was between them, or how the dolphin knew his mind, but he became aware, with a sense of slow wonder, that Flite's spectacular display was a farewell performance. He had understood Matthew's grief — he knew the dangers — and he was going away. Whether it was the normal time for his migration south, Matthew would never know, but it was somehow clear to him that the dolphin's time of departure had come, and this last marvellous sharing of joy and the breathless ride on his back was Flite's final gift of love.

'Goodbye then, Lord a-Leaping Flite,' he murmured, half-smiling, and clasped the beautiful, lissom body in his arms. 'Thank you for everything you've taught me . . . I shall never forget you.'

Flite seemed to shiver a little in his arms and lean against him a little closer. Then he turned in the water so that the great head came close, and for a moment the two of them — dolphin and boy — gazed at one another in love and trust, in perfect understanding.

At last the long, sensitive beak moved gently forward and touched Matthew's face, the wide smile rested on him like a final benediction, and the long, silvery shape of the wild dolphin turned in an incandescent swirl of bubbles and swam away into the vast jade and indigo depths of the wide Atlantic.

Flite had gone.

PART II

ETERNITY'S SUNRISE?

The Captain was looking out of his window. He had been ill again lately, and confined to bed, but now at least he was up and sitting in his chair, and he could see the sea. He always felt better when he could see the sea.

It had been another golden autumn day, but now it had clouded over, and a sharp offshore wind had got up, lifting the surf into restless white crests. He saw the boy go by, head down into the wind, walking fast — and something about the set of his shoulders troubled the old man. The thin figure seemed too tense, braced against pain and pursued by furies. No one that young ought to look so beset.

He watched the boy fight his way on against the wind to the far end of the long surf beach and then turn back when he reached the rocks and come steadily towards him with his uneven stride, across the firm wet sands near the water, head still down and heedless as he came.

He watched him drawing nearer, and then pressed the bell on the wall beside his chair. When the cheerful face of the young chambermaid came round the door, saying: 'Yes, Captain?', he beckoned her over and pointed at the beach below.

'Emma, is there someone who could run an errand for me?'

'I 'spect so, Captain. I could find somebody, surely.'

He nodded. 'That boy. Down there, walking alone. I want to see him.'

The young country face smiled at him, seeming unsurprised. 'Right-o, Captain. See what I can do.'

She bounced out of the room, still smiling and cheerful, and the Captain returned to his window-watching.

Presently he saw the girl herself go running out of the hotel gates, tying a scarf over her head against the wind as she went. She climbed down the steep steps to the beach and ran diagonally across the sand to reach Matthew as he walked by. He saw them meet, and for a moment the boy looked up towards the hotel and the Captain's window, and then the two figures turned and came towards him, side by side.

Soon, there was a knock at his door.

'Come in, Matthew,' he called. And when the boy stood there hesitantly in the doorway, he added: 'It's good to see you.'

'They tell me you've been ill.' The grey-green eyes were fixed on him reproachfully.

'Ancient history. Better now.' He jerked an imperious thumb at a nearby chair. 'Come and sit down. Could do with some company.'

Matthew obediently sat down and looked at the old man with attention. He was shocked to see how much older and frailer he looked this time. Clearly, the illness he dismissed so lightly was not something trivial.

'Won't I tire you?' he blurted out, anxious about that fragile air.

The old man laughed. 'Tougher than I look.' He fixed Matthew with a shrewd and penetrating stare. 'So — tell me what's new?'

Matthew met his stare for a moment and then looked away at the sea beyond the hotel windows. He sighed. 'New? . . . Well, it all seems to be partings at the moment.'

'Such as —?'

'Oh — first it was Madge and Jim and the kids. And then Tudor Davies.' He flashed him a grateful smile. 'It was good of you to arrange that.'

The Captain merely grunted.

'And then today, it was Petra's turn.'

'Who's Petra?'

Matthew paused, surprised. 'Didn't you meet her? Skip's girlfriend? She's a marine biologist or something. Into whales and such.'

The old man nodded. 'Think I did see her with him once — at the Club. Blonde?' He remembered the two heads very close together, blonde and tawny, bent in secret discussion or private dreams under the lights of the Club bar. But she had kept her face hidden.

'Blonde,' agreed Matthew. 'And smashing to look at.'

There was something in his voice that made the Captain glance at him more sharply. 'And she's gone. Where?'

Matthew shrugged. 'Where her work takes her. She said something about the Pacific.'

'And Skip will miss her?'

'A lot, I should think.' He looked at the Captain with a rueful grin. 'They were — as the saying goes — very close.'

There was another unspecific grunt. But the Captain was no fool. 'Will *you* miss her?'

Matthew answered calmly enough. 'Oh well — yes, a bit. She was very kind to me.'

The Captain was silent for a moment. Then he shot Matthew another hard look. 'Well then — who else has gone?' For something had to account for that air of acute desolation.

The boy seemed to freeze into himself for a moment. But then he turned and allowed his friend the Captain to come close. 'It's Flite,' he said.

They talked for a long time about the dolphin and then Captain St George said with surprising gentleness: 'You did the right thing, boy. But are you sure he's gone?'

'Oh yes.' Matthew sounded quite certain. 'He said goodbye to me. I'm sure of it.'

The Captain's smile was only faintly quizzical. 'Talked to him, did you?'

Matthew blushed a little. 'Oh yes . . . all the time.'

'And he answered?'

The thin wash of colour deepened on his cheekbones, but he was not really embarrassed. 'Well — yes. I thought he did . . . At least, we communicated — somehow.' He looked at the Captain with honest eyes. 'I mean — words are only one way . . . They kind of spun into my mind — or his . . . I don't know which.'

The Captain sighed. 'We none of us understand the mind of a dolphin.'

Matthew agreed. 'Of course, he might have been going anyway. It's the time of year for migration. Petra told me . . . But I'm sure he understood me. And I'm sure he said goodbye — in his own way.'

There was a bleakness in his eyes that made the old man's own heart ache. But then, strangely, the bleak look of loss seemed to change and soften, and the boy said suddenly: 'He'd disapprove of this, though.'

'What?'

'This — regret.' He looked at the old man beside him, painfully trying to put impossible things into words. 'Flite didn't believe in regret. It was something outside his experience. He believed in *now* — today!'

The old man nodded slowly.

'Instant joy . . . ' Matthew murmured.

'What did you say?'

'It was what *you* said. Instant joy. Don't you remember?'

The Captain thought about it. 'Yes. I do . . . Those children on the beach — and that little fella, what was his name?'

'Jampy.'

'That's it. Jampy. Jumping up and down like a jack-in-the-box.' The old eyes lit with humour. 'Irrepressible, that one.'

Matthew smiled. 'Yes.' Instant joy, he thought. That was what Flite taught me. But I don't know how to hold on to it . . . And I suppose I shouldn't try.

'It will come back,' said the Captain, as if he had spoken. Then he looked round the room as if searching for something, and added abruptly: 'Over there — on my table. Blake. I was reading it this morning.'

Mystified, Matthew fetched the book for him, and waited while the parchment fingers turned the pages and found the place.

'Here,' said the Captain. 'Hackneyed, of course, but still true.' And he held out the open book for him to see.

Matthew looked down at the printed words on the page.

> *He who binds to himself a joy*
> *Does the wingéd life destroy.*
> *But he who kisses the joy as it flies*
> *Lives in eternity's sunrise.*

Tears stung his eyes as he read the famous words. He had a far-off picture in his mind of Flite, leaping through the waves across a gleaming pathway on the sea, swimming and swimming, away from him and always towards the sunrise . . .

'That's your Flite speaking,' said the Captain softly.

But Matthew could not answer.

At length, when the silence had become less fraught, the Captain said briskly: 'Well, then, Matthew. What now?'

The boy seemed to return from a long way off. But he smiled at the old man and said honestly: 'I don't know.'

'Will you stay down here?'

Matthew hesitated. 'Not for much longer. The doctors say I'm almost fit now. But I promised to help Skip with the decorating. And —' he looked at the Captain a little shyly, 'I daresay he could do with a bit of company right now.'

The old man smiled. 'That figures.'

'The only thing is —' The boy paused awkwardly.

94

'Yes?'

'I ought to get some kind of a job. But I don't suppose it's easy down here in the winter.'

'Not that easy, no. Even the locals find it hard.'

Matthew nodded. 'Maybe I'll have to wait until I get back to London.'

'Will you go back to Madge and Jim Farley?'

Once again he hesitated. 'Yes. To see them. Especially over Christmas, with the kids and all. That's why I need some money.' The fleeting grin came back. 'But to stay — no.' He looked at the Captain, willing him to understand. 'I need to be independent.'

The old man understood all too well. 'It won't be easy, though, on your own.'

Matthew agreed.

'You should have accepted that insurance money.'

'I know I should.' He sounded both obstinate and apologetic. 'But it made me feel sick, somehow . . . I'd much rather earn it.'

'I don't blame you.'

Matthew breathed a sigh of relief. It surprised him to find how much he cared what the old Captain thought of him.

'All the same —' the old voice spoke cautiously. 'I'd like you to promise me something.'

'What's that?' Matthew sounded equally cautious.

'Keep your options open.'

'What does that mean exactly?'

'Oh — just don't take any final decisions too soon. I mean — if you get a job somewhere, or knock about the world for a bit, or anything you fancy — you can still take an A-level or two and go to university later on. Or do some kind of training or other. There's nothing to stop you doing it when you're twenty — or thirty, for that matter. Is there?' The fierce old eyes were bright with challenge.

'No, I suppose not.' Matthew knew he sounded unconvinced and rather luke-warm.

'Brains are meant to be used,' growled the Captain. 'So is talent. God-given, your Tudor Davies would say. Not to be wasted!' He glared at Matthew, and then relented and smiled instead. 'Just keep an open mind, that's all I ask.'

'I'll try,' said Matthew, not quite knowing what pledge he was giving. It occurred to him, though, that the Captain was taking an extraordinary amount of trouble over a tiresome teenager he scarcely knew.

'Computers,' said the Captain suddenly. 'Why didn't I think of it?'

Matthew looked at him enquiringly.

'Good at them, aren't you?'

'Fairly.'

'Well, then.' He leant back in his chair, as if he had said enough.

'Well what?' asked Matthew, mystified.

The old man waved a hand towards the door into what Matthew had supposed was his private bathroom. 'In there. Have a look.'

Matthew went over and peered inside. But it wasn't a bathroom at all. It was a small dressing-room that seemed to have been turned into an office. There was a telex and a fax machine in one corner, and beside them a desk with a telephone, a few tidy papers, and a neat computer screen and manual set at one end of it. On closer inspection, it seemed a simple enough piece of software, and one he was quite used to handling.

He went back to the Captain and stood beside him, still puzzled.

'Could you handle it?'

'Oh yes.' He waited for an explanation, but when none was forthcoming, he asked: 'But what for?'

The Captain grinned. 'Keep tabs on 'em, boy. That's what.' Then, seeing Matthew's bewilderment, he laughed and spelt it out for him. 'You know about shipping?' He did not wait for Matthew to answer. 'Keep an eye on what's happening. Each day. Only way to run a business.' His shrewd glance met Matthew's puzzled one with amusement. 'Most days, I ring head office in London. They tell me what's going on — any problems — loading and unloading — accidents — strikes — whatever. I feed it all into the computer. That way, I know at once where everything is.' He paused, and added with a vague wave of his hand: 'Only a small travelling gadget, this one. Keeps me in touch. At home, I have a much more complicated system.'

Matthew nodded. And waited.

The old man looked at him approvingly. The boy did not waste time asking unnecessary questions. 'But since I was ill, I got behind. Everything's out of date. The whole system's shot to hell. Understand?'

'Yes.'

'Could you put it right?'

'If you give me the facts —'

'We'll get 'em from head office. Plenty to feed in.' He shot a swift, assessing glance at Matthew's expressive face and added casually: 'Pay you the going rate.'

Matthew protested at once. 'There's no need for that.'

'Yes, there is. A job's a job. Four pounds an hour. Two hours a day. Take it or leave it.'

'It's too much.'

'Rubbish. You'll earn it. I'll see to that.' His glare was very convincing, but Matthew didn't believe a word of it.

'I don't know what to say.'

'It's a good offer.'

'Yes, but —'

'But what?' The glare was even fiercer.

Matthew shook his head and said gently: 'Isn't it time you went south — like Flite?'

The old eyes looked astonished, and then suddenly misted. 'Are you trying to push me out, boy?'

Matthew smiled. 'Only — like I pushed Flite out.'

Captain St George was absurdly touched — and therefore gruffer than ever. 'See here, young man. I've been coming back to this place every summer for years now. Sentimental reasons. Most of the time, I told you, I've been damned lonely. This year, for once, I got interested in a couple of things. Decided to stay on a bit, that's all. Anything wrong in that?'

Matthew looked down at him, still half-smiling. 'Only if it makes you ill.'

The Captain snorted. 'Irrelevant. I've enjoyed myself.' Then, seeing that Matthew still looked unconvinced, he added slyly: 'But I could do with your help — just for a couple of weeks.'

At this, Matthew capitulated. 'All right.'

The Captain held out his hand. 'Deal?'

'Deal,' agreed Matthew, and clasped the frail fingers in his own.

★　★　★

Skip did not come home till very late that night. In fact, he did not come home at all, and Matthew finally went to bed and left the verandah light on — as much to cheer himself up as to see Skip home. It was raining hard, and the wind blew great gusts of rain and sea-spray against the windows. Matthew pictured Flite out there in the turbulent darkness of the sea, battling his way south against the winter storms. Was he safe? Was he lonely out there in the watery wastes of the deep Atlantic? Or had he joined a school of his friends, and were they all travelling cheerfully together, careless of the storms, leaping through the waves as joyously as ever? He hoped so. Oh, he hoped so. No harm or fear or memory of sadness should ever come to that loving, joyful creature.

He sighed, admitting that sadness had indeed overtaken him, and fell into an uneasy sleep where dreams of Flite haunted him and he swam through endless deep-sea surges and towering wave crests, searching for the blue-black shadow of a dolphin that was never there . . .

Towards morning, he woke suddenly at the sound of cautious footsteps on the verandah, followed by something heavy falling, and a muttered curse. He got out of bed and went through to the verandah door, pushing it open against the wind and driving rain.

'Skip? Is that you?'

A fierce spatter of rain drove into his face, blinding him so that he almost fell over the dark figure hunched on the verandah floor.

'Skip? What the hell are you doing down there?'

The pale blur of Skip's face looked up at him in the gloom. 'Looking for my key,' he said vaguely, and went on sitting there in the rain.

'I left the door open, you clot.' Matthew shook his head in exasperation, and then reached behind the door for a spare oilskin before dashing out into the rain to seize Skip by the shoulders.

At first he thought he was merely drunk, and set about getting him inside without too much fuss. He was used to dealing with drunks. He had often put his mother to bed after a heavy night — and her boyfriend(s), come to that. It didn't bother him a lot — except that this rather brought it all back, just when he was beginning to forget it.

But then something about Skip's heavy limbs and his vague attempts to help himself made Matthew wonder. He got him successfully into the dim passage-way and steered him towards the kitchen. Once through the door and under the light, he had another look at him, and was appalled by what he saw.

Skip was soaked to the skin — and covered in mud, even up

to the sodden shoulders of his anorak. Rain dripped in rivulets off his hair and down his face, and something which looked ominously red was mingling with the streaks of mud on his forehead and trickling into his eyes.

'My God,' said Matthew. 'What's happened to you?'

'Mud,' explained Skip, with extreme lucidity.

'I can see that,' agreed Matthew. 'Where's the jeep?'

'Wrapped lovingly round a tree when I saw it last.'

'Where?'

'Somewhere near Tresillian Head — I think.'

Matthew stared at him. 'You walked — *from Tresillian?*'

'Well, I didn't fly,' growled Skip, and lurched towards the nearest chair.

'Are you hurt?' Matthew put his arms out swiftly to steady him.

'Not so's you'd notice. Bang on the head, that's all.' He shook the mixture of rain and blood out of his eyes, and clutched at the back of the chair with his mud-caked hands. 'Lucky, really,' he added, in a chatty voice, and passed out cold on the floor.

Matthew took one look at him and went swiftly to work. First, he stripped off all Skip's wet clothes, peeling them off his cold, uncaring limbs, and wrapping him in a couple of heavy blankets which he grabbed off the nearest bed in the long, club dormitory. Then he propped Skip's head on a cushion, and fetched a basin of water to bathe the cut on his forehead. When he had got rid of the mud, he found that the wound was not very deep, but there was a flap of loose skin still oozing blood, and a large egg-shaped lump which was rapidly swelling and turning black.

Having cleaned him up as much as he could, he began to worry about his continued unconsciousness, and the coldness of his body. He wondered if he ought to leave him there on the kitchen floor, or try to get him into his bed — and whether he could find such a thing as a hot bottle among Skip's spartan belongings.

He was just considering the possibility of filling an empty cider bottle with hot water and wrapping it in a woolly hat, when Skip opened his eyes and said: 'Soup.'

Matthew grinned his relief, and went over to the cooker. 'Certainly, sir. Soup coming up.' He had opened a tin of tomato soup earlier in the evening for his own supper. There was plenty left, and he only had to warm it up. All the same, he kept a wary eye on Skip as he lay there, and wondered if that blazing pallor indicated shock, and whether he ought to ring the doctor.

'Help me up,' demanded Skip, vainly trying to get some strength into his legs.

'You stay there,' ordered Matthew. 'Till you get this down you.'

'Can't drink soup lying down.'

'I'll get some more cushions.'

He fetched two more fat velvet ones from the clubroom, and propped Skip up against them. 'Can you manage like that?'

'I suppose so,' Skip grumbled, lying back mutinously against his cushions and trying to look in control of the situation. But the world kept going out of focus, so he wasn't very successful.

'Here.' Matthew handed him the bowl of soup. 'Get outside of this.'

He gave him a spoon, but he noticed that Skip seemed to have some difficulty in wielding it. 'You've hurt your arm as well,' he said.

Skip moved it gingerly up and down, and made a face about it. 'Must've wrenched it on the steering wheel,' he muttered. And then, explosively: 'So damn *stupid!*'

'Skip, anyone could —'

'I've been driving up and down these bloody cliff roads for fifteen years. Never hit a thing — and one small strip of mud on the road . . . ' He waved the spoon a little too wildly, and cursed as pain shot through the damaged muscles.

'Eat your soup,' said Matthew. 'I want to get you to bed.'

Skip glared at him, but he was too tired to protest, and meekly finished his soup without another word.

That meekness worried Matthew more than anything else. 'Should I ring the doctor?' he asked, voicing his doubts aloud.

'Tomorrow.' Skip put down his empty mug with rather a clatter. '*If* it seems necessary.' He frowned, making a huge effort to concentrate. 'And we'd better tell Bob Harris at the garage — and maybe Old George at the police station . . .'

'Is the jeep off the road?'

'Yes. Nearly off the cliff.'

Matthew shuddered. 'No need to tell anyone tonight then.' He bent down and put his arms round Skip's back and shoulders. 'Come on. You'll be better off in bed.'

Somehow, he got Skip to his feet and half-carried him through to his bedroom, where he unceremoniously heaved him on to his bed and pulled the covers over him. 'Are you still cold?'

'No.' But Skip's teeth were beginning to chatter.

Matthew looked doubtful. 'Alcohol? After a bang on the head?'

'No.' Skip's eyes were closing. 'I'll be all right . . . '

But Matthew was not satisfied. He went off and got his make-shift hot bottle and stowed it beside Skip's cold, shivering body.

'Thanks . . . ' murmured Skip, but he was already far out.

Matthew stood there, irresolute, looking down at Skip's bruised and ashen face. The tawny tongues of hair lay limp against his head, and he looked suddenly young and vulnerable, lying there. Matthew felt a curious wave of affection and pity wash over him as he remembered that Skip had said goodbye to Petra that day, and did not know when he would see her again . . . Just as Matthew had said goodbye to Flite — and might *never* see him again . . . Skip must be riven with the same enormous sadness. And probably made careless by his own distress of mind, so that he was unwary and slow to react when he met that fatal streak of mud on the road . . .

'Don't worry,' drowsed Skip, aware of Matthew still standing beside him. 'Better . . . in the morning.'

'Of course,' agreed Matthew. 'Yell if you need me. I'm not far away.'

'Far away —' sighed Skip, and turned his face to the wall.

★ ★ ★

In the morning, Matthew took charge. He rang the garage and the police station about the jeep as early as he could, and then rang the doctor. He knew him anyway, because he was a regular visitor to the Aqua Club, and had been overseeing the treatment for Matthew's legs. Now he said briskly that he'd be over during the morning, and to keep Skip quiet — if that was possible — meanwhile. But that was easy, for Skip slept on undisturbed. Matthew had another look at him, and was a little troubled to see that the blazing pallor was still there, and the bruises looked blacker and bigger — but his breathing seemed all right, and Matthew guessed he was mostly just exhausted.

Then he thought of the Captain and his promise to go over to the hotel and help out with the computer. But he couldn't leave Skip. Not at the moment. After considering the matter over a cup of tea in the kitchen, he decided to ring the hotel and leave a message — even though it was only a few hundred yards away across the beach. Having done that, he felt better. He didn't like disappointing the Captain — or seeming ungrateful about the offered job. He knew very well the old Captain was making special concessions on his behalf.

He looked out of the window across the dunes and the wet sands beyond towards the little cluster of houses above the seawall, and wondered if the old man was all right. He had seemed very fragile yesterday — his hands had looked almost transparent resting on his stick . . . But that word transparent reminded Matthew of Skip's face, so he went to have another look at him. He was still asleep.

Skip's window looked straight out to sea, and Matthew stood there for a few moments, staring out at the dark horizon. Was Flite out there? . . . He was probably many miles away by now — far across that wild, churning sea . . . It was dreadful how much he missed him. He ought not to be so sad. He ought to be glad he'd gone. Glad he was safe. The world was still good out there (he hoped), and Flite was probably enjoying it. Rejoice, rejoice, sang Flite into his mind, leaping like quicksilver . . . But it was somehow a receding, sorrowful sound that faded with the retreating tide . . .

It occurred to him that if he could be so churned up about Flite's departure, Skip must be feeling much worse about Petra's, and he wondered idly in his mind how Petra felt about it, and how she could just go like that, and why — if they were so close — she couldn't feel that something was wrong with Skip. Maybe she could, but she was half-way across the Atlantic by now, he supposed — like Flite.

At that moment, the phone rang in the office and he ran across to answer it in case the bell woke Skip. 'Yes?'

'Is that — Skip?'

'No, it's Matthew.' But he knew that voice. He couldn't mistake it. '*Petra*? I thought you'd gone.'

'My flight's delayed. Is Skip there?'

Matthew hesitated. 'Yes . . . but he's asleep.'

'Asleep?' She knew Skip's habits — his busy working day. It was totally unlike him. 'Is he all right?'

Matthew heard the anxiety in her voice, and was absurdly glad for Skip. She did care, after all.

'Not entirely, no. He turned the jeep over on the way home last night.'

'Oh my God. Is he hurt?'

'Not a lot. Mostly bruises and a bang on the head. But he walked about fifteen miles.'

'No wonder he's asleep. Have you had the doctor?'

'He's coming this morning. I thought he ought to have a look at him.'

She seemed to sigh on the line. 'Good boy, Matthew. Then I won't disturb him. Just tell him I rang.'

'No,' said Matthew, suddenly knowing what he must do. 'Don't ring off. He'll want to talk to you.'

'But —'

'Hang on,' he commanded, and went to wake Skip. It took some doing, but finally he convinced him that Petra was really on the line, and got him somewhat groggily across to the little office where he collapsed into the nearest chair.

'Petra? What are you doing in England?'

Matthew watched the smile grow in Skip's eyes, and then tactfully went away and left him alone. But he didn't dare go very far, because it was clear to him that Skip really was pretty shaky and would need steering back to bed. However, he was greatly cheered when a smiling Skip put his head round the door and said: 'You can stop skulking out there.'

'Back to bed,' commanded Matthew (he was being very forceful this morning). 'Doctor's orders. Could you eat anything?'

'*Anything*,' agreed Skip fervently.

Matthew laughed. 'You must be better.' So he saw him safely back into bed and went off to cook bacon and eggs.

He didn't know what Petra and Skip had said to each other, but whatever it was, Skip looked a different person, and the light was back in those sea-blue eyes.

★   ★   ★

The doctor, when he came, pronounced mild concussion and ordered Skip to stay in bed for two days. 'And if you get any double vision or anything unusual, you'd better go and get an X-ray,' he added, eyeing Skip severely.

Skip agreed, sounding deceptively meek.

Then Dr Thorpe turned to Matthew. 'How are those legs?'

'They're fine now,' Matthew smiled. 'Even Skip and the physio team have let me off the hook.'

The doctor grunted. 'A bit uneven still?'

103

'A bit.'

'It was a bad break, you know — that right one. But you're young, and with any luck it'll grow that extra inch. Keep up the swimming, though.'

'Yes.' Matthew sighed. He could swim in the pool. Or alone in the winter sea. But it wouldn't be the same. *Oh Flite, where are you? Are you safe?*

Dr Thorpe was a squarish, bluff man, as weathered as the Cornish cliffs he trudged up and down and the tough seafaring folk he served. He was splendid in emergencies, and had little time for megrims. But he knew Skip and what a tireless and rock-steady man he was, and he knew Matthew by now and that he wasn't what he called 'a whingeing boy.' So he was kind to both of them in his crisp, uncompromising way, and went off twinkling behind his glasses and promising to look in again to see that Skip was behaving himself.

'Well,' said Skip, 'it looks like you're the boss for a day or two. Can you cope?'

'Of course,' grinned Matthew.

'Mrs Hesketh will be in tomorrow. She'll shop for us, as well as clean the place up.' He looked at Matthew doubtfully. 'I could get Mary to come in an extra day?'

Mary, the club secretary, only came in once a week in the winter months, just to keep the paper work in order. She was a nice enough girl, Matthew thought, even if she did get in a muddle over the computer — but he couldn't see how she could help right now.

'Don't be daft!' he said. He'd looked after himself without much help from his mother for most of his young life. He could surely look after Skip for a few days. 'I was thinking,' he added, glancing at Skip in a tentative way, 'you know you said I could help with the decorating —? I could slap a bit of paint on the club room, with you giving orders from the sofa?'

Skip stared at him in astonishment.

'I mean,' went on Matthew lamely, 'that way, you wouldn't feel so idle.'

'*You* wouldn't feel so idle, you mean,' said Skip. Then he laughed. 'All right. I suppose it'll keep me out of mischief.'

'That's what I thought,' said Matthew, looking sublimely innocent.

★   ★   ★

There wasn't time to swim or to think of Flite during the next few days — and in a way, Matthew was glad. Working himself into the ground had always been his way of blocking out unhappiness — even when he was quite a small boy. The more bizarre his mother's lifestyle became, the more he buried himself in books, or his computer, or, later on when his hands got big enough, in the painful repetitive practice that learning the guitar demanded. If all these activities failed to overcome the unacknowledged ache of loneliness, he would clean the flat. No one else ever did, so it was usually pretty filthy — and he rather enjoyed getting it straight. Scrubbing was a cinch for getting rid of aches — of any kind.

So now, he found himself caught in the same absurd pattern of distress. The more he missed Flite, the more he scrubbed down walls and ceilings and slapped on paint, and cooked and cleaned for Skip, and rushed over to the hotel to deal with the Captain's computer.

This last task he found increasingly fascinating, and his respect for the Captain and his enormous business interests grew. He found that it was not only shipping he had to deal with, but the consortiums that manufactured the cargoes — oil companies, wheat-growers, mining companies, timber growers, tractor builders — almost every side of commercial life seemed to be involved, and share prices were all mixed up in it, too.

He asked the Captain once, rather shyly, whether his shipping empire had got smaller in recent years — like so many other shipping companies hit by air travel and air freight.

But the Captain smiled and said: 'Not really, Matthew, because I'm a wily old bird, and I knew which lines to get rid of. Big passenger ships are out — their days are over, I'm sorry to say. But the demand for smaller holiday craft keeps increasing.'

Matthew nodded.

'And then there's freight. You can't beat container ships for bulk carrying. Even the biggest planes can't really compete. Same with tankers.'

He glanced at Matthew, watching the receptive young mind take in the details of his complicated business. The boy really was pretty bright. It was a pleasure to teach him. 'The secret of business success, Matthew,' he told him, the shrewd old eyes crinkling in a smile of pure mischief, 'is to be *flexible* — and a step ahead of your competitors, all the time!'

Matthew laughed. 'On your toes?' He thought the old man must have been pretty sprightly in his time — and still was, in some respects.

'Oh yes.' The smile grew. 'A merry dance — if you can stand the pace.'

One way and another, Matthew learned an awful lot in a short space of time about how a big shipping empire worked, and he was constantly surprised at how much of all this information the Captain kept in his head, without referring to his computer for help.

In fact he vaguely suspected that the Captain scarcely needed his help at all, and was perfectly capable of feeding all the information into the system himself. But all the same, he seemed to be glad of his company, and clearly enjoyed explaining things when Matthew failed to understand. But he also did get very tired suddenly, and Matthew learnt to watch for the signs of fatigue, and to say cheerfully: 'I think we'd better stop now. I'm getting boss-eyed.'

The Captain usually surrendered with a good grace, though not in the least prepared to admit that he was tired, of course, and Matthew learnt how to make him his favourite 'coffee with a dash of rum' in the electric teasmade by his bed.

He wondered sometimes why it was that a man so rich and so powerful was so alone. Didn't he have any family? Any friends? Why did he come down here to stay at the rather shabby little hotel, and sit alone on a bench in the sun, with no one to talk to but a rather clumsy boy with damaged legs? These questions often came into his mind, but he did not ask them. He understood that the Captain would talk about business, or Matthew's own problems, or Flite, or almost any wider topic — but never about himself. He respected that — and kept to the rules. But he couldn't help wondering.

He said as much to Skip one evening, when he was busy finishing off a second coat on the bar-room ceiling.

'Skip —?'

'Mm?' By now Skip considered himself totally recovered, and was busy rubbing down the bar counter.

'About the Captain —'

'What about the Captain?'

'Well, why is he here on his own? Doesn't he have any family — or anyone who cares about him?'

Skip's face seemed to become strangely closed and bleak, and he didn't stop his fierce rubbing. 'Apparently not.'

Matthew had a sudden desire to drop the paintpot on Skip's head. 'Honestly, Skip, you're as close as a clam.'

'Sorry.' He stopped scrubbing at the wooden surface and looked up at Matthew with an apologetic grin. 'What can I tell you? . . . He's been coming down here every summer for — oh, a good many years now. Longer than I can remember. He never has anyone with him — but some of the older villagers say he used to come with his wife long ago. Since he no longer brings her, I presume she's dead, but he never talks about it.'

'Didn't he have any children?'

There was a fractional pause, and then Skip said in a voice even tighter than before: 'I told you — he never talks about it.' He glanced at Matthew's outraged face, and then relented a little. 'I believe — the villagers say — there was a daughter. But she went off.' He gave another vicious swipe at the bar counter. 'And then, of course, there's Conrad.'

'Who's Conrad?'

'You may well ask. Whether he's a nephew, or just one of the Captain's business managers, we don't know. He comes down sometimes, and argues with the old man, and everyone at the hotel gets very nervous.'

'Why?'

'Because the old man is frail. A row could kill him. And Conrad provokes him.'

'Deliberately?'

Skip shook his head. 'How should I know? . . . All I can say is, he comes and there's an almighty dust-up, and then he goes away, and the Captain is usually ill for days afterwards. We all dread his coming.'

'Can't he be stopped?'

Skip's eyebrows went sky-high. 'Give orders? Interfere in the Captain's private affairs? You must be joking.'

'No, but I mean, the doctor could —'

'He's tried. Believe me. Last time it nearly killed the old man. Thorpe told him he wasn't to let Conrad set foot in the place again, and the old Captain just laughed and said: "Try and stop him!"'

Matthew swore mildly, and actually did drop a spot of white paint on to Skip's clean bar counter. Skip looked down at it and swore too.

'I don't know what's got into everyone,' grumbled Matthew. 'There's the old Captain up there, as lonely as hell, and doing nothing about it, except letting some idiot come and barrack him and make him ill. And there's you —' He broke off, not knowing whether he dared go on.

'What about me?'

'You, down here, in the same boat and doing likewise. It's so damn silly.'

'Yes,' agreed Skip, rather too meekly.

'I mean — it's such a bloody waste.' Matthew sounded quite violent.

'Yes. It is.' Skip's voice was suddenly no longer meek at all. It was even more taut with anger than Matthew's.

Matthew glanced down in surprise, and then climbed off his ladder and laid down his can of paint and his brush. 'I'm sorry, Skip. I oughtn't to say anything, I know. But it's just —' He looked at him with a kind of exasperated honesty. 'I'm stuck with being on my own, and I *can't* do anything about it. But you're not, and you *can!*'

Skip blinked. 'Can I?'

'Well, you could go after her.'

He sighed. 'It's not as simple as that.'

'Isn't it? When you get down to basics?'

Skip put down his sandpaper block and turned to face Matthew. The sea-blue eyes were dark. 'Petra has a problem of her own that I can't resolve for her. She has —' He hesitated a little and then went on awkwardly: 'She has divided loyalties.' He paused again, as if attempting to explain the inexplicable. 'She thinks she's right. I think she's wrong.'

Matthew nodded. 'So?'

The blue eyes widened. 'So — she's got to work things out for herself.'

'Why?'

Skip looked confused. 'What do you mean — why?'

'I mean, why can't you work it out *together*?'

There was a startled pause. 'I — Petra's very independent. I can't interfere.'

Matthew wanted to shake him. 'She's probably dying for you to interfere. Aren't women supposed to like the macho type? Man of action stuff?'

Skip began to laugh.

'. . . sweep her off her feet, and all that?'

Skip's laughter grew. 'I never knew you were such a romantic.'

Matthew dismissed it, smiling with sudden shyness. 'I don't know anything about women.' Except one, who was a tramp, he thought bleakly. Nothing romantic about *her*. 'But still —' he glanced again at Skip, this time with hidden mischief: 'It seems chicken not to try.'

Skip took a half-hearted swipe at him, still laughing. 'Chicken, am I?'

Matthew dodged. 'Not in most things,' he admitted, grinning.

'Nor are you, come to that,' Skip acknowledged, aware that Matthew had just dared quite a lot on his behalf. 'In fact you're rather good in emergencies, aren't you?'

Matthew's grin faded. 'Oh — that's only because it's the only time I ever feel wanted.'

Skip stared at him, arrested. It was suddenly clear to him with a jolt of understanding, how it must feel to be alone in the world, with no family at all, and why Matthew was so contemptuous of his and Petra's indecision. *'The only time I ever feel wanted . . .'* he thought. How awful. And how stupid can you get?

'Shall I make some coffee?' asked Matthew, looking at Skip's stricken face with some shame. 'We've done enough for today.'

'*Quite* enough,' growled Skip severely, and laid a friendly arm round Matthew's paint-spattered shoulders. 'Let's go and sit in the sun.'

★　★　★

The sea was winter-dark, and cold in spite of the sun when Matthew slid into it from the familiar place on the rocks.

He didn't really want to go in, knowing Flite would not be there, but something compelled him to call his own bluff. He had to brave the loneliness of that empty sea. He had to practice what Flite had taught him — to rejoice in the moment, to love the sea for itself alone, and not long fruitlessly for a blue-black shadow that did not come.

It is enough to be alive, he told himself sternly. To be here in the sea, to be free to swim and marvel at its ceaselessly changing beauty, to be part of it — now. Today.

Today, today! echoed Flite's voice in his mind. That's it! Today!

But it was no good. He couldn't bear it. He couldn't rejoice without him. Always, in spite of himself, his eyes kept searching through the dark green depths for a long, slim shadow gliding between the rocks and drifting sea-wrack below the surface of the quiet bay.

It was empty — empty and sad. Full of deep echoes of sorrow that he could not escape . . . Even the seals seemed to have gone — no longer bobbing in the swell or hauled out on their own small rocky island beyond the point.

Oh Flite, he said. I miss you so. It's dreadful to be so lost without you, but I can't help it. Are you safe? Are you leaping and playing in the sun? Resting in warm soft seas? Diving in fathomless deeps, and breasting the tall sea-swells?

There was no answer. Of course there was no answer. The sea was empty and cold. But somehow, a strange conviction that his beloved dolphin was safe seemed to reach him through the water. He did not understand it, but the feeling grew within him — a tide of unexpected warmth and certainty. Whales, he knew, could reach each other with their songs across thousands of miles of ocean . . . Maybe dolphins could too? He did not know . . . But something was reaching him through the limitless deep-sea swell, something that spoke of comfort and reassurance. Flite was safe and happy. Swimming south, always south, with his companions, carving a path through the blue-dark spaces of the wide Atlantic — rejoicing all the way. Rejoice, rejoice, sang his voice, through the surge and sweep of the waves. Rejoice! it called again, on a fading uprush of spray . . .

Comforted, Matthew turned on his face and swam for the shore.

★ ★ ★

During Skip's brief spell of incapacity, Matthew discovered that the village of Porthgwillick had a heart. When the last of the summer visitors drove away in their cars and trailers and shiny coaches, the little community drew together and settled down to its winter occupations. Matthew had been so wrapped up in his own concerns and his enchantment with the dolphin, that he had paid little attention to the world around him, and he was ashamed to admit that he had scarcely noticed the sturdy villagers with their sea-dark watchful eyes. But now he saw them, and they all spoke to him in their soft voices and asked about Skip. The two old fishermen who sat sunning themselves outside the Seamen's Union allowed themselves a couple of

110

creaky smiles, and offered Matthew a pot of goose-grease ointment to rub on Skip's bruises.

'Works a treat,' said one, fixing him with his far-seeing seaman's gaze. 'Allus used it after a rough night at sea.'

'Ar,' agreed the other. 'Takes off the wust.' His glance was even more filled with ancient memories and long distances. 'You tell 'im, boy.'

'I will,' agreed Matthew, repressing a private grin when he thought of what Skip's reaction would be.

In the tiny village shop, Mrs Merrifield gave him a free packet of Skip's favourite extra-strong mints and a bunch of grapes 'just come in from Penzance'. She also asked earnestly whether Skip was behaving himself and going to bed early, like he should, instead of gallivanting all over the place, like usual.

Out in the street, two young fishermen from the next cove round the point stopped and handed Matthew a couple of fresh mackerel, and asked him to tell Skip not to worry about the boat repairs yet, they would keep.

When Matthew looked slightly puzzled at this, one of them added, smiling: 'Skip's a good boat-builder. Like his Dad. Always helps us out in winter. Didn't you know?'

Matthew shook his head, adding yet another facet to the composite picture of Skip and his many talents.

'Gets very ratty, mind, if we doesn't do as he says,' volunteered the other, grinning. 'Likes to be boss, Skip does.'

Matthew could agree with that, and grinned happily back, before setting out once more to make his way back to Skip. But on his way to the clubhouse, he was overtaken by a boy in traditional black leathers on a motorbike, who said over the roar of his own engine: 'Tell Skip we've put off live music night for a coupla weeks.' He flashed Matthew a brief, shiny smile and added: 'OK, is he?'

'Nearly,' Matthew told him, juggling wildly with the mackerel and the grapes.

The boy gave him a quick, approving nod and zoomed off in a roar of exhaust that split the quiet village street with ear-splitting noise.

He had nearly got to the dunes below the verandah, when three little girls rushed up to him, panting. One was carrying a dish wrapped in a cloth, and the other two were dangling school satchels. All three were dark-haired, blue-eyed and brown with sun and salt sea winds.

'Mam sent Skip a stargazy pie,' said the first round-faced child, smiling up at Matthew with undisguised admiration.

'And she said to tell 'im, we'm not coming till next week,' added the second, smiling even more angelically.

'Coming where?' asked Matthew, mystified.

'Swimming,' all three chorused.

'Skip runs a class in winter,' explained the third child kindly. 'In the pool. Badges, he gives us, and all. Is he better then?'

'Nearly,' Matthew repeated, trying to balance the pie on top of everything else. He wondered whether Skip would be able to face those little gaping fish-heads sticking out of the pastry.

'Goodbye,' chorused the girls, their smiles resting adoringly on Matthew's bewildered face. 'We're glad you're looking after him,' and they scampered off in a scatter of sand and half-suppressed giggles.

'Phew,' said Matthew, climbing up the steps to Skip who was laughing at him from a chair on the verandah. 'If I'd known you were so popular, I'd have taken a truck.'

'What's for dinner, then?' asked Skip, still laughing.

'Stargazy pie and extra-strong mints,' said Matthew. 'Oh, and two mackerel and a bunch of grapes.'

'Is that all?'

'Well, you could start with this.'

'What is it?'

'Goose-grease. For bruises. Guaranteed cure.'

'Ugh,' said Skip, and went on laughing.

★ ★ ★

When Matthew went up to the hotel, an atmosphere of mild chaos seemed to have overtaken it. Emma, the chambermaid was rushing upstairs with a tray of tea, John, the barman and general porter, was trying to pour out a stiff whisky for someone and answering the phone as well, and Milly, the proprietress, was literally wringing her hands and saying: 'Oh dear. Oh dearie me. He'll be the death of him, for sure. I never should've let him go up.' And upstairs, Matthew could hear the sound of raised voices and a stick banging furiously on the floor.

'What is it?' he said. 'What's happened? Is anything wrong with the Captain?'

'It's that Conrad,' explained Milly, still wringing her hands.

'He's that persistent. I told him the Captain wasn't too well today. But he would go up. And now listen to them!'

Matthew listened, and did not much like what he heard. 'I thought the doctor said he wasn't to come any more.'

'So he did. Don't mince words, don't Doctor Thorpe. But it didn't do no good.' She looked at Matthew despairingly. 'That Conrad, he won't take no for an answer, see? . . . And I don't know what to do.'

'I do,' said Matthew. He suddenly felt tall and brave and very angry. No one had the right to make the old Captain ill. But no one. 'Give me that drink,' he said.

He stormed up the stairs, and paused outside the Captain's door, shocked by the anger in himself, and by the anger in those raised voices behind the door.

'I'll thank you to mind your own business,' said the Captain's voice, very clipped and cold. 'I am perfectly capable of managing my affairs, and when I want any advice from you, I'll ask for it.'

'That's just the trouble,' replied a new voice, louder and less disciplined than the captain's. 'You never *do* ask, and you never do consult me.'

'Why the hell should I? It's my company, and I'm not too senile yet to be capable of running it.'

'I'm beginning to wonder about that,' snapped Conrad. 'Since this merger offer came up, you've done nothing but block it.'

'That's because I don't want it,' barked the Captain. 'We are perfectly all right as we are. Solvent, profitable and stable. I don't trust these fancy fellas an inch.'

'Just because you are old-fashioned and hidebound,' snarled Conrad, 'doesn't mean the entire company has to be.' The rasp in his voice seemed to get rougher every minute. 'They are a reputable group, and they offer good terms.'

'They are *not* a reputable group,' countered the Captain. 'I happen to have had them investigated. They are extremely suspect, and their finances are not at all secure. I won't have it, Conrad, and that's final.'

'Well,' said Conrad, and the rasp was quite nasty now, 'of course if you *want* to hold the company back from expanding . . .'

'I want nothing of the sort. I want to hold the company back from entering into a shady deal which will not help us at all in the long run, and will only succeed in ruining our reputation as a business of rocklike steadiness and integrity.' The Captain's voice, too, had an edge to it now. 'Maybe that is something you are incapable of understanding.'

Matthew heard Conrad draw a sharp breath of outrage at this, and thought he had better go in before they actually came to blows. He pushed open the door, and marched up to the Captain's chair, brushing past the pink-faced, angry man who was standing over him.

'Captain, I've brought your drink. And it's time to run the evening computer programme. Are you ready?'

The Captain looked at Matthew in astonishment, and then a slow twinkle began deep down in his eyes. 'Quite ready, Matthew. Are we late?'

'Almost,' said Matthew, and handed the Captain his ebony stick. 'Head office will be waiting for your call.' He stood beside him squarely, still holding his stiff whisky-and-soda in one hand, and waited for the old man to get to his feet.

Conrad looked at them both, openmouthed, but before he could say any more, the old Captain simply walked out of the room into his little office, leaving Matthew to get rid of his unwelcome guest.

'Have you far to go?' asked Matthew politely, holding the door open for Conrad with the clearest of gestures. 'I'm sure they'll get you a taxi downstairs.' He had not looked at Conrad very closely yet, being almost too angry to do so, but now he saw a big, plumpish man with receding brownish hair, a thin, petulant mouth and rather small, quick-moving eyes that looked somehow hot behind their blue stare. 'This way,' he said.

Somehow mesmerized by Matthew's extreme politeness, Conrad began to go out of the door towards the stairs. But at the last moment he called over his shoulder: 'You've not heard the last of this!'

'I'm sure I haven't,' agreed the old Captain, from the other room. 'Goodbye, Conrad.' The dismissal was final.

There was nothing left for the hapless Conrad to do but go away. He went, muttering darkly about 'obstinate old men', and giving Matthew a hot and angry glare in passing. But he knew when he was defeated, and did not try to prolong the argument.

Matthew breathed a sigh of relief, and went into the little dressing-room in a hurry. The old Captain was sitting in his

114

chair, sipping the stiff whisky he had brought him, and looking very tired.

'Are you all right?' asked Matthew, anxious about that white look of stress.

'Will be in a minute,' growled the Captain. 'Thanks to you.'

They looked at each other and laughed. Then Matthew got to work on the computer, reasoning with himself that the Captain could rest while he was busy, and would clearly rather be left alone for a while.

He did not try to bring up the question of Conrad, but in the end it was the Captain himself who spoke of it.

'Ambitious, that one is, d'you see? . . . Makes him aggressive.'

'That doesn't give him the right to wear you out with arguments.'

'True.' His grin was mischievous. 'He thinks it's for my own good.'

Matthew snorted. 'Oh, does he!' Then he looked curiously at the old Captain. 'Is he — part of the family?' He supposed that might account for his rudeness, he reflected grimly.

'Sort of. Distant.' The Captain wasn't giving much away. 'But he's also one of my managing directors. Thinks he knows it all, stupid fella.' The grin was not in the least malicious now. 'When as a matter of fact, I knew all about how to run this business when he was still in short pants.'

Matthew laughed. 'Is he really a — a threat?'

'No.' The old voice was quite calm. 'I hold all the strings — including the purse strings. All he can do is fulminate from time to time. It soon dies down.'

'Does — do head office know about this — um — proposed merger?'

'Oh yes. And they know my opinion of it.'

Matthew nodded. 'Do they agree with you?'

The Captain's grin got suddenly wider. 'They do. They were the ones who did the research.'

'Oh well, that's all right then.' Matthew was still looking at him, still assessing that blanched look of strain. 'So long as it doesn't bother you.' He hesitated, with his hand on the computer keyboard. 'Should I feed in his visit?'

'Why not?' shrugged the Captain. 'Occupational hazard — ambitious underlings with an eye on the main chance. Put him in!'

Matthew did, while still keeping an eye on the Captain's blazing pallor.

'Godsend,' said the Captain suddenly. 'D'you know that?'

Matthew turned hs head and smiled. 'I only saw him out.'

'*Only?*' The Captain began to laugh again. 'You should've seen his face.'

'I did!'

Suddenly they were both giggling like naughty schoolboys, and Matthew was relieved to see the tension recede from the old man's face, leaving it curiously relaxed and cheerful.

It was while Matthew was checking the final day's share prices, that the phone call came.

'Would it be possible to speak to Matthew Ferguson?'

'Er — yes, I mean, speaking . . . ' Matthew glanced wildly at the Captain. 'He wants to speak to *me*.' He sounded totally incredulous.

'Well, speak to him!' the Captain growled, suppressing another mild twinkle.

'I tried to reach you at the Aqua Club,' went on the pleasant voice. 'They told me you might be here.'

'Oh.' Matthew gulped. 'Who — who is this?'

'Why, your solicitor, John Harvey. I have some unexpected news for you.'

'Yes?' Matthew was still bewildered.

'We have traced a relative of yours — in America.'

There was a pause. So long a pause that John Harvey said sharply: 'Matthew? Are you there?'

'Yes, I'm there.' There was a smaller pause, and then he asked in a stifled voice: 'Wh — what kind of relative?'

'A connection of your father's.'

'My *father's?*' His voice was even fainter. 'I didn't know he had any. I mean, I never knew anything about his family.'

'So I understand. But she exists, I assure you.'

'She?'

'A Mrs Madeleine Grant. She was married to your father's brother, which makes her a kind of aunt.'

'*Was* married?'

'He died, I believe, some years ago. She is now married to an American living in San Diego.'

'San Diego?' He still sounded vague and shocked. 'That's — that's a long way away.'

'It is. But she wants you to go over and visit her — with a

116

view to offering you a permanent home. She is prepared to pay your fare.'

Matthew's head spun. 'I — are you sure of all this? It isn't a joke?'

'It isn't a joke.' John Harvey's voice was firm and reassuring. 'Perhaps you'd better come up to London to see me, and we can discuss it.'

'Yes.' He sounded curiously reluctant. 'But not yet.' Once more he glanced in wild appeal at the Captain, who had politely moved away out of earshot. 'I can't leave here yet,' explained Matthew lamely. 'I have a job to do.' And there's Skip, he thought. I can't leave Skip on his own yet. He'll mope. And work too hard. 'I — I was thinking of coming to London for Christmas,' he said. 'To see Madge Farley and the kids. Could I come and see you then?'

'Certainly.' John Harvey's voice held a trace of surprise in it. 'Are you sure you don't want to come right away?'

'No. I mean, yes, I am sure. There are things I have to do here first.' He let his appeal to the Captain come out into the open. 'Perhaps — would you like to have a word with Captain St George? He'll explain to you.'

'Very well.' Harvey seemed unperturbed. After all, he was a friend of Verney St George. It was the old man himself who had arranged for Harvey to represent Matthew in the first place.

'John?' growled the Captain. 'Good to hear from you. What's all this?'

Matthew, remembering the old man's scrupulous politeness about eavesdropping, went into the bedroom to make the Captain's special coffee and a dash. He thought they could probably both do with it.

'Matthew?' called the fierce old voice in a few minutes.

He came and stood in the doorway, balancing two cups of coffee.

'You could go now if you want to. I could manage.'

'No.' Matthew shook his head decisively. He gave his friend the Captain a shy, fleeting smile. 'I'll go when you head for the sun.'

They grinned at one another, and the old man turned back to the phone. 'John? He says no. But I'll see that he gets in touch before Christmas.'

There was a murmured reply, and the fragile hand put down the phone. Matthew saw that it was trembling very slightly.

117

'Here,' he said. 'I put in a good dash. Thought we might need it.'

The Captain laughed. but his eyes were curiously misted with an old man's tears.

★ ★ ★

Matthew did not tell Skip about the relation in America at first. Nor did he discuss it with the Captain. He did not want to talk about it — in fact, he found himself curiously reluctant even to think about it. A relation? Someone he'd never met . . . who had never got in touch all these years? And why should they want to do so now? Out of duty? Prompted by the lawyers? He hadn't got any money, so it must be duty. And he didn't want to be someone's 'duty'. The whole thing repelled him, somehow, and he felt filled with a fierce determination not to be taken over by some do-gooding stranger. He wanted to stay alone — alone and independent, with no ties and no obligations, so that no one could get at him. He was tired of being pushed around, tired of feeling guilty about a mother who had never really wanted him, and whom he had never tried very hard to get to know. Tired of being ruled still by that tyrannous tie of 'family obligation', and tired, too, of being dependent on other people's kindness — however well-meant. He didn't *want* people to be kind to him, or to be sorry for him and his solitary state. He liked it like that. He didn't need their charity or their concern. He could manage perfectly well on his own. (Though even then he felt guilty about being so ungrateful for everyone's concern and kindness, and that only made it worse.) But one day, perhaps, he told himself, he might find someone who would care about him just for himself, and not because they ought to. Someone like Flite, who would come joyously to meet him with no other motive than delight in his company. Someone like Flite.

That was it, of course. He missed Flite badly, and somehow nothing in the dull grey world away from the sea seemed anything like so real or so warm as that loving companionship he had known in the green-glass freedom of the wide Atlantic.

So it was with a shock of terror that he heard Skip say one morning at breakfast: 'They've found fifteen dead dolphins washed up on a beach.'

'*Fifteen?* . . . *Where?*'

'In France — on the Brittany coast.'

118

Matthew felt himself go cold with dread. Brittany wasn't that far from Cornwall . . . And *fifteen*? That was a massacre — a whole school, probably . . . 'What did they die of?'

Skip shrugged. 'Too early to say — pollution of some kind, probably.'

'Or the seal virus?'

'Possibly.'

Matthew was already on his feet, looking as if he was going to take off for Brittany that moment.

'Hang on,' said Skip, and laid a hand on his arm. 'Have some sense.'

'But — but I must know.' He sounded quite wild.

'I'm doing my best,' Skip told him. 'If you'll only listen.'

Matthew subsided.

'Marine biologists are a clanny lot. They're in touch all over the world. D'you follow me?' He didn't wait for Matthew to answer, but went on: 'I've got on to the local boys, and they've asked their French friends to photograph them before they're disposed of.'

'Disposed of?' Matthew's voice was bleak.

'Well — you can't leave fifteen dead dolphins to rot on a bathing beach, can you?' He glanced sympathetically at Matthew's stricken face. 'They'll take samples, of course, and do tests. And maybe they'll find out what killed them — or maybe they won't. But they'll do their best to take note of any identifying scars and marks.' Once again the sea-blue eyes rested on Matthew with kindness. 'It's the best I could do.'

Matthew swallowed. 'How — how soon? When will they know? Can I see the photos?' He looked round in a desperate, driven manner as if he might find an instant means of transport to France lying on the clubhouse verandah.

'Give me a chance,' said Skip, smiling a little. 'The Captain's got everything we need, hasn't he? They can send photos through on Fax, I think. We'll go up and see him in a minute.' the smile tugged at the corners of his mouth, and he added with a flick of mischief: 'And I daresay he'd charter a yacht for you, if you asked him.'

'Don't be daft,' said Matthew automatically — but he began to feel a little better. Perhaps it wasn't Flite after all. There must be hundreds of dolphins around the shores of France. And there were a lot of bottle-nose dolphins in the Mediterranean as well, he knew. Maybe it would be all right . . . Well, all right for Flite who was his friend and dear companion . . . But it was

119

not all right for all those others — those fifteen beautiful bodies washed up on the shore.

'Come on,' urged Skip. 'Stop moping. We'll go up and see him now.'

★   ★   ★

They waited all day for news, and in the meantime Matthew decided to stay and get the rest of the Captain's work in order. He could not somehow bring himself to go away from the Fax machine or the Telex that might clatter into life any minute — and even Skip seemed inclined to hang about, looking anxious.

It was during one of the lulls in work that the Captain suddenly tackled Matthew about America.

'What are you going to do about San Diego?'

Matthew gave him a look of muted anguish and sighed. 'I — don't know.'

Captain St George was not a stupid man. He could see that the boy was under some kind of stress, and his gruff voice came out surprisingly gentle. 'What bothers you about it?'

'A lot of things.' Matthew spoke almost reluctantly. How on earth could he explain to a man like the Captain, who had anything in the world he wanted, what it was like to be totally dependent on other people's charity? Everything on earth — except a family, said his mind, remembering suddenly the Captain's admitted loneliness. And here was he, Matthew, rejecting the only chance of family life he had . . .

'I suppose it's — because of how things *were*,' he said obscurely. 'I mean — I was never much good at it.'

'Good at what?'

'Family feeling, and all that.' He seemed embarrassed by his own clumsy tongue, but he was determined to be honest with the Captain. He deserved it. 'In fact, I don't think I like the idea of family ties much at all.' His voice was bleak. 'I mean, my mother couldn't really do with me — I cramped her style. But because she was my mother, she felt *obliged* to do something about me. And I — I didn't get on with her very well at all, in fact, most of the time it was a total disaster. So I mostly opted out. But then I felt guilty. And so did she.' He looked helplessly at the Captain. 'Stupid, isn't it?'

The Captain made a non-committal noise in his throat which might have been a growl or a snort of disapproval. 'So?'

'So — these people — this aunt-by-marriage or whatever in

120

San Diego. She doesn't know me. I don't know her. She's never tried to contact us all these years. So why now? Just because a lawyer told her to? Out of a sense of duty? . . . That family tie bit again?' He shook his head in fierce denial. 'I don't want it. I don't want to be someone else's *duty*.'

The Captain could understand that. Very well. But he said mildly: 'She might be just inquisitive.'

Matthew actually laughed, which was what the wily old man had intended anyway. So he followed up his advantage by saying, still in that deceptively mild manner: 'Well — what *do* you want?'

'To be free,' said Matthew, thinking of Flite. 'Free and uncluttered . . . To get a job and manage my own life. And not be beholden to anyone.'

The faded blue eyes looked into his with sympathy. 'It's a lonely sort of life, with no ties, you know.'

Matthew suddenly smiled. 'I didn't say no ties. I meant no built-in ones. I think — I think you should care about someone because you want to — not because you have to.'

The Captain nodded. 'Like Madge and her kids?'

'Yes.' Like Flite.

'What about Skip? You've been good to him when he was laid up.'

'He's been good to me.'

'Obligations again?'

'No,' said Matthew, trapped by his own unwary tongue. 'Of course not.'

'What about me?' The tired eyes were suddenly bright with challenge.

Matthew began to stammer. 'But you know — I can't begin to — I mean, you've been wonderful to me —'

'You've done a lot for me, too.'

'That was — work. You paid me.'

'You offered to do it for nothing, remember?'

'That was because —'

'Obligations again?' The eyebrows went higher and higher.

Matthew floundered. 'You know it wasn't —'

'What I'm saying is,' the old man told him gently, 'it isn't always as simple as all that — is it? It isn't always cut and dried.'

There was a pause, while Matthew considered this. It was true. He had begun with a sense of obligation, certainly. Kindness repaid — consideration due — and self-respect restored.

121

But now it wasn't that at all. Of course it wasn't. It had become much more. And the Captain knew it. Probably Skip knew it, too. Only he had gone on blundering about, proud and prickly, when what he had wanted was there all the time for the asking. He was ashamed of his stupidity.

'I am a fool,' he said humbly.

The old man grunted. 'We all are, Matthew — where human relationships are concerned. What I am saying is — I think you should give San Diego a try. You never know. This aunt or whatever — she may be lonely, too.'

Lonely, too. It was no good trying to fool the Captain. He knew very well what it was all about.

'Besides,' he went on, 'it's an excuse to travel. See a bit of the world. San Diego is a lovely place — if a trifle dangerous.'

'Dangerous? Why?'

'Very laid back. Full of drugs for the asking. You'd have to watch it, or you might find yourself drifting around there for ever.'

Matthew said surprisingly: 'It interferes with my fingers.'

'What?'

'My mother used various things, besides pot. I tried them a couple of times. But it made my fingers clumsy. Music doesn't let you *blunt* things.'

The Captain nodded. 'Good thing you've got the guitar, then.'

They looked at each other and grinned. It seemed to Matthew that the Captain's warning had been given, and for some reason Matthew's obscure answer had reassured him.

At that moment both the Telex and the Fax machines began to clatter. The photos were coming through.

The Telex said: 'Authorities insist on burial this evening. Photos not very conclusive.'

The photos were reasonably clear, if a bit grainy, but it was true — they were not conclusive. Marks and scars looked curiously blurred and not easy to distinguish. Matthew pored over them anxiously, and then passed them to Skip who had returned to see how they were getting on.

'I can't be sure,' muttered Matthew, shaking his head. 'I can't *see* a scar like Flite's. But I can't be sure.' He looked at Skip with desperate appeal. 'Can you?'

Skip also studied the photos carefully as they came through. But after a time, he also shook his head. 'No. Not positive.' He sighed. 'I'd like to know what they died of.'

122

Matthew's face was bleached with longing. If only he could reach those beautiful lifeless creatures and touch their pale throats with his fingers as he had so often with Flite . . . He would know then. But Flite had been alive and joyous when he had last touched that pulsing throat with its cross-shaped scar . . . Alive and joyous . . . Could he be one of those long, sparkless bodies lying so quiet on the shore? And oh, how all that quenched and purposeless beauty made him ache with pity, whether it ws Flite or not . . .

'Skip,' said the Captain suddenly, 'what about St Just?'

Skip looked at him. 'You mean —?'

'Your friend, Mark. He could do it.'

Matthew stared from one to the other, bewildered. 'St Just?'

'The airfield. Skip knows one of the pilots.' The Captain was waving an imperious hand at Skip. 'Ring him now. No time to lose.' He glanced sideways at Matthew's face, now even paler with rising hope, and the imperious hand descended and touched him gently. 'Don't worry, boy. We'll get you there somehow.'

★   ★   ★

It didn't really seem possible to Matthew, but there they were, airborne in a little plane bound for the Channel and the coast of Brittany. They came down at Dover for customs clearance, which didn't take long and seemed to be minimal, and then took off again in the neat small plane without much delay.

He looked down at the blue-black waters of the sea and wondered where Flite was. If he was alive. This was only a small sea — quite narrow here between Britain and France — but even so it looked immense, stretching to far horizons. What would the Atlantic look like, with its enormous, stormy expanses? How would it feel to Flite, swimming and diving and leaping into the blue air for breath, swimming and swimming, tirelessly, away from danger, away from the clumsy, blundering creature on two legs who loved him . . . Away — further and further away — never to be seen again . . .

'Nearly there,' said Skip, pointing to a long, dark spit of land jutting out into the sea.

Matthew pulled his thoughts back, guiltily reminding himself that he *wanted* Flite to be swimming away from danger — alive and safe. Not dead on a Brittany beach. Brittany. The coastline looked very much like Cornwall — rocky and black against a churning, surf-strewn sea.

The little plane came down on a small, quiet landing strip, with a couple of hangars and a tin shack of a customs house at the end of the runway. There was a little knot of people waitng for them, and as they climbed down from the plane, a figure detached itself from the group and came forward.

'I'm Pierre,' he said, speaking excellent if slightly accented English, and held out his hand to Skip and then to Matthew. 'Clearance came through from Dover. The Douanier knows about you. It won't take long.' He turned back to the others of his group and added: 'We are all in the cetacean protection game, so you are in good hands.'

Matthew said awkwardly: 'It's very good of you to arrange all this —' Just for the sake of identifying one wild dolphin, he meant to add, but somehow his throat closed tight and he could not say it.

Pierre was right, and the formalities did not take long. Skip's friend, the pilot, Mark, decided to come along too and see what happened. He did not make any stipulations concerning the return journey, but he and Skip seemed to have an understanding about hours of daylight and night-flying, so Matthew did not feel anxious. In fact, he was so concerned about reaching the dead dolphins that nothing else seemed to matter at all.

In a short while, the small party climbed into a waiting Range-Rover, and drove off down the straight French road towards the coast. After a few miles, they turned off the main road down a narrow lane and finally bounded and rattled across a rutted farm track on to some grassy dunes. Pierre, who was driving, turned his head and smiled at Matthew. 'Not long now.'

Matthew nodded. He would soon know. Whether Flite was alive or dead. One way or the other. But, of course, his mind told him, this was only *one* hazard, one chance Flite might have had to take among many. There were countless other dangers he had to face. If he was not here among these stricken creatures, he still might be lying dead on another shore . . . or in the fathomless deeps of a different ocean . . .

'Come on,' said Skip, touching his arm. 'No time to waste.'

They climbed out on to sandy tufts of grass, crossed another windblown ridge of yellow-brown sand-dunes, and stood looking down on a flat curve of empty beach. Empty, that is, except for one jeep and a bulldozer moving slowly along the far end of the shore close to the rocks, and a curious line of blue-black shapes lying close to the water in motionless abandon.

'*Diable*, they're here already!' exclaimed Pierre, and started running down the beach, shouting and waving his arms.

Matthew and Skip ran after him, and the rest of the party followed, also running. They reached the far end of the bay where flat ridges of scaly rocks edged the sea, stretching backwards into low, shale-strewn cliffs. There, Pierre was arguing fiercely with the driver of the jeep, waving his hands about and pointing at the quiet line of dead dolphins on the shore. He was a handsome man, in a thin, Gallic sort of way, with wild brown hair and a beard to match, and the sun made reddish glints in both as he tossed his head in furious argument.

At last, the jeep-driver capitulated with a shrug and a faint grin. '*Alors, j'attends. Mais dix minutes seulement. D'accord?*'

'*D'accord,*' agreed Pierre, unwillingly, and turned to Skip, his dark eyes still sparking with anger. 'We'd better hurry.'

The whole party advanced on the pitiful line of dead bottle-nose dolphins. One by one, they bent over them, searching for identifying scars. Some of the dolphins lay sideways on the sand and could easily be examined, but some were face downward and had to be turned over. It took two of them, grasping the dorsal fin and the graceful tail-fluke, to move the heavy bodies until the pale under-belly and throat were exposed.

Two of the party, who seemed to be more scientifically equipped and businesslike than the others, went about with small cases and instruments, taking samples. They did not speak much, but got on with the job as quickly as possible.

To Matthew, it seemed the worst ten minutes of his life. They were all so beautiful, so spread out and quiet in innocent death. Each one of them as lissom and powerful as Flite, and probably each one as loving and full of joyous life as he.

One by one, he laid his fingers against pale throats and felt for that telltale cross-shaped scar. And one by one, he dismissed them with a flick of relief, because the long, slender under-jaw did not have what he was looking for.

A flick of relief? But he was ashamed to feel relief, really. For they were all just as splendid as Flite — all just as deserving of life — just as perfectly made for the perfect element they lived in.

By the time he reached the last one, tears blurred his eyes, and his hands shook uncontrollably. He and Skip turned it over, and once again — one last time — his fingers searched and probed that silken skin.

There was no scar. It was not Flite. His search was over. For a time, at least. But these others? How did they come to this? This dreadful, ignominious end — just a heap of flesh to be bulldozed into the sand . . .

Blinded, he turned away. 'No,' he said, choking. 'Not Flite . . . ' And then, turning rather desperately to Pierre, he asked the fatal question: 'How did they die?'

Pierre shrugged again — that all-embracing Gallic gesture — but there was sympathy in those shrewd brown eyes. 'We've taken samples. And done one section. So far it looks as if they drowned.'

'*Drowned?*'

The Frenchman glanced in rather helpless anger at one of his companions — a tall, spare woman who had helped to turn over some of the heavy, uncaring bodies. 'Martha?'

'Nets,' she said briefly, speaking in a clipped, rather mid-Atlantic accent. 'We thought the purse-seine nets were mostly in the Pacific. But —' Like Pierre, she gave a small, exasperated shrug, 'there are big fishing interests muscling in around these coasts, too. They're dredging the ocean-floor dry with their huge trawl nets, scraping everything off the bottom so that nothing is left alive. Nothing! And as they pull up their bloody nets, the dolphins and even small whales get caught and can't come up to breathe. It's appalling.' She glanced round at the line of quiet bodies. 'Look at them! Probably all thrown back as they released their catch. Dropped back, already dead. And the sea brought them to shore.'

As she spoke, the jeep-driver signalled to his mate in the bulldozer and spoke over his shoulder to Pierre. '*Alors, on va.*'

Matthew turned despairingly to Skip. 'Do they have to?'

'What else can they do?'

Matthew did not know. But he felt, obscurely, that something else ought to be done to honour these beautiful dead creatures — something other than shovelling them like so much carrion into a hole in the sand . . .

In life they had been noble, powerful animals, filled with strength and grace, and with the unconscious dignity of a great wild creature at home in its natural element. It seemed all wrong that such power, such grace and beauty, such unclouded innocence, should be so wantonly destroyed, so swiftly shoved out of sight. Got rid of, with no word of pity or sorrow for

126

their plight — no acknowledgement, even, that fifteen living, breathing, sentient creatures had ever existed as separate individuals, swimming free in the wide dark seas of the world.

'I ought to —' he began helplessly, and made a curious, defeated gesture with his hands.

But the woman, Martha, turned on him sharply. 'Scatter flowers on their grave? Sing them requiems?' She seemed so angry that he almost expected her to hit him. 'How will that help them? Sentimental gestures do nothing, except perhaps ease your conscience!' Her eyes were cold with contempt. 'What we have to do is *stop it.*'

'How?'

The little band of conservationists seemed to draw together and look to Pierre as their spokesman.

'Talk!' he said. 'Speak! Write!' He glared round at his friends. 'What we *are* doing — some of us.' His eyes flashed fire at Matthew, challenging him to join them. 'Tell everyone. Take photographs. Get it on the media, one way or another. *Shame* them into doing something about it.'

'Can they be shamed?' asked Skip. 'There's too much money in big fishing.'

Martha was about to expand the argument, when the pilot, Mark, said easily: 'I hate to break up this discussion, but I have to get these boys home.'

Instantly, Pierre's mobile, fighter's face changed. 'Of course,' he said. 'We'll run you back to the airport.'

'And get that boy a drink,' added Martha, an unexpected gruffness in her cool, clear voice.

The others glanced kindly at Matthew, and he in turn looked miserably back at them, ashamed of his weakness.

Up till now, he had been so desperately concerned about the dolphins and Flite that he had hardly noticed the people around him at all. He was ashamed of his obsession. Here were a whole lot of busy people who had gone to a lot of trouble to help him — and he had scarcely been aware of their existence, let alone thought to thank them. Of course they had been engaged in their own research, too, but even so they had gone out of their way to make things easier for him.

Now he looked at them attentively for the first time, and wondered why he had been so blind. There was Pierre, the leader — bushy-haired and rangy, seeming relaxed and easy but permitting fierce anger to erupt when needed. And Martha — long and thin, with square-cut brownish hair, very dark brown eyes, almost black when they were angry, and a kind of leashed impatience with the stupidity of mankind that was burning her up with cold fire. Next to Martha was a stocky German called — as far as Matthew could understand — Bogle. He was very strong, where moving dolphin carcases was required, and he had clever, blunt hands. Matthew knew about hands. He always recognized a craftsman's strength and precision. Was he a surgeon, perhaps? . . . And with him, the youngest and least authoritative of the party, was a blond Swedish biologist called Eric. He may have been the least responsible, but he was also closest to Matthew in age, and possibly in sympathy, for now he laid a large, friendly arm round Matthew's shoulders and said: 'We will go find some cognac, yes?' and led him forcibly away to the jeep.

While they were all standing round having a farewell cognac beside the tiny airstrip, Martha suddenly said to Skip: 'You know Petra Davison, don't you?'

Skip seemed to go very still. 'Yes. Why?'

'Best expert we've got on cetaceans. She'd be interested.'

'I expect she would.' Skip's voice was non-committal.

'Won't you tell her?' asked Matthew, looking at the group of experts. After all, Skip had told him they were all in touch with one another.

Pierre looked doubtful. 'It'll be on the computer — when we get the results. She can find it if she wants it.'

'We could tell her,' said Matthew, with intent.

'Do you know where she is?'

'Skip does.'

Skip looked mutinous. 'Somewhere in the Pacific, I believe. Doing a whale survey. Not easy to reach.'

'You could if you tried,' muttered Matthew, glaring at him.

But it was no use trying to bully Skip. He would do things his own way, regardless. Matthew might as well keep his mouth shut, for all the good it did. He sighed, and swallowed his cognac in one gulp so that it made him choke. Petra had loved Flite, too. She would be glad, like last time, that he hadn't been a casualty of this endless war.

'Time to go,' said Mark. 'Come on, you two. I've got a date tonight.'

As they turned to go, Martha spoke to Matthew abruptly. 'It's a mistake to get too attached to one creature, you know.'

'I know,' agreed Matthew helplessly. But what could I do? He sought me out in the first place . . . and I loved him. And

I think he loved me, too. 'What can I do?' he said aloud, meaning something quite different.

'Just *talk*,' answered Martha. 'Like Pierre said. Keep on keeping on. We'll win them round in the end.'

'I'll try,' promised Matthew. But would it save Flite? Was he alive still, out there in the echoing deeps? Could he still feel the pull of Matthew's affection following him like a shadow in the sounding spaces of the ocean?

Not a shadow, thought Matthew. I mustn't pull at him. I mustn't cloud that marvellous instant joy. Let him alone. Let him go free. He is better without me now.

Sadly, he climbed back into the little plane. He knew he should be rejoicing. Flite was safe, so far as he knew. But he could not help grieving for those others who no longer cared whether they were safe or not. He gave one last, anguished glance at the flat French fields and the long straight road to the beach — to the long, lonely beach, empty now, he supposed, except for a few motionless grey shapes and a bulldozer digging a hole . . .

No flowers or songs, Martha said. We've got to stop it. *Stop it.*

But all the same, thought Matthew to himself, I'll play for them tonight. At least I can do that. Maybe, somewhere in the wild deeps, they will catch an echo of it. The dolphin-soul will hear.

The little plane charged merrily down the runway and lifted into the air.

★ ★ ★

The Captain demanded a detailed account of their Brittany investigation, and when Matthew had finished, with Martha's final words to him, the old man nodded agreement and said: 'Yes. Well, that's one worry off your mind. Now perhaps you'll pay some attention to your future.'

Matthew looked startled. 'What do you mean?'

'Your lawyer friend has been on to me. When are you going to London?'

'I thought — the day before Christmas Eve.'

'That's two days from now.'

'Is it?' The expression on Matthew's face became one almost of panic. 'I didn't realize . . . Skip's got a music-night tomorrow. He wanted me to —'

The Captain was looking at him quizzically. 'You don't want to go, do you?'

'No. Not really.'

'You must, Matthew. It's important.'

'I know.' He met the Captain's alert blue gaze with painful awareness. 'What will you do?'

The old man shrugged. 'Go south. High time I did, anyway.'

'Alone?'

The blue eyes clouded a little. 'Why not?'

'At *Christmas*?'

There was a fractional pause, and then Captain St George said neutrally: 'It doesn't make much difference to me, nowadays.'

Well, it should, thought Matthew. And I'm going to do something about it. 'Would you be going through London?'

'I might.'

'Could I — would you come and see Madge and the kids on Christmas Day — if asked?'

'I might.'

Matthew laughed. 'Skip might come too, if pushed.' He almost waited for the Captain to say: 'He might.' But the old man didn't rise this time. He just went on looking at Matthew thoughtfully.

'It'd be quite a — a —'

'Family occasion?' suggested the Captain innocently.

Matthew had the grace to blush. But then he said with sudden belligerence: '*Chosen* family.'

It was the Captain's turn to laugh.

★ ★ ★

Skip was busy turning the club music-night into a farewell party for Matthew, and had given him strict instructions to be there early, and get his guitar 'all tuned up'.

But Matthew had something else in mind first, and he took his guitar and wandered off to the far edge of the rocks where the seals could hear him — if they were still there. Where Flite could have heard him and come joyously to meet him, not so long ago . . . He stood looking out to sea for a moment, and then he settled down to play those fifteen dead dolphins to their rest. No flowers, no songs, said Martha. But it was all very well. He couldn't let those lost, beautiful creatures slip into oblivion without one passing salute.

It was a calm night. The sea was winter dark, and smooth

130

as polished silk. A pale December sun was sliding down into the west, laying bars of white-gold on the inky water. It looked lonely out there — lonely and vast and empty. No Flite anywhere. Matthew shivered a little, and began to play.

It was peaceful, though, all that echoing space — plenty of room for the notes to fall gently on the listening air . . . They would lie quiet now, those lifeless dolphins, untouched by any further fear . . .

He played Granados — de Falla — everything he could remember . . . Maybe it was a rehearsal for the evening ahead, but it was a private concert, too.

After a time, he became aware that the darkening water was not empty any more. There were listening heads breaking the surface, staying motionless in the swell to hear Matthew's music.

'Hallo,' he said, smiling. 'You've come back, have you? Don't look so astonished. It's really quite a good sound.'

He struck one more singing bass chord, and then launched into a final piece of Villa-Lobos. It was the last bit of his repertoire that he could remember, so he played the repeats to make it longer. The seals did not go away. They stayed upright in the water, their great liquid eyes fixed on the source of this fascinating sound on the shore.

'Well, that's all, folks,' said Matthew, somehow curiously cheered by the seals' silent company. 'Have a good winter — and give my love to Flite, if you see him.'

The seals did not answer. They waited till he got to his feet and turned his back on the sea. Then, one by one, they dived through the twilight ocean and swam away.

* * *

Skip's music nights were famous along the coast. People came from all sorts of small outlying places to join in. The local folk group, which was pretty bad but made up in noise for what it lacked in talent, always began the proceedings. They shouted a lot of local songs and sometimes put on funny hats and a bogus Cornish accent, and everyone loved them. But besides them, there were other visiting groups. Sometimes a silver band from a nearby town, or a travelling pop group between gigs, and one or two would-be pop singers who yelled happily and tunelessly into the mikes. And when they sang, everyone sang. The noise was deafening.

131

This time, as the folk group thumped its way through the range of good 'yelling songs', Matthew found himself strumming along with them for what Skip called 'a bit of a play-in'. But then, to his surprise, a small visiting jazz group got up on to the clubroom stage and invited Matthew to join them. This was quite a different matter. These were skilled and subtle improvisers, weaving intricate, intoxicating patterns with a piano, a double-bass and a clarinet, and Matthew had the time of his life. When they had happily embroidered their way through various old numbers and one or two new ones, the clarinet player paused for breath, loudly demanded beer, and under cover of the general racket said to Matthew, smiling: 'You're good, kid.'

'So are you,' retorted Matthew, flexing his fingers which ached a little with the excitement of being extra stretched.

'Good?' said Skip, coming up with beer all round. 'You should hear him on the classy stuff.'

'Well, why not?' grinned the clarinet player, taking a long swig of beer.

'Oh no,' protested Matthew, embarrassed. 'Not in — not now.' And then, seeing their raised eyebrows, he added lamely: 'They don't want to be serious tonight.'

The pianist, Len, looked up and pretended to take enormous umbrage. 'You think we weren't serious?'

Matthew laughed. 'I'll say. You had me scared rigid I wouldn't be able to keep up.'

'You did OK,' pronounced Len, nodding a wild head of hair. 'Didn't he, George?'

George, the bass player, took a long swallow of beer, mopped his brow with a red silk handkerchief and then carefully polished the strings of his double-bass. 'OK,' he growled. 'Not everyone can let go and impro.' He went on polishing his sweat-streaked instrument, and added in an even deeper growl: 'So play, man.'

Matthew looked doubtfully at the sea of cheerful, beer-swilling faces. But then, unaccountably, word seemed to have got round and they fell suddenly silent, looking up at Matthew expectantly.

'Come on, Fingers, give us the hard stuff,' shouted a voice from somewhere.

'The real McCoy,' added another.

'The works,' put in a third.

'Fingers Ferguson, give, give!' they chanted.

132

'You better get going, man,' muttered George. 'You wanna get lynched?'

So Matthew got going.

It was his farewell to them, after all, and he had got strangely fond of these tough, warm-hearted people. Strangely fond of Skip, and old Captain St George, who was there quietly in the background, watching the proceedings with his blue-eyed, quizzical stare.

All right, said Matthew, so I'm fond of them. In spite of what I said about no ties. Why not? Like the Captain said, it's not as simple as that. And since I can't tell them so in any words that won't embarrass them, I'll play it to them. Like I did to the seals. Like I did to Flite. Perhaps they'll understand. 'The Maiden and the Nightingale', he thought. They'll understand that. All that deep, dark sadness, the surge of longing behind those rich, pulsing chords . . . and moonlight, moonlight pouring down on silver olive groves, making the ache and pull of love still stronger, still more sorrowful . . . And then the bird, the tireless, brave little bird, singing and singing out there in the dark, pouring out ecstasy into the scented night air that smells of wild herbs on the slopes of hot hillsides and jasmine in shaded gardens, and fountains beneath the lemon trees of quiet courtyards . . . The small brown bird with the voice of love, singing and singing in the heart of the dark . . .

He only played that one piece to start with, enough to stir them up, he thought, and maybe after that, if they were bored, they could all shout for drinks and forget to ask for an encore. He had not meant to get so carried away, either, but then the music was stronger than he was. And perhaps it would do them no harm to feel the power and spell of Granados tonight.

But when he stopped, there was a moment of deep, unbroken silence, and then they asked for more, and went on asking for more until he had played almost everything he knew, and some he didn't know too well, including the new ones brought down for him by his old friend, Tudor Davies.

At last he spread out his hands and said, smiling: 'Sorry. Don't know any more,' and laid his guitar aside. But then he remembered that he was going away tomorrow, so he picked it up again and began to play 'Sailing, I am sailing . . . ' for them to sing. In a moment or two the jazz group picked it up, and after them the folk group and then everyone who could sing or play anything joined in. And then they progressed from

133

'Sailing' to 'Rio Grande' and got even louder. The noise was terrific.

> 'Then away, boys, away —' they yelled.
> 'Way down Rio,
> So fare you well, my pretty young gels
> For I'm bound for the Rio Grande.'

It's not so far out, either, thought Matthew. The other side of America . . . and then he remembered how he had played it before when Petra was leaving, and how sad she and Skip had been and how cross he had felt with the two of them wasting their chances . . .

He looked round for Skip rather guiltily, wondering whether this age-old song of parting would upset him. But Skip was singing lustily with the rest of them, and waving — of all things — a pair of stiff, brand-new jeans in one hand.

'These are for you,' he said, when the singing subsided.

'Why?'

'Because you ruined yours painting my ceiling.'

Matthew began to protest, but he saw a dangerous gleam in Skip's eye, and gave up.

'And this here is to go with it,' added a group of Skip's 'yelling boys' — waving a startlingly bright T-shirt with the words: 'Porthgwillick Aqua Club' emblazoned across it.

Looking into their laughing, determined faces, Matthew knew better than to refuse. 'Well, thanks,' he said, laughing too. 'At least you'll see me coming!'

One of them, a close friend of Skip's, looked at him seriously. 'Will you be coming back?'

The question hung in the air, fraught with extraordinary tension. 'Of course,' said Matthew, glancing swiftly at Skip. 'Of *course* I will.'

'That's all right then,' they cried, and launched drunkenly into 'He'll be coming down the mountain when he comes —'

Matthew couldn't think of any way to finish the evening adequately, so he went outside and had a fierce argument with himself about getting all worked up about nothing.

Skip came out and found him there, and a different argument began. Or it may have been the same one under a different guise.

'Can you come up to London for Christmas Day, Skip?'

'No.'

'The Captain says he might come.'

'I can't, Matthew. I've got a children's party for the village kids.'

'On *Christmas Day*? You can't have. They'll all be at home with their families.'

Their families.

'Well — Boxing Day, actually. But I have to get it ready.'

'No you don't. I'll help you before I go. *Please*, Skip. It'd be —' Well, why not say it out loud? 'It would be like a — a family party of our own.'

Skip hesitated. Then he remembered Matthew's history, and he knew suddenly why this mattered and he must not say no.

'OK. But I'll have to get back.'

'Of course,' agreed Matthew, rejoicing. (Rejoice, rejoice. Today, today!)

'The more we are together,

Together, TOGETHER —' shouted the yelling boys.

'Come on,' said Skip. 'They're getting maudlin in there. Time to throw them out.'

★　★　★

In London, Matthew dutifully phoned John Harvey, the solicitor, and fixed a morning appointment after Christmas, and then made his way to Madge's new address. It was not far from his old haunts in Pimlico, and he even passed the street where his mother's flat had been. But he did not go to look. Instead, he quickened his stride, and loped along, swinging his bag and thinking of Madge's kids, wondering whether they would remember him and what kind of a welcome he would get from Jampy.

But when he got to the door of the flat, a distraught Madge came rushing out to meet him, and clutched frantically at his arm.

'Oh God, Matt, it's you. Have you seen him?'

'Seen who?' Matthew was bewildered.

'Jampy. He's gone off. Missing all day.'

'*Jampy? Missing?*' He looked at Madge in horror.

'Why didn't you come sooner?' she cried, raging at him 'It was you he wanted. He kept on and on. "When is Matt coming?" . . . And now he's gone off to look for you, and I don't know what in hell to do.'

'To look for me? Where?' He was still bewildered.

'How the hell should I know? . . . Just gone to find you — that's what the other kids said.'

Matthew took Madge firmly by the arm and led her inside her own front door. 'Sit down, Madge, for God's sake. Now let's get things straight. Jampy went off — when?'

'This morning. I was doing the washing. Donna and Danny were at school. He was playing out front. When I went to call him in, he was gone. One of the other kids told me he said he was going to find Matt, he was tired of waiting, he said.'

Matthew thought swiftly. 'Have you tried the old flat?'

'Yes. Jim went round there. And the bed-sit, though he wouldn't go there, he hated it.'

'What about the school? Did he go to see Donna?'

'No. They haven't seen him. No one has.' Her voice rose dangerously. 'Oh God, Matt, what will happen to him? He's only three — out there in the streets on his own.'

Matthew was still thinking furiously. 'We went down to Cornwall by coach, remember? Does he know where the coach station is?'

She looked doubtful. 'He might. We go past it sometimes, especially if I take him with me to the shops.'

Matthew nodded. He had just come from the coach station himself. It was a much cheaper way to travel than the train. Could he have passed little Jampy, vainly trying to find him in all that jumble of people and traffic?

It's logical, he thought. Jampy's no fool. He might've thought I'd come that way. Or he might try to get on a coach himself. I wonder if he could read 'Cornwall'? Probably not. But he might guess. Or ask . . .

'I'll go back and look,' he said, making a swift decision. 'It's the best bet we've got . . . He wouldn't try the trains, would he?'

Madge looked even more distraught. 'Oh God, I hope not.'

'Where's Jim?'

'Out looking.'

'What about the other kids?'

'Checking with all their mates round here. Jim told them not to go any further.' She took a shaky breath. 'Can't . . . c–can't lose *all* of 'em, can I?' She began to weep helplessly.

Matthew laid an arm round her shoulders and hugged her close. 'We'll find him. Jampy's tough. He won't come to any harm.'

He began to go out of the door, but Madge clung to him. 'What shall I do?'

'Stay here. Be here. He might come back on his own. Have you told the police?'

'Jim has.' She gulped. 'They're out looking, too — in a Panda car.'

'Well, I may be luckier,' said Matthew, and went off at a run.

Yes, at a run, he told himself thankfully. I can really run now. Thanks to Skip and the swimming — and Flite. I'm cured!

He ran.

At the coach station in Victoria, there was the usual organized chaos of thrusting travellers with heavy suitcases, queues and wailing children. Matthew shoved his way through the crowds, searching every patient line of people at every terminal, and every corner of the cafeteria and the windy forecourt where the coaches came in.

There was no sign of Jampy. He even went to the enquiries office and the complaints desk to ask if any small, wandering, unattached boy had been seen. Not today, said the clerk, smiling. They quite often did get lost children brought in, or reported missing. Did he want them to put out a tannoy?

No, said Matthew, trying vainly to explain that he didn't even know whether Jampy was here or not. The desk clerk looked at him oddly and went back to his papers, obviously thinking: 'Passengers! They get nuttier every day!'

Matthew went outside once more and systematically searched the whole place all over again. But there was no Jampy.

He stopped to think, trying to put himself into the shoes of a small, determined boy who only knew that Matthew lived in Cornwall. And that coaches went to Cornwall. Coaches. How else could one get there? Trains? Cars? Lorries? *Lorries*?

He suddenly had a very clear picture of Jampy jumping up and down outside the little farm shop by the campsite in Porthgwillick, watching the farmer unload a sack of potatoes from his laden truck.

'All-for-us, all-for-us?' Jigging like a yo-yo.

'No, my handsome. Some for you, and some for London.'

'Some-for-me and some-for-London?' Another couple of jumps in the air. (He was a bit like Flite, come to think of it.) 'Goin'-to-London-to-see-the-queen?'

'Not today.'

'Tomorrow?' A twirl and a hop.

137

'Ay. To market tomorrow.'

'To-market, to-market, to-buy-a-fat-pig?'

And the farmer laughing: 'That'd be the day!'

And then Donna, who liked teaching them nursery rhymes and tried to be a good little mother, jogging the baby up and down in her arms and chanting: 'Home again, home again, jiggety jig.'

'Home-again?' Jampy jumping up and down again.

'Ay. There and back again.'

'There-and-back-again?'

There and back again.

Matthew went off at a run again and arrived back at Madge's flat, out of breath and urgent. 'Do you still shop in the market?'

'What?'

Matthew had done two paper rounds in those streets. He knew all the little local shops and the stall in the small street market near his old flat. But Madge was looking totally distraught and did not understand what he was saying.

'Your veges!' He wanted to shake her. 'Where d'you buy them?'

'Veges?' She stared at him open-mouthed. Jampy was missing, possibly run-over, or kidnapped, or murdered, and Matthew talked about *veges*?

'Yes, veges. D'you go to the market?'

She nodded, still bewildered. 'Why?'

But Matthew did not stop to answer. He went off again up the street. He knew the market and most of its traders, from his school-days before the fire, when he used to run errands for them and buy himself a hot dog from the corner stall instead of the dinner his mother had forgotten to provide.

Now, several of them greeted him like an old friend.

'Matt boy, where you bin?'

'Good to see you, Matt. Legs OK now?'

He hardly dared to stop and answer the pleasantries, but he knew that these were the people who could help him. The market traders were shrewd and observant. They had to be. They watched what was going on — and they knew all their regular customers. If Jampy was anywhere about, they'd probably have seen him.

'Madge's kid? The cheeky little-un? Plenty of lip? No. Ain't seen 'im today.'

'Jampy? The one we calls The Bouncer? No. Not today.'

But someone thought he'd seen him over by the fruit stall, talking to old George.

'Old George' — who was surprisingly young, not a day over forty, squarish and solid and very much on the spot — said yes, he thought it was Jampy. Small and talkative? Never still for a minute? That's 'im. Gotta watch these kids. Get their hands on an orange and run off soon as your back's turned.

'Not Jampy,' said Matthew firmly. 'He doesn't steal.'

'Well, maybe not,' conceded George grudgingly. 'He was after sumfink else.'

'What?' Matthew almost snapped his head off.

'Wanted to hitch a ride on a lorry, didn't 'e? Little tyke. I told 'im to go 'ome.'

'Did he?'

George shrugged broad and unconcerned shoulders. 'Couldn't say. He run off somewhere.'

It was the same all round the market. Some had seen him. Some hadn't. Some couldn't remember if it was today or yesterday. One or two said the kid had asked about lorries and rides. And one, the man on the chip-stall who had a sack of uncut potatoes round the back, said the nipper kept asking about cornflakes.

Matthew stared at him. 'Not cornflakes,' he said. 'Cornwall. That's what he was asking about. *Cornwall.*' He looked round wildly at the crowded street scene in despair.

Then a woman from the bric-a-brac stall said cheerfully: 'They only comes back when we're packing up.'

'What do?'

'The lorries and trucks. We're open late tonight. Christmas, see? . . . They won't be back till sevenish.'

She smiled at Matthew out of button-bright brown eyes and pushed back a tangle of wispy dyed hair. 'He won't get far, luv. No one in their right mind'd give a lift to a kid that young.'

No one in their right mind. Matthew shivered.

He had been round every stall and was wondering where to try next when he noticed a jumble of sheds by the corner where the lorries loaded and unloaded. There was a litter of broken boxes, cartons, dilapidated trestles, and old coat-hangers lying about on the ground, and a high pile of rotting left-overs from the fruit and vegetable stalls, mixed up with waste paper and smashed fruit baskets. He went a bit closer to have a look, thinking it would be logical for anyone as determined as Jampy to wait where the lorries turned round and loaded up. He might

139

even try to smuggle himself on board, if no one was willing to take him . . .

There was no one near the pile of rubbish on one side. Nor on the other. Nor in the first shed with the broken roof . . . And then he heard it — the sound of a small boy's furious sobbing from behind a pile of sacks in the corner of the second shed. '*Will* go!' he raged. '*Will*-damn-go!' And the sobs grew louder.

'Jampy!' Matthew called softly. 'Is that you?'

He went round the corner into the other shed and pulled the pile of rotting sacks away. And there was Jampy, grubby, tired and dishevelled, with one grimy fist stuffed into one eye, and tearstreaks mingled with market mud all down his face, and — at the sight of Matthew — even more furious.

'Where you *bin*?' he sobbed. 'You never come — not never. I bin lookin' for you. Lookin' and lookin'.'

'*You've* been looking!' answered Matthew, too astounded by this attack to be angry. Then he laughed and scooped Jampy up in his arms and hoisted him on to his shoulders. 'So have we all,' he said, still laughing. 'Everyone looking for everyone! Come on, soldier. Your Mam's having kittens back home!'

He went out into the market with Jampy riding high, rejoicing all the way. (Oh Flite! . . . Rejoicing all the way!)

Everyone in the market rejoiced with him. A small, mischievous kid had got himself lost and now he was found, safe and well. It was something to be thankful for these days, especially at Christmas. Someone thrust some left-over sprigs of holly into Matthew's spare hand, and someone else gave him a bunch of mistletoe and a spanking kiss to go with it, and hung a piece of bright red tinsel round Jampy's neck. And Sheila, the bric-a-brac lady, ran after them with a silver gas-balloon which said 'Happy Christmas' on one side and 'SANTA LOVES YOU' on the other.

It was like a triumphal procession, and though Matthew knew Jampy had caused a lot of trouble and anxiety, he somehow hadn't the heart to scold him.

'Home again, home again, jiggety jig!' he chanted, remembering with thankfulness what had made him know where to find him.

But for some reason, for Jampy this was the last straw. He looked down at the top of Matthew's head, and burst into howls of anguish.

'Hey!' Matthew tried to glance up at the outraged purple face above him. 'What's up now?'

'No pig,' howled Jampy.

'What?'

'Wasn't no fat pig.' The sobs of outrage almost choked him. 'And no one wasn't going home-again, *not no one*.'

Then Matthew understood. 'Well, I know somene who's going home again, double quick,' he said.

Jampy stopped howling in the middle of a sob. 'Me?' He considered the matter, one fist still in his eye. It hadn't occurred to him that home could be in two places at once.

'Yes, you, you twit. Stop bawling, and hold on tight. We're going to run all the way home.'

'Run-all-the-way-home!' crowed Jampy, his smile coming out like the sun. And he held on tight to Matthew's hair and rode his shoulders like a laughing charioteer.

★　★　★

Madge, when she saw them coming down the street, didn't know whether to laugh or cry. In fact she did both, and rushed out to hug them and scold them and shower them with tears of relief.

Donna and Danny came running out too, with Kirsty, not to be outdone, crawling along behind them; and Jim, who had just come back from another fruitless search, promptly went in and opened his Christmas bottle of ruby port.

'Celebration,' he said, by way of apology. And Matthew did not contradict him.

★　★　★

One way and another, it was a pretty good Christmas, what with Skip coming up for the day, and the old Captain being there as well — though he nearly didn't manage it, he told Matthew, because of another row with Conrad who wanted him to go to the south of France. However, he *was* there, and smiling quizzically at everyone in his usual quietly acerbic way. But for Matthew it was an occasion inescapably tinged with sadness, for he knew it would be a long time before he saw all these friends of his again. Perhaps a very long time if this aunt of his insisted on him staying with her in America. Still, he didn't want to cast a blight on the festivities — especially as

141

he had been the one who insisted on this family gathering. Family? . . . Well, they were much more like his family than this unknown woman in San Diego . . . So he determined to enter into the spirit of the occasion, and make it as cheerful a day as possible.

Madge had cooked a huge Christmas dinner for everyone, and there was a present for each of them under the tree, in spite of the fact that money was tight, as usual.

Matthew got a new sweater from Madge, and so did Skip because he had been good to Matthew, and anyway she liked knitting. The kids had bought Matthew some vivid purple socks with orange clocks because they looked 'nice and bright', and Jim gave him an extra dollop of ruby port when no one was looking.

Skip had brought the two boys toy boats to sail on the pond in the park ('but don't fall in!'), and a shell necklace for Donna which made her preen like a princess, no less — and baby Kirsty had a rubber fish that swam in the bath.

The Captain's present to the children enchanted all of them. It was a globe of the world which lit up when you plugged it into the mains, and included a small computer keyboard with the names of towns and countries on it. When each name-key was pressed, the location appeared on the map as a flashing red dot, and the seas and oceans came up as blue arrows. Jampy was fascinated.

Matthew secretly blessed the Captain for his tact. Madge and Jim were touchy enough about accepting things, but this gift reflected the old man's own world of shipping and journeys, and was so patently educational that no one could object or complain of extravagance.

Matthew had chosen his own contributions carefully, too. Madge had a small (inexpensive) brooch with a seagull on it, to remind her of Porthgwillick. Jim had a new pipe, because it kept him calm in the face of family chaos. And the children had a Lego fort, like the castles they had built in the sand, with a real portcullis and a drawbridge that let down, and a whole lot of knights and soldiers and horses with pennants flying and even some pea-shooting cannon to defend it. Now, he watched all the excitement with a sense of extraordinary rightness and content, and submitted meekly to being used as an enemy supply-train being potted at by the cannon, a siege-tower to be charged at by the horses, and even a hill for Kirsty to crawl over . . . This is how it ought to be with a family, he thought.

Everyone relaxed and cheerful — no one getting at anyone (and no one drunk or angry) — and a feeling of warmth all round that nobody bothered to analyze. It was all too easy to feel as if he belonged here and could stay with Madge and the kids for ever.

And to add to the general warmth came the surprise of the day — a visit from his old teacher, Tudor Davies, who brought him a new set of guitar strings, and two more Granados pieces to learn, and stayed to have tea with them all before going down to wild Wales for the rest of the holiday.

He gave Matthew a beaming smile and said: 'Boyo, you look a new man.'

'Do I?'

'Hundred per cent fit, and raring to go!'

Matthew laughed. But he wasn't raring to go. That was the trouble. And that was why there were still tensions, even in this easy, undemanding place. Of course there were. Particularly when Madge was so pleased with her new flat and so busy showing it off, with side-long grateful glances at the Captain for his (supposed) intervention on her behalf.

'Look, Matt, this is a sofa-bed. You can sleep here any time. And there's a room on the next floor coming up any day now, and the Council said you could probably have it if you want it.'

Matthew smiled and nodded, saying nothing yet about America. He didn't want to spoil Christmas, and his eyes met the Captain's in silent appeal. Skip knew about the tensions too, of course, and there also seemed to be some unexplained extra ones between him and the Captain. For when some laughing comment was made about Jampy's escapade, and the Captain said Madge was very forgiving, Skip looked at him with sudden intensity and seemed about to make some sardonic retort. But in fact he said nothing, and Tudor Davies, who was no fool about unspoken tensions either, innocently interrupted by asking Matthew to play for them.

Matthew looked at his old teacher and smiled. 'I'll play the two new ones you brought me last time — just to show I *have* practised! But then I think it'd better be carols, since it's Christmas.'

Tudor nodded happily.

Even the children listened while Matthew played. They were used to hearing him thrumming away downstairs in the old flat, and they didn't mind if it was 'serious stuff' or not. It was all music to them. But soon they were all singing carols together, with Tudor Davies leading them in his warm Welsh tenor, and Skip and even the Captain joining in. When someone demanded 'The Twelve Days of Christmas', Matthew agreed without demur, but his hands almost faltered when he got to twelve lords a-leaping and he thought of Flite leaping through the wild Atlantic as he swam farther and farther away. But he went on, reminding himself sternly that he was happy *now*, and Flite would not countenance any looking back.

'I must be on my way now,' said Tudor at last, just as Jampy was finishing off an extra out-of-tune 'Noël' of his own. 'Come and see me off, Matthew?'

Obediently, Matthew followed him down the stairs. But at the street door, Tudor paused and said seriously: 'So you are off to America then, boyo?'

'Looks like it.'

'You want to go?'

Matthew shook his head. 'No. But I suppose I've got to give it a whirl.'

'That's it. Never know till you try. I only wanted to say this to you: Any kind of trouble, you can always come to me. You know where to find me.'

Matthew stared at him, speechless.

'Haven't got a great deal of cash, look you. Schoolmasters don't amass fortunes. But you need help — you get stuck out there or anything — you tell me, see?'

This time Matthew managed a nod. Then he blurted out one word: 'Why?'

Tudor pretended to be enormously affronted. 'Why? The boy asks me *why*? With a talent like that at risk? I'm a teacher, remember? Can't bear things going to waste.' A mischievous grin cancelled out the spurious rage. 'Besides, it'd be a good investment, wouldn't it?'

'D'you think so?'

It was a serious question, and Tudor recognized it. He gripped Matthew's arm in friendly reassurance. 'I do think so, boyo. That's the point, isn't it?' He gave the arm a little final shake. 'So keep playing. That's all I ask.'

'I will,' Matthew promised, knowing he was somehow making an unbreakable commitment.

Tudor seemed satisfied. He let his grin grow wider, murmured: 'God bless,' and hurried away.

Then it was Skip's turn. He merely screwed up his eyes in

144

his famous all-embracing smile and said: 'Remember, the club's always open — and the sea's always there.'

Matthew sighed. 'I know.'

'And maybe Flite will come back in the spring.'

A sudden wild hope stirred inside Matthew. 'Do you think so?'

Skip's smile grew compassionate.'It's possible. They often do return to old haunts.' He hesitated,and then added: 'Particularly if they've got attached to someone.'

Attached to someone, thought Matthew . . . Yes, it's like an umbilical cord, pulling and pulling — only I don't know where it wants me to go . . . Oh Flite, where are you?

But Skip was now holding out something and looking almost shy about it. 'If you go down to the whale-watch in Baja California, you might meet Petra. It's not all that far from San Diego.'

Matthew took the slip of paper from Skip's firm brown hand. 'Is this her address?'

Once again Skip hesitated. 'Not exactly. But she said she could be reached there. Messages would get to her.'

'I see.' Matthew looked at him hard. 'Any message from you?'

Skip's sea-blue eyes seemed to cloud with pain for a moment. But he only said, carelessly enough: 'Oh, just tell her I'm the same as ever. Nothing's changed.'

'Nothing's changed,' repeated Matthew dutifully, and privately thought to himself: I wish to God it would! Then some imp of mischief made him ask innocently: 'If I get into a real jam out there, would you come to the rescue?'

Skip laughed. 'I shouldn't think so. Too expensive.' Then he grew serious for a moment, the strong brown face looking almost stern while he thought about it. 'But, yes — if you were desperate, I dare say I might . . .'

Matthew's grin was still full of mischief. 'Oh good. I'll try to pick a really fierce jam.'

'Don't you dare,' growled Skip. Then, surprisingly, he put an arm round Matthew's shoulders and hugged him hard. 'I hope it all works out for you, Fingers. Let me know how it goes.'

'I will,' answered Matthew, helplessly making more unbreakable promises. But while he was speaking, Skip sprang down the steps and went rapidly away down the street without looking back.

And finally, it was the old Captain. In the mysterious, quiet way in which his high-powered life was ordered, a chauffeur-driven car had set him down at Madge's door, and now it had returned, as quietly and mysteriously as it went, and stood waiting for him at the curb. So now he went slowly down the stairs, and stood leaning on his stick and looking at Matthew out of his shrewd, faded eyes.

'Now, listen to me, Matthew. You know how I'm placed — and most of the details of my business. I've not tried to smother you with offers of this or that. You've got to find your own feet.' He grinned suddenly, remembering the halting, pale boy who had hobbled to meet him on the sea wall not that long ago. 'But just remember I'm there. Head office can always reach me. If things don't work out in America, I've no doubt we can find you a job over here.' His glance was calm and undemanding. 'I know you want to be independent, so I'm not offering anything at present. But if the time comes — don't be too proud to ask.'

That was it, of course. *Don't be too proud to ask* . . . That fatal flaw of pride, ruinous pride, had been the cause of endless suffering — endless loneliness . . . He couldn't tell the boy, of course. But maybe he could prevent him from making the same mistake.

'Will you — will I see you again?'

The question hung in the air between them. It suddenly seemed to matter enormously to Matthew that he shouldn't be saying a final farewell to this fierce, solitary old man.

'I dare say —' murmured the Captain, 'if you don't leave it too long.'

'Will you go back to Porthgwillick — next year?'

'Possibly.'

'Please —' began Matthew, and then, greatly daring, said what was in his mind. 'Please be there —'

'Do my best,' growled the Captain. But there was a hint of uncertainty in his voice that made Matthew afraid. 'You'd better have this,' added the old man, not wanting to prolong things. 'I won't guarantee air fares, but this will get you a passage — of a sort — on any of my ships, anywhere.' He held out a small embossed card with 'St George Shipping Lines' printed on the top, and his own name, Verney St George, Chairman, in neat letters below it. Underneath, he had written in his fine, spidery hand: 'Free passage for Matthew Ferguson to any destination,' and signed it with an indecipherable flourish.

Matthew was overwhelmed.

'Might be a tanker, mind,' he added, twinkling at Matthew. 'Or a container ship. Don't get refrigerated.'

Matthew tried to laugh. But it came out like a gulp. 'I — I can't begin —' he tried.

But the old man cut him short. 'Don't. We don't need flummery, you and I. Go and spread your wings, boy. Learn to fly. Come back when you're a true high-flier.'

'I will,' said Matthew for the third time, and knew that this was the most serious promise of all.

The old man nodded, tapped him on the shoulder with his stick, and climbed into his car.

Matthew stood on the pavement and watched him go, feeling that some vital part of his own life was slipping away from him in that quiet, fast car. He lifted his hand in farewell, and saw a faint flicker of an answering hand against the window in response. Then the dark Mercedes turned the corner and was gone.

★ ★ ★

Matthew did not tell Madge about America until after his visit to the solicitors. This, he discovered, was even more cut-and-dried than he had expected. His future was laid out before him, tidily and neatly, without any consultation with him. His air ticket had been bought. A certain sum of money had been sent to him for 'travelling expenses'. He would be met at the other end. And in the meantime there was a letter for him to read from his aunt-by-marriage, Mrs Madeleine (Della) Grant.

John Harvey, the solicitor, was as quiet and prim as ever, but there was sympathy in his intelligent brown eyes as he handed Matthew the letter. Even to him, the arrangements seemed rather cold and bleak.

Matthew opened the letter in silence. So far he had not said anything except 'Yes, I see', to all the directions.

Dear Matthew (said the letter, in a round, rather childish hand) I hope all the arrangements will be satisfactory, and you will have no difficulty travelling. We are looking forward to seeing you over here. San Diego is a beautiful city, and I hope you will like it. Yours sincerely, Della Grant.

That was all. No word of family feeling or friendly welcome.

Just polite and rather distant. Oh well, thought Matthew, with a mental shrug, what did I expect? They don't know me. I've been wished on them by these well-meaning lawyers. Why should they be welcoming?

But it didn't make the prospect of travelling all that way to meet them seem any more inviting. A cold feeling of dread and mistrust seemed to settle inside him. He wished with all his heart that he didn't have to go. That he could stay with Madge and Jim and the kids, where at least he knew he was always welcome and could be some use — especially to that unruly little terror, Jampy. Yes, Jampy. What kind of a scene was he going to make when Matthew told him he was going away again? . . . He shuddered at the thought, and closed his mind tight against the knowledge that he would mind leaving Jampy behind, too.

' . . . anything else?' John Harvey was saying.

Matthew blinked. 'Sorry?'

'Is there anything else you want to know?'

Matthew considered. 'Yes. What happens if we don't get on? If it doesn't work out?'

The solicitor nodded. 'I thought you might want to know that! Well, of course, at sixteen you can decide for yourself what you want to do.'

'Can I? Don't they have — legal rights over me till I'm eighteen?'

'Not unless they apply to be appointed your legal guardians, or for adoption papers, and they haven't done that yet.'

'Could they?'

'Oh yes. But my guess is, they'll wait and see.' His brief, unexpected smile flickered out. 'After all, they are as much in the dark as you are.'

'Yes, of course.' Matthew saw the justice of that. 'Well — I'll just have to play it by ear.' A thought struck him. 'That air ticket — it's one way, I suppose?'

'I'm afraid so, yes.' But Harvey knew what was bothering Matthew, and went on to reassure him. 'However, I have that small amount of money of yours in trust, remember? Maybe you wouldn't refuse to use it if it meant you could get home?'

Matthew had the grace to look a bit ashamed of himself. 'Maybe I wouldn't,' he conceded, and smiled a lopsided smile.

'That's all right, then,' said John Harvey briskly. 'Just send an SOS to me, and I'll see that you get it. But — may I suggest that you do give the American visit a fair trial first?'

'Yes,' agreed Matthew. 'I intend to.'

★　★　★

When he told Madge and the kids, the expected scene from Jampy came with a vengeance. He stormed and yelled, and looked at Matthew out of outraged, tear-filled eyes that clearly said: 'Traitor!' and lay on the floor and kicked and refused to be comforted.

'You promised!' he sobbed. 'Come home, you said!' He rolled over and glared at Matthew. '*Can't* go away again!'

Matthew tried patiently to explain about his aunt, about a family of his own, about a new home in America. But that only made it worse. Jampy just yelled louder and stamped his feet and said: '*This* is home!'

Matthew looked helplessly at Madge. He didn't dare say what was in his mind — that he agreed with Jampy. This was home. This small, drab council flat, bursting with children and toys and washing, and Madge struggling to keep order and do two jobs at once, and Jim patiently smoking his pipe in the corner when he wasn't lending a hand with the baby or the endless cleaning . . . No room to turn round, no privacy — let alone anywhere Matthew could practise his guitar — and only a hard sofa-bed to sleep on . . . But nevertheless, warm and friendly and undemanding — home.

'Never mind, Jampy love,' said Madge, gathering the small boy up like an untidy parcel and hugging him close so that the wildly flailing arms and legs stuck out round her like a wriggling octopus. 'He'll come back.' She met Matthew's anguished look with perfect understanding. 'He knows this is his home, too.' She spoke quite calmly, as if stating an irrefutable fact.

'Home-too?' repeated Jampy, fixing Matthew with one stormy red eye and keeping his fist in the other.

'Home too,' agreed Matthew, and turned away hastily to stuff things into his hold-all before he disgraced himself in public and howled as loud as Jampy.

Jim Farley watched him in silence, and then took his pipe out of his mouth and added just two words to Madge's statement. '*Don't forget.*'

PART III

HE WHO BINDS TO HIMSELF . . .

The flight to San Diego was long and uneventful. He had to change planes in New York, and had a moment of panic when he didn't know where to go. But he was shepherded along with the rest of the passengers and was soon in the air again. The only glimpse of New York he had was of that famous skyline, sharply etched in bright winter sunshine, and making strange cubist patterns against a blue frosty sky.

He was even more dazzled by his first sight of San Diego. It seemed to be all blue sea and white buildings and golden sunlight — the city skyline floating on the bay like a brilliant mirage.

He arrived in a bewilderment of sun and shadow, and emerged in the airport terminal too dazed to look out for anyone meeting him. He went through customs and immigration still in a daze of confused images, clutching his passport and his all-important green card in a nervous hand. But at last he heard a voice behind him say in a crisp, English voice: 'Matthew? Matthew Ferguson?'

He turned sharply, and found himself looking into the eyes of a tall, elegant woman dressed in a white trouser-suit with lots of gold jewellery glinting at him in the sun. She had a squarish face which looked dependable enough, and grey eyes a bit like his own — and equally anxious. Her hair seemed to be ash-blonde fashionably tipped with silver on the curling fronds that framed her face, and her mouth, which was now attempting to smile at him encouragingly, was wide and not ungenerous, but curiously guarded, somehow.

She, for her part, saw a tall, shy boy with his father's deep grey-green eyes, and the same gold-bronze hair that sprang away from his forehead in the same kind of unruly crest. He looked tired and discouraged, she thought, and there was a wary look in those clear, light-changing eyes, and a set to his mouth that was both determined and braced for hurt. It was a face just settling into the firm lines of young manhood, already promising good looks and strength, and it was so like his

153

father's — the young man she used to know — that she caught her breath in surprise.

'You *must* be Matthew,' she said, holding out her hand. 'You can't be anyone else.'

'Why?' he answered, taking her hand and finding it warmer and friendlier than he expected.

'You're so like your father,' she said. And then, seeing the sudden bleak look of confusion on his face, she decided to take charge and not waste any more time. 'Come along. Is that all the baggage you have?' She hustled him out into the brilliant sunshine and into a bright green roadster with an open roof.

She drove fast, in a stream of moving traffic, with the blue Pacific appearing in gleaming vistas in between wide streets and piercingly white buildings. 'You'll have time to explore tomorrow,' she said, waving a dismissive hand at the inviting glimpses of sea, bright yachts in the bay, and tall masts and cranes down by the busy port. 'Right now, I guess you could do with a shower and some English tea.'

He caught her sideways glance at him and grinned. 'You sounded almost American then. But I thought —'

She answered at once: 'Oh yes, I'm English. A Londoner, like you. Till I married your father's brother — your Uncle Ned, that was. We went to live in Edinburgh then.' Once again she gave him that half-questioning, sideways glance, and then added ruefully: 'But since then — I've been out here so long, I almost feel American sometimes.'

'Do you miss England? — Or Scotland, I mean?' He didn't know what made him ask — except that he missed England already, even in all this sunlit splendour, and he couldn't think why.

'Yes. Sometimes.' Her mouth seemed to clamp shut then, as if he had touched on a subject that was taboo. But presently she waved her hand again at an approaching interchange with wide avenues branching off it, and said briefly: 'We live in a condo — down here.'

They duly arrived at a neat condominium of apartment blocks surrounding a central grassy square flanked by palm trees leaning towards the sun and the flawless blue of the sky above them.

The elevator took them to the third floor, where Della opened an outer door into a large, sunny apartment. There was a big living room with windows all along one wall, and a glimpse of the always-present Pacific between two other tall white apartment blocks. Beyond this was an opulent-looking double bedroom with satin swathes, and a smaller single one which also had a thin blue slice of ocean appearing between white walls. This room was furnished simply, with a bed and its own little washroom, a built-in wardrobe and a small white-painted desk to work at. There was a bright Indian rug thrown over the bed and on one wall a picture of a yacht heeling steeply into the wind.

'Yours,' said Della. 'Hope you've got enough room for everything.' She glanced at his small hold-all and smiled. 'Doesn't look as if you've brought much.'

Matthew did not say: 'It's all I possess'. He thought she probably knew.

'Come on through when you're ready,' she said over her shoulder. 'I'll let you settle in. Des won't be back till late, so we'll have time for a chat.'

What does 'a chat' mean? wondered Matthew grimly. Awkward questions about my mother? . . . And I wonder if she'll talk about my father? No one ever has before. A sudden passionate longing to know more about this unknown shadowy figure beset him. He had never known him — never really understood what had happened to him. He could scarcely remember him at all, except as a vague, unsmiling shape that his mother had shouted at. But then she had shouted at everyone. And they had mostly shouted back. Curiously enough, though, he couldn't remember his father's voice at all.

Sighing, he gave himself a mental shake, stripped off his crumpled, travel-weary clothes and stepped into the shower. Afterwards, he dressed carefully in the only other pair of jeans he possessed and the new T-shirt with 'Porthgwillick Aqua Club' to give him confidence, towelled his hair dry into even more unruly burnished tongues, and went to find Della.

She was in the kitchen-diner, frying him eggs, pancakes and hash-browns. 'Sit down,' she directed, jerking a thumb at the shiny barstools by the long counter. 'Hope you're hungry.'

Matthew didn't know he was till he began eating. Then he found he couldn't stop till the plate was empty. 'That was smashing,' he said gratefully.

Della was looking at him with curious uncertainty — wondering, perhaps, how much she ought to say to him. 'I'd better explain the set-up here,' she said at last, smiling at him, but with the same unexplained anxiety behind it. 'Des and I are both out all day, at work. I come home around five. Des, he

155

comes all hours. He's in insurance, and goes out on calls every goddam place under the sun.'

'What do you do?'

'Oh, I work in a downtown boutique. It's OK — not too hard except in a sales rush — and I enjoy meeting folks.'

Matthew nodded.

'So, you're free to do what you want by day —' Her smile was still a shade cautious. 'Lots to see in San Diego. You ought to take in the Zoo, it's famous. And Sea World. They have killer whales and things.'

'And dolphins?'

'Oh sure. Dolphins. You like dolphins?'

Matthew swallowed. 'I — got to know one once — in Cornwall.'

'A wild dolphin?'

'Yes.'

She was looking at him in surprise. 'Well, these are pretty tame, I guess. They do tricks and so on. And come when they're called.'

Flite came when he was called, thought Matthew. And even when he wasn't. But I can't tell her so. She wouldn't understand.

'We usually eat in, latish. Though sometimes we eat out by the beach. Des likes seafood. Do you?'

'Like seafood?' Matthew's thoughts were whirling. 'Oh. Oh yes.'

'I see you've brought your guitar. The lawyer told me you played real good — and I ought to let you keep it up. That so?'

Matthew nodded. It was good of John Harvey to have done that for him. Paved the way. Maybe he'd be able to practise here in the daytime while everyone was out.

'Des doesn't like too much noise, evenings,' she said, sounding anxious again. 'Unless he's got his favourite ball-game on — then he wouldn't hear an earthquake coming.'

They laughed together, both a little shyly, but Matthew understood that Della's warning had been given.

'About your schooling —?' she began suddenly, an apologetic frown creasing her brows. 'Do you want to go on to college?'

'No.' Matthew was quite definite. 'I wouldn't mind a computer course at night-school or something. But I want a job.'

'At sixteen?'

'Aren't there any?'

'Sure. Not very special, though. Don't lead anywhere much. Don't you mind?'

He shrugged. 'So long as I'm independent.'

There was a gleam of sympathy in her eye. 'You don't like being — beholden is the old-fashioned word, isn't it?'

'No. I don't.' Then he looked confused. 'But that doesn't mean —'

'You're not grateful. I know.' She was silent for a while and then said abruptly: 'You don't have to feel grateful, Matt. I want to do this. I was — very fond of your father.'

Matthew's eyes went cloudy with appeal. 'Can you tell me about him? . . . I know so little.'

She was staring beyond him, down a long, dark road of memory, and she started when he spoke. 'What? . . . ' She put up a hand and brushed the silver-gilt fronds of hair off her forehead, almost as if brushing away memories she could not bear. 'Oh, he was — young and rather handsome when I knew him. I married the older one, Ned — so I didn't meet Michael till the wedding.'

'Michael. Was that his name?'

She looked up, out of a dark abyss of recollection. 'Didn't you even know that?'

He shook his head. 'My mother never talked about him.' He saw her lips clamp shut again at the mention of his mother, and thought desperately: What can I do to make her talk? Any mention of my mother seems to make everyone clam up. 'What did he do?' he asked, at length.

'Do?' She sounded vague. 'Oh. He was a civil engineer. Transport. Roads and so on — bridges and things.' She smiled suddenly, a radiance of memory making her look all at once much younger and softer. 'And stars.'

'*Stars*?'

'He loved astronomy. He took me to look through that huge telescope once — the one at Greenwich Observatory . . . Only, I think it's been moved some place else now.'

'Astronomy?'

'Yes. Quasars and light-years. You know — maths. I suppose it goes with engineering.' She looked at him, with a strange light of recognition in her eye. 'You've got it too, haven't you? . . . Computers and such?'

But Matthew was still pursuing a thought, and ignored this. 'Was he any good?'

'As an engineer — or an astronomer?'

157

'Either?'

She laughed. 'Yes. Pretty damn good at both, I'd say. His bridges won prizes, I think.' Her eyes were unwary for once, full of dreams. 'He was always very bright, Ned used to say. We couldn't understand why he —' She stopped, confused.

'Why he married my mother?' He paused, and at last dared to ask what he had always wanted to know: '*Did* he?'

She looked astonished. 'Marry her? Oh yes. Whatever made you think —?'

Matthew shrugged. 'I don't know. She never talked about him. Never told me what happened, really . . . I just — wondered?'

'It didn't work out, Matt. It couldn't have, really. They were so different.' She glanced at him again speculatively, wondering how much to say. 'You must've realized —?'

'That my mother was a tramp?' His voice was flat. 'Oh yes. There were always boyfriends. Always someone new. They never lasted long.'

She nodded silently. Then she said with abrupt kindness: 'Didn't you mind?'

He shrugged again. 'Not really. I never knew anything else.'

I never knew anything else. Della Grant shivered at the tired, worldly-wise acceptance in the young voice. What a bleak and loveless life this boy had lived till now. And could she make it up to him at all? Now, when it was so very much too late to give him back his childhood? Could she at least give him some stability and affection here? . . . *Affection?* Or would he refuse to accept it — like his father before him?

'Well,' she said, trying to be practical and kind, as she knew she should, 'no good dwelling on the past. You're here to enjoy yourself a little for a change. I suggest you spend a few weeks getting to know yor way around before you look for a job. There's no hurry.' She ventured another, friendlier smile. 'We're not short of a dollar or two, Des and I. And we'd like to see you have a good time. OK?'

Matthew agreed — inwardly sighing because once again the subject of his father had been closed before he could get at the truth of it.

Awkwardly, Della laid a hand on Matthew's shoulder. 'No need to take decisions right away. Let's get to know each other first, shall we?'

He looked up and answered her smile with a tentative one of his own. 'Why not?' he said, and left it at that.

★ ★ ★

Des, when he came in, was large and hot and hearty. He clapped Matthew on the shoulders, saying: 'Hi-ya, kid,' called loudly for a cold beer, and flopped into a chair.

Matthew was too shy to say much and waited for Des to make the overtures. But the big man seemed to accept his presence with careless unconcern, and went on with his own normal evening's routine without question.

By this time, sleep was beginning to catch up on Matthew. He reckoned vaguely that by English time it was probably about four in the morning — the next morning at that. But here in San Diego it was still broad daylight and the sun was casting a golden evening aura over the bright city and its blue, smiling bay.

'Della,' said Des, lazily waving his beer, 'I guess we might eat out at the Beach tonight. Kinda celebrate.'

Della hesitated and glanced at Matthew's face. She knew how weary and jet-lagged he must be by now.

'I don't know, Des. Matt's probably tired.'

'Sure, he's tired,' agreed Des, laughing hugely. 'Best way to deal with jet-lag is ignore it.' He got heavily to his feet and gave Matthew another hearty slap on the back. 'OK, Matt?'

'OK,' said Matthew wearily.

'Getta view of the city,' added Des, grabbing his car keys and his wallet and stuffing them into a back pocket on his bulging hips. 'See where you are, kiddo. Try out some sea-food, OK?'

'OK,' agreed Matthew, for the second time.

★ ★ ★

Matthew realized from the first that he would have to make his own friends. And it wasn't that easy. Della and Des were out all day, and in the evenings they either stayed in and had friends round, or went out to one of San Diego's many beach-side restaurants and joined other groups of friends for a meal. But these were mostly people of their own age who were kind enough to Matthew but treated him rather like an extra tame exhibit in San Diego Zoo. Some of them did have teen-age kids, who occasionally joined them but mostly went off in their own noisy gangs to their own haunts. One or two of them did ask Matthew along, but he found himself strangely reluctant to

159

become drawn into their pursuits — their hang-gliding and wind-surfing, their endless beach games and barbecues, their discos and smoky bars and latest crazes in break-dancing and crack or their successors . . . 'I am becoming a prig,' he said to himself, knowing these careless, golden young people found him awkward and stiff. But then he remembered to bring his guitar next time, and from then on, particularly at the beach after a barbecue, he drew in his own small circle of devotees, and people forgot about him being strange and prickly.

Des, for his part, obviously trying hard to play the benevolent uncle, insisted on taking him out at weekends to the Zoo and Sea World. As if, thought Matthew wryly, I was a small boy being taken out at half-term. San Diego Zoo, however, was so spacious and well organized that he almost forgave them for keeping wild animals in captivity. But Sea World was another matter. He had tried to avoid the daily shows of killer whales and dolphins jumping through hoops, but Des insisted jollily that it was Spectacular, kid, and he would love it. He hated every minute of it. He wanted to get down into the water and open the sluice gates and set them all free. He wanted to make all the crowds go away and stop their silly shouting. He wanted to clasp those driven creatures in his arms and say: 'It's all right. you needn't do any more tricks to please your keepers. You needn't be pushed around and cajoled and bullied and demeaned any more. You're free to go. And the great wide ocean out there is cool and quiet — waiting for you.'

But he couldn't. Of course he couldn't. There they were, these tamed, well-trained, graceful creatures, leaping and diving to order, playing their appointed games and doing their brilliant acrobatics, and coming up for applause with their ingratiating smiles fixed on their faces — and he, watching them, wanted to curl up and die of shame. How could we? he thought. How could we reduce these glorious creatures to such servility? How can they bear it? . . . Or have they forgotten what it was like to be free — to be their own master out there in their own wild wilderness? If I could just reach out, he thought, and take one flipper in my hand, or touch one dorsal fin, and tell them . . . But what could I tell them? That mankind isn't so awful as they think? Or that being safe and fed in a tank, with thousands of staring eyes and shouting mouths directed at them is better than swimming free?

And probably, he thought, if you let these ones go now,

they wouldn't survive. They wouldn't know how to fend for themselves. Or would they?

'They enjoy it, you know,' said Della, who had seen Matthew's face and knew a little about how he felt.

'Do they?' snapped Matthew. 'How do you know?'

The question hung in the air between them, and Des, picking it up, said cheerfully: 'Oh, they're all clowns at heart. They *love* performing. Look at them!' He grinned, and gave Matthew a playful dig in the ribs. 'They know what's good for them.'

Matthew sighed, and just stopped himself saying: 'Do they?' again. Then he caught the eye of a girl who was standing near the rail next to him — not sitting in her seat like the gawping crowds, but looking as if she was on the point of walking out. She was slim and brown, with a tangled stringy mane of dark hair, and a rather angry-looking mouth, and her bright, observant eyes seemed to spark with impatience. In fact, her whole supple young body in its brief shorts and shirt seemed strung with the same enormous impatience.

'Pathetic, aren't they?' she murmured. And Matthew didn't know if she meant the dolphins and killer whales, or the audience oohing and aahing at them. Then she jerked her thumb at the exit. 'Coming outside?' she asked, and moved away.

'Excuse me,' he said politely to Des, wondering if he could get outside without being sick, and followed the girl out of the noise and heat of the arena.

She was waiting for him outside, and with her were two young men, a bit long-haired, and older than Matthew, wearing shorts and Hawaiian shirts and sporting the golden, all-over tan that San Diegans all seemed to have.

'I'm Tracey,' she said, and then waved a careless brown hand at her two companions. 'Bud and Spike.'

'Hi,' they responded lazily, crinkling up their eyes against the sun in smiles that were almost real.

Matthew's own smile was cautious. 'Matt,' he volunteered, somehow feeling it fitted better with this company.

'Animal rights,' added Tracey, without any other explanation — and then dismissed her two colleagues with a nod. 'See you tonight then. My place. At eight.'

They nodded cheerfully, grinned at Matthew, and after a brief consultation went off in different directions and climbed into two different cars in the parking lot.

The girl, Tracey, watched them go and then turned to Matthew. 'Didn't like it much, did you?'

Matthew shook his head. 'All that in there? . . . It seems so — degrading, somehow. Dolphins are such — such noble creatures.'

She looked at him in astonishment. '*Noble*? . . . Well, yes, I guess so . . . and whales.' She was still staring at him. Then she said abruptly: 'English?'

He nodded.

'How come you know about dolphins?'

He smiled. 'They do come to our cold English waters — sometimes.'

She stared. 'You seen them?'

He hesitated, wondering how much to say to this blunt, forthright girl. 'I — knew a wild one once, yes.'

She waited, but when he failed to say any more, she gave a quick nod to herself, as if this confirmed something in her assessment of him. Then she said, even more abruptly: 'You seen the greys going down?'

He looked bewildered. 'The greys?'

'Grey whales. Wild ones,' she added, a sudden note of bitterness in her voice. 'Going down the coast.'

'Oh.' He was still bewildered. 'No.'

'Come with me.'

He paused, wondering what to do about Della and Des. Then he thought: what the hell. They saw me go out. They won't worry.

But Tracey had not even waited to see if he was following her. She was already climbing on to a small moped and signalling to him to get on the back. They whizzed out along the coast road to Point Loma, where there were already a small number of visitors looking at the view of San Diego spread out along the bay. But some of them were not looking at the white-and-gold city on their left. They were looking out to sea, where in the beguiling calm of the blue Pacific, a slow, swirling line of dark grey humps moved steadily down the coast towards Baja California. From time to time they came up to blow, then curved over into a massive, glistening wall of greyish-white bulk, and dived deep, sending a huge shower of spray up with the rising tail-fluke which came out of the water like a vast, branching tree.

Matthew was enthralled.

'Where are they going?' he asked, aware at once that their purpose was fixed, their journey imperative and laid down by countless years of custom.

162

'To Scammon's Lagoon,' said Tracey. 'And a couple of others in Baja. To breed. All the way from the Bering Sea. Every year the same.'

'Marvellous,' breathed Matthew.

'Sure is. No one knows quite why. Or how they all know where to go.'

Matthew stared out to sea at the slow, long line of dark humps in the water. 'Follow-my-leader?'

Tracey laughed. 'Could be. They swim in groups, mostly. I guess they tell each other — the old mothers tell the new ones it's safe down there.'

'Is it?' Matthew's face was anxious.

'Oh yes. It is now. They're protected. Even the whale-watch is restricted — in case it scares them. Too many little boats buzzing about . . . The mothers can get dangerous when their offspring are threatened.'

'I don't blame them.'

She was looking at him thoughtfully. 'You oughta go down there.'

'Where?'

'Scammon's Lagoon. See for yourself.'

'I'd love to.' He sighed. 'But —'

'You're with your folks. I know. I saw them.' She made a face at him. 'Can't you break loose?'

He hesitated. 'It's — not that easy. Things are a bit — er — complicated.'

She nodded, accepting it. 'When aren't they?' But there seemed to be a gleam of some other resolve in her eye.

'Will you be going down?' he asked suddenly, not quite knowing what he was starting.

Her expression changed. All at once she looked older and rather stern. 'I might. But I got other things to do first.'

'Such as what?'

It was her turn to hesitate. 'You into Animal Rights?'

'Not yet. But I'm willing to learn.'

She nodded. Then she raised a slim hand and pointed down the coast. 'See that line of stuff? Closed area. US Navy. You know what their latest gimmick is? Training dolphins to dive deep and recover bits of nuclear warheads off subs — and to act as guard patrols against frogmen.'

Matthew was horrified. '*What?*'

'They buy them from the Japs. Dolphins can go real deep,

163

you know. Deeper than the Navy realized. So — now the training starts. You can imagine what their life is like.'

'I can.' Matthew's face was grim. 'It's obscene.' Then he asked, looking at Tracey hard: 'So what can we do about it?'

'Protest,' she said at once. 'Carry banners. Get the media in on it. The more noise the better. And perhaps —' But she broke off there, and seemed to change her mind.

A far off voice in Matthew's mind echoed from the shores of Brittany where those fifteen dead dolphins had lain. '*Talk! Speak! Write!* . . . Shame them into doing something about it.' And Skip's voice, dry and sorrowful at once: '*Can they be shamed?*'

'If you're interested,' Tracey was saying, 'there's a meeting at my place, Friday week. To plan a march. Coming?'

'Yes,' said Matthew decisively.

Satisfied, she gave a little nod and turned back to have a last look at the patient line of grey whales swimming steadily away down the sunlit coast of California. Grand and stately, stronger than the tides themselves, nothing deflected them from their purpose . . . She wished she was as strong, and as single-minded.

★　★　★

Della and Des did not seem particularly annoyed that he had walked out of Sea World. They accepted that he had felt sick, and assumed that the heat had got to him.

But when he mentioned Tracey and her meeting, Des was definitely none too pleased. 'You want to watch it, kid, with that bunch. Trouble-makers, all of 'em.'

'But I —'

'Hoodlums and layabouts. Think they can change the world by violence.' He took another swig of ice-cold beer — there was nearly always a beer-can in his hand — and waved his other hand dismissively. 'Leave it out.'

Matthew glanced at Della in appeal. But she was scrabbling in her handbag for a cigarette, and gave him a neutral shrug.

'Their ideals may be OK,' she said, still scrabbling, 'but they do kinda get themselves a bad image. You know — cutting fences, and opening cages, and even throwing a bomb or two. Leads to God-almighty trouble. Des is right. Better steer clear of that lot.'

Matthew's mouth shut in an obstinate line. If the two of

them had known him better, they might have recognized the signs. But they didn't. He said nothing. But he made a quiet resolve in his own mind to slip off on his own when the time came.

★ ★ ★

When he had endured as much idleness and sightseeing as he could bear, he enrolled in a computer course for one night a week, and then went downtown and found himself a job.

Mosky was a shrewd, stringy Jew who ran a café-diner with a bookstore on the side — or it might have been the other way round. He looked Matthew up and down and said abruptly: 'Speak.'

'What?'

'Speak. Enunciate. Give.'

Matthew looked bewildered. 'What do you want me to say?'

Mosky grinned. 'You done it, kid. It's the English accent I want.'

Matthew found Mosky's grin encouraging. 'Why?'

'You kin read, I take it?'

'Of course.'

'No "of course" about it. Most kids can't these days — or won't.' He waved an expressive brown hand at the rows of books on the shelves that Matthew glimpsed through an archway beyond the café tables. 'Gotta be flexible. They want a burger — you get it. They want Marcel Proust — you find it. Follow me?'

'Yes.'

'But you don't bring the book to the table. Grease-and-tomater all over the dust jacket. You take the guy to the book. See?'

Matthew nodded.

'You know San Diego?'

'No. I'm new here.'

Mosky wagged a wise head. 'I guessed so. You gotta learn, kid. You gotta learn fast.' He looked out at the street where the downtown crowds sauntered by, and then turned back to Matthew. 'Folks come in here, they want directions. Mostly tourists — and mostly lost. You gotta put 'em right.'

Matthew looked a little alarmed. He didn't dare seem over-confident with those clever brown eyes watching him. 'I — I'll

165

do my best. You'd better lend me a guide book, and I'll learn it by heart!'

Mosky laughed. 'You do that, kid. But, most of all, you get out there yourself and look. Take the bus — take the trolley — go duck around the bay. It's an easy city to learn — all coast roads and horizontals. Shiny-clean and not a twist among 'em. You from London?'

'Yes.'

'I was in London once.' He seemed to pause there and go into some dark thoughts of his own. But then he came back to Matthew, flashing his impish grin at him, and saying briskly: 'When can you start?'

'Today,' said Matthew promptly. He rather liked Mosky. He knew this was the job for him — if he could do it.

Mosky clapped him on the shoulder. 'Attaboy. I thought the English were supposed to be work-shy.'

'Not me,' said Matthew simply. 'I'm broke.'

The two pairs of eyes met. They understood one another.

'Come meet the guys,' said Mosky, and led him to the long counter-bar with the line of hot-plates and micro-ovens behind it. 'This is Joe — he cooks; and Allie, she waits tables; and Merc, he clears up. But we all do what's needed. OK? Guys, this is Matt.'

The three of them looked up and nodded cheerfully, and went on with their work. The morning rush was on, and it was clear that none of them had time to stop. Joe was long and thin, and busy turning burgers with a long, flat spoon on the sizzling hotplate. Allie was brown and plump, with long brownish hair tied back in a bright green bow. And Merc, who seemed almost submerged in a mound of washing-up in the double sink, was square and sweating, with powerful arms plunged into soapy water, and a face suffused in steam that yet managed to flash him a quirky smile.

'Hi.' Matthew sounded shy. 'Can I help?'

Merc stared at him. 'Jeesus. Someone's offerin'.' He reached out one soapy hand and flung Matthew an apron. 'Help yourself.'

'That's it. Get stuck in,' approved Mosky, and went off smiling to himself. Matthew's job had begun.

At the end of the first week, he took some of his wages back to Della, and provoked a major row.

'What d'you think I am, a child exploiter?'

'I'm not a child, Della.'

166

She looked at him, and her smile seemed to change subtly. 'No,' she conceded softly. 'You're not, are you?'

There was a curious little silence. Matthew felt uncomfortable under that altered gaze. But he still held the dollar bills out to her in his hand. 'Please,' he said.

'I can't take your money, Matt.'

'Yes,' he insisted. 'You can. Just for my keep. It'd make me feel better.'

'Would it?' She did not really understand this. How could she? Life had always been comfortable and easy for Della. But she tried very hard to put herself in Matthew's place. To have no one — and nothing of one's own. To be dependent on other people's kindness and goodwill. To belong nowhere. To expect nothing from anyone . . . And to be independent enough to *need* nothing from anyone. yes, she could see how it would be.

'All right,' she said at last. 'I guess you win. But only a small amount, mind. I won't take advantage.'

They glared at each other for a moment, and then began to laugh.

Really, Matthew thought, she's quite pretty when she laughs — and she's beginning to get my point of view.

He's a good kid, thought Della, and not bad-looking when he stops being so goddam serious. And, truth to tell, he's so like Michael, I find it hard to refuse him anything.

But she didn't tell Des about the money. Des was funny about being the boss — the main provider. He didn't even like her working, much. He might take it amiss, and she didn't want any trouble.

* * *

Tracey's pad was in a downtown apartment block between a bank and a group of shiny neon-lit bars and restaurants. Its concrete approach was cold and faceless, and clearly none too affluent.

The 'meeting' seemed to spread all over the shabby living room and the half-screened kitchen with its hard yellow bar-stools and stained worktop. People draped themselves on chairs, on sofas, on beanbags, on the floor, and even propped up the walls. There was a haze of smoke and the unmistakable sweet smell of pot in the air, and there were empty glasses and coffee cups strewn in all directions. To Matthew the company all seemed absurdly young, laid-back and nonchalant, and not in

167

the least like a bunch of ardent activists. They scarcely even looked up when he arrived, but went on lazily drinking beer and smoking something that Matthew didn't think was tobacco . . . It looked as though the meeting had already been going on some time — and might go on for ever.

'This is Matt,' said Tracey to the room at large. 'He's English — and into dolphins.'

Matthew winced a little, and wondered what 'into dolphins' really meant. The two blond boys she had introduced before as Bud and Spike looked up vaguely and said 'Hi,' before going on with their own rather monosyllabic conversation. And then, as an afterthought, Spike offered Matthew a hand-rolled cigarette and said casually: 'Smoke?'

'No thanks.' Matthew shook his head, feeling too virtuous and far outside this cosy little group. But he was very wary of those innocuous-looking rolled-up cylinders.

Tracey looked at the assembled company through narrowed eyes, and then turned on Spike with sudden venom. 'You can cut that out.'

'What?' He looked up at her with wide, innocent eyes.

'You heard. You go on a demo with that stuff on you, you'll get busted real good.'

Spike shrugged in lazy unconcern. 'No demo here.'

'You leave it out, Spike, you hear? All of you. *Leave it out.* We're into something serious this time. No one's to be caught with crack or anything else. It only takes one bust to give us all a bad image. We need to be squeaky-clean this time, understand?'

There was a vague murmur which did not satisfy Tracey, and she leaned forward and snatched Spike's cigarette out of his hand and flung it into the kitchen garbage bin.

'I mean it,' she snarled, and glared round at the others. 'We don't know if we're watched here, like last time, or not. Protests around a naval base are hot stuff. If they come in here on a search, where'll you be?' The silence seemed a little more alert by now, and several pairs of lazy blue eyes in suntanned faces took on an almost intelligent expression.

'Now, listen.' Tracey shook out her mane of hair and got down to business. 'Listen real good. It's *Friday.* Friday week, OK? . . . That's the twelfth. Gives us time to get out the posters.' A few heads nodded. 'And hand out leaflets.' A few more heads nodded. 'Assemble at my place and march downtown first.'

'*Only* march?' said one, sounding disappointed.

Bud and Spike glanced at one another and then across at Tracey. But she seemed to ignore them.

'*March*,' she ordered. 'With banners. "Save the dolphins" — all that jazz. We got enough?'

'Could make a coupla more,' volunteered a thin girl with mouse-brown straight hair, wire-rimmed glasses and a nervous grin.

Tracey gave her an approving nod and turned to Matthew. 'You coming?'

He looked a bit uncertain. He badly wanted to know what else they were planning to do besides march, and what that odd glance between Spike and Bud signified. 'I'm working till four,' he said.

Tracey nodded, seeming unconcerned. 'Then meet us at Ocean Beach. We'll be about there by then, ready for Point Loma and Fort Rosencranz.' She glanced balefully at the roomful of lazy people. 'That is, if any of you can get yourselves together by then.' She added, by way of reassurance to Matthew more than anyone, 'The police know our route. There'll be no trouble — unless we make it.'

Matthew did not quite know how to take that. So he merely said: 'I'll be there if I can,' and left the difficulties of life with Des and Della unexplained.

'OK,' she agreed, and quite deliberately dismissed him, and most of the rest of the meeting with him. 'Better spread now. Gotta talk to Spike and Bud — about leaflets.'

Matthew noticed then that there was a copier in one corner of the room, and a pile of papers spilling off the table on to the floor.

'Here,' she said, grabbing one and handing it to Matthew. 'Dig this. See you Friday week.'

He knew from the look on her face that she and Spike and Bud were planning something else, but she had made it very plain that he was not wanted on that trip — whatever it was. Maybe she didn't altogether trust him yet, and he couldn't blame her. Anyway, something within him decided he was rather glad not to know what they were up to. So he turned away, grinned over his shoulder at them collectively and non-committally, and said nothing more at all.

★　★　★

169

Back at Della's apartment, Matthew let himself in and slid unobtrusively off to his own room without saying anything. To his relief, Des appeared to be out, and Della was banging about in the kitchen.

He got out his guitar rather guiltily, for he had been neglecting it lately, and began to play the new piece by Rodrigo. It got hold of his fingers, and a sudden wave of dreadful nostalgia swept over him. He longed to be back home again in grey old London, within reach of his good friend, Tudor Davies — within reach of Madge and the kids, and Jampy interrupting his practice with endless questions and irrepressible jumps and jigs . . . He didn't belong in this bright, affluent city with its dazzling beaches and yacht harbours, its heedless golden boys and girls . . . Somehow, its sparkling brilliance filled him with terror. It was too clean, too beautiful, too smart . . . And even though he was near the dolphins and killer whales of Sea World, and the great grey whales of the pacific — his own loving, graceful companion, Flite, seemed farther away than ever . . . Flite had nothing to do with those grinning vaudeville displays, or the gawping boatloads of whale-watchers ducking around the bay — or even the doomed dolphins training in deep water at the secret naval station. Flite was somewhere out there, a long way north in the cool Atlantic, swimming free — with no shadow of man's exploitation to hold him back from his natural destiny . . . Or was there? Did the growing shadow of destruction reach even there? Matthew hoped not. Oh God, he hoped not . . .

There was a tap on the door, and Della's elegant head came round it. 'Can I come in?'

'Of course.' Matthew looked guilty. 'Was I too loud?'

She smiled and strolled over to sit on the edge of his bed, crossing her slim brown legs and leaning back to look up at him. 'No. I like to hear it. Your lawyer was right, you play real good.'

Matthew was relieved.

'It's only Des who —' She did not finish it, but instead fished in her jacket pocket and brought out a yellowing envelope. 'I thought you might like to have these.'

Matthew took the envelope from her. Inside it were two faded photographs. One of them showed a young man with curly bronze hair and a curly smile to match. He was leaning against some kind of bollard, and screwing up his eyes against the sun. The second photograph showed the same, smiling young man, arm-in-arm with a slightly older and more serious-looking version of himself on one side, and a young, also smiling woman on the other. He looked at it more closely and recognized the woman as a youthful version of his aunt Della — a softer, gentler version, perhaps, but with the same slightly arrogant tilt of the head.

He looked at her enquiringly. 'Is that — my father?'

She sighed. 'Yes — that's Michael. Standing by one of his bridge supports or something . . . And that's Ned, my late. And me, of course — when young . . .'

Matthew was staring at the stranger in the photograph. There was no stirring of recognition inside him — scarcely even a flicker of relief that he knew at last what his own father looked like. Only a vague feeling of disappointment that it didn't mean more to him. It ought to, but it didn't. Here was a picture of a man he didn't know, living and working and laughing into cameras before Matthew was even thought of . . . Or was he alive then? He didn't know. He was ashamed to find that he didn't much care, either . . . He looked a nice enough guy — pleasant and alert and no doubt good at his job. But he was a stranger.

'Would you like to have them?'

He started. 'Oh. Yes, I —' But there had been a softness in Della's eye as she looked down at them, a hesitation in her decisive voice that made him wonder. 'Have you got other copies?'

'No.'

'Then —' He handed them back to her, smiling. 'Maybe we could get them copied?'

She seemed relieved, and held them in her hand, looking down at them thoughtfully. 'I guess we could.'

'He looks — a nice guy.' It sounded painfully inadequate.

'Yes,' she said. 'He was. And very like you.'

'Really?' Matthew leaned over to have another look. Like me? But I don't have that air of confidence, he thought. That look of belonging in the world . . . Perhaps I will one day . . . 'It's difficult for me to see it,' he said lamely, and laughed a little. 'I don't really know what I look like.'

Della smiled at him with unexpected warmth. 'You look real good to me.'

Matthew was embarrassed. But he dearly wanted to know a bit more about his father and that unexplained car crash. The trouble was, how to get it out of Della when she clearly didn't want to talk about it.

'I suppose he — had to travel about a lot, with that kind of job?'

Della's smile was abruptly dowsed, and he could see that he had said the wrong thing again. But before she could reply there was the sound of a slammed door and a shout from the living room. Des was home.

He came lazily to the doorway of Matthew's room and stood looking in at them. There was not exactly suspicion in his glance, but a certain watchfulness that made Matthew uneasy.

'Anyone alive round here?'

'Yes, Des, of course. I was just — giving Matt a couple of old photos.'

Des snorted contemptuously. 'Not playin' around with that old crap again? Why don't you leave the past where it's at, Del. Dead and buried.'

Della looked shocked. 'Des — it is Matt's father.'

Des shrugged massive shoulders. 'So it's Matt's pa. Then. But now it's today.'

(Today, today! sang Flite, far down in Matthew's mind, stirring an ache of longing for that joyous, uncomplicated company).

'*Today!*' repeated Des, glaring at Della. 'And I'm hungry. So get yourselves together, guys, we're goin' out.'

Della put the photographs in her pocket and almost scuttled out of the room to find her handbag. Her face was closed.

Matthew got up and laid his guitar on the bed with careful hands. He did not look at Des. It was becoming obvious to him that there was something about the past that Des resented — even disliked — and Matthew himself was part of it. When he thought about it, the future here didn't look very rosy, and it was clear to him that he'd better keep out of Des's way as much as possible.

'You and Della go,' he said. 'I've got some work to catch up on for my class.'

'Suit yourself,' shrugged Des, and sauntered off, leaving the door wide open.

But when they had gone, Matthew went down to Mosky's and offered to lend a hand on the late shift. He needed the company.

Because of his hours at Mosky's and his evening classes, Matthew had taken to swimming very early in the morning. He preferred the beach then anyway, when it was empty and quiet. It seemed a little nearer to his own windswept Cornish beach and the small bay behind the rocks where the seals came to listen to his music, and the gentle presence of Flite the dolphin filled the day with joy.

Here the sea was bluer and the sands were whiter and never entirely empty, though they stretched for mile after gleaming mile. But at least in the cool morning ocean he felt less cut off from the world he once knew. There were seals here too — he often saw their round heads bobbing in the bay. And pelicans. Sometimes the sky was alive with them, wings flashing in the sun, and there were usually a few strutting about on the sands. And out there, not far beyond the point, the great grey whales were swimming steadily southwards, curving and arching through the water, unhurried and unafraid . . . While somewhere out there, far out in another ocean, Flite was swimming too, arching and curving, leaping and diving — rejoicing all the way . . . Unhurried and unafraid? . . . He hoped so. Oh God, he hoped so — and he sent urgent and unanswered waves of recognition and reassurance out into the deep Pacific swell, reaching out through the echoing wastes of water to one solitary dolphin swimming alone in another hemisphere where it was night while this was day . . .

Sunrise was nearly always clear and beautiful in these washed Pacific skies, but one morning it was so spectacular that it took his breath away. Great wings of glowing cloud stained the horizon with crimson veils, and even above his head small brush-strokes of pink and scarlet fire were stippled across the robin's-egg bowl of dawn. And as he turned on his back in the shot-silk water to look up, he saw the whole white and gold city skyline flushed with a rosy incandescence as the light grew in the east.

He lay watching it from the lift and fall of the ocean almost with disbelief as the blaze grew in the sky and laid fiery fingers of light on the sea all round him. He seemed to float in sunrise, and the ocean burned with flame from shore to shore. 'Eternity's sunrise . . . ' said the old Captain's voice in his mind.

Flite, he thought. Have you seen such a dawn as this? Yes, of course you have — many such dawns on your journeying

173

through the great ocean spaces of the world. Seen them and leapt in the air to meet them, lifting you head to the fiery sky and diving deep in the flame-drenched water. Leaping and diving, filled with joy as it flies. Yes, Flite, rejoicing all the way . . . And I want you to know that I am rejoicing too.

He went to work in a dream, his head full of flamingo skies and garnet waters, and tried to concentrate on serving hash-browns and eggs sunny-side-up, and waffles drowned in maple syrup. When the first rush of breakfasts was over, he drifted into the bookstore side to see whether Mosky had a copy of Blake on his shelves. He had just located it when Mosky's voice spoke behind him.

'Don't tell me I gotta customer?'

Matthew turned, smiling. 'Is it such a shock?'

'*Poetry?* I might drop dead.'

'Then I'd better put it back,' said Matthew, looking concerned. But he still held the book in his hands.

Mosky's laugh startled the few remaining café customers who looked up and smiled. 'You like Blake?'

'I don't know. I was looking for something —' Matthew hesitated. But somehow he knew he could say things to Mosky that he couldn't speak of to anyone else. 'Something about . . . *eternity's sunrise.*'

'"From the Notebook",' said Mosky promptly. 'Here, I'll show you.'

He took the book from Matthew and leafed through the pages until he found the passage. 'This what you want? . . . "*Joy as it flies*" . . . ?'

Matthew looked down at the words, remembering with a lurch of awful homesickness the Captain's old, brusque voice, and Flite's joyous, unquenchable delight in living as he leapt and dived in the sun.

'That's it,' he murmured, and bent his head swiftly over the page to hide his absurd tears.

Mosky sighed. 'He's right, I guess. But as for joy — it sure does fly.' He glared at Matthew. 'Talking of which, you workin' today or not?'

Matthew laughed. 'Can I buy this first?'

'Sure can. Discount for staff. But if you read it here, you're fired.'

They were walking back past the tables, still laughing a little together in a curiously companionable way, when a young blond boy looked up with a mouthful of waffle and said: 'Matt-the-Whizz. Where's your guitar?'

Mosky stopped and looked from the cheerful boy to Matthew. 'You play guitar?'

'*Does* he?' drawled the lazy voice. 'Man, he's class. Beach guru, that's who. Draws 'em in like crazy.'

Mosky glared at Matthew even more fiercely than usual. 'Bring it down tonight — you hear?'

'Yes, but —' protested Matthew.

'But what?' The glare was still dangerous.

'I — I play classical mostly — not pop.'

'Who says I want pop?' growled Mosky. 'Just bring it — or you're fired. OK?'

'OK,' agreed Matthew, smiling sweetly. 'I will.'

★ ★ ★

There began for Matthew a strangely divided existence. In the early mornings when he swam in the ocean, he was himself, full of dreams and the aching pull of longing to find Flite. During the day, working at Mosky's, he was mostly a pair of hands and a pair of legs, with occasional sardonic gleams of humour from Mosky, and a few snatched moments of friendly backchat from his overworked companions. One evening a week, he was all head and cool thought over his computer course, though on the whole he found it not very challenging unless he fed in some much more complicated data than they expected. He met a few of his fellow students, but they were mostly older than he was and, to his way of thinking, a bit slow, except for one — a thin, stringy man with pebble glasses and a permanent stoop from hunching over his own computer all day. He said: 'Call me Pebbles. Most folks do,' and Matthew never did discover his real name. But he did discover quite a few bits of useful information from him, and decided that the man was a lot brighter than he was himself at computer studies, and that was very good for him.

And then there were the evenings when he took his guitar down to Mosky's. He was all fingers then — fingers and a head full of sounds and patterns, and a heart that kept getting in the way and turned his music into something that hurt. After the first evening, he didn't make any concessions to his audience. He just sat in his corner with his foot on a stool, and played. He played everything he knew and loved, wandering from the early lutanists to calm, measured Bach and on to Spanish fire and back again to tidy Vivaldi; and sometimes the ache and pull of Granados and Villa-Lobos got so bad that he felt drained and tired and could not play at all. Then Mosky would send young Allie over with a cup of coffee, and she would smile and say: 'Sounded real good, Matt,' — or sometimes Mosky would come over himself, look him over, and say brusquely: 'Go on home, kid. You're bushed.' And Matthew would go walking through the shiny neon streets, the flashing club signs and sauntering crowds of downtown San Diego, his head still too full of music for him to see the world at all clearly, and that feeling of fierce and lonely concentration still not quite letting him go.

It didn't leave much time for Della and Des, and though he felt a bit guilty about that, in a way he was rather relieved. The antagonism he had sensed in Des seemed to be growing rather than receding as he got to know him, and Della seemed more brittle and unpredictable than ever — one moment almost too affectionate and full of sentimental references to his father, and the next, offhand and unreachable. In fact, he decided, he wasn't really getting to know either of them at all. They both put up defences in their own way, and Matthew failed to understand them. He sighed to himself about this, remembering somewhat wryly how he had hoped against hope that this new start with new relations might have given him the family life he had always wanted and always just missed . . . But then he gave himself a shake and told himself that nothing was ever given to anyone on a plate, it had to be earned — and he would try for a bit longer to get through to these two difficult people before he gave up and went home . . . Yes, that was it. Went home. For he was beginning to realize now that this restless, bright-coloured life was not for him, and it would never do. He needed the quiet empty beaches of winter Cornwall, and the comfortable shabbiness of London, and the tough, open-hearted ordinariness of people like Madge and Jim . . . Still, he would give all this a bit more of a whirl, since the old Captain had told him to — and then he could go home.

He forgot all about Tracey and the Dolphin Demo until someone thrust a leaflet into his hand in the street. Then he felt a lurch of guilt — not so much at forgetting Tracey and her longhaired hangers-on, as at failing to remember the plight of those other dolphins being trained to make use of lethal weaponry in the deep waters of the naval experimental station . . .

176

He would have to join the protest — however little good it did. For Flite's sake, he would have to join it. Once again he thought of the marine research team on that Brittany beach, and Martha's bitter voice saying: '*What we have to do is stop it.*' And Pierre, their leader, saying: '*Take photographs. Get it on the media . . . Shame them.*' And Skip, doubtful and sardonic: '*There's too much money in big fishing.*'

And there was a lot of money, he supposed, together with a lot of absurd futuristic defence policy, mixed up in this naval experiment with dolphins — and he doubted very much if 'they' could be shamed. But he had to try — along with Tracey and her followers, even if they did seem to him vague and disorganized and not very practical. '*Muddle-headed idealism and no sense . . .*' He could hear the old Captain's dry voice pronouncing judgement, and he rather agreed with him. But all the same, for Flite's sake, and for all Flite's innocent companions in the wide seas of the world, he had to try.

He worked his shift at the restaurant, and then left his guitar with Mosky for safe-keeping. 'I may be late tonight,' he explained. 'Got something to do first.'

Mosky merely raised eloquent eyebrows and refrained from saying 'You're fired.' But he stowed the guitar safely away behind the counter in his bookstore where it was quiet and there was no chance of getting coffee poured over it. Satisfied, Matthew gave him a lopsided grin of thanks and went off to find the march.

At Ocean Beach, to his surprise, there was quite a sizeable crowd assembled, banners aloft, and the different groups already marshalled into reasonably manageable marching order. They had already marched through the town and were now taking a breather and re-assembling for the more serious march down the coast to the naval base. He found Tracey giving last minute instructions to Bud and Spike, and to the mouse-brown girl who was still adjusting a couple of new banners.

'Now, see here, Matt,' Tracey snapped, 'any trouble, you just scram. You with your green card and all — you get picked up by the Feds, they'll deport you right back where you came from.'

'The Feds?' Matthew was interested.

'Naval establishment. Sensitive area.' Tracey spoke laconically. 'But even the locals would be a drag. You get caught, you don't know me. You don't know *anything*. You're just a dumb student out on a demo. Get it?'

Matthew nodded. 'What about the others?'

Tracey laughed. 'They're just dumb students anyway. Come on, we gotta move.' Someone gave Matthew a banner, and at a signal from Tracey, they all moved off quite slowly and peaceably, changing '*Save the Dolphins*' as they went. Matthew found himself marching beside the brown girl, Stephi, on one side — and on the other, a thin, leggy boy who said he was known as Beaks and he was more into whales than dolphins, but he thought this was an OK target.

Matthew wondered what an OK target was?

The march progressed cheerfully enough. Some of the students sang the old campus songs, and changed 'Where have all the flowers gone?' to 'Where have all the dolphins gone?' which went down rather well. Passers-by and beach parties smiled indulgently at just another student demo, and some of them accepted a leaflet and even stopped to read it, but for the most part they let the marchers pass and went on with their own lives, regardless. Matthew felt like shaking some of them, they looked so heedless and complacent, so glossy and suntanned, intent on their evening's lazy pleasures — while out there, somewhere in the deep recesses of the ocean, dolphins were being schooled and ordered in the observance of the killing rituals of mankind . . . He would have liked to take the lot of them to that beach in Brittany where those helpless, beautiful creatures lay, destroyed . . . These people who went happily out in little boats to watch the whales go by — and did not seem to remember that countless more whales, and dolphins, too, were being slaughtered every day of the week . . .

'No deal gettin' broody,' said the brown girl, thrusting a banner into someone's face on the roadside. 'Sing! At least it gets 'em lookin'.'

So Matthew sang with the rest of them, and chanted 'Save the Dolphins', and went on marching past the glittering bay and along the road to Point Loma.

From there, after another brief assembly stop while someone from an environmental group harangued the crowd in a voice that no one could hear, and most people got out sandwiches and coke and munched through the speaker's impassioned appeal, the marchers turned south and went on down the edge of the Cabrillo Highway towards the gate to the naval station. It seemed to take a long time, as they all walked very slowly, and dusk was beginning to creep into the shadows on the road.

Matthew and his group were fairly near the back, so they

could not see what was happening. The march continued as slowly as ever, and everyone just went on walking and singing and waving their banners in the blue evening air. It was almost dark by now, and several of the stragglers at the rear had brought torches to warn approaching cars of the marching columns ahead. But some, Matthew realized, had just sloped off and given up and gone home. It was a long walk.

They had just begun another verse of

> *Where have all the dolphins gone?*
> *They've been slaughtered, every one . . .*
> *Oh when will they ever learn,*
> *When will they ever learn?*

when a commotion seemed to break out in front. People ahead started pushing backwards, and the marchers at the rear went on pushing forward, so that something like a heaving football scrum began to develop. Shouts were heard, a few strangled oaths, and then the sound of security whistles, alarm bells and police sirens.

'What's happening?' asked Matthew breathlessly, being shoved and pushed from either side.

'Trouble,' said Stephi, and put down her banner. 'We'd better scram.'

'But —' protested Matthew.

'Tracey's orders,' snapped Stephi, seizing Matthew by the hand and yanking him out of the struggling mass of marchers. 'Go, man, go!'

But Matthew stood still, looking down the road to where lights were flashing and people were shouting.

'What were they trying to do?' he asked.

Stephi shrugged. 'Hand in a petition, Trace *said*. But I guess they tried a break-in somewheres else — that's Trace's style. Sounds like it failed anyways. Come on, Matt. She hasn't lucked out this time.'

'But —' he stalled again, 'won't she need help?'

'Not from you, she won't. Trace can take care of herself. Let's go. I gotta see you safe.'

Defeated, Matthew turned to go, and found that all the marchers were running away in the dark. It seemed an ignominious end to a worthwhile protest.

At this point, a police car screamed up alongside the dispersing column and two men leapt out and started running towards the nearest of the protesters. The retreating marchers saw them coming, and ran even faster, but two of the stragglers were too slow and were hauled back, kicking and struggling, to the squad car, where they were roughly bundled inside and the doors slammed on them.

'Hey!' said Matthew, starting forward. 'They haven't done anything —'

'Shuddup!' hissed Stephi. 'They'll grab you too.'

'But —' Matthew was outraged. 'They were only *marching* —' He shook off Stephi's restraining hand and tried to push forward again. If he was going to join in a protest — he was going to protest. 'Listen,' he began, 'they're only kids . . . '

But his voice was drowned with the booming voice of a loud-hailer which suddenly sprang into life on the roof of the squad car.

'Disperse!' it shouted. 'Disperse real quiet. Anyone running will be picked up.' There was a burst of crackling, and then the voice added: 'Stragglers could cause a serious accident. Disperse quiet. Go home.'

The squad car, lights blazing, cruised on down the road, with its two captives huddled inside. Frightened runners mostly slowed down and tried to walk nonchalantly away. One or two went on running and disappeared in the shadows. The squad car went after them.

'What will happen to them?' Matthew stared after the retreating tail lights.

Stephi shrugged. 'Taken in for questioning.'

'And then?'

'They'll let 'em go.'

'No sweat,' added Beaks cheerfully. 'Can't hold 'em for marching.'

Matthew stood, irresolute and troubled, on the dark road. Then he turned round and started back towards the head of the march where he thought Tracey had been.

'Matt, no —' Stephi grabbed his arm none too gently.

Once more Matthew shook her off. 'I must — I must see what's happened to Tracey —'

'*No!*' snarled Stephi, tugging at him again. 'You won't be any goddam help.'

'Let go!' Matthew panted, now thoroughly roused, and feeling rather foolish.

'Hey, come on, man.' Beaks also tried to drag him away. 'Too late for heroics now.'

As he spoke, there was another small rush of running marchers from ahead. They all surged past, pounding down the road in silent panic, and after them came another squad car, cruising slowly, and in front of it, another couple of sweating police, also running. Several of the escaping protesters cannoned into one another, swearing at each other in the dark, and two of them fell over in a struggling heap almost at Matthew's feet. The police were not far behind, but before they could catch the stragglers, Matthew leapt forward, jerked the fallen students to their feet and sent them lurching on into the darkness with a fierce and urgent push.

The police had seen him by now, and were rapidly closing in on a likely-looking trouble-maker, when another bunch of stragglers hurled themselves out of the darkness knocking him to the ground, and went on running, trampling on him with their squashy trainers as they ran. The breath was knocked out of him and he was just attempting to get to his feet, when Stephi's hand came out and yanked him sideways into deeper shadow.

'This way —' she said, and Beaks added from Matthew's other side: 'Beach track not far from here.'

They stumbled along in the dark, through scrubby wasteland and backlots, for what seemed an achingly long, jolting run, and finally found themselves walking on sand. The flashing lights and shouts still went on behind them, and Matthew felt ashamed to be leaving Tracey to face them alone.

'She'll get by,' said Beaks, steadying Matthew as he tripped over a rock. 'Tracey's used to trouble. No big deal.'

But Matthew, hearing the hidden menace behind that smooth police voice over the loudspeaker, thought there probably was.

'We got transport in Ocean Bay,' urged Stephi, pushing ahead in the dark. 'Better get there fast.'

It seemed a long time to Matthew, stumbling along on dark paths and bits of roadway he did not know, but eventually they came out into the wide well-lit streets of Ocean Bay. His two companions did not pause but made straight for a parking lot where they had left their mopeds. Matthew suddenly realized that he had been escorted and looked after from the first — and though he was secretly rather touched at Tracey's concern for him, he was also a little annoyed at being considered so green and in need of protection.

But Stephi, the brown girl, was a lot brighter than she looked, and laid a friendly hand on his arm as she got on to her moped. 'You go charging off like a white knight, Trace'd be in more trouble, Matt. She's gotta think of herself as well as you.'

'Yes, of course,' said Matthew, sounding absurdly crestfallen.

'Disappointed heroes,' added Beaks, in his dry drawl. 'All of us. You're not the only one.' He gave Matthew a brief, gritty smile and climbed on to his moped.

'So long, guys,' he called, lifting a hand in mock salute, and rode away.

Stephi pulled Matthew on behind her and roared off after him.

When Matthew finally got to Mosky's, he was tired, grubby and upset. Mosky took one look at him out of shrewd, assessing eyes and said: 'Sit down. I'll getta coffee.'

He did not ask any questions, except after a few minutes of watchful silence: 'You fit to play?'

'I will be in a minute,' said Matthew, gulping his coffee.

Mosky slapped him on the back, making him choke. 'Atta-boy!' he grinned, in his usual parody of Hollywood style, and went away and left him in peace.

Matthew had thought he would play very badly that night, for his hands were still shaking — whether with anger or frustration he did not know. But in fact the music, as usual, took him away from the confusing conflicts of the day to a place that was ordered and perfect, a place where beauty was not destroyed by heedless hands (except his own), and the spirit of a wild dolphin leaping and dancing in the uncharted oceans of the world could sing into his mind and lift his heart to a strange, ecstatic joy that shone through every note.

He went home tired but contented and thankfully slid into bed without having met either Della or Des on the way. But as he was just drifting into sleep, he heard his door open softly, and Della came in and stood looking down at him as he lay, tousled and drowsy in the half-light from the landing. She was wearing a long, shimmering kind of robe, and her ash-blonde hair was spread round her face in a kind of silvery halo.

'Matt?' she whispered. 'You all right?'

'Sure,' he answered, puzzled by her softened appearance and the strange look of unwilling recognition in her eyes.

He could not have known, of course, how he looked to her — young and tired and defenceless, and so like his father . . . but something about her approach troubled him, and he sat up rather quickly and asked: 'Is anything wrong?'

'No,' she sighed. 'Nothing's wrong, Matt.' She came forward and perched herself on the end of his bed, and one hand came out and almost absently pushed the hair back out of his eyes. 'You were late tonight, that's all. I got kinda worried.'

'I went on rather late at Mosky's,' he explained.

She nodded, and fell silent, as if pondering something that was difficult to express. Finally she said, with a strange note of appeal in her voice: 'Are you — are you happy here, Matt?'

Matthew gulped, trying to get his weary mind into focus. What could he say? He knew very well that things were not going to work out between him and Des, and this new, rather beseeching Della filled him with dismay, though he was not quite sure why. 'I — sure,' he said helplessly. 'It's different, of course. Takes some getting used to . . . ' He tried a lopsided smile. But he suddenly felt that smiling was not a good idea, and lay down again, looking exhausted and bewildered, both at once.

'Never mind,' said Della softly, 'I can see you're tired . . . ' She leaned forward and kissed him with a curious, lingering sadness. Matthew just managed not to flinch, but somehow he felt frightened.

'Goodnight,' he said, and turned on his side away from the light filtering in from the hallway.

He heard Della sigh again, but she did not say any more. The silence seemed to go on and on, but presently she rose to her feet and went quietly away.

Matthew did not sleep for a long time, but when he did, he was constantly running away from pursuit down dark paths that had no end, and searching desperately for the shadow of a dolphin in an empty sea.

* * *

It was a couple of days after this that the stranger came into Mosky's. He stood there quietly looking round for a few moments, until he spotted Matthew playing his guitar in the corner. Then he sat down at a table to listen. Quite a lot of the customers listened to Matthew these days — news had spread about the English boy who could play guitar like old man Segovia himself. (Well, not quite, but almost.) So they ate their burgers and drank their coffee in respectful silence — or at least talked in subdued murmurs, while Matthew's music fell with surprising sweetness and clarity on the listening air.

If the stranger was surprised at Matthew's skill, he did not show it. He sat there impassively, drinking a quiet cup of coffee, and waited for Matthew's fingers to get tired. But presently, as Matthew came to the end of his last piece and spontaneous applause broke out, the man rose to his feet and went across to speak to Mosky who was officially busy at the till, but secretly enchanted by Matthew's sorrowful Granados and hardly able to change a dollar.

Mosky looked up, startled, when the stranger spoke, and then nodded doubtfully and looked across at Matthew who was putting his guitar away in its case.

The tall, quiet stranger strolled across to Matthew and offered him a coffee.

Matthew looked as startled as Mosky, and hesitated. 'Thanks, but I —'

'It's OK, I've squared it with your boss.'

'Oh. All right, then.'

He followed the stranger to an empty table near the bookstore end of the café, away from the main crowd of customers, and sat down.

Mosky came over with two cups of coffee in his hands and paused by the table, looking at Matthew rather anxiously.

'Don't keep him long. He gets tired, playing.'

Matthew stared up at him, surprised. Mosky's clever eyes seemed to be signalling some kind of warning, but he couldn't guess what.

'I won't,' said the stranger civilly. 'This won't take long.'

His voice, Matthew noticed, was deep and oddly attractive, and its accent seemed to be mid-Atlantic softened by some kind of hidden warmth rather than true American. He did not say any more after this initial response, and seemed to be waiting for Mosky to go — and after a second's hesitation, the observant Jewish face seemed to settle into its usual lines of resignation, and Matthew's boss turned away.

'Now,' said the stranger, smiling pleasantly, 'let me introduce myself. My name is Morris. Commander Morris. I have an official capacity, but I am here — er — unofficially.'

'I see,' said Matthew, who didn't see at all. He was looking at the stranger attentively now, and he saw a man of quiet middle age, with brownish hair going grey at the edges, a firm, rather squarish face and a mouth that could be very stern and straight, Matthew thought, but was now smiling very faintly, matched by a pair of grey, extremely intelligent eyes that had a quality of cold steel about them but were also at present reflecting the same faint smile.

'I want to talk to you,' began Morris gently, 'about dolphins.'

Matthew jumped a mile. 'What?'

'You were, I think, taking part in that abortive march?'

Matthew hesitated. He wondered who this man was, and whether Tracey and her friends were in real trouble — and if anything he said now might make things worse for them. There had been some headlines in the local press about that march and an attempted break-in to the naval base. It had even been briefly reported on the local television channel, and there had been some lively discussion about the dolphin question, at which Matthew had secretly rejoiced. Any publicity might help, he thought. It was consistent with what Pierre had said . . . 'Tell everyone . . . Get it on the media. *Speak!*'

'Yes,' he said, and his head went up in a curiously fighting pose which Morris found oddly touching, though he didn't, of course, allow it to cloud his judgement of the matter in hand.

'But you weren't involved in the attempted break-in?'

'No.' Matthew was still thinking furiously. 'I didn't even know it was going to take place. I don't think anyone did.'

'Except the perpetrators?'

Matthew shook his hed. 'They were mostly kids — college kids out on a demo.' He looked at the cool grey stranger in front of him and tried a fleeting grin. 'They didn't mean any harm.'

The calm face before him did not change. 'Breaking into a military establishment is a serious matter, you know.'

'So is training dolphins to take part in lethal acts of war,' said Matthew.

'Ah.' Morris nodded at him. 'You have strong views on this matter?'

'I do, yes.' Matthew took a deep breath. 'Listen,' he said. ('*Talk! Speak! Shame them!*' said Pierre in his mind). 'I got to know a wild dolphin once — on the Cornish coast . . . ' He stalled there, wondering how to go on. How to tell him what Flite meant to him. Whatever he said would sound corny. But then he remembered Pierre and forced himself to go on. 'He was the gentlest, most loving creature I've ever known. And the — noblest.' He glanced rather wildly at Morris and plunged on. 'He wasn't aggressive. He didn't kill for fun. He ate fish when he was hungry, but mostly he just played . . . ' Once more he drew breath and willed himself to go on. 'And he was *free* — like your grey whales coming down. Free and powerful and splendid. He used to come through the water to meet me of his own free will and — and greet me like a brother . . . ' His voice almost wavered there, and yes, he knew it sounded corny, but he added one more phrase: 'Full of innocent welcome.'

The two pairs of eyes met and locked.

'How could anyone want to harness that innocence and turn it into a weapon?' accused Matthew, now sounding like an avenging angel.

There was a shaken pause. At last Morris spoke. 'You are an eloquent advocate.'

Matthew looked suddenly embarrassed. 'To tell you the truth, I didn't know I could say all that.' Then he added swiftly: 'But I meant it.'

Morris smiled. 'I can see you did.' He seemed to ponder the matter for a while before pursuing it further. Then he said, still in that gentle, unemphatic voice: 'Tell me, whereabouts were you in the march?'

'At the back.'

'So you could not see what was happening up front?'

'No.'

There was another fractional pause. 'But if the organizers had asked you, would you have tried to break in with them?'

Matthew considered. 'I don't know what they were trying to do. But if they actually thought they could release the dolphins into the ocean — yes, I would.'

Morris nodded again. 'But of course they couldn't.'

'No. I suppose not.'

'You see, Matthew,' said Morris softly, 'there are other arguments. The naval authorities would say they are protecting the world against nuclear submarine attack — and any means they use to safeguard their defence is justified.'

Matthew looked obstinate. 'That's their judgement. I don't believe mankind has the right to order other creatures to do his dirty work. It's obscene.' He looked at Morris again, urgently. 'I mean, who are we to tell the dolphins what to do? We aren't God.'

'No,' sighed Morris. 'We aren't God. That's been our mistake all along — to think we were.'

The silence between them was somehow a great deal more friendly. But Morris still had a question to ask. 'You're not a Communist, I take it?'

186

Matthew looked astonished. 'A *Communist?* I thought all that was exploded with perestroika.'

Morris was unperturbed. 'Not entirely, Matthew. There's Cuba, remember.'

Matthew was still mildly astonished. 'Sorry, I don't believe in politics much. Why?'

'People who break into military bases sometimes have other motives than altruistic concern about dolphins.'

'Oh. I see.' Matthew actually laughed. 'Reds under the bed? You can't be serious?' But he saw by Morris's expression that he was, so he hastened to add: 'No ulterior motives. And I don't believe the others had, either.'

'You think the girl — Tracey Holland — was sincere?'

Matthew hesitated. He saw the trap Morris had set. If he defended Tracey now, he was admitting that he knew her and that she was the ringleader in this affair. But if he denied all knowledge of her or her motives, he was quiet clearly marking himself as a liar, and a disloyal one at that.

Morris was watching him with a half-smile. He did not miss the struggle in Matthew's mind. 'I should be honest, if I were you,' he said in that gentle voice which was somehow more menacing than anger. 'We know quite a lot about Tracey Holland already.'

Matthew sighed. 'I thought you probably did. Is she in serious trouble?'

Morris picked up the spoon from his coffee cup and looked at it intently. He seemed to be weighing possible replies in his mind. 'It depends,' he said neutrally.

'On what?'

'On what we think of her motives. You haven't answered my question.'

'I've only met her twice,' said Matthew slowly. 'No, three times counting the beginning of the march when she was organizing everyone. But I'd say she was honest about what she believes — whether right or wrong. She was as concerned as I am about the fate of the dolphins.'

Morris inclined his head in a small nod of agreement.

'And she took me out to see the grey whales going down — I felt then that she . . . *cared* about wild creatures in a sort of personal way that most people don't.'

Once more the small, affirmative nod. 'Did she ever talk to you about — taking violent action?'

'Oh no. She was very careful to keep me out of it. I did feel —?' He paused, not sure how to go on.

'Yes?'

'I did feel, once or twice, that she was probably planning something beyond the ordinary march — she and a few of the others. But nothing was ever said.' He stopped again, and then added, on impulse: 'But I don't honestly think she had a thought in her head about the *military* implications. She's probably as good an American as you are.'

'I'm English, actually,' murmured Morris, and the faint smile was back in those steel-grey eyes. 'But I will repeat — you are a good advocate.'

Matthew shook his head. 'I don't know. The animal rights people have been wrong before. I mean, releasing mink into the wild, and letting out infected rats and so on — and even letting off bombs. In England they get into trouble, too, don't they? But at least they make people aware of what's going on.' Pierre's deep, Gallic voice kept coming back into his mind. '*Talk. Tell everyone.*' 'I — I met a marine biologist once,' he said, sounding suddenly shy.

'Where was that?'

'In Brittany. We were examining some dead dolphins on a beach. He said . . . the best way to help was to tell everyone.' He looked straight at Morris with sudden challenge. 'That's what Tracey was trying to do, I think. Just make enough fuss to get people talking. She's just a — just an ordinary girl who feels passionate about things — not a terrorist or an old-fashioned Russian spy.'

Morris laughed. 'You may be right.' He had found out what he wanted to know, and Matthew had unconsciously established his own innocence in this affair. But there were warnings that had to be given, all the same. 'You could be in trouble with the immigration authorities, you know, if you get mixed up in "subversive activities". How would your parents feel about that?'

'I haven't any parents,' said Matthew flatly.

The expression in Morris's eyes seemed to change. 'Then —?'

'I'm just staying over here — for a while.'

Morris looked at him quietly. 'Could you tell me about that?'

There was a moment's hesitation, and then Matthew said in a strange, sharp tone: 'Yes. If you stay neutral.'

'What does that mean?'

'I'm sick of people being sorry for me,' he snapped. Then he added in an apologetic tone: 'Sorry. I know I'm touchy.'

'I promise not to be touched,' said Morris solemnly. 'Go on.'

So Matthew told him. He told him the whole of it. And Morris kept his promise and his face neutral — and what he felt inside he did not say.

At last Matthew finished with the awkward words: 'She's very kind to me — Della Grant . . . though I'm not quite sure why.'

'And Desmond Grant?'

That was the crux of the matter, really, and Morris had unerringly put his finger on it.

'I think he resents me a bit.'

'And you're not quite sure why, either?'

Matthew grinned. 'Exactly.'

'So — does it look to you like a permanent arrangement?'

For some reason Matthew did not hesitate at all this time. 'No. I don't think so.'

Morris did not comment on this. 'So what will you do?'

Matthew shrugged. 'I promised the old Captain I'd give it a whirl — so I will. Then — who knows? I — I suppose I'll go home and get some sort of job.'

'Will you take up Captain St George's offer?' He was holding the Captain's small card in his hand, looking at it with interest.

'I don't know. I might. Depends where I land up.'

'It's a damn good offer, you know. He's a pretty remarkable man.'

Matthew's face lit up in a sudden smile. 'Do you know him?'

His questioner blinked at the unexpected flood of light in Matthew's sombre young face. It transformed the boy, he thought. 'I have met him,' he said carefully. 'He is pretty well known in most parts of the world.' He handed Matthew back the precious little card and said kindly: 'Take care of that. It may come in very useful.'

Matthew nodded, sternly pushing back an engulfing wave of longing for that quiet Cornish beach and the Captain's fierce old eyes looking into his, instead of these cool, assessing grey ones opposite.

If Morris noticed the bleakness of loss in Matthew's expression, he did not remark on it. Instead, he got quietly to his feet and held out another small card of his own. 'You have been very frank with me, Matthew. I appreciate it. I have to tell you that your movements — and Tracey Holland's — may be watched for a while, but don't let it worry you. Things will die down in due course!' The quiet flick of amusement was back in his voice, but then he grew serious again for a moment. 'In the meantime, if you need any assistance — or advice — you can always contact me here.'

Matthew took the second card and looked at it carefully. It said simply: '*Commander J.S.Morris, RN*' but gave the address of the US Naval Base at Fort Rosencranz. 'You said you were English,' he said, mystified.

'Let's say — transatlantic,' smiled Morris. 'Liaison,' he added softly, by way of explanation.

Matthew nodded and put the little card in his pocket. 'I don't know why you're taking all this trouble,' he grumbled vaguely.

'Liaison,' repeated Morris, smiling more openly this time.

Matthew looked up and found that Morris was still holding out his hand. Confused, Matthew held out his own and met a surprisingly firm and friendly grip.

'Meanwhile, steer clear of trouble,' murmured Morris. 'Good luck.' And he strolled away past the busy café tables and merged neutrally into the San Diego crowds in the evening streets.

Behind him, Mosky said anxiously: 'OK, Matt?'

Matthew looked at him and grinned. 'OK,' he agreed. 'By the skin of my teeth!'

★   ★   ★

But when he got home that night to Della's apartment, it wasn't OK at all. Des was waiting for him, with a face like thunder.

'What's this about the AR Demo?'

Matthew stood still. 'What about it?'

'Two guys came looking for you. About the Demo. That's what.'

'*Two?*' Matthew's eyes went wide. Then it wasn't Morris who had given him away. He wondered who they were?

'Yeah, two.' Des was glaring at him, his eyes almost black in his accusing face. 'Feds, I guess. And I don't like goddam police nosin' about in my apartment!'

'I'm sorry —' began Matthew.

'Sorry!' snarled Des. And then the explosion came.

Matthew listened to it in silence. He supposed he deserved it, but he had looked after himself for so long that he found it hard to see himself in terms of 'a dependent' who had to do what he was told.

'Stuck-up, snotty-nosed English kid . . . come swanning out here and think you can do what you goddam please . . . no regard for anyone but yourself . . . ' Des's voice raged on. 'And I don't want a goddam hoodlum in my house.'

Matthew said mildly. 'I'm not a hoodlum, Des. Honestly. I only went on the march. I wasn't in on the break-in.'

'Just as well,' snapped Des, 'or they'd send you right back home like unwanted baggage — and they'd be goddam right.'

Matthew could not help reflecting that Des's vocabulary seemed rather limited, but at the same time he felt a curious coldness building up inside him. 'Is that what you want?'

Des paused in mid-tirade, red-faced and angry still, and by now beyond caution. 'You bet it is, kid. Della brought you out here. It was her decision, not mine. I never wanted it. I don't go with her still livin' in her goddam past.'

Matthew went pale. 'What do you mean?'

'You're a substitute lover-boy, son. Didn't you know?' The angry little eyes raked him contemptuously. 'She wanted your father, and she couldn't have him. You'll do instead.'

'But that's crazy.' Matthew was so white by now that even Des faltered a little. 'Sure, it's crazy. People do crazy things outa remorse.'

'*Remorse?* Why?' And when Des hesitated, Matthew repeated it, getting angry too. '*Why*, Des? Isn't it time you told me what really happened?'

Des looked at him warily, aware of the boy's growing anger — and then shrugged his fat, sweating shoulders. 'OK I'll tell you.' He waved his empty beer-can at Matthew, and spoke with laconic precision. 'Della married your Uncle Ned — the older brother. But she went overboard for young Michael as soon as she laid eyes on him. He was having a rough time with your mother —' He glanced again at Matthew, with the same wary bravado, and went on: 'So Della invites him up to stay with his brother in Edinburgh. I guess she rather threw herself at his head — Della's like that when she's got a fixation. And so she got him into bed someways or other. Ned came in and found them. Big scene. So Michael goes off, all kind of uptight and guilty, and drives his goddam car straight into a truck.'

Matthew sighed. It was a long, shaken sound, and a whole lot of bright heroic images of his father seemed to shrivel and die in its wake. Heroes were just like other men. Fallible.

191

Easily led. Ordinary feet of clay . . . 'How awful.' It sounded painfully inadequate.

'Yeah. Della never stopped blaming herself — never stopped trying to make it up to Ned.' He stared moodily out, away from Matthew's shock-dilated eyes. 'And never stopped loving the other guy,' he added in a growl of sardonic bitterness. 'Like a goddam movie!'

'But surely —?' He did not quite know how to say it.

'Oh, sure, she's happy enough with me, I guess.' He shrugged again, and then went on roughly: 'Leastways, she was — till you came along. That kinda stirred things up all over again, when they were good and buried. And I don't like it.'

'No,' agreed Matthew coldly. 'Nor do I.'

Des looked startled. 'You don't?'

It was Matthew's turn to let private bitterness surface. 'How d'you think it makes me feel? . . . I'm me, Matthew. Not my father. All that old history — I don't want any part of it.' He sighed again. It would be nice, he thought dispassionately, to be wanted for himself, without any ulterior motive or any sense of obligation — and not be used to fulfil some absurd and useless fantasy. But it didn't seem likely to happen to him, somehow. Maybe it never happened to anyone, and openhearted, unsought-for love was just a myth . . . Except, of course, with Flite, who had raced towards him in the wide, open seas, alight with love and welcome, and never asked for anything in return . . .

'I'm sorry,' he said, looking directly at Des with candid, troubled eyes. 'It's no good, is it?'

'No, kid,' agreed Des, already regretting his anger, but realizing it was too late to take back anything he had said. 'I guess it's no damn good for any of us. I'm sorry, too.'

*　*　*

It was very late when Della came in, and the row between her and Des began. By then, Matthew had already decided what he must do — only he hadn't reckoned on overhearing so much of the row, and it made him feel worse than ever.

'How *could* you?' screamed Della. 'How could you do this to me?'

A rumble of protest from Des.

'And to him, as well! He's only a kid.'

192

More rumbles which exploded into: 'He wanted the truth, and he damn-well got it.'

'I didn't think you could be so cruel.'

'Time there was some plain sense around here.'

'What will he think of me? How can I face him after this? You bloody fool, you've wrecked the whole thing . . .'

That was it, of course. She couldn't face Matthew. Matthew couldn't face her. The whole thing was, in truth, well and truly wrecked.

He was used to rows — his mother's endless rows — and he hated them. Especially the last one that had led to that awful tragedy in the fire. And this one was all mixed up in tragedy, too — and it was clear to him there would be more if he stayed here. More endless rows. More sudden silences, and taboo subjects, and difficult, painfully self-conscious conversations. He couldn't bear it. Raised voices and black tensions. No. He couldn't bear any more. It would destroy him. And, as far as he could see, it would destroy Della and Des as well. It was quite clear what he must do.

He waited till all the shouting died down and the apartment sank into night-time stillness. Then he got up, packed his few things in his duffle-bag, picked up his guitar and crept out into the living room, making for the outer door. But a thought tugged at his mind, and he paused by Della's desk, picked up a sheet of paper and the ballpoint lying beside it and wrote her a note.

'*Thanks for everything. Sorry it didn't work out. Matthew.*'

Then he thought doubtfully: That's a bit bleak. And she'll worry. Maybe even send the police after me. (But they may be tailing me, anyway!) I'd better say something sensible.

Matthew was a responsible boy on the whole. He had seen with Madge how a good parent worried about her children. (Not like his own mother who never seemed to give him a passing thought.) He liked Della, and he didn't want to put her through any more hassle. It seemed to him that she had enough to contend with already. He hesitated uncertainly for a moment, and then added a postscript:

'*Going to visit a friend in Baja. Will contact you before I go home.*' Better make it clear that he was going home. Decisions taken. No more arguments. Easier that way . . . Yes, that sounded reasonable. And it was more-or-less true. He hoped.

Satisfied, he laid the note down on the living rom table. Then he quietly let himself out of the apartment and took the elevator down to the street.

It was still dark, and he wasn't sure where he was going. But he knew his way to the beach, and the sea was cool and forgiving — and blessedly neutral. He would swim a bit and wait for daylight. Then he could go to work at Mosky's and plan something or other. Tomorrow was another day. Or today, rather. Yes, today, today! . . . And somewhere out there in the dark oceans of the world there was a creature that he loved — and who had loved him, without any strings at all.

He reached a quiet stretch of empty beach — empty except for a few shadowy mounds of lovers or people sleeping rough — and laid his duffle bag down with his guitar. For a moment he was frightened at leaving that precious guitar unattended. Supposing it got stolen? He would never be able to replace it. But there was no one about. Everything seemed calm and silent.

Sighing, he went out into the quiet sea, and let its water lift his tired body, its ceaselessly whispering voice soothe his aching mind . . . Flite, he said, turning under a wave, it doesn't matter where you are. I can still love you . . . No one can take that away, can they? . . . The sea gave him no answer, but it rocked him gently in its arms and demanded nothing . . .

At Mosky's, Matthew suddenly realized that he could not stay. Des and Della knew where he worked, and they would come looking for him. So he did his best to explain the situation to his shrewd old boss, and tried not to see the reproach in his eyes.

But those eyes were difficult to avoid, and he realized as he was explaining — somewhat lamely — that they were not so much reproachful as anxious.

'You in trouble, kid?' said Mosky, ignoring all the stumbling excuses. 'That guy that came lookin' for you — was he trouble?'

Matthew shook his head, smiling a little. 'No. Funnily enough, he wasn't . . . It's not that kind of trouble, Mosky.' He paused and then added, still half-smiling: 'He was on about dolphins.'

Mosky's clever brown eyes widened. 'You on that march?'

'I was.' And something about Mosky's concern prompted him to add awkwardly: 'I care about dolphins.'

'Why?'

'I knew one once . . . a long time ago.' It seemed a long time

194

ago, but the sudden reminiscent glow that came into his face startled Mosky.

'Kinda friend of yours?'

'Kinda.' The glow was still there — incautious and somehow touching. 'That Blake you found for me — remember?'

'Joy as it flies.' Mosky was no fool.

'That was him — my dolphin . . . Flite, I called him.'

Mosky nodded a sage head. 'Put us to shame — creatures.' He was silent, respecting that glow and waiting sadly for it to fade. When it had, he said briskly: 'So if it's not dolphins — what's eating you?'

Matthew grinned somewhat painfully. 'It's — a family matter.' He supposed it was family — though the thought made him shudder slightly, especially after Des's laconic explanation: *'You're a substitute lover-boy — didn't you know?'*

Mosky was still looking at him. 'They know you're taking off?'

'I left a note.'

The grizzled head nodded again. He was a family man himself. He didn't like kids taking off without a word. 'So where you headin'?'

'Baja California. To see the whales.'

'Scammon's Lagoon?'

'Yes.'

'Well, just you look out for yourself, kid. Wild country that — and hot. Very hot in the desert.'

Matthew looked startled. 'Desert?' He realized th͏ ͏ ͏e didn't know very much about Baja California really — only as a magical place of lagoons and warm seas where the whales found sanctuary for breeding . . . But it was winter now — in so far as they had any winter. So even if there were deserts, surely they wouldn't be hot?

'Any dough?' Mosky was asking, still in his dry, rasping voice.

'Mosky!' Matthew was shocked. 'You pay me plenty. And I've saved some.'

'Huh! That won't go far.' He reached out to his own till and took out $100, holding it out in an imperious hand. 'Here.'

Matthew stared at him. 'I don't need it, honestly.'

'You do, too.' He sounded almost angry. 'Work it off when you come back.'

'Suppose I don't come back?'

'You will, kid,' said Mosky, suddenly grinning. 'Sure as hell, you will.' He thrust the notes into Matthew's unwilling fingers. 'And meantime — look after yourself real good. And keep that guitar by you. It'll always earn you a meal or two.'

'Even in Mexico?' Matthew was smiling, too.

'Anywheres,' stated Mosky flatly. 'The way you play. *Anywheres.*'

'I hope you're right,' said Matthew piously, with a private blessing in his mind for Tudor Davies and his cronies (and the Captain?) for this invaluable asset, and the freedom it gave him.

'Mosky, I — thanks for everything.' He was suddenly shy.

'Aw, shucks,' said Mosky, putting on a western drawl to cover for him. 'You brung me custom, kid. I ain't grumblin'.' He waited to see Matthew laugh, and then added his café's regular farewell. 'Have a nice day.'

Matthew grasped his hand, suddenly too full up to speak, and went out into the street without looking back.

He looked very young and vulnerable standing there with his duffle bag in one hand and his guitar slung over his shoulder — young and thin and lonely — so that Mosky sighed and shook his head as he looked after him. But then a customer from his busy restaurant called for attention, and he hurried away.

Outside, among the purposeful crowds hurrying to work before the day got too warm, Matthew felt even more isolated and aimless than usual. He paused to take stock of his own thoughts, and then went into a travel agent's to get a tourist visa for Baja. One of the guide books he had read for Mosky had told him this was the thing to do, and it would not be difficult. It also told him that the border crossing at San Ysidro where the trolleys went to was quieter and less likely to hold you up. But first he had something else to do. He had to find out about Tracey.

He arrived at the apartment block and climbed the stairs to Tracey's front door without being challenged by any mysterious observer, though he supposed if they were watching, they would be carefully unobtrusive. He rang Tracey's bell and waited somewhat nervously for someone to come. What if Tracey was in prison or something, and the apartment was occupied by some of Des's hated 'Feds'?

But in the event it was Tracey herself who opened the door, and when she saw Matthew she was furious.

'Go away, you mutt. You're not supposed to know me.'

'Sorry,' said Matthew, holding his ground. 'I wanted to know how you were.'

'Well, you can see. I'm OK. Now get going before they find you here.'

Matthew's mouth set into an obstinate line. 'Not till you tell me what happened to you.'

Tracey raised her eyes to heaven and swore. 'Jee-sus, don't you ever learn? You better come inside.' She pulled him into the narrow passage that led to the living room and slammed the outside door.

'Now,' she said, sounding belligerent and cross, 'for your info — I got busted and I got fined, and I gotta keep the peace for a year.' She grinned suddenly and added: 'I guess that'll be the hardest.'

Matthew laughed, relieved to find her so relaxed about it.

Then Tracey went into the attack. 'How come you're not at work?'

Matthew sighed. 'I left.'

'You quit?' She looked at him incredulously. 'You're nuts. It was a real cinch, that job.'

'I know,' said Matthew sadly.

'So what happened? Were you fired?'

'No. Nothing like that. I just — had to leave.' He looked at her, not knowing how to explain. 'In fact, I'm leaving San Diego.'

'Why?'

'I — where I was staying didn't work out.'

Tracey nodded, not asking any awkward questions. 'Where will you go?'

'Down to Baja, I think.' He was still looking at her.

'Whale-watching?'

He hesitated. 'Partly. But I've got a friend down there — I think.'

'You *think?*'

'Well, she said she'd be there — sometime about now.'

'She?' snapped Tracey suspiciously.

'Petra Davison. She's a marine biologist. Studying whales.'

'Oh. I see.' Tracey sounded a shade less fierce. There was a pause, then she added: 'How're you gettin' there?'

Matthew shrugged. 'Trolley to the border. Then we'll see . . . Hitch, I suppose.'

There was another pause, and then Tracey said cautiously: 'I might come, too.'

197

Matthew's face lit up. 'That'd be great.'

She shook her head at him. 'It might not be — for you. But I guess if we get together *after* the border, they can't say anything.'

'*They?* Do they really exist?'

It was Tracey's turn to shrug. 'How should I know? That guy, Morris, said — '

'Oh. He came to see you too, did he?'

She looked startled. 'Were *you* questioned?'

'Oh yes.'

'Where?'

'At Mosky's.'

'Christ!' she said, sickened. 'And I thought I'd kept you out of it.'

'You did,' agreed Matthew. 'He was really quite nice to me.'

'*Nice!*' She glared. 'Worst of all, that kind. Pussy-footing around. I don't trust 'em a goddamed English inch.'

Matthew laughed again. 'I don't think he'll bother us in Baja. You coming or not?'

Tracey took time to consider, twisting a strand of tangled hair in her fingers as she thought about it. 'I guess it's a good idea to get out of here for a while. I'll meet you the other side — with the Fly. It'll get us there — but it'll be kinda rough.'

'I don't mind.' He sounded quite calm and cheerful.

Tracey scowled again. 'Your folks know where you're headin'?'

'They're not my folks,' he said automatically. 'But, yes — I left a note.'

She gave another small nod of approval, but made no comment.

'Anyway,' Matthew was suddenly indignant, 'I don't see why you're bothered about *them*. You seem to come and go when you like.'

'I'm older,' said Tracey flatly. 'I left home a long time ago.' Her mouth clamped tight shut in a forbidding line, and she said no more.

Matthew ignored the scowl and asked, smiling: 'OK. When'll we meet?'

'Tomorrow.' Tracey's scowl seemed even fiercer. 'Gotta tourist card, have you?'

He waved it at her. 'All in order. I'll go down to San Ysidro today.'

'Got any dough?'

'Enough.' He sounded almost as clipped and forbidding as Tracey.

'Matt,' she protested crossly, 'you'll need to sleep some place. And eat, remember? Every goddam day.'

'I'll manage,' said Matthew, and turned to go. 'See you tomorrow.'

'There's a youth hostel at Tijuana,' she said, looking at him severely. 'I'll pick you up down there in the morning.'

'All right. Stop fussing.'

'And buy a water bottle.'

'OK, OK!'

'Gotta sleeping bag?' She saw him hesitate, and went on without letting him speak. 'Better take one of mine. I keep several here for the gang.' She yanked one out of a corner and gave it to him. Then, seeing his mutinous face, she took a step forward and laid a hand on his arm. 'You gotta take care, see? You could do without any more trouble right now.'

'So could you,' growled Matthew, and gave her a fleeting grin. 'See you, then.' And he tucked the sleeping bag under his arm and slipped quietly out of the apartment and went away down the street, carefully not looking back to see if anyone was watching him. Or following him.

Tracey looked out of the window after him, checking too. But no one seemed to be about. Like Mosky, she sighed as she saw Matthew's retreating figure going down the street. He looked small, and defenceless, somehow. Vulnerable. Well, she would do what she could to keep trouble off him.

Presently the slight figure paused at the intersection, lifted a hand in mocking salute to anyone who might be watching, and then turned the corner and disappeared from view.

PART IV

THE WINGÉD LIFE DESTROY

He did not linger in San Diego. It was better to cut loose and get going right away, he told himself. So he made his way downtown to the Santa Fe depot and got the trolley to San Ysidro. It was a journey that intrigued him, since the cheap fare brought a mixture of returning Mexicans, daytrippers to the border, impoverished students and a few hardy backpackers intent on 'doing Baja' by way of alternate thumb-jerking and hard slog.

Matthew listened to the mixture of languages and wished he had learnt a bit more Spanish at school. His knowledge so far was mostly connected with Spanish guitar music and its romantic titles and mood directions. Not much use on a trolley-ride, or for buying a meal somewhere. *Andante melancólico, amigos. Con molta fantasía* . . . No, he didn't think it would help much.

But the crowd around him seemed cheerful enough, and friendly when he gave them the chance. He got off at San Ysidro with a chattering group of Mexicans and followed them through customs where his passport was examined and his tourist card stamped with a valid visa. So far so good.

He crossed over the pedestrian bridge into the outskirts of Tijuana, and asked a passing tourist the way to the youth hostel, only to be told that he would have to re-cross the river on another bridge further south, as the hostel was 'way out in a park on the Avenida Padre Kino', or else go back and get a blue and white Central Camionera bus to the Sports Centre.

Matthew thanked the rangy American who smiled at him out of a suntanned face and told him to have a nice day. But the idea of the youth hostel somehow didn't fill him with enthusiasm, so he decided to go on into Tijuana and have a look round and maybe head for a beach. He always felt better near the sea. And he was very conscious of his slender resources, in spite of his brave words to Tracey, and he thought sleeping out on the beach would do perfectly well and be a lot pleasanter than a crowded hostel dormitory.

He wandered on, getting hotter and thirstier with every step

203

and every rising cloud of dust from a passing car or lorry. He found that downtown Tijuana was much like downtown everywhere else — shopping malls and crowds and tourist shops and cafés, all looking new and prosperous; and beyond them shanty-town squalor all looking shabby and forgotten. He avoided a ride on a *burro* painted in black and white stripes like a zebra, with a persistent photographer beside it, and he side-stepped a street trader trying to sell him a *sombrero* in absurdly gaudy colours — but he did stop at a tempting stall selling hot and sizzling *tacos* when the spicy smell of cooking became too much for him.

He seemed to walk for a long time, admiring the bright Mexican colours of the crowds and the stalls full of painted pots and vivid striped blankets, the sudden glimpses through arched doorways of cool courtyards and flowery balconies, and an occasional brown child washing something in a painted china bowl . . . But at last he came to the new Bull Ring by the Sea, and the Pacific Ocean gleaming serenely before him.

He turned southwards along the beach, looking for some-where quiet, but it was almost impossible to find an empty place until he had walked quite a distance from the cheerful holiday crowds of Tijuana. At last he paused by a quieter stretch of sand where there was only one beach party of young people enjoying a make-shift cook-out, and beyond them a few fishing boats and the remains of a derelict fish-camp hut on the edge of the shore. Inland, beyond the sandhills, he could just see a caravan and trailer park with a dirt track leading off the winding toll-road that followed the coast to the south.

He set down his duffle-bag and his guitar case, and lay back on the sand to rest his aching legs. They still hurt him some-times when he walked too far. But now a problem assailed him, and he sat up again, wondering what to do about it. It was the same as before in San Diego. He badly wanted to swim — to get rid of the dust and heat of travel, even from that not very strenuous walk through Tijuana city. But if he swam, what about his guitar? His money and passport he had learnt to keep on him in a waterproof pouch tied into his swimming trunks. He had done this, prudently, from the first day he arrived in San Diego, having been severely lectured about pickpockets on the beach. But the guitar was different. He couldn't swim with a guitar round his neck, even if he could have kept it watertight. He had managed it once, alone on that night-time San Diego beach. But here?

He was looking round him in some bewilderment, when one of the young crowd from the beach barbecue strolled over to have a look at him.

'Going far?'

Matthew shrugged. 'Down to Scammon's Lagoon — if I can get there.'

'Whale-watching?'

'Yes.'

The tall, blond boy nodded. 'Take you a while — hitching.'

'I guess so,' agreed Matthew, unconsciously slipping into American idiom.

'You play that thing?'

'Sure.'

The boy considered him, head on one side, lazy blue eyes surprisingly alert and sympathetic. 'Hungry?'

Matthew sighed. 'I could do with a swim more.'

The pale gold head nodded again. 'We'll keep an eye on your stuff. Then you can play for your supper.' He was laughing now and holding out a sunburnt, sandy hand. 'Deal?'

'Deal,' agreed Matthew, smiling, and grasped the thin brown fingers in his. Then, joyously, he threw off his dusty jeans and T-shirt, and plunged into the cool Pacific.

He felt better in the sea. More himself, somehow, and less like a lost and rootless stranger in a strange land. The sea was the sea, anywhere in the world — bluer and warmer here than in the dark Atlantic that he knew, but still the same restless, endlessly moving, surging and receding living force that held him and cradled him in its arms and flung him breathless towards the shore in a smother of surf and spray and glinting sunlight. He felt nearer home here — almost home altogether — and nearer to the far-distant, leaping shadow of a dolphin that came smiling to meet him, alight with love and welcome . . . Oh Flite, he thought, where are you? In what deeps of blue-green space are you swimming now?

He had not until now admitted to himself how disappointed he had been over the way things had turned out with Della and Des. Disappointed, yes — and shaken. He hadn't really expected it to work out, of course. Things rarely did work out the way you expected. But all the same, he had hoped — he had almost allowed himself to believe — he might have been able to make a go of it, might have been welcome, might have become part of a real family unit at last . . . Childish of him. Idiotic, really, to expect two total strangers to want to give a home to an awkward sixteen-year-old. Why should they? . . . And all that stuff about Della's past — the emotional overdrive she went into — it was all impossible and hopeless, and somehow vaguely unhealthy. Not that he believed Des much about that 'substitute lover-boy' stuff. But still, it was a bit alarming. Shocking, really — though of course he was a fool to be shocked at anything at his age, wasn't he? All the same, he knew he had been right to get out while he could, before things got any worse . . . Only, where was he to go from here? There didn't seem to be any place where he felt he truly belonged . . . except in the sea with Flite — and he couldn't exactly turn into a marine creature himself, however much he might like to . . .

That brought him to think about Petra. Petra the dedicated marine biologist who yet had time to be extraordinarily kind to a shy, rather dazzled teenager who had never dared to come close to anyone so golden and so beautiful before . . . Petra, who even so had really no eyes for anyone except Skip — Skip, who was almost as golden and beautiful as she was herself.

Honestly, said Matthew to himself, allowing another wave to break over his head and hurl him towards the shore. I don't know what I want to go and see her for. It isn't me she wants. But perhaps she'll tell me what to do next. She has a lot of plain common sense inside that golden head of hers.

A bigger wave than usual pushed him in the back and shoved him sprawling into the shallows, as if to say: Stop being so sorry for yourself. Get on up the beach and start living!

Obediently, Matthew picked himself up and made his way back to the little party on the beach. His guitar was still there, and so were his dusty clothes. But the air was still warm even though the sun was going down, and he did not bother to dress. He simply took his guitar out of its case, sat down on a rock, and began to play.

The group of young people had been busy grilling burgers and fish over a smoky fire, but now they turned to him in wonder and forgot to go on talking. They almost forgot to go on cooking, and only just rescued some blackening steaks in time. Matthew ignored them all, oblivious of everything except the gleaming wood of his guitar and his own fingers moving on the pulsing strings . . . He forgot that he was alone on a strange shore with not much money and no certain future — and no one in the world who cared what happened to him now. He forgot that he was tired and hungry, and had nowhere to sleep that night. He forgot everything except the music that flowed out from under his hands into the sunset silence of a Pacific beach . . . He was totally engrossed, totally happy, and nothing in the world mattered, except the voice of Villa-Lobos that laid a dark dream of sorrowful enchantment on the listening air.

At last, his fingers grew tired and came to an end, and he withdrew from the dark dream to see a ring of faces looking at him with a mixture of awe and wonder in the flickering firelight, and beyond them the sunset sky deepening into swift night as the fiery glow in the west began to fade.

'Wow!' breathed one of the listeners, and sighed, and said no more.

'How come you're wandering about loose,' said another, 'when you play like that?'

'I like wandering,' answered Matthew, and laid his guitar carefully in its case and wiped it lovingly with the only clean handkerchief he possessed.

'Have a burger,' said the boy who had first spoken to him, smiling. 'Must be starving after all that,' and he busied himself ladling a mixture of fish and steak and half-blackened burgers on to a tin plate.

Matthew ate gratefully, and soon they were all talking again and plying him with questions about Scammon's Lagoon and the whale-watch, and where he learnt to play guitar like that, and what he was doing wandering about alone, and what England was like, and was it true it was always raining or foggy and you never saw the sun? And why was he interested in whales, anyway?

When he talked of dolphins and told them about Flite, they were surprisingly sympathetic. There were dolphins round here, they told him, lots of them. And even more in the Sea of Cortez, if he went over to the other side of Baja. People said they got quite friendly, and came inshore to play with the swimmers. He ought to go over there and see for himself.

Yes, agreed Matthew, he ought to . . . But, somehow, he did not want to. All the other dolphins in the world would not make up for Flite and the joyous companionship he had shared . . . But he kept these thoughts to himself, and merely smiled and agreed that he ought to visit the Sea of Cortez as well as Scammon's Lagoon, if he got the chance.

He played for them again before the party broke up. But at last they began to drift away, some to the trailer park beyond the dunes, and some to parked cars along the edge of the

207

highway. One of them, Harley, the friendly boy who had first invited him over, offered to put him up in his tent in the caravan park, but Matthew refused, explaining that he rather fancied sleeping out on the beach and watching the stars.

They did not press him, seeming to respect his need to be on his own, and went off into the windy darkness, calling goodnight over their shoulders.

'Watch out for scorpions!' called one, over his shoulder.

'And crabs!' added another voice, fading into the distance.

Presently, Matthew was alone — absolutely, blessedly alone on a wide, starlit beach with only the sound of the surf for company. He lay down on the cool sand and turned his face to the sky, looking up into chasms and deeps of space, darker and wider than any ocean, their fathomless distances filled with a myriad points of light.

My father loved stars, he said. He was glad Della had told him that. Not glad about all the rest he had learnt about that shadowy figure — the one he had secretly dreamed of and looked up to all these years . . . But about the stars, he was glad. It made his father seem more real somehow, more actual — though, *actually*, astronomy was a very abstract subject, he supposed, difficult and strange, and full of surmise and unresolved enigmas . . . But all the same, it brought his father nearer. He, too, had a mathematical mind that wanted to go further than finite thought . . . Up there, among those glittering galaxies, there were huge mysteries to explore. He would like to go there one day — one day, up into those distant spaces, farther than the farthest ocean, than the farthest wave breaking on the farthest shore . . .

Patiently, the old Pacific kept breaking gently against the sand, and lulled in its eternal music, Matthew slept.

★ ★ ★

When Della read Matthew's note, she was distraught, and an even bigger row with Des blew up.

'Now look what you've done!' she screamed. 'Driven the kid away. I suppose that's what you wanted!'

'Of course it wasn't,' snapped Des. 'I wanted to let in a little daylight round here, that's all.'

'But what'll become of him?' wailed Della. 'Where'll he go? He's far too young to take off on his own.'

'He'll manage.' Des was at bay now, red-faced and angry,

too. 'He's no fool, that one. And he's been lookin' after himself most of his young life with that tramp of a mother to contend with.'

'But not in a strange country — with no one to turn to.'

'For Pete's sake, Dell, kids do take off at that age — they do it all the time.'

'He's got no money.'

'Didn't he save any outa that crappy place he worked?'

'Not a lot. He gave me most of it.'

'*What?*'

That sparked off another burst of anger and insults flew across the breakfast table, followed by a plate of pancakes and an ashtray.

Finally Della said, more soberly: 'We'll have to tell the lawyers in London he's gone off.'

'Why?'

'We're responsible for him, Des. We agreed to look after him, remember?'

'*You* agreed,' said Des sulkily. 'It was never my idea.'

Della sighed. 'I know you never liked having him here — but he's a good kid. He didn't do you any harm.'

'I don't like resurrecting the past,' growled Des. 'All that guilt-and-nostalgia syndrome is over. *Over*, see? And I don't want you being reminded of it every goddam day of the week.'

Della looked at him. 'The past is never over, Des. Matthew's alive, isn't he?' Her face paled even further at the next thought. 'At least, I hope to God he is.'

'Sure he is,' said Des comfortably. 'And he'll show up one day soon — you'll see.'

'No thanks to you if he does,' she spat at him. And then, with sudden uncertainty: 'Had I — oughtn't we to tell the police?'

'No!' bellowed Des. 'I've had enough of those goddam Feds poking their noses in here. He's told us where he's heading. He says he'll contact us again. What more do you want?'

'I want him back here — safe and sound,' cried Della, and burst into noisy tears.

Des patted her awkwardly and let her sob on his shoulder. Then he said, into the subsiding storm: 'Leave it out, Dell. He'll be back, and then we can all think again . . . Much better let him have his fling. It'll be all right. Everything will be fine, you'll see.'

Della sniffed and muttered: 'I hope to God you're right.'

But she did what Des wanted her to do. Nothing at all.

★ ★ ★

Matthew woke very early, before sunrise, to the sound of surf and the cries of seabirds. There were some brown pelicans strutting along the shore, and above his head a few more wheeled and dived for fish among the screeching gulls. He went down to the edge of the water and stood looking out to sea before deciding whether to plunge in for a morning swim or not. That surf looked tricky.

Far out, he could see a couple of fishing boats rocking at anchor while the men hauled in their nets, with a cloud of seabirds round them after the discarded bits of their catch. And beyond them, much further out, was a long line of dark fins and humps steadily moving south. The grey whales were still swimming patiently onwards to their chosen breeding ground.

Scammon's Lagoon, thought Matthew. I wonder if Petra will be there? Well, I'll soon find out.

He was still staring out towards the stately progress of the whales, when a smaller, livelier line of dark fins came close in behind the fishing boats and started lifting up into the air.

'Dolphins!' breathed Matthew, watching the gleaming bodies glint in the sun as they leapt and dived round the boats. 'A whole school of them!' He was suddenly assailed by a terrible longing to leap into the sea — to swim out to those dancing shapes and ask them whether they had seen Flite on their travels.

But they aren't even bottle-nose dolphins, he told himself. And they live here in the south Pacific. How could they know about Flite, thousands of miles away in the dark Atlantic?

But all the same, something tugged him towards those shining creatures out there in the bay, and he left his belongings lying on the empty sand, guitar and all, and plunged into the smiling Pacific.

He did not dare swim out too far, not knowing the tides and currents on this rocky coast. Skip's early training had taught him caution in strange seas. But he did let the big Pacific rollers wash over him and lift him in their arms. Maybe the dolphins would see him and come to have a look at this clumsy invader of their territory. They were inquisitive creatures, he knew, and usually unafraid of human beings. (To their cost!) And their sense of fun often seemed to overcome any doubts they might have had about their own safety . . . He swam slowly

210

in the translucent water, and looked up at the morning skies already flushed with sunrise, and waited.

Sure enough, in a little while there was a splash beside him and a puff of air as a sleek body surfaced to have a breather. He turned in the water to look, and another lissom shape curved round a wave and leapt into the air close beside the first one, and then cut the water like a gleaming knife-blade in a steep, effortless dive under Matthew's feet. Soon he was surrounded by leaping, diving bodies alight with spray-shimmer in the first rays of the sun as it rose behind the hills of Baja. Springing into shining arcs, sinking beneath the next crested wave, chasing each other's shadows and racing like dark arrows through the green-gold depths, they turned in swirls of rainbow spume to laugh at Matthew as they flashed by.

'Oh,' he cried to them, with his mouth full of spray, 'aren't you *beautiful!* What a marvellous way to greet the morning. I wish I could leap like that!'

Well, come on then, try! they called to him. The sun is up, the day is here. Today, today! See how we leap, how we take the crest of the waves, how we fly like seabirds through the blue air. See how we dive, deep and straight, to the secret spaces below, to the blue-dark, echoing ways of the ocean we know and love . . . And see how we come swinging back in a sparkle of bubbles to dance round you, to swerve and curve, to rise and fall, and brush close and dart away, to play, to tease, to encompass you in our joy . . .

Come on, they called to him, come and play. The day is here. Sunlight is on the sea. The world is all blue and gold, alive with newness, just born, just begun. Today, today! Rejoice like us. Today!

Why, thought Matthew, enchanted, they speak the same language as Flite! There is no distance between us at all! And, caught up in their joyous celebration, he answered their call and turned in the water to join in their glorious game.

He seemed to be surrounded by smiling faces, long, slender bodies, and sharp dorsal fins. They wove a charmed circle round him, and leapt into spectacular displays of prowess for his delight, turning their laughing faces to him for approval after each pirouette and swift spiral, as if to say: Aren't I clever? Don't you admire my skill? I am a master among the waters. I can do anything — I can go anywhere — I can breast any wave, and reach the farthest deeps, and leap for the sky! The sea is my kingdom, and it is wide — wide and deep and

211

strong . . . and its strength upholds all its creatures in its tireless arms. See? Like me? Rest in it — and play in it — rejoice in its power, like me. Like me! Rejoice!

Matthew rejoiced. But he did not try to touch the dolphins as they played round him. Once or twice a sleek body brushed close in a daring swerve, but it swung away again very swiftly, and Matthew understood that he must keep his distance. They did not know him as Flite had known him, and though their smiles were almost as welcoming, the strange unspoken communion that he had known with his Cornish dolphin was not there among these friendly Pacific creatures.

Maybe, he thought, if I could swim with them every day, it would come. They don't altogether trust me yet. Who could blame them? . . . But he knew, even in the midst of his delight in their playful antics, that what he had known with Flite was rare and precious, and perhaps never to be found again.

You are very handsome, he said to them, swimming round in circles to admire them, and I am delighted to meet you all, but where is Flite? Do you know? You are all friendly and welcoming, which is more than I deserve, and I know there is some strange kinship between us, but Flite was like a long-lost brother to me, and I loved him.

Loved him? they called, smiling. Love is *now*. Not *then*. The ocean loves us — we love the ocean. Our world is full of love — full of joy. Can't you see it all round you? Love us *now*. Love the air, and the sun, and the ocean. Love us all. Now!

Matthew sighed, and swallowed a whole lot of sea. They did not know where Flite was. They did not care. They leapt in the sun and smiled, rejoicing with every fibre, every nerve and sinew of their ecstatic bodies — and after they had filled Matthew's earthbound body and mind with light and swirling rainbows and joyous delight in living, they turned, as one, and headed out to sea, and left him floundering in the shallows.

The sun had climbed over the brown hills by now, and laid bright bars of gold on the water and on the wet sands as Matthew waded to shore. His head was still full of bright images, smiling faces, flashing bodies, and upflung cascades of iridescent water, so that he felt dazzled and strange — filled with a mixture of dolphin-joy and curious sadness which he did not understand.

He stumbled a little as he reached the shore, and turned to look back at the sungilded Pacific where, a few moments ago, he had been so happy, surrounded by those gleaming, rejoicing

212

bodies. It was empty now, but far out, round the fishing boats, he saw a glint of leaping light and dorsal fin as the dolphins returned to their earlier haunts.

'Beautiful,' he murmured, and rubbd a salty hand over his stinging eyes.

He wasn't aware that he had spoken aloud until a voice answered him from behind. '*Sí. Muy bellos, los delfines — e muy alegres!*'

Matthew turned in astonishment. A Mexican fisherman was standing beside him, one brown hand grasping a bucket of fish, the other clutching a blue-grey bundle of net slung over his shoulder, dark hair tangled with salt sea spray, and black eyes smiling at the young *gringo* who was enchanted by *los delfines*.

'*Pescado?*' he asked, swinging his bucket. 'You would like a fish?'

Matthew shook his head, inwardly cursing himself for being so improvident. He had no matches, no way of lighting a fire — no provisions of any kind with him, not even a jar of instant coffee. 'No matches,' he said, shrugging sadly. '*No fosforo,*' he added, grabbing wildly at his schoolboy Spanish. (Or should it be *cerillo?*)

The fisherman was still smiling, intent on offering some kind of morning comfort to this shy boy who liked dolphins. 'I cook,' he said, and jerked his head towards the derelict fish-camp hut. 'You come, *sí?*'

'*Sí,*' agreed Matthew, wondering why he should be so favoured.

The fisherman ploughed on across the sand to the hut, took out an ancient key and opened the bleached wooden door. Inside, Matthew saw, the hut was not derelict at all. It had a couple of sleeping mats in one corner, a primitive stove and tin sink in the other, and a series of crates and fish-boxes to sit on. Obviously, the hut was still used by the fishermen as an emergency stop-over during their long stints at sea.

In a short time — or so it seemed to Matthew — there was a tin jug of coffee heating on the stove, and the fish were being grilled on sticks over an open driftwood fire just outside the door.

'I am Felipe,' announced the fisherman, presenting Matthew with a tin mug of scalding coffee.

'*Gracias,*' said Matthew politely. 'I am Matthew.'

'Ah. Mateo.' A brown, calloused hand came out, and Matthew shook it, smiling.

213

Felipe was eyeing Matthew's guitar in a speculative way. 'You play the pop?'

Matthew's smile grew. 'No. I play classical. Villa-Lobos?' He wondered if a Mexican fisherman would ever have heard of him, but the brown face lit with instant comprehension. '*Sí, clásico*. He is great, that one. You will show me?'

'I will show you,' agreed Matthew.

He only played one piece — 'Aubade', he thought it was, and that was appropriate too — but that was enough to enchant the Mexican and make him his friend for life.

'Have a fish,' said Felipe, holding out a crisp brown offering. 'Have two fish.'

'One will do,' protested Matthew, laughing, and laid his guitar carefully down beside him.

They ate companionably, sitting on upturned fish-boxes by the open door, and watched the early sun gild the tops of the waves as they crested and rode the incoming tide.

'*Muy alegres*,' repeated Felipe, his eyes on the water, and Matthew was not sure whether he meant the waves that broke so joyfully on the morning shore, or the leaping dolphins that swam in them out in the sunlit bay. *Alegres*, he thought. Joyous. Perhaps he means all of it.

'They came very close,' said Felipe softly. 'You are much honoured.'

Matthew looked at him in surprise.

'They do not come for everyone,' he went on, still speaking softly. 'But they are very — *amigables* when they wish to be.'

'I know,' said Matthew.

The fisherman glanced at him out of alert black eyes. 'You know?'

'I knew one once — long ago.' (It seemed long ago.)

'Here? In the *Pacífico*?'

'No.' He was still watching the blue waters of the bay and the fishing boats with their cloud of gulls, but his eyes saw another shore and a darker sea, and a blue-black darting shape that came joyously to meet him without being called. 'In the Atlantic — in England, far away.' Far away . . . The words echoed in his mind like fading music. '*Amigables*,' he murmured. *Amigables* and *alegres*. Yes. That was how they were. Friendly and joyful. And he strained to see those gleaming bodies leaping in the sun.

'You will go back?' said Felipe suddenly.

Matthew nodded. 'I will go back.'

'And he will come, your *delfín*.' It was not a question. It was a statement of fact, and Matthew looked at him, startled.

'I don't think so. It was too long ago.'

'He will come,' stated Felipe, still looking out to sea with his tranquil, unhurried gaze. 'They remember — *los delfines*. And they are, like I said, *amigables*. If he loves you, he will come.'

Matthew took a gulp of hot coffee and nearly choked. He was ashamed of the surge of tears that threatened to engulf him. 'I hope you're right,' he murmured, and tried to restrain his longing to leap into the sea again and swim and swim until he found Flite again in the deep waters of a distant ocean . . . Then he noticed how high the sun was getting in the morning sky, and he said regretfully to his new companion: 'I must go now. I have a friend waiting.'

'Where?'

'At the CREA Youth Hostel — the other side of town.'

'You must take a bus,' said Felipe seriously. 'A Central Camionera, down the Avenida Niños Heroes. On that, you will arrive.'

Matthew thanked him, and did not know what to do about the fish and the coffee. But when he put his hand on his money bag, Felipe grasped his fingers in a firm, hard grip and pushed them away.

'We are friends, Mateo, are we not? *Amigos*. Like *los delfines*. *Sí?*'

'*Sí*,' agreed Matthew, smiling, and picked up his guitar and left Felipe still sitting on his fish-box, gazing tranquilly out to sea.

* * *

When he got to the youth hostel in the Sports Complex, the Fly was parked outside near the cafeteria, and Tracey was inside drinking coffee and looking distinctly angry.

'Where've you been?' she demanded, as soon as he came in sight. 'What the hell've you been doing?'

'Sleeping on the beach,' said Matthew sunnily. 'Sorry.'

'You're crazy,' she snarled. 'You know that? Anything could happen to you out there.'

'Well, nothing did.' He smiled at her, trying to assess how angry she really was. Not very, he thought, and he smiled some more.

'You eaten anything since yesterday?'

215

'Sure.'

'When?'

'Er — some folks having a cook-out gave me supper.' His grin got wider at her exasperated expression. 'And a Mexican fisherman gave me a fish. I did fine.'

'You sure did,' conceded Tracey grudgingly. 'Nothing lifted?'

'Lifted?'

'Stolen, you mutt.'

'Oh. No. In fact, they loooked after my guitar for me.'

'Jeesus!' she exploded. 'The guy's an idiot.' She leaned forward earnestly and spelt it out for him. 'It's not safe to leave your things around when you're travelling.'

Matthew sighed. 'They were OK. Everyone was very friendly.' (Including the dolphins. But he did not want to talk about them.) He glanced at her warily, seeing her impatience simmering beneath the surface. 'But I guess you're right.'

'You bet I am.' Tracey's scowl almost relented. 'Have some coffee.' Then, as his hand strayed to his money-bag, she added hastily: 'On me.'

'No.' Matthew was quite firm. 'On this trip, we share.'

'But —'

'I pay my way, Tracey — or we split.'

She looked at him, surprised at this sudden declaration of independence. 'OK, OK. Get yourself some coffee. We gotta long way to go, and it'll be hot and bumpy inland. Did you get that water-bottle?'

'Yes, I did. And I stopped downtown and got some instant coffee and two plastic mugs and a sort of kettle — oh, and some matches.' He grinned at her astonished face. 'Plenty of driftwood on the beach.'

'We're not going on the beach,' she snapped. 'We're going by road. Inland.'

'At night?' Matthew's voice was pleading. 'It'll be much cheaper . . . Two of us together will be safe enough . . . ' He watched the doubts chase themselves across her mutinous face. 'And I — we've come down here to be near the sea and the whales haven't we?' (Near the dolphins?)

She seemed to hesitate and then give grudging consent. 'OK.' Her shrug was ungracious, but there was a gleam of mischief in her eye. 'As a matter of fact, I brought a tent — in case of emergencies. But if there's scorpions or snakes, I'll run screaming.'

'There won't be by the shore.' Matthew's tone was confident, but he wasn't a bit sure he was right. He would just have to be extra vigilant, that's all.

'Go get that coffee,' growled Tracey. 'Can't sit here all day.'

Obediently, Matthew did as he was told.

★ ★ ★

Matthew's first view of the Baja peninsular was somewhat oblique. The Fly buzzed and rattled along the coastal toll-road, which Tracey had grudgingly taken at Matthew's insistence, and the hard little wheels seemed to jar his spine with every pot-hole, so that he had to cling on to Tracey in a fiercely upright, cramped position for fear of falling off. He had to sit on the rolled-up tent, and even under two sleeping bags the metal tentpole seemed to be far too near his behind for comfort. If he turned his head to the right, he caught tantalizing glimpses of the blue Pacific, interspersed with sparse headlands, low scrub and endless cactus and sharp-looking stiff grasses. The colours seemed to be mostly greenish-grey with sandy brown rocks in between. If he turned his head to the left, the land became rolling and empty, and the cactus plants became taller and more strange, and beyond this desert-like inland plateau there rose a chunky range of lion-coloured mountains. The few trees — mostly palms —seemed to be concentrated round the shiny white restaurants and hotels that lined the beaches wherever they were accessible to the American tourists. For the rest, there were only the endless cactus plants that sometimes grew hugely tall and spiky with tufts of pale yellow flowers on their hairy stalks, and sometimes spread out into great barrels of vicious spines that looked alarmingly prickly to walk among.

Occasionally, as the road came near to the sea on rugged clifftops, Matthew could look down on rolling surf and gleaming sands, and once he saw a couple of sea-lions hauled out on the tawny rocks, sunning themselves.

'Oh, stop!' he called over Tracey's shoulder. 'I want to look.'

Obediently she stopped, but she grumbled all the same. 'Can't stop for every goddam bit of wildlife in Baja!'

'Just this once,' pleaded Matthew, climbing off the Fly to look over the cliff. 'I've never seen wild sea-lions this close before.' He looked down at the gleaming grey-brown bodies below him, and the largest one lifted a languid head off the flank of its mate and looked back at Matthew with a surprisingly alert, inquisitive gaze.

Tracey, ever practical, was rummaging in her well-stocked bags, and presently brought out a can of coke. 'Here,' she said, breaking it open. 'You said share. But don't take all day. We gotta get on.'

'Why?' asked Matthew, still staring down at the sea-lions. But he took a grateful gulp of coke, and handed the can back to her, smiling.

'Because,' said Tracey crossly, 'we wanna get some place where we can eat — before we die of exhaustion.'

Matthew laughed. But he climbed back on to the Fly and made no further protest. Tracey was an old campaigner — she knew about distances and limitations. She was also very aware of the Fly's bony structure and the ferocious battering it gave to its passengers. So she stopped frequently at the small coastal communities on the way to Ensenada, and spent what Matthew privately thought was far too much precious money on *tacos* and soft drinks, and even American burgers at one of the camp-site cafés. However, he had to admit that the small stops did relieve his backache, and the dry, dusty road made him all too willing to swallow quantities of liquid — of whatever kind.

When they got to El Mirador and stopped to look at the view of the blue and gold Bahia de Todos Santos and the wide ocean beyond, Matthew saw that a whole lot of other travellers had also stopped to admire the spectacular beauty spot, and one of them turned to him and said, smiling: 'Makes the goddam bumps worth while, I guess.'

Matthew agreed and stood for a moment looking out to sea, almost too dazzled to see clearly. He didn't really want to leave it at all and buzz his way on to the busy streets of Ensanada. But Tracey was adamant. They had to get 'somewheres safe to stop' before nightfall.

They did not stay in Ensenada, in spite of its waterfront and elegant fleet of yachts and charter boats. In fact, Tracey seemed in even more of a hurry than usual, and turned her back on the beguiling glitter of white boats and blue water, and chugged on down the road to La Bufadora before stopping to rest at all. Here, they joined another group of gawping tourists looking at the upflung clouds of spray from the blowhole and the delicate rainbow that hung over the blown spume glinting in the sun. But it was almost sunset by now, and after a few moments of awestruck silence, Tracey growled something about looking for a campsite and dragged Matthew away.

In the end, they compromized. Tracey insisted on putting up the tent in a small official campsite overlooking the sea. Matthew insisted on sleeping out on the beach.

'There's showers. And toilets,' pointed out Tracey, ever practical. 'I like things civilized.'

'Sure,' agreed Matthew reasonably. 'And I like stars.'

She shot him a surprised glance at this, but made no further protest, and volunteered cheerfully to share his camp fire and try out the new kettle.

They sat gazing at a spectacular Pacific sunset burning away over the sea, and drank their coffee in companionable silence, until Tracey said suddenly: 'What if it rains?'

Matthew laughed. 'Does it ever here?' He was feeding the fire with bits of sunbleached wood from broken fish-bozes, splintered deck planks from long-gone wrecks, the dried, twisted branches of forgotten trees and the spiky limbs of dead cactus that littered the shore. Everything around him looked dry and brown, even the coarse grasses on the dunes were shrivelled to a stiff, brittle fringe. The merciless noonday sun of Baja left little green except the enduring cactus plants that grew everywhere, even on the edges of the rocks.

'There are winter storms,' insisted Tracey. 'Sure, it rains. Like hell.'

'Then I'll get wet.'

She snorted. 'Then you'll come in the tent. That's what it's for.'

'All right, all right,' he smiled at her, and poured some more hot water on to some more instant coffee and handed her back the plastic mug.

But he wondered, rather uneasily, what was expected of him on this trip. Sharing a tent in a rainstorm was one thing, but sleeping together was something else again . . . And anyway, sex in a sleeping bag was not exactly easy for a start, and not at all romantic. He gave himself a mental shake and told himself to stop worrying. Tracey already treated him like a rather tiresome stray dog she had taken in tow, and he was two or three years too young for her, anyway. She was not likely to have any amorous yearnings about a sixteen-year-old boy who was all arms and legs and as green as the Baja grass wasn't. No. It was probably all right.

Tracey was watching him with a sardonic gleam in her eye.

'No strings, Matt. I'm not into casual sex if that's on your mind.'

'No one night stands?' He hoped he sounded offhand and adult, but he doubted it. You couldn't fool Tracey.

'With AIDS where it's at in San Diego? You must be joking.'

Matthew tried not to sigh with relief. He also tried not to blush, but he failed. 'I — er — I'm not into it either.'

She grinned. 'Just as well.' She stirred her coffee vigorously with a piece of twig and then asked in a casual voice: 'You gotta girlfriend back home?'

He shook his head. 'No.'

'Why not?'

The question startled him. He thought for a moment and then answered slowly. 'I don't know . . . I think I got turned off all that — rather early on.'

'How come?'

He was staring out beyond Tracey now at the darkening sea, seeing a different place and a different time — the bleak walls of their tenement block and his mother's endless procession of men who were always there when he got back from school, and usually half-dressed and half-drunk at that. 'My mother had boyfriends.' He broke a piece of wood in two with sudden violence. 'They were always — underfoot.'

'Off-putting, I guess.'

'Somewhat.' He was silent for a moment and then said abruptly: 'It killed her in the end. Or perhaps I did. I don't know.'

She was staring at him now, but more in bleak sympathy than surprise. 'So what happened? Hadn't you better tell me?'

He told her — briefly and starkly, and without self-pity. 'I thought they were out,' he said. (How many times had he said it to himself?) 'But they were having it off in the bedroom. They never noticed the fire — till it was too late.'

'Oh my God.'

'I might have guessed,' he added bitterly. 'It was the usual pattern. I *ought* to have guessed. But I didn't.'

Tracey did not argue about this. She was a practical girl and accepted actualities. Matthew felt guilty. So. She knew about feelings of guilt, too. The thing was, to get on with living — now.

'So you came out here. And that went wrong, too?'

'Yes.'

'Wasn't she good to you?'

Matthew winced. 'Too good,' he said.

Tracey's eyebrows went higher. 'Like that, was it?'

'She got me confused with my father. Her substitute lover-boy, Des called me.'

Tracey swore softly. 'That makes two of us.'

Matthew blinked. 'What?'

'On the run from sex-mad relations.' She was laughing, but her eyes were hard.

'You too?' His mind came back sharply from his own problems. He had wondered where Tracey's family was — why she lived alone in San Diego — what she was doing with her life besides going on Animal Rights marches. And whether she had a permanent boyfriend among that sleepy rabble of hangers-on.

'Who?' he asked, all at once being as blunt as she was.

'My mother took up with a creep,' she said flatly. 'A creep who liked little girls.'

'Oh Christ.'

'Couldn't tell her, of course. Would've broken her up. If she'd believed me.'

'So you ran.'

'So I ran.'

'All the way to San Diego? What d'you live on?'

'Student loan. And I work nights — like you. I get by.'

Matthew sighed. 'Do you — keep in touch?'

'Nope. I cut loose so I cut loose. I'm a big girl now, Matt. She thinks I'm an ungrateful brat. I think he's a shit. We don't talk. What is there to say?'

Matthew saw the logic of that. But then he thought about loneliness, and wondered some more. He was lonely. He had found more true companionship among the dolphins than with human beings. But he was young and rootless and shy. Tracey was older. She should have been able to put roots in her life by now.

'Don't you have a boyfriend?'

Her face seemed to close in the firelight. 'I did.'

'What happened?'

'Oh, he — went off.'

'Why?'

'I guess he just loved boats more than me.'

'*Boats?*' He remembered suddenly how Tracey had turned away with inexplicable impatience from the sunlit harbour at Ensenada with its fleets of yachts and charter boats. There was a naval base there too, and he had wondered vaguely if Tracey was still nervous of being followed by those faceless men in San Diego who might think she was planning another raid.

'What boats?' He was still pushing past her reluctance to talk.

She shrugged. 'Any boats. He always wanted to sail — round the world, he said. So when this guy came along and offered him a share in his boat, he couldn't resist it. Why should he?'

'How long was he — were you together?'

'Nearly two years.'

It was Matthew's turn to swear softly. 'The bastard.'

'I don't know. I guess he got his priorities right.'

Matthew had his doubts about that, but he did not say so. Instead he murmured: 'I wondered why we left Ensenada in such a hurry.'

'Lots of ocean-going boats put in there. It's the sort of place he might show up.'

'I thought it might be the naval base.'

She stared and then laughed abruptly. 'Oh that. *Mexican* navy.'

'No dolphin training?'

'Not that I've heard.' But the familiar glare of outrage was back in her face. 'Much worse things happen to dolphins than that out here.'

Matthew was shocked. '*Here?* But I thought they rather liked dolphins . . . The fishermen, I mean.'

'Yeah. The small local fishermen. The dolphins lead them to the tuna . . . And the yachts. Some of them say they even follow dolphins through the shallows round the islands — use them as pilots. They seem to enjoy showing them the way.'

Matthew wasn't surprised. 'That figures. So where's the threat?'

'The big guys. The trawl fleets — the floating fish factories. They use huge drift nets — and some of them still use purse-seine nets. You heard of those?'

'Yes. Petra told me.'

'Who? Oh, your marine biologist. Yeah, she'd know.'

'They drown,' he said, remembering Petra's strong, compassionate voice speaking with such anger and outrage. 'They cry in the nets when they can't get out to breathe. You can hear them crying . . . and then they drown.'

Tracey glanced at him in bleak agreement. 'Yeah. They drown. And when they come up against the drift nets, they tear their fins off, trying to get out. Hundreds of them.'

Matthew stared out to sea. Those smiling, friendly creatures he had met in the sunlit sea only this morning? Would they get caught in the lethal nets too? 'What can we do about it?' He was suddenly desperate to be some use.

Tracey shrugged again. 'The usual. Yell. Shout. March. Scream.' She grinned at him fleetingly. 'Get arrested. Your friend Petra probably knows the odds. There's a fish quota — like a whale quota. And a dolphin-kill quota, too. But they don't stick to it, of course, and who's to know? You can't go aboard every trawler and count every catch.'

'I'd like to —'

'Sail out there like a shining crusader and cut their rotten nets to ribbons. I know. So would I, too. But you can't beat the big guys. You can only shout.'

They were silent for a while, each of them contemplating with some bitterness the power of the big consortiums and the small man's slender chances of making them change.

'What's his name?' asked Matthew suddenly.

'Who?'

'Your boyfriend's.'

'My ex,' she said firmly.'Mitch.'

'Mitch?'

'Well, Mitchell Anstey, to be precise. Family rich and classy. Too good for me. But everyone calls him Mitch. Why?'

'I just wondered.' He was half-smiling at her in the dark. 'Maybe if he turned up he could take us out to the nets and I *would* have a go!'

'That'd be the day,' she snorted, and rose to her feet, brushing sand off her shabby jeans. 'Well, I guess I'm bushed, Matt. I'll leave you to your stars.'

She strolled away then from his bright little fire, and disappeared up the track through the dunes to the campsite beyond.

Matthew sat on alone and watched the starlight glint on the sea. It was dark out there — dark and calm. He hoped the dolphins were safe — swimming quietly in the lightless depths of their own great ocean.

Be safe, he said. Be happy. I'll do what I can for you. When I can. If I can . . . And tell Flite I love him — if you can.

There was no answer from the sea — only the gentle splash of the waves on the darkened shore. But its quiet music soothed him. Presently he lay down under the stars and slept.

223

This pattern repeated itself for several days. Knowing the short-comings of 'Fly-travel' as she called it, Tracey set the day's mileage limits fairly short, and there was time to swim and wash off the dust at the end of each bone-shaking stretch of road. The distances seemed quite long enough to Matthew anyway, and he began to realize that travelling down even half of the Baja peninsula was a huge undertaking.

In Maneadero they stopped at the immigration checkpoint, having been warned to do so by some passing Americans, and got their tourist cards stamped before buzzing on through the quail-filled hills around Uruapan. Here Tracey stopped and bought strawberries from a wayside stall, and then insisted on going to look at the sea-urchin factory 'to give them a breather'. To Matthew's disgust, Highway I stayed firmly inland without any tantalizing glimpses of ocean for a long, dusty stretch of passably good road, but eventually even Tracey got tired of brown hills, endless cactus, and the terraced vineyards of Santo Tomás and headed back towards the sea at Puerto San Isidro — where she bought lobster *burritos* before finding a campsite near the beach. Matthew adored the lobster *burritos*, but the sea was even better.

In San Antonio del Mar, Matthew learned how to go clam-digging, and how to steam his catch over his campfire, and the friendly American who taught him also showed him how to cast a short line over the rocks for the small fish that swam close inshore. (I could survive on my own, he thought exult-antly. But he didn't know yet how tough this wild country could be.)

In San Quintin it rained — a sudden winter storm rode out of the sea, blocking out the entire landscape with a fierce curtain of stinging fury. Tracey took one look at it and refused to camp anywhere, stamping off to find rooms in a cheap rooming-house and a large, hot Mexican supper which even Matthew had to admit was worth the three precious dollars he handed over. But he missed the sea and his nightly stargazing, so in the morning when it was fine again, Tracey relented and bumped on down to Santa Maria beach where they could swim. The surf was a bit high after the night's storm, but the sea was as blue as ever, and far out Matthew could still see an occasional hump of blue-black whale swimming steadily southwards towards Guerrero Negro and Scammon's Lagoon. But however much he dived and swam through the waves and strained his eyes gazing over the dazzling ocean, he could not see the dolphins anywhere, and this time they did not come.

But there were seals in the bay, not far out, basking on a long spit of rock, and one or two swam inshore to have a look at the stranger blundering about on their terrain. Matthew was reminded of the seals on the shiny black rocks of Cornwall, and how they had come to listen when he played his guitar to them — how they had gazed at him with huge, enquiring eyes, just like these inquisitive Californians. On an impulse, when he came out of the water, he fetched hs guitar and sat down close to the edge of the sea on an outlying rock and began to play. He thought perhaps the roar of the surf would be too powerful for the thin sound of guitar strings, but sure enough the round dark seal heads came nearer, and the beautiful liquid eyes stared up at him in astonished wonder.

Tracey was astonished, too. She had not heard him play before, though several of her gang of hangers-on had gone down to Mosky's to listen, and had reported back to her that 'Matt played real good'. Now, she waited till he grew tired of sitting on a hard rock and the enchanted seal-heads had drifted away, and then said drily: 'You often give seal recitals?'

Matthew laughed. 'I used to — back home.'

Back home. He was suddenly assailed by longing again for the cool, rocky shores of Cornwall, and Skip's astringent presence, and Madge and the kids, with Jampy hopping up and down and shouting: 'Me too!' . . . and the Captain looking at him out of his shrewd old eyes . . .

'Hey!' said Tracey. 'Come back. We gotta get moving.'

'Sorry.' He gave her a lopsided grin and scrambled to his feet.

'Short run today,' Tracey pronounced as they climbed back on to the Fly. 'Last chance for sea. Tomorrow we go inland — and it's going to be tough.'

'How — tough?'

'Windy. Dusty. Thirsty. And empty. Desert country. Nowhere to stop.'

'Long stretch?'

'Too long. So today, we take it easy. Just as far as El Rosario.'

'OK by me,' agreed Matthew, who would have liked to dawdle by the sea all day.

The Fly coughed and puttered into life, and they bumped back on to the road in a cloud of sand and dry Bajan dust.

That evening, Tracey left Matthew to put up the tent and have his usual swim, while she went back to town to get petrol and supplies for the long trip next day.

'Make the most of it,' she said, waving a hand at the ocean. 'You won't see it again till Guerrero Negro.'

Matthew made the most of it. He swam and dived till he was tired. He watched the brown pelicans diving for fish, and he stalked the fiddler crabs on the beach and wondered if they were good to eat. He collected driftwood and made a fire, and watched the lizards on the rocks while he waited for his kettle to boil. He also watched a thin brown rattlesnake (he thought it was a rattler) slither quietly away behind a convenient stone. So far, he reflected, they had not seen many of the hazardous creatures they had been warned against. No scorpions or tarantulas, no black widows, and no rattlesnakes about to strike — only this long, thin brown thing wriggling away very fast, not hissing at all, and making for the green mats of cactus on the dunes behind the piled up stones at the edge of the shore.

He leaned forward to put some more bleached driftwood on the fire, and wondered again — somewhat guiltily — what to do about postcards home. In San Diego, he had been rather good about it, sending a brightly coloured picture of some sort to Jampy every week. But down here in Baja he was faced with a dilemma. If he sent one from here, he would have to explain what he was doing. And if he did that, he would have to admit he had left the protection of Della and Des . . . All these explanations were too complicated for a mere postcard — and a card from Baja with no explanation would only disturb them . . . He supposed he could just say: 'Having a wonderful time' and let them assume he was on holiday . . . But they might get worried and start asking questions, Madge would be sure to smell a rat . . . And she'd bother that solicitor till she found out what was happening. No, better do nothing about it and wait till he was back in San Diego on the way home . . . The way home? He hadn't the least idea how he was going to afford the air fare. Or maybe he could use the Captain's precious card and cadge a passage on a ship . . . a container ship or something? But where did the shipping go to from San Diego? Probably to Japan or somewhere . . . It would be a long way home.

At this point in his reflections he became aware of three things. The kettle was boiling over, the light was going from a fiery sunset sky, and he was looking straight at a scorpion which had come to investigate the food packages lying on the sand. The creature had its tail ominously curled upwards ready to strike, and he wondered how fast it could move when it decided to attack.

He leapt to his feet and seized a solid branch of driftwood in his hand. But the thing was hard to kill, and he was sweating by the time it lay twitching on the sand.

Then he looked up at the darkening sky and began to worry about Tracey. She should have been back long ago. She always made a point of setting up camp before dark, and not wandering off after that in case they got lost.

Where was she? Had she run into some kind of trouble in El Rosario? Surely not. It looked a harmless little town, and the Mexican people there seemed friendly enough. Maybe the Fly had broken down on the way back . . . Perhaps he ought to walk along the dirt track road that led back to the town and have a look . . . ?

He took the kettle off the fire, piled on a few more bits of fuel to keep it going, and set off away from the beach along the dusty track, with Tracey's torch in his hand. Now that it was almost dark, he began to notice the night creatures of Baja emerging all round him in the cactus scrub bordering the dirt road. There were strange rustlings and scrabblings among the loose stones. A small, furry-looking animal — probably a jack-rabbit — bounded away from his torch-light. The creaky, monotonous voice of a Scops owl called from a tall *cardón* cactus nearby, and far away, echoing across the hills, he heard the thin howl of a coyote. He had heard them before, late at night while he was lying safe in his sleeping bag on the beach, but they had never sounded so menacing and eerie as they did tonight. And there was still no sign of Tracey — no sound of the returning Fly.

It was a clear night, and by now the moon was rising, climbing up behind the hills to cast bright radiance and sharp shadow on the empty landscape. The tall shapes of the *cirios* and *cardones* became threatening, almost manlike silhouettes, and even Matthew's own shadow seemed huge and frightening. Even so, he kept the torch beam moving ahead of him, aware now that there might be unknown hazards in the deep pockets of shadow that lay along the edge of the moonlit track.

He walked on, turning the torch beam from side to side ahead of him in case of trouble, but in spite of its probing light, he nearly stepped on another snake writhing its way across the path on some purpose of its own. Not a rattlesnake, he thought. Something different. Thin and green. And deadly?

He had gone about half a mile in this cautious fashion when the dirt road took a sudden bend, and his torch-beam, swinging ahead of him, picked up something bright and metallic gleaming in the moonlight. He began to run then, and came up to it breathless and frightened. For it was the Fly — lying on its side in the dust, and beyond it, in a patch of deep darkness, lay a crumpled heap that was Tracey.

He bent over her in terror, shaking her by the shoulder. 'Tracey? *Tracey!* Can you hear me?'

For answer, she turned slowly on to her back and groaned.

'*Tracey!* Are you hurt?'

He tried to feel whether anything was broken or ominously out of place, but her arms and legs seemed intact at least. Maybe she was just dazed, he told himself, and looked down at her limp body spreadeagled before him and wondered what to do.

'Tortillas,' said Tracey in a blurred voice.

'*What?*'

'Somewhere . . . ' she sighed a little, and moved her head from side to side. 'Find them, will you?'

Matthew put his arm under her shoulders and lifted her head up a little. 'Never mind that. Are you all right?'

She seemed to consider the matter drowsily, flexing her limbs slowly and straightening her back before trying to sit up. 'Yeah,' she said at last. 'Must've hit my head . . . ' She leant tiredly against Matthew's arm for a moment and then began struggling to get up.

'Take it easy,' said Matthew. 'Sit still a minute and get your breath back.' He felt her relax again, as if glad not to have to make the effort to move, and her acquiescence worried him. It was not like Tracey to accept orders from anyone — least of all, him.

'What happened?' he asked, hoping to keep her resting for a bit longer.

'Something ran out across the track.'

'What was it, could you see?'

'No. Biggish — kinda like a dog.'

'Coyote,' nodded Matthew.

'I swerved and the Fly hit a rock and turned over.'

'And you went headfirst into the nearest stone.'

'I guess so.'

Matthew shone the torch on her face for a moment. 'Can't

see a bruise anywhere. Oh yes, I can. You've got a sizeable egg up there.' He reached out a gentle finger and touched her forehead very lightly, but even so she winced.

'Ouch. Do you mind?' Then she looked at Matthew's anxious face and began to laugh. 'Tracey bites the dust . . . Come on, Matt, it's no big deal.'

She scrambled to her feet then, and stood weaving slightly in the brilliant moonlight.

Matthew went over to retrieve the Fly, and stood looking down at it doubtfully. 'Doesn't seem to be damaged. Can you manage it?'

Tracey took a couple of unsteady steps forward, and then stopped, shaking her head. 'Too woosy. you'd better put me on the back.'

Matthew was alarmed. He'd never driven the Fly before — didn't even know how. And even Tracey said it had a will of its own. 'Me?' he squeaked, protesting. But then he saw that there was not much alternative. Tracey was clearly too shaken to walk, and the Fly was very heavy to push along this uneven track with Tracey sitting on it.

'OK,' he agreed, with misgiving. 'Just show me.'

'Throttle, gears, brake,' said Tracey laconically, and climbed on the back without more ado. Then she climbed off again and started looking around her on the dusty ground.

'What on earth are you doing?' Matthew was astride the Fly by now, and just daring to start the engine.

'The tortillas —'

'Damn the tortillas,' he said. 'Come *on*.'

But Tracey was not to be deflected. She searched the ground until she found the greasy packet, still wrapped in its protecting paper. 'Too good to waste,' she muttered, shaking off some predatory ants who were just about to have a banquet. Then she climbed back on to the pillion seat, shaky but triumphant.

The Fly came back to life with its usual exasperated cough, seeming no worse for its spill on the hard ground, and — cautiously — Matthew set off down the track towards the beach.

The little fire was still burning when they got back, and Matthew set about brewing some strong coffee for Tracey. He also insisted that she strip off her torn jeans and jacket so that he could inspect her for damage. Both her knees were grazed, there was a darkening bruise on one thigh, and the palms of her hands were raw, but there did not seem to be anything serious.

'You didn't fall into a cactus, anyway,' he grinned. 'That would have been much worse.'

Tracey grunted, and winced when he touched her. He was bathing the various cuts with hot water from the kettle, and now he stooped to have another look at her hands. 'Or did you? Have you got any prickles in there?'

'Don't fuss,' snapped Tracey, and snatched her hands away. 'They're OK.'

Matthew was not entirely convinced. Better have another look at them in daylight. Right now, it was clear that Tracey was still a bit shocked and needed to sleep it off.

They ate the squashed tortillas with their coffee, and watched the moonlight over the sea in peaceful silence. Then Matthew glanced at her and murmured shyly: 'Better get some sleep . . . It's been quite a day.'

Tracey nodded and moved rather stiffly and painfully to get to her feet. But Matthew suddenly leaned forward and hugged her close for a moment, muttering into her tangled hair: 'Glad you're safe.'

Tracey looked at him in astonishment. But she didn't say a word.

He watched her go, rather unsteadily, into the tent, and then — offering the only comfort he dared — reached for his guitar and played her to sleep. Or he hoped he did. (Like Jampy and the others, long ago, in the crowded little flat upstairs.) His fingers got a bit nostalgic then, and he sat long beside his dying fire in the bright Bajan moonlight, and the sound of his music fell softly and gently on the air, drifting into a fading whisper that merged with the voice of the sea.

★　★　★

In the morning Tracey did not emerge at her usual painfully early hour, so Matthew left her sleeping and went down to the sea for his morning swim. He remembered to kick out at the sand and tread cautiously in case of sting-rays as he waded out, but nothing troubled him except one scuttling crab and a small silver cloud of little fish that swam round his feet and tickled his toes. Soon he was swimming with them, happily idling in the shallows and watching the pelicans dive after the silvery shoal and come up with a beakful of breakfast. He smiled at their comical fish-crammed faces, thinking somewhat ruefully of the fate of those engaging little fish, but then he remembered that Flite ate fish too — of course he did, like all the dolphins. That was the way life was in the ocean — the dolphins went after the tuna, and men went after the tuna, too and caught the dolphins as well . . . Dog eat dog. Fish eat fish. Man eat everything . . . He sighed, and turned on his side for a moment and looked out to sea. But there was no sign of the dolphins this morning. Nothing except a calm bright sea and a few wheeling gulls. He turned again in the clear water, and began a long slow crawl. He felt good in the water — free and strong in an element he loved, and when he looked down there was a whole world of colour and secret life below him waiting to be explored . . . But he still missed Flite — even in these smiling, translucent depths.

He came out close to a deep inlet by some rocks further down the beach, where a weather-worn fisherman was hauling some green nets and yellow rope into his boat. Matthew stopped to look. Those nets wouldn't hold a dolphin if it was desperate to get out, he was sure. But maybe the fisherman would know where the purse-seiners were — or where the deadly drift nets hung like invisible death traps in the smiling sea.

'You want to go shark fishing?' enquired the Mexican, in passable English, and flashed him a crooked, salty smile.

'No-o.' Matthew hesitated, wondering how far out the shark fishers would go. Was this solid-looking boat really ocean-going, or was shark fishing an inshore pursuit?

'The tuna boats — the big ones that use purse-seine nets — how far out would they be?'

'Ah.' The fisherman's cheerful smile turned into a ferocious scowl. 'The sea-robbers, the pirates, with their draw-strings and their wheels and winches —' He lapsed into a string of Spanish oaths which Matthew scarcely needed to translate. 'They take it all,' went on the fisherman, after exhausting his repertoire of curses. He waved an expressive brown hand at the innocent sea. '*All.* They sweep the sea clean. They destroy all the fish stocks.'

'And the dolphins.' Matthew's face was almost as grim as the fisherman's.

The Mexican stopped for a moment in his tirade, and then nodded vigorously. '*Sí* — even *los delfines*. They all die — the big fish, the small fish, the lobsters, the crabs, *los delfines*, they all die.' He rubbed a frustrated, salt-caked hand through his hair. 'Some nets even scrape the seabed and leave nothing alive. It is death to the sea . . .'

Matthew said, persisting: '*How far out?* Could you find them?'

The brown, angry eyes glanced at him warily. 'I could find them, God's curse on them — but what could I do? They are too big for me.'

'I want to see for myself.' Matthew sounded oddly fierce and demanding. 'Then I can — I can tell people about it.'

It sounded very lame to him. But he looked at the seamed Mexican face before him with sudden wild appeal, willing the angry fisherman to understand. After all, their anger was the same, though the Mexican cared more about his fish catch than the dolphins. '*Tell people*,' he repeated, desperate to be understood. 'We have to *tell* them — it's all we can do.'

The ferocious, sun-dried scowl seemed to grow blacker than ever. But there was a spark of something else in the shrewd brown eyes, and a curious, dry acceptance in the swift shrug of his shoulders. 'I go shark fishing. It is possible my boat might go further out than usual. She can manage the *Pacífico*, this one . . . If you wish to come . . . ?'

'How much?' asked Matthew, frantically counting dollars in his head.

The fisherman was regarding him with the same black stare of rage, but there was the same faint spark there too, deep down. 'For *los delfines*? . . . We call them our luck, you know. They lead us to the tuna. We do not like to see them destroyed. He pondered a little. 'You could haul nets?' He eyed Matthew's thin frame with some doubt.

'I could haul,' agreed Matthew.

The fisherman grunted and turned to look out at the blue Pacific, shading his eyes against the sun. 'They are out there somewhere — the spinners and the white-sides . . . That means the tuna are there, too. Not far away.'

Matthew was wondering in sudden dismay what to do about Tracey, when her voice spoke behind him.

'What's not far away?'

'The tuna —' Matthew spoke with meaning, knowing Tracey would catch on. 'And the dolphins . . . ' He looked from Tracey to the fisherman, not knowing what more to say.

'I am Pepito,' announced the fisherman, suddenly remembering his manners and holding out a calloused hand. 'And this is my brother, Guillermo. Hey, Guillermo, wake up. There is a

232

lady present.' And he leaned over into the boat and gave something inside a hefty shake.

A large, sleepy head emerged, and two eyes as brown and alert as Pepito's fixed themselves on Tracey first, and then on Matthew, with friendly interest. '*Buenos días*,' he said, and yawned hugely.

'You must forgive,' excused Pepito, spreading his hands and his shoulders in a wide, expressive shrug. 'We have been out all night laying the nets. We only came back for an extra one.' He gave his brother another push and added playfully: 'Hey, Guillermo, I take on another crew since you sleep all day. He will haul nets while you snore.'

Tracey turned to Pepito with her most devastating smile. 'I can haul, too.'

He glared at her. 'A lady? Never.'

'I am as strong as Matthew.' She glared back.

Pepito raised his eyes to heaven, and then called over her head to his brother. 'Two crew, Guillermo. You can go back to sleep till tomorrow.'

'*Mañana*,' yawned Guillermo, and climbed out of the boat to shake Tracey's hand, and then Matthew's, with solemn courtesy. 'You wish to see sharks?'

'No,' Matthew answered carefully. 'Dolphins.'

Guillermo's dark face changed. 'Ah. *Los delfines* . . . *La fortuna del pescador* . . . ' He glanced at his brother, and messages seemed to pass betwen them.

'The tuna fleet . . . ' Matthew's voice was anxious. 'Can we find it?'

'We can try,' growled Pepito.

'Sure we can try,' agreed Guillermo, and climbed back into the boat and began to coil up the yellow rope, yard by yard.

★ ★ ★

On reflection, Matthew thought this day out on the sea might be just what Tracey needed after last night's mishap. She was very pale this morning, with heavy shadows under her eyes, and the bruise below her hairline had turned very black overnight. But she was still her brisk, bossy self, and before they left she had insisted on packing up the tent and persuading Pepito to let them leave all their belongings, including the Fly and Matthew's guitar, in one of the empty fish-camp huts at the end of the bay. Pepito cheerfully stowed them away and

233

locked the door of the hut behind him with a big, old-fashioned key. After this, Tracey seemed curiously exhausted, but she said nothing about it and climbed into the boat without another word. Once there, however, she seemed to throw off her tiredness, and chattered away to Guillermo while he continued to lay out the nets along the deck of the *Isabella* as she chugged steadily across the bay. But Matthew wondered how Tracey would be when the sturdy fishing boat left the shelter of the cliffs and headed out to sea. The Pacific looked all smiles this morning, but he suspected it would feel a good deal choppier out in the real ocean.

They went first to their own fishing grounds to drop the extra net. Matthew found that the green bundles were not lying in a haphazard heap, but laid out in carefully organized swathes so that they fell neatly overboard on to the calm sea, spreading out as each alternate float and weight balanced it in the water. They left a marker float with a small red flag on it that fluttered bravely near the other two nets, and then Pepito turned the *Isabella* towards the open sea and said: 'We will pick up our catch on the way back.' He looked at Matthew and then added carefully, fingering the rest of the net lying at the bottom of his boat: 'This is good net. Not too fine. The drift net pirates use terrible nets.'

'Terrible?'

'*Terrible*.' His glare was ferocious. 'So fine, so thin it is invisible. It hangs in the sea like a — a *mortaja*.' He shook his head fiercely. 'Everything gets caught in it — everything dies. *Ballenas, delfines*, everything . . . They get tangled in the nets, they swim into them because they do not see them — and they drown.'

Matthew nodded. 'I know.'

The fisherman turned his angry head. 'You know?'

'Someone told me about it.'

Pepito looked at him hard, sighed and rubbed a frustrated hand over his wild hair. 'It is very tough, this net. Sometimes even our boats get tangled in it. A knife will not cut it, so now we always carry these.' He picked up a lethal-looking pair of scissor-shears and waved them at Matthew. 'I am the leader of our *sindicato*,' he explained, still waving the shears with alarming fierceness, 'and we have to protect ourselves.'

Matthew could see the sense in that. 'Do they use drift nets round here?' he asked, persisting in his own quest. 'Or the purse-seines?'

Pepito shrugged. 'Both. Either. I do not know. Sometimes it is one kind, sometimes another. But the drift nets are the worst.' He shrugged his powerful shoulders. 'They are — how do you say? — *ilegal* now for most countries, but they are still used, of course — and our own trade is lost as well as the lives of the *delfines*.'

Matthew nodded again. It was difficult to talk against the noise of the engine, the sound of the wind, and the lurching of the *Isabella* as she took the ocean swell.

Pepito beckoned him nearer with a salty brown hand. 'I can go near to the big trawlers — the factory ships — but not too close. They are not kind to small boats that interfere with their catch.'

Matthew understood very well that Pepito's boat was his living, and he would not want to risk any trouble.

'The other day, one of our boats was run down,' he growled, shaking his head again even more fiercely. 'And the pro-testers — the Greenpeace — they were almost capsized.' His voice rasped in the wind. 'Devils, they are — they care for no one else on the seas.'

'Not too near,' Matthew agreed, shouting into the wind. 'I only want to look.'

The *Isabella* ploughed on, straight into the choppy Pacific swell. And Tracey got steadily paler and more silent. Matthew asked her once if she felt all right, but she nearly bit his head off, so he said nothing more. He guessed she had a raging headache anyway after that bang last night, and feeling seasick wouldn't help, but she clearly didn't want any sympathy.

The sea was still that miraculous Pacific blue, and the sky was clear, but the wind had got up and there was quite a swell. Waves reared up and looked ominous and threatening, as if about to swamp the *Isabella* in tons of surging water, but the sturdy boat always seemed to breast them or plough straight through them in cascades of spray, giving herself a little shake of satisfaction as she rode triumphantly out of the next alarming trough.

'She is tough, my *Isabella*,' yelled Pepito, accurately assessing Matthew's thoughts.

Matthew grinned. 'I'll say. She rides the seas like a dolphin.'

Pepito's crooked smile flashed out, white teeth gleamed in a brown face, and he raised himself a little and pointed forward out to sea. 'They are there — *los delfines* — see? That means the tuna are there, too — the yellow-fins, the skipjacks.'

'And that means —?'

'Sí. The pirates — and their nets. Guillermo!' He waved an arm at his brother and pointed again towards the choppy horizon.

Guillermo understood him and nodded a shaggy head. 'I watch!' He shouted. 'I look! I am *desvelado!*'

The *Isabella* took an extra large sea over her bows, and spray fell in an iridescent shower over everyone. When they had shaken themselves like wet dogs, Guillermo suddenly shouted: '*Ahí!* There!' and pointed to the south of the boat.

Pepito acted instantly, and swung the nose of the *Isabella* away northwards. He knew how wide and how lethal these outspread nets could be.

Matthew looked over the side and saw a long line of cork floats stretching as far as his eyes could see, and threading between them a wicked-looking thin wire cable.

'Purse-seine,' grunted Pepito, and kept his boat well away from its cruel embrace. He jerked a thumb ahead, and Matthew saw that there were a number of spinner dolphins leaping in and out of the water. They were clearly excited and distressed, but they were keeping their distance from the deadly stretch of netted sea. 'They are the lucky ones.' shouted Pepito. 'They have sense. But their friends have not.' He kept the *Isabella* cruising gently along the edge of the huge nets, but his eyes were searching ahead for any sign of the trawler whose vast fishtrap lay across her path.

Matthew was watching the dolphins intently. They kept diving and leaping near the nets, thrusting at the cork floats with their beaks and then turning away, only to swim back in a more furious and anxious attack the next time.

Their friends are trapped inside, he thought. I have heard people say they try to help them — that they are upset when they hear them cry. He leaned over farther to have a closer look, and Tracey's hard hand came out and grabbed his arm.

'Don't do anything crazy, will you?'

Matthew turned his head to look at her fleetingly. 'They're crying in there,' he said. 'I can hear them.'

And he could. He was sure he could. In the midst of the slap of the waves, the shriek of the wind and the creaking planks of the *Isabella* and her steadily chugging engine, he was sure he could hear the whistles and clicks and calls of communicating dolphins, and beyond them the desperate cries of their trapped companions, unable to escape, unable to breathe.

236

As he watched, he saw the cork floats begin to move, and the drawstring wires at the edges of the floating nets begin to close inwards towards some unseen force that was pulling them away across the water. He could not yet see the trawler — the nets must be enormously wide — but she was there all right, not far away.

'They're pulling in,' shouted Pepito, and turned the *Isabella* even further away, knowing the dangerous tug of those unseen cables, and the turbulence the nets' withdrawal would cause.

The spinner dolphins seemed to get even more agitated, and butted helplessly at the retreating nets in renewed frenzy. One of them came up out of the water close to the bows of the *Isabella* and seemed to look straight at Matthew with desperate entreaty. Help us! it seemed to be saying. Our friends are dying in there. Help them to get out! Help us!

Matthew could not bear it. Their voices seemed to be all round him, calling and beseeching, echoing in his head like one long cry of pain. He turned frantically to look for some kind of tool or weapon he could use against that lethal netting, and found himself staring down at the gleaming scissor-shears that Pepito had shown him. He leant swiftly down and snatched them in one grasping hand, and then — without stopping to think — leapt overboard into the turbulent sea.

Behind him, the two Mexicans shouted, and Tracey made a fruitless grab at him as he leapt — and then they could only watch in horror while Matthew fought with the sea and the retreating purse-seine nets, pursued by the anxious spinner dolphins left on the outside.

There followed, for Matthew, a timeless interval of frantic chaos. Waves broke over his head. Wild wind and watery darkness engulfed him, and blind rage consumed him. He reached the retreating wall of nets and hacked and sawed with furious urgency at the tough nylon fibres. Beside him, he was dimly aware of dark dolphin bodies also butting at the cork floats and the ever-closing curve of the purse-seine as it was pulled in. But Matthew's rage seemed to have given his flailing arms and slashing shears extra strength, for all at once a section of the net below the surface parted, and a great gush of fish and trapped dolphin bodies surged out into the water round him, overwhelming him in a tidal wave of wriggling silver, swirling tail flukes, dark dorsal fins and thrusting snouts, and blow-holes gasping thankfully at new air . . .

The weight of their surge was so great that Matthew sank

237

under it like a stone, and floundered with bursting lungs in the seething water, unable to reach the surface. But as he struggled painfully towards the light, he felt a firm nudge behind him and another at his side, and two blue-black shapes swam close to him and pushed him steadily upwards till the gold and silver sparkle of sunlight on water was just above him and his head broke the surface into blessed air. The sound of the sea and the voices of the dolphins seemed to be all round him now, not all crying out in trapped desolation, though he thought there were still some calling desperately to him from a long way off, but nearer they seemed to be talking to each other, whistling and clicking in strange patterns of echo and re-echo, long cadences of sound rising and falling, mingling with the ceaseless rhythm of the waves, the deep voice of the ocean swelling and dying in his ears . . . Two great gulps of air Matthew took, and then he sank again among the mass of escaping bodies, and again those two blue-dark shapes came close and nudged him upwards towards the light. He thought this time he would never reach it, the pain in his lungs was beyond bearing and he was dying . . .

Round him the dolphin voices seemed to grow louder and clearer, multitudinous and inescapable — the voices of all the sea creatures in the world, the great whales, and leaping dolphins, the sword-fish and tuna and the smallest flying fish, all calling to each other across the watery wastes in an endless stream of anguished communication . . . I am dying, said Matthew. Soon I shall just be part of the ocean . . . then I shall understand their language. I don't feel afraid with all these voices round me . . . Flite, where are you? Maybe soon I shall find you . . . I will find you when I drown . . .

But he did not drown. Again, two powerful dark bodies pushed and nudged his half-conscious body, lifting him in the water, forcing him steadily upwards, and this time a hard and horny hand came down out of nowhere and grabbed him by the hair. He was heaved up, limp and defeated, and deposited face downwards on the wet planks of the bucking *Isabella*. Then the same hands pushed down on his back and his aching ribs, forcing the water out of his lungs till he lay coughing and retching with returning life. It hurt to come back. He wasn't even sure he wanted to. Out there, somewhere, were the creatures he loved, the voices he knew, and something inside him wept for the understanding he had nearly reached, and now would never know . . .

Then Tracey's voice, shaking with rage and possibly something more, said close to his ear: 'You goddammed lunatic!' And Pepito, sounding equally angry, growled: '*Loco* English!'

'I'm sorry,' choked Matthew, trying to sit up. 'They were crying, you see . . . '

They were all looking at him in disbelief. But Pepito suddenly laughed and said: 'I am not sorry. You cut a damn-big hole in their nets!'

Guillermo was still looking at Matthew in a somewhat awestruck way. '*Los delfines*,' he said. 'They brought you back. You are — *afortunado*.'

'We will not be *afortunado* if they find us here,' rasped Pepito. 'Now we go back to our own nets, pretty damn quick.'

Matthew was too tired to answer. But he managed a watery grin.

Back at their own fishing grounds, the brothers went calmly and confidently into action. Matthew insisted on helping to haul in the nets, saying he had promised, and anyway it would warm him up. They looked at him doubtfully but did not demur, and Tracey silently came up beside him and took her share of the weight. Some of the smaller fish they threw back, and a horde of screaming gulls immediately descended on them, fighting among themselves over the discarded scraps. But the larger fish and the sharks were soon piling up on the wet floor of the Isabella.

Matthew saw that the sharks were not very big — not more than three or four feet long, though they had powerful jaws and their teeth looked fairly lethal. He was not too happy about those limp and lifeless bodies — they too had died suffocating in the nets, since sharks, he knew, had to keep swimming to take in oxygen. And their voices must have been calling among all those others in the deep recesses of the ocean . . . But Pepito seemed to know his thoughts, for he said as he hauled one more long black body out of the nets: 'We only take what we need. Not like the pirates who sweep the whole sea clean . . . ' He looked down at the silvery harvest at his feet and added: 'This will feed all the village.'

Matthew nodded, and leaned over to help Guillermo haul in the last of the nets. 'And now we go home,' Pepito grinned. 'And if anyone asks, we have been here all day. It takes time, shark fishing.' He winked cheerfully at Matthew and went forward into the little wheelhouse to start the engine.

Matthew turned to Tracey somewhat anxiously. 'They won't get into trouble, will they?'

'I shouldn't think so,' growled Tracey, putting on her most ferocious scowl. 'But you will when I get you back on dry land.'

* * *

That evening there was a party. Guillermo had gone off to fetch the fish truck, and when he returned, bumping down the rutted track to the edge of the beach, there were several friends with him to help load the catch.

'We have an ice-house in our village,' explained Guillermo, heaving the last of the sharks on to the battered old truck. 'The women will cut them up. Now I go.' He grinned at Matthew, who had been helping to load the silvery haul into the fish boxes lying on the sand. 'But I come back. There will be fish for supper. And lobster. you will come?'

Matthew looked round for Tracey, but she was already busy collecting her own gear from the empty fish-hut, and seemed wholly preoccupied in disentangling the tent, so he answered for her. 'Sí. We would love to come.'

Pepito, who was swilling out the bottom of his boat with sea water, looked up and added: 'Your *guitarra* — we will have some music?' And when Matthew nodded a little doubtfully, he grinned and remarked to no one in particular: 'We have something to celebrate — *no?*'

But when they were alone, setting up the tent, Tracey made it clear that she didn't think it was a cause for celebration. She tore Matthew off a strip and told him he was irresponsible, reckless and downright dangerous.

Matthew was mystified. 'But you weren't averse to breaking into a naval base. That's much more dangerous.'

'No, it isn't. I wasn't likely to get drowned.'

'You might've got shot.'

Tracey snorted. 'Some chance!'

'Or landed in jail.'

'At least it wouldn't have been a *Mexican* jail.' She glared at him. 'Do you realize — if they'd caught you, there might've been a political incident.'

Matthew laughed. 'Oh, come off it. One small tear in a mile-long net?'

240

'You don't understand — these fishing wars are apt to get very tough. Did you see the trawler at all?'

'No. Did you?'

She shook her head. 'Too far off — and too choppy. But Pepito did.'

'What nationality?'

'Couldn't tell. He says they are often Japanese — and sometimes American.'

'*American?*'

'Yeah. Big factory ships. All the gear heavily mechanized. Huge catches processed on the spot — nothing much left for anyone to see. The little guys like Pepito simply can't compete.'

'No wonder he was pleased about the net.'

'He was *not* pleased,' snapped Tracey. 'He was scared witless. We all were.'

Matthew's mouth twitched to a grin. 'Sorry. I didn't think you cared.'

Tracey glared even more fiercely. 'You didn't think, period.'

Matthew nodded. 'That's true. They were crying out there, you see. Couldn't you hear them?'

'No,' she growled. But the bright anger in her eyes was subsiding.

That was it, Matthew was thinking. With those sounds in my ears, how could I stop to think? They were calling to me. I *had* to do something. I *had* to.

But aloud he only said mildly: 'Well. It's over. No big deal.'

'Don't ever do it again.'

He shrugged. 'I probably won't get the chance.'

She softened a little. 'I can see your point, Matt. But we've got to find other ways.'

'Sure,' he agreed. 'I know. It was just — I couldn't sit there and do nothing.'

Tracey looked at him. 'Not your scene, passive observer, is it?'

'No,' he sighed. But then he remembered that Petra spent most of her time being just that — a passive observer on whaling ships, on deep-sea trawlers, on wild and empty shorelines . . . in Scammon's Lagoon? But then she was a trained observer, an expert in her field, and she had a voice that people would listen to . . . And Pierre had said: 'All we can do is shout . . .'

But I'm too small, said Matthew angrily to himself. Too

241

small and too unimportant. No one will listen to me. What can I do?

Tracey saw the doubt and despondency in his face, and thought maybe she had been too tough. But before she could say any more, Pepito's voice spoke behind her. 'We are cooking. Are you coming?'

'*Sí* . . . ,' said Matthew, remembering his manners. '*Gracias.*' And he picked up his guitar and turned to walk back across the sand with the burly fisherman. Tracey followed them without a word.

So the party began.

While the fish was cooking, someone else brought out a guitar, and the Mexicans, led by Guillermo's strong tenor, began to sing their own songs. Matthew struggled gamely to keep up. He did not know their songs, but he had a good ear and he could mostly guess what was coming next and embroider round it. And in between songs, they passed round the beer.

Then someone asked Matthew to play for them. He considered whether to match their songs with English pop, but in the end settled for his own favourites. He played them best, anyway — and he remembered that the other Mexican fisherman at Tijuana had liked '*clásico.*' So once again it was Granados and de Falla and even Bach, and he did not even notice the astonished silence that settled on his listeners. They were naturally courteous, and listened in grave and somewhat awestruck attention, and when he paused for breath and to ease his fingers, they passed round the beer and begged for more.

Then everyone was eating lobster and fish and clams, with some spicy tortillas that Guillermo had brought from the village to add to the feast — and they passed round the beer. And somehow the singing broke out again, and Matthew found himself both playing and singing and laughing in between.

When the tequila came out, Matthew glared at Tracey and leaned towards her muttering: 'Not after that crack on the head,' and she retorted: 'Not after being half-drowned!' But they both accepted a small tot in a tin mug, promising themselves it would be the last.

After that it was a glorious haze of laughter and singing, and more fish and more tortillas, followed by bitter-sweet coffee and more cans of beer.

Matthew looked round at Pepito's smiling face in the light of the kerosene lamp, and from him to the circle of other

242

brown, salt-seamed faces happily singing round him, and his heart suddenly seemed to clench with unexpected affection. He didn't know these people, but somehow he loved them — all of them, with their tough, work-weary bodies and their child-like delight in simple things, their kindness and generosity to an awkward English boy who nearly got them into awful trouble. He didn't know how to tell them this — of course he couldn't — so he simply played his heart out for them on his guitar, the only gift he could give.

At last Tracey murmured something about 'a long trip tomorrow', and they found themselves being escorted back to the tent by several still-happily-singing companions whose arms were draped lovingly round Matthew's and Tracey's shoulders.

'*Mateo*,' crooned Guillermo into his ear. '*El afortunado —*'

The lucky one? I suppose I am, thought Matthew. I didn't drown, at least.

'*Amigo de los delfines*,' added Guillermo, who was feeling very sentimental by now, and still a little awestruck by the happenings round the purse-seine nets.

'I hope so,' answered Matthew aloud, smiling back. Oh, I hope so.

On the other side, Pepito growled: '*Viva la liberdad!*' and waved his beer can in his free hand. Then he winked hugely at Matthew's surprised face and slapped him on the back with such mighty affection that he nearly fell over.

The fishermen deposited them safely by their tent, called loving *buenas noches* across the moonlit sands and departed singing into the night.

Tracey stood looking at Matthew for a moment, and for some reason in the bleached light of the moon her face looked strangely young and vulnerable.

'Matt?' she said hesitantly, then leant forward and grasped him fiercely by the shoulders. 'No more goddam heroics, you hear me?'

Matthew laughed. 'Some chance!' he said, and, greatly surprising himself, leant even closer and kissed her on her blanched, upturned face.

Tracey blinked, glared in fury, and then laughed. 'It's the tequila talking,' she said, and turned swiftly away to her tent.

Matthew let her go, and presently lay down in his own sleeping bag, unconcerned by wandering crabs or lizards (but with a passing shudder at the thought of black widows or scorpions), and stared up at the stars. They were very bright tonight, and they reminded him somehow of home — of the Cornish cliffs and pale, washed sands, and the dark spur of rocks where Flite came to greet him . . . And Skip, whose lean brown body was as tough and salt-stained as these wiry fishermen's, and whose eyes had the same serene delight in simple things . . . Except when they looked at Petra, and then they smouldered with all kinds of hidden fires . . . Petra . . . And that led to wondering whether she would really be down in Guerrera Negra at the whale-watch, or at the address nearby that he had been given. And would she be glad to see him? Would she, in fact, have time to waste on a boy she scarcely knew — let alone be able to tell him what to do next?

I have to get home somehow, he told himself. I have to go back. I see that now. And there's Madge and the kids to see. Jampy will be asking all sorts of awkward questions — or he may be forgetting me altogether. I have to go back.

But the stars didn't seem to care much about his problems. They shone on above his head, brilliant and changeless, undisturbed. And into his mind came the voice of a dolphin. Not those anguished cries of despair he had heard in the deep Pacific swell, but a different voice he knew, from far away. Today, today! said Flite, calling to him across the winter seas of home. Why worry about tomorrow? Today you are alive. The stars are bright. The sea is at your feet. Joy is all around you. Today!

Smiling a little, Matthew turned over and slept.

★　★　★

Back home in London, Madge turned over in bed and said to Jim: 'I'm worried about that boy.'

'Which boy?' Jim mumbled, half asleep.

'Matt, of course. Who d'you suppose?'

Jim yawned. 'What about him?'

'He hasn't written. Jampy's right upset about it. Every week that postcard come — like clockwork. Matt was that good about it.'

'Boys forget sometimes.'

'Not Matt. He promised Jampy.'

'Maybe he's busy.'

Madge snorted 'Too busy to write a postcard?' She turned over again and stuck a bony elbow into Jim's shoulder-blade. 'I think somethink's up. I gotta feeling.'

244

Jim groaned. he was used to Madge's 'feelings'. 'That lawyer chap might know.'

Madge agreed, grabbing Jim by the arm in her excitement. 'You're dead right. I'll ring him in the morning.'

But in the morning it was not so easy. By the time she had got Jim off to work and the older kids off to school, parked Jampy and the baby with a downstairs neighbour, and run down the road to the pay-phone on the corner, she realized she did not know the solicitor's number and would have to look it up in a phone book. The first three phones were vandalized, the fourth had no phone book, and when she at last found a useable phone book, she realized it was impossible to find a solicitor called John Harvey unless she knew the name of his firm and its address — which she didn't. She did however know Skip's number in Cornwall, and after counting out her money, she tried that. But by now it was getting late in the morning, and Skip had already gone out to one of his swimming-therapy classes at the local hospital.

Frustrated, and somehow even more anxious about the unreachable Matt, Madge picked up her money and determined to try again on her way to work in the evening. But in the evening Jim was behind schedule coming home, Jampy made a scene about going to bed and kept on about Matt's postcard not coming, the baby decided to have a good yell as well, and Madge was nearly late for work. She had to run all the way, so she decided to ring Skip on the way home instead.

It was nearly ten o'clock when she got away from her office cleaning, and she was afraid Skip would have gone out again to something or other, but after a long time his cheerful voice answered, sounding close and warm, and accompanied by even more cheerful background noises from the club bar behind him.

He listened to Madge's breathless anxieties about Matthew, and promptly said: 'I'll see what I can find out. Can I ring you back?'

'No,' said Madge. 'I'll have to ring you again. Will tomorrow night be too soon?'

'Do my best,' answered Skip. 'Don't worry, Madge. I'm sure he's OK.' And then the pips went, and before Madge could insert any more money, they had been cut off. Sighing, she went home to another restless night.

Skip, meanwhile, did not waste any time trying to trace John Harvey, of Harvey and Harvey, somewhere in London, he simply rang the number the old Captain had given him, and left a message that asked for Harvey's number as enquiries were being made about Matthew's welfare. It was a bit presumptuous, he supposed, to bother the old man, but he had his own reasons for wanting to keep in touch.

The result, very swiftly, was a terse phone call from the Captain himself, from somewhere in the south of France.

'What's all this about, Skip?' he rasped, and it was clear from the tone of his voice that he was as absurdly anxious about the boy as Madge was — or Skip himself?

When Skip explained, he said at once: 'Leave it with me. I'll get Harvey on to it right away. I'll be in touch,' and rang off.

Skip was left smiling a little at the autocratic ways of rich old men, and the thread of genuine concern that came through that incisive voice.

John Harvey, on receiving barked instructions, wasted no time either, but rang San Diego in the late afternoon, which would make it about Della's breakfast time.

He was astonished to be met by a rather blank and breathless voice saying: 'Matt? Oh — he's not here right now.'

'Not there?' queried Harvey, his voice carrying the same upward curve as his eyebrows. 'Where is he then?'

'I —' She seemed to hesitate, and to sound oddly at bay. 'I don't know exactly, somewhere in Baja California, I guess.'

Harvey was scandalised. 'You *guess*? Don't you have an address?'

'No. No, I don't.'

There was a moment of mystified silence, and then Harvey spelt it out carefully. 'Let me get this straight. You sent for Matthew to come over to stay with you — with a view to making his permanent home with you in San Diego — yes?'

'I guess so — yeah.' She was beginning to sound scared — and even more defensive.

'You accepted responsibility for his welfare and safety?'

'Yeah.'

'And you tell me you *don't know where he is*?'

There was another pause while Della took a gulp of control. 'I — there was a bit of a disagreement here — with my husband. Matt just took off.'

'I *see*,' said Harvey, sounding very grim indeed. 'And you have no idea where he went?'

'He — he said in his note he was going down to visit a friend in Baja. I didn't know he had a friend down there, but I guess he must have some address to go to.' She took another nervous

gulp of air and added: 'He said he'd be in touch again before —
before he went home.'

'Oh,' said Harvey, without being able to avoid some sarcasm.
'So he mentioned going home, did he?'

'I'm sorry,' wailed Della. 'It was a misunderstanding. You
know how touchy boys are.'

'You should have told me.'

'Yeah, sure I should. But Des said — my husband said —
boys often take off for a spell and come back, and we'd better
wait and see.'

Harvey's disapproval could be felt down the line. 'I shall have
to inform the authorities,' he said severely.

Della trembled a little, not sure who he meant by the authorities. But Harvey went remorselessly on.

'He is a British citizen — and a minor. *Someone* must take
responsibility. In the meantime, if you hear anything from him,
let me know at once. *At once*, do you understand?'

Della understood. She understood too that she was in serious
trouble, and so was Des. And she was scared.

She was even more scared when later that day a quiet, softly-
spoken man strolled into the boutique, smiled a very gentle,
very dangerous smile, and held out a card to her which said
simply: 'Commander R.J. Morris, RN' and a private telephone
number.

'Mrs Della Grant?' he asked, with the utmost politeness.
'Forgive my intrusion. I was wondering if by any chance you
had heard from your nephew lately?'

'My — my nephew?' Della squeaked. 'Oh, you mean Matt?
No — er — no, we haven't.'

'Still on a trip south, is he?' purred Morris, his eyes very
bright and still as they watched her nervousness grow.

Della swallowed hard. 'In — down in Baja, yes.'

'Still with his girlfriend, I take it?'

She jumped a mile. 'What girlfriend?'

'Oh.' Morris's steady stare seemed to be laced with faint
amusement now. 'You didn't know about that?'

Della wordlessly shook her head. Girlfriend? Matt? . . . She
didn't think he'd shown any interest in girls — up to now.
And, all things considered, and the way things were, this bit
of information seemed to her the last straw. When she had
offered him — well, what had she offered him? More than a
home, more than affection, more than ordinary love . . . And
he had run screaming — *with a girl his own age.*

'According to our information,' explained Morris precisely, 'Matthew crossed the Mexican border on his own one evening, and was joined next day by his young friend Tracey Holland on a motor scooter.'

'Tracey Holland? Isn't she the girl who—?'

'Yes. The girl who is an animal rights activist and who was recently arrested for attempting to break into a military establishment.'

Della went visibly pale. 'Are they — is Matt in any kind of trouble?'

'Not that I know of. They didn't try to stop off at the Naval Base at Ensanada, if that's what you mean.'

'Well, thank God for that,' Della breathed an audible sigh of relief.

'No, as far as our reports go, the two of them have simply been having a holiday, seeing the usual sights, camping on beaches, and going steadily southwards.'

'To the whale-watch,' said Della suddenly. 'I remember him telling me he was interested. Isn't it down there some place?'

'Guerrero Negro, yes. Scammon's Lagoon. Is that where they're heading?'

'I — I guess so.'

'He didn't tell you his plans?'

'He didn't tell me a thing,' snapped Della, sounding both angry and sulky at once. 'He just took off.'

'I see,' murmured Morris, very much in the same tones as Harvey had used earlier. He was looking at her with a kind of studied calm. 'He is outside our jurisdiction, of course, in Mexico. But if he should get into any trouble down there, it could be very serious for him, you understand.'

Della nodded. 'That girl — she'd be the trouble-maker. Not Matt.'

Morris smiled. 'Family loyalty isn't a bad thing.'

Della suddenly felt enormously guilty at that remark. Family loyalty? How loyal had she been to Matt, her nephew — to Des, her husband — or even to her long dead lover, Michael?

'But, as a matter of fact,' Morris was continuing, 'according to your nephew, Tracey Holland is sincere in her beliefs and not just a hoodlum hooked on demos. In any case, her latest brush with the law will have made her pretty wary, I dare say. She won't be looking for trouble.'

'I hope to God you're right,' breathed Della.

'Oh, I'm sure I am,' said Morris, the smile in his voice too by now. He gave Della one more shrewd and piercing glance and added softly before turning away: 'Well, do let me know if you hear from him, won't you? I shall be most interested to know where he gets to. *Most* interested.' And he wandered away out of Della's expensive boutique, pausing to admire a particularly fetching little number in black velvet and beads as he went.

Behind him, Della found she was shaking so much she had to sit down on the only chair in the salon. She felt quite faint. After a moment's frantic reflection, she decided that she must tell Des what had happened without delay. So she gave up work for the day, apologized all round, and hurried out into the bright San Diego morning.

★   ★   ★

Much further south, on the road to Guerrero Negro, it was an even brighter morning — windy and fierce, with the dust blowing off the desert lands beside the road, and the sun beating down out of a hard blue sky. It was winter, so the temperature was not all that high, but even so Matthew felt parched and dried up in the relentless wind, and wondered how it would be in high summer when the sun was really hot. Almost unbearable, he thought; for this bumpy, wind-scoured journey was bad enough. Even the forests of tall *cirio* trees and *cardón* cacti seemed dried up, standing in stark, fantastic groups against the flat brown hills and the strange, piled-up boulders and thrusting clumps of barrel cactus that made up this bitter desert wilderness.

Tracey allowed them a rest-stop wherever one presented itself, bought cold drinks and filled up their water bottles, and then pushed on again with grim determination. She knew the dangers of this bleak, difficult stretch of road. If anything, the wind seemed to be getting stronger, and by the time they reached their second stop, at Cataviña, it seemed to be blowing a hurricane.

'Come on,' snapped Tracey, pushing Matthew back on to the Fly, and handing him yet another can of coke. 'We can get back to the sea before dark, if we keep going.'

They kept going — grinding along the merciless highway in the teeth of the gritty wind — until, towards evening, they turned off the main road for the little fishing village of Santa Rosalillita. Here at last they bumped down a track to the beach, and Matthew thankfully fell off the Fly and plunged his aching body into the cool Pacific swell.

He came out to find Tracey standing curiously still, staring at the cluster of fishing boats round the little harbour, and the gleaming white hulls of a couple of ocean-going yachts tied up among them.

'What is it?' he said, seeing her expression. 'Something wrong?'

'No.' Her voice sounded strained and rather distant. 'No, I guess not . . . ' She turned away rather abruptly and began to unpack the tent. 'Just — I just thought . . . ' She did not go on, but Matthew finished it for her.

'You thought you recognized one of the boats?'

She went on shaking out the groundsheet in case of scorpions or spiders, and muttered into the unfolding canvas. 'Guess I was wrong.'

'You're tired,' stated Matthew. 'Why don't we go into the village and see if we can get something to eat?'

'You go,' said Tracey, still keeping her head down. 'Bring back some tortillas or something. I'll — I've got things to do here.'

Matthew made no comment. But when he got back from the village, carrying two fish and a handful of spicy tortillas, he saw that Tracey was not waiting for him by the tent, but far out along the beach sitting alone on a rock and gazing out to sea. He did not go after her, but busied himself getting a driftwood fire going, and setting his two fish to cook over it, speared on a couple of sticks, as the Mexican fishermen had taught him to do. He thought Tracey would probably come back when she saw the fire, and sure enough she returned, silent and unsmiling, just as he was beginning to worry about the fish being overcooked.

When they had finished eating, Tracey suddenly said: 'Play something, Matt. I got shadows.'

Matthew reached for his guitar, wondering which piece was the best shadow-chaser. An old pop-song? A bit of hotted-up jazz? A Mexican folk song? (He was getting good at those now.) Or should he just play what soothed him most — what his fingers liked best?

He drifted quietly from one thing to another, while the fiery sunset faded in the west, and Tracey sat staring into the fire, her expression remote and rather stern. She showed no particular interest in his choice of music — but by this time Matthew had almost forgotten her and was playing for himself alone.

They neither of them noticed the tall, fairhaired stranger who came up behind them and stopped to listen — who listened and stared, and stared again, and then spoke in a lazy drawl when Matthew came to an end.

'Hey, man, you sure can play that thing.'

Tracey, by the fire, seemed to freeze into utter stillness. In the deepening twilight Matthew saw her face go pale and bleak with shock.

'Hi, Trace,' went on the stranger softly, and sat down on the sand beside her. 'What are you doing down in Baja?'

Tracey did not answer at all — so Matthew replied quietly for her. 'Whale-watching. When we get there.'

'Guerrero Negro? I'm going down there myself. Maybe we could travel together.'

'No, we couldn't,' said Tracey, turning round and glaring. 'Matt and I are on the Fly. No room for anyone else. And anyway, Michael Anstey, if you think you can stroll outa my life one day and stroll into it again another, you gotta nother think coming.'

The young man laughed, not in the least put out. 'Not strolling, Trace. Sailing. I was kinda offering you a lift.'

'No thanks,' said Tracey, and got rather pointedly to her feet. 'We got other plans.'

Matthew added, trying to be polite: 'You going down to see the whales, too?'

'Nope.' Mitch shook his head, and a whole shower of firelit sparks glinted in his fair hair as he did so. 'Need a spare part for the engine. They tell me the salt fleet have a maintenance depot, and I might get what I want down there.' He was looking at Tracey in the flickering firelight, and Matthew fancied he was not quite as confident as he sounded. 'Tracey . . . couldn't we meet up some place?'

'We could not.' Her voice was flat with suppressed anger.

'Don't be mad at me,' he begged, smiling at her mutinous face.

'Go away, Mitch,' she growled. 'Go practise your charm on some other poor mutt.' She turned away to go into her tent, and Mitch got to his feet in one lithe movement and laid a sunburned, detaining hand on her arm.

Tracey reacted like a spitting cobra. 'Take your hands off me!' she hissed. 'Get lost, Mitch. Nobody wants you here. *Get*

251

lost!' And she disappeared inside her tent and zipped up the entrance smartly in his face.

Mitch looked unexpectedly shaken by this. He rubbed a rueful hand over his face and said to Matthew in an apologetic murmur: 'Sorry. I guess I spoke outa turn . . . ' and he wandered off down the beach without another word.

Matthew did not know quite what to do next. He supposed Tracey was best left alone to get over her private rage. So he sat on alone by the dying fire, and played a few more soft and dreaming phrases to the quiet night sky.

She would probably feel better in the morning.

But in the morning, Tracey was still white-faced and mono-syllabic. She got very brisk and business-like about setting off on the Fly, and then buzzed angrily down the road at a punishing pace which made Matthew's bones ache more than usual. She did not let them stop at Santa Rosarito, but forged grimly on down Highway I till they reached the 28th Parallel, where she did allow them to take a short break and a long cold drink at the hotel bar. Then it was on to Guerrero Negro, and a pause to draw breath, shake out cramped limbs, and ask the way to the whale-watch. But even here Tracey did not seem inclined to stop for long in the town, tired though she was. She pushed on down to the lagoon and followed the tourist route to the whale-watching area at its southernmost tip. It was a long way down, and both she and Matthew were almost paralyzed with weariness and stiffness when they finally arrived. But at last she stopped among the growing numbers of visiting whale-watchers camping on the shore.

Matthew was amazed by what he saw. The whole lagoon was dotted with whale heads or rising tail-flukes, long, sleek backs and small, accompanying calves. There were boats out on the water, filled with fascinated watchers, and Matthew saw one or two people lean out from their boats and actually touch the huge, barnacle-encrusted flank of a passing whale. The calm, slow-moving creatures seemed totally unafraid of the outboard motors — and of the people themselves. Since Scam-mon's Lagoon became a nature reserve and the whales were protected, they had clearly learned that this was a safe environment and they were not under threat from human beings. But Matthew wondered whether this innocent acceptance of man's goodwill ought to be encouraged. What would happen when the mothers got out to sea again on the long migration north with their unwary offspring? Might they not be less cautious, more dangerously trusting than they should be, when they came near to other boats that were not so harmless, to other men that were not so benign but still hunted the grey whales in the deep reaches of the sea?

Or, thought Matthew, remembering the fine, entangling mesh of those lethal nets he had already met, might they not even just blunder into a crippling ensnaring shroud in those smiling seas they loved?

He shuddered once, thinking of the oceans outside this charmed circle, and then fell to watching the great, placid creatures with enchanted eyes.

'Oh,' he breathed, watching in breathless amazement as a mother and baby swam quite close. 'Can we go out in a boat now?'

'You go,' said Tracey, busy with her tent. 'I want to get fixed up here.'

Matthew looked at her closed, bleak face, and decided that she still wanted to be left alone. So he went down to the next boatload and paid out some of his precious money to join the party.

The next hour was one of total enchantment for him. There was a curious serenity and patience about the great sea creatures as they lazed and swam and helped their young to the surface for their first vital breath. They were so perfectly co-ordinated and smooth in every movement — every turn and roll of their massive bodies, every lift and fall of their wide tail-flukes, every slow-drifting glide and tilting dive of their gleaming flanks in the still waters of the lagoon. Sometimes they came up within feet of the boats and seemed to eye the occupants with mild curiosity. But they never came too close or upset the boats, and they seemed totally unharassed by all the gaping faces, and totally unbelligerent in the face of all this invasion of their privacy.

Matthew was not sure in his own mind that he altogether approved of this growing invasion of the quiet lagoon. He wasn't even sure he ought to be gawping in a boat himself (though the boatman volunteered the information that tours were restricted nowadays, as were the noise levels of the outboard motors, so that the whales should not be too much disturbed). But in the face of such majesty, such pure and mighty strength, he felt very small — and somehow rather ashamed to be so intrusive. This was the mother whales' chosen breeding ground — this safe, unbroken stretch of water, enclosed and protected from the wild Pacific swell. In this sunlit, buoyant sanctuary the mothers could give birth, and their calves could grow, unmolested. Did they really not mind the boatloads of staring faces, (however restricted), the flashing cameras and sputtering engines, the excited chorus of awestruck exclamations? Wasn't it somehow a loss of dignity for the beautiful creatures to be subjected to this mindless invasion?

But then, watching the smooth, unhurried progress of those majestic blue-black shapes in the water, Matthew suddenly realized that there was no loss of dignity for them. They were too big — too powerful — for it to matter. The puny squeakings and rattlings of men did not touch them at all. They were beyond their reach. They lived in a world of deep, sounding spaces and fathomless dimensions, pursuing their own quiet lives with calm deliberation, moving in massive, undeviating strength through the ancient patterns of birth, migration, life and death as it had been laid down for them since time began when 'that great leviathan' swam in the deep. To them, Matthew supposed, the antics of these noisy tourists was no more tiresome than a flock of screaming seabirds squabbling over a shoal of fish — and rather less important.

Humbly, not looking at his fellow-watchers, Matthew stretched out a hand and touched one vast, rubbery flank as it came close. I want to tell you, he said, I don't mean to intrude. I think you are beautiful and magnificent beyond belief. Please forgive us for being so inquisitive.

But the great cetacean sailed quietly past them, its huge eye observing them with placid unconcern, and behind it swam a young calf, dutifully close to its mother's side, and neither gave any sign that they heard Matthew's plea.

My dolphins would have heard me, he said, watching with a curious sense of loss as the heedless whales sailed by. They would have answered. Flite would have come leaping to tell me he did not mind — that he was glad to see me . . .

But even so he reached out again to touch the great long back as it slid effortlessly through the translucent water, and a strange thrill of power seemed to course through his fingers from that vast, lissom bulk.

You may not be so joyous or so *amigable* as my dolphins, he said, in awe, but you have the strength and power of all the oceans in the world in your bodies, and you fill me with wonder, but I do not understand you at all!

And then the mighty tail-fluke came up and gave a gentle

twist in the air, and there was nothing left in the water but a swirl of foam and a fading blue-black shadow.

Matthew did not even notice when his boat turned for home and landed its load of bemused and enchanted passengers on the shore.

When he got back to Tracey, he saw that Mitch was there again. His fair, sunbleached head was bent close to Tracey's and he was making some kind of impassioned appeal. But Tracey did not seem impressed. She listened to him impassively, her face expressing nothing more than its usual scowl of disapproval, and gave no sign that Mitch's powers of persuasion were winning her over. All the same, Matthew reflected, she *was* listening — which was more than she had done yesterday. It occurred to him that he'd better make himself scarce — for a while at least.

He skirted the two of them silently and reached for his guitar through the tent flap before sidling off down the crowded shore to join some other American sightseers. He was almost out of sight — and earshot — when Mitch caught a glimpse of him and remarked in a rather venomous voice to Tracey: 'I hadn't realized you were into cradle-snatching.'

Matthew paused. Then he swung his guitar on to his shoulder and turned back to look at Mitch with a cool, grey-green gaze that raked him from head to toe and made him feel as if he had been dowsed in the waters of the lagoon itself.

'*Whale-watching*, Mitch. Not cradle-snatching. There is a difference.' His voice was cold. 'Though I daresay the whales have doubts about it.'

Mitch opened his mouth to answer, but Matthew forestalled him, still speaking in that light, ice-cold voice. 'They only bother with the males once, you know. After that they are perfectly self-sufficient on their own.'

He grinned at Tracey, who was looking almost as thunderstruck as Mitch. 'I might have a yen for Trace,' he admitted, smiling, 'since she's extremely yennable — but what the hell, freedom comes first. Ask the whales.'

He turned and went then, still smiling rather dangerously, leaving the other two speechless behind him.

Maybe they'll get together, he thought. And maybe they won't. But that guy Mitch has got a hell of a nerve. Perhaps that'll make him think twice . . . And meantime, it looks like an evening elsewhere for me.

He wandered down the shore-line and joined a cheerful group

of whale-watchers who were having a cook-out. They were friendly and welcoming, full of talk about the marvels they had seen, and generous with offers of slightly burnt fish and sooty burgers. Matthew unslung his guitar and began to play.

When he stopped, they looked at him with awe, and piled his plate with even more food. 'Gee,' they said. 'Guitar-players are a dime a dozen out here — but no one plays like that!'

Matthew grinned politely, and took a large bite of fish. He decided he was hungry — and wondered fleetingly if Tracey had thought of eating yet, or was she too tied up in argument with Mitch to think of anything so mundane as food?

The party round the barbecue began to sing then, and Matthew strummed along with them happily, somehow wanting to prove to them that he was not too high-powered to bother with their pop songs . . . They reminded him a bit of the yelling songs at home, and he was suddenly acutely homesick for a cool Cornish beach and Skip's crinkle-edged blue eyes and cheerful laughter . . . The beer got passed round then, and the singing went on a long time, till the fire died down and the brilliant stars of Baja garlanded the sky.

The lagoon was shadowy now, lit with faint gleams of phosphorescence where a fish jumped or a whale passed by, pushing a glinting bow-wave before it. Matthew sighed, watching the darkening water, and knew it was time to make for camp. But what camp? His sleeping bag would be inside the tent. Tracey always made a point of keeping it safely zipped away until he climbed into it — in case of scorpions and tarantulas, she said . . . But if she and Mitch were in there together, he couldn't exactly barge in and demand it . . . Well, he'd just have to lie down on the shore and hope for the best . . . But first he might as well make a quiet reconnoitre to see what was happening.

He left the singing Americans and wandered off by himself in the direction of Tracey's tent. There was a small dying fire outside it, and beside it was his sleeping bag, carefully rolled up, with a large stone on top of it. There was no sign of Tracey. Sighing with relief, he began to unwind the sleeping bag, but a sound from within the tent made him pause. It wasn't two people talking, or even two people making love — he knew what that sounded like from those early days with his mother. It was the sound of one person crying — and Tracey never cried.

He didn't know what to do. Should he ignore it? Tracey was

proud. She wouldn't like him to see her defeated by anything. But it was such a desolate sound — this low, muffled weeping — and somehow he couldn't just sit there and let it go on.

He debated within himself and then decided to make up the fire and brew some coffee in their battered camp kettle. When it was ready, he went over to the tent, pulled the zip down a little and put his head through the gap.

'Tracey? Come on out. I've made coffee.'

There was a moment's silence, and then Tracey's voice, husky and strange, came from the darkness. 'Go away.'

'No,' said Matthew, struggling to sound firm and masterful. 'Not till you've drunk this. Come on. I bet you haven't eaten anything either.'

There was a grumbling and upheaving from within, and then a dishevelled Tracey crawled out backwards and sat down by the fire, keeping her face hidden in a tangle of hair.

'Here,' said Matthew, handing her a plastic mug full of scalding coffee. 'And I saved you a couple of corn pancakes from the cook-out. I'm afraid they're a bit burnt.'

Tracey made no comment, but took both the mug and the scorched pancakes without protest.

Matthew waited till she'd begun to eat before he went into the attack. 'Trace — isn't it about time you made up your mind?'

'What?'

She looked unexpectedly young in the dim glow of the fire — young and tear-stained and terribly uncertain. Not a bit like the tough, uncompromising Tracey he knew. More like a bewildered child, adrift in a fierce and overpowering tide-race with no sense of direction at all. Terribly lost and terribly torn — and years and years younger than him.

He was suddenly enormously angry with her — and that made the whole thing a lot easier. Here am I, he thought, dying for some roots — some kind of commitment — someone in this God-awful empty world to care about — and here's this stupid girl with it all on a plate, and she won't accept it.

'I don't understand you at all,' he said, stabbing viciously at the fire with a piece of stick. 'What's wrong with second thoughts, anyway?'

Tracey was stunned by his bluntness. 'What?' she repeated, startled.

'You and Mitch.' He was too angry now to be cautious. 'I

257

don't know what's with you two — but it's obvious you both want to get together — so what's stopping you?'

'He walked out on me, remember?'

'Well, he's back, isn't he?'

'And I'm supposed to welcome him back with open arms?'

'Why not?' Matthew flung out a challenge. 'If you want him?'

She was silent, suddenly seeing a different course of action to the cold, barren one of furious pride she had set herself. Mitch? Back again in her life? . . . All the warmth and fun he had brought into her world before . . . would it be possible?

'The whales,' said Matthew, apparently speaking at random. 'You haven't even looked at them yet since we came . . . They don't go in for these tiny tantrums.'

'Tiny tantrums?'

'On their scale —' he waved a hand at the dark lagoon and the sleeping grey shapes within its quiet waters. 'You told me first, remember? . . . They choose a mate without any fuss. They swim thousands of miles to get here to have their young — and thousands of miles back again to their summer feeding grounds. They are up against huge issues of time and space — dangers and losses — whalers and drift nets. They don't waste any time arguing about whether to get together or not. Life's too short, and too precarious.'

Tracey was staring at him now as if he was a stranger. 'I've never heard you talk like that before.'

'No,' agreed Matthew flatly. 'And I don't suppose you ever will again. Got carried away. Sorry.'

'It's OK.' Tracey's voice was suddenly soft. 'You kinda made sense.'

Matthew laughed. Then he thought he'd better press home his advantage. 'Is he coming back?'

She nodded, and began to prod the fire as Matthew had done earlier. 'Tomorrow. He's waiting for that spare part. Then he has to sail the boat back to San Diego.'

'And I suppose he wants you to go too?'

Tracey sighed. 'I guess so.'

'Well, why not?'

She looked astounded. '*Why not*? What about you?'

'I'll be all right.'

'On your own?' Her tone was sharp with disbelief.

'Petra's place is only a few miles from here.'

'How will you get there?'

He grinned at her outraged face. 'Walk. Take the local bus. Hitch.'

'I suppose you could have the Fly.'

It was his turn to look astounded. 'I could not. No licence, no insurance. And anyway, I'd probably wreck it.' He glanced at her warily. 'Can't you take it on the boat?'

'Oh yes, I guess. But I don't like it.'

'Don't like what?'

'Dumping you.'

'I've told you — I'll be fine.' Matthew wondered if Tracey realized she had already made her decision. 'You got me safely here — where we meant to be. Now it's your turn to have some fun.'

'I don't know —' She sounded suddenly weary, heavy with doubt.

'Sleep on it,' said Matthew, knowing the battle won. 'And come whale-watching in the morning. It's what we came for, after all.'

'Sure,' agreed Tracey, pushing the hair out of her eyes and smiling a tired smile.

'They'll put things in perspective.'

Tracey actually laughed. 'You're quite a guy, Matt, d'you know that?'

'You're not so bad yourself,' retorted Matthew, and watched her blunder wearily away and disappear inside the tent.

It was quiet now on the shore. The lagoon lay still and dark with no moving shapes upon its surface, and above it the stars burned very bright.

Perspective, drowsed Matthew. Whales and stars. And dolphins. Dolphins, who know joy as no man ever does . . . Who make their choices without fear, and come racing towards you, alight with love and welcome . . .

A small night wind ruffled the water, and in the silence one bird called. Beyond that, nothing stirred.

★ ★ ★

In the morning, true to her word, Tracey came with Matthew to look at the whales on the first boat that went out.

She gazed in awe at the huge dark shapes and their smaller offspring swimming close beside them, and marvelled at the effortless ease with which the mothers turned their vast bulk to make a protective barrier between their newborn calves and

259

any danger that might threaten them. Like Matthew, she stretched out a hand to stroke one smooth, glistening flank as it swam close, and like Matthew she was utterly enchanted by what she saw.

When they returned to the shore, Mitch was standing there waiting for them. He looked strangely nervous and uncertain, standing there, with his blue eyes screwed up against the sun as he tried to pick out Tracey from the crowd of returning whale-watchers. And Matthew found himself liking Mitch the better for that air of doubt and uncertainty.

But Tracey did not immediately go towards him. Instead, she turned to Matthew and said simply: 'I guess you were right.'

He nodded. 'Cut us down to size, don't they?'

'They sure do.' She was looking at him now with some anxiety. 'Will you be OK?'

'Sure.'

'Get in touch when you get back?'

'Sure,' he repeated, smiling.

But she was not convinced. She reached into a pocket in her jeans and brought out some money. 'You'd better have this. I shan't be needing it now.'

'I'm all right,' protested Matthew. 'I've got enough to get to Petra's.'

'Maybe you do,' she retorted. 'But you have to get back somehow, don't you?'

Matthew saw the logic of that, but he was still reluctant.

'I'd feel better about it,' Tracey added, scowling furiously. 'Come on.' And she thrust the notes into his hand. 'You can always pay it back later,' she added, omitting to say that if he did she would at least know he had come back safely.

Matthew capitulated, and she gave him a brisk, approving nod. Then, seemingly as an afterthought, she put her arms round his neck and kissed him soundly.

Matthew blinked.

'You take care now, you hear?' she told him. 'And I hope you find what you're looking for.'

Mitch was regarding all this with some astonishment. But at last he said mildly: 'Do I take it you're coming?'

'You do,' said Tracey shortly. 'The Fly's all loaded. Get on.'

Mitch walked over to inspect the Fly, which had been left in charge of one of the boatmen, and eyed it doubtfully. 'Will it carry us both?'

'It'll get us back to the boat. What more do you want?' She climbed on and gave an imperious jerk of her head at Mitch. 'OK?'

'OK,' agreed Mitch, without much originality, and somehow folded his long legs on either side of the Fly and clasped Tracey cheerfully round the waist.

Tracey turned her head to smile at Matthew, and lifted a hand in salute. Then she kicked the engine into life, and the Fly whizzed off in a cloud of sand and desert dust.

Matthew was left standing by the shore, staring after them. He waited until they were out of sight and the noise of the Fly's engine puttered into the distance, and then he picked up his guitar, slung his sleeping bag on his back, and set off to look for a lift to the main road.

Now he was really alone.

★ ★ ★

The carload of Americans who picked him up were going back to Guerrero Negro, so Matthew went with them. He wanted to buy a few things from the store anyway, and he also wanted to ask how to get to Petra's address.

The young gang of Americans had either been drinking tequila all night or had started very early in the morning, for they were pretty drunk by now, very boisterous, and still passing the bottle round. They were also smoking rather questionable home-rolled cigarettes. They all piled out of the dust-streaked Ford and surged into the nearest café-bar. Matt went too, hoping to find someone who could point him in the direction of Bahia Tortuga.

He detached himself from his noisy companions and their cries of 'Hey, man, the party's just starting,' — and went over to talk to the Mexican behind the bar. He had just got out the bit of paper with Petra's address on it, when a fight broke out behind him. There was a crash of overturned chairs, a string of oaths, both American and Spanish, and the unmistakable sound of blows. He swung round, astonished, and the Mexican behind the bar called out to someone in the kitchens rather sharply and came round to the front, untying his apron and rolling up his sleeves, obviously preparing to throw the trouble-makers out. Matthew saw then that he was a powerful, square-cut figure, with very broad shoulders and strong-muscled arms like knotted mahogany. His face was equally tough — black

261

eyes snapping fire, black moustache bristling, black hair standing on end in a belligerent crest. As he came forward, there was another crash from the café floor.

'My guitar!' said Matthew, seeing that trouble was coming. The burly Mexican beside him grinned and seized the guitar from Matthew's hands and stowed it swiftly at the back of the long shelf behind the bar.

By this time, the fight was spreading. It had begun when one far-too-merry American boy made an amorous pass at a dark-haired Mexican girl who happened to be with her own boyfriend at the next table. Exception was taken. Insults were exchanged. The American was far too drunk to be conciliatory, and his friends rallied round him. So did the Mexican's *amigos*. The air hummed with antagonism.

'*Gringos!*' spat the Mexican. 'Who wants them?'

It seemed that no one did, for the rest of the café habitués set about throwing them out with a will. Bodies began to be hurled about in all directions. Tables turned over. Crockery flew in the air and smashed on the floor. A fighting couple lurched into Matthew and knocked him over, and as he fell he saw the sudden flash of a knife-blade in the Mexican's hand.

'Look out!' he shouted as he went down. 'He's got a knife.'

He didn't much like these loud-mouthed tourists and their loutish manners, and the present trouble was clearly their fault, but even so, he had to warn them.

However, he needn't have worried, for his tough friend from behind the bar simply chopped down with his hand once, very hard, and the glittering knife-blade clattered to the floor.

Then everything seemed to happen at once. The barman seized the fighting American by the collar and slung him out on to the street. The knife-wielding Mexican slithered past Matthew just as he was getting to his feet and shoved him down again so that he hit his head against the wooden bar rail near the floor. At the same time, he felt a hand yank swiftly at his moneybag which was hanging round his neck under his open shirt. The leather thong snapped and the hand snatched at the pouch. He put up his hands and tried desperately to hold on to it, but he was too late. My money! he thought. What shall I do?

By this time there were shouts in the street, and sirens and whistles blowing. It was clear that the fighting Americans were going to be picked up by the local police. In fact, they were fighting their drunken way straight into their hands.

Matthew got groggily to his feet, and found the grinning barman beside him. 'My moneybag!' gasped Matthew, clutching at the broken thong. 'All I possess!'

The big Mexican looked at him. '*All*?'

'All in the world,' said Matthew, appalled at the thought.

'I will get it back,' stated the barman. 'I know that one.' He paused, looking out into the street, and then turned back to Matthew urgently. 'You can play that thing?'

'My guitar? Yes.'

'Then play. Now.'

'What?' Matthew was mystified.

'Now. The police will come in here soon. You play. You are with us. Not with the other *gringos*.'

'I wasn't with them anyway. I'm English, not American.'

'*Inglés*? Good. Then you play. I get your money back — *sí*?'

'*Sí*,' agreed Matthew fervently.

It was an extraordinary scene. As soon as the offending Americans had been ejected, the Mexican customers picked up the chairs and tables, brushed off the broken crockery, and sat down again as if nothing had happened. Matthew went round behind the bar and got out his guitar. He looked inside the lid of the case where there was a small pocket, and made sure his passport and visa were still intact, breathing a small sigh of relief that he'd had the sense to hide them there. Then he got hold of a chair and a small lopsided stool, and sat down to play.

The Mexicans looked up and smiled unconcernedly and went on with their conversations and their interrupted meals. Matthew kept his head down and played. He did not look up when the local police came in, laughed with the habitués about the crazy *gringos* who drank too much tequila, asked a few cheerful questions, and went away again, still laughing.

Matthew went on playing. He had begun by feeling rather scared and shaken — the loss of his money was serious for him, and also his head still sang with the impact of that wooden rail. But as he played, the music steadied him — as it seemed to steady the other people in the café, and by the time his friend the bartender came back, Matthew was far out in de Falla, and had forgotten his own troubles.

'Here,' said the barman, and slapped down Matthew's moneybag on the table beside him. 'It is all there. Domingo did not have time to spend it. Besides, the police were outside.'

Matthew's hands faltered and slid to a stop on the strings. His smile was full of relief. 'How can I thank you?'

The big Mexican laughed. 'Hammer Gonzales, that's me.'
He held out one hard hand and gripped Matthew's thin one in
a grasp of iron.

'Is that what they call you?'

'Some people. I was a champion once.' The large grin was
back. 'And you?'

'Oh, I'm Matthew.'

'Mateo. Mateo Guitarra.' He nodded approval. 'It is good
that you kept playing. It made things — *normal*, you understand?'

Matthew understood. 'What will happen to the Americans?'

'Those *gringos*?' He shrugged. 'Perhaps a night in the *calabozo*.
Perhaps a fine. Perhaps nothing.' His square brown face was not
censorious. 'They were young — and tequila is very strong . . .
Besides, we need the tourists, whatever my friends might say.'
Here his cheerful grin faded for a moment, and he laid a brown
finger on Matthew's moneybag. 'That one — Domingo — you
must understand, he is very poor. He is also a bad one — but
it mostly because he is poor. And he thought you were with
the drunken *gringos* — to him, all *gringos* are rich.'

Matthew nodded. 'But this is not a poor town, is it?'

'No. The salt works employs many people. But there are still
fishermen — and their living depends on their catch. Sometimes
there is nothing, you understand?'

'Is it getting worse? The big factory ships—?'

'*Sí.*' He nodded a fierce and angry head at him. 'Each year
the catch is smaller.' Gonzales looked at him in some surprise.
'You know about this?'

'I have met it before — the tuna nets. The drift nets, the
purse-seines — and the dolphins.' His face was grim.

'Ah. *Los delfines*. The fishermen's luck, we call them. If they
go, the luck goes with them.'

'I know,' said Matthew. When Flite went, my luck went
with him, too . . . He could not keep the sadness out of his
voice.

'Where do you sleep tonight?' asked Gonzales suddenly.

Matthew was startled. 'Oh, I — I usually sleep on the beach.'

'But here there is no beach. Only salt pans. And the port.'
Gonzales was smiling again. 'So tonight you sleep here.' It
seemed to be a command rather than a suggestion, and Matthew
suddenly realized that Hammer Gonzales was the owner of this
café, and not just a barman at all. What's more, he seemed to
be looking at Matthew with real friendly concern.

'Where were you trying to go?'

Matthew had almost forgotten his original request. But he found the slip of paper in his pocket and held it out for Gonzales to see.

'Bahia Tortuga . . . ?' Gonzales frowned. 'That is difficult country, Viscaino. Desert country, very barren, very dangerous.'

Matthew looked obstinate. 'I've got to get there somehow.'

'Maybe there will be a fish-truck,' said Gonzales, sounding doubtful. 'I will find out for you tomorrow.' Then the doubt seemed to clear from his seamed brown face, and the wide grin returned. 'Now I think you will eat, and then you will sleep. Sí?'

Matthew put his guitar away, and found that his feet were crunching on broken crockery. 'First,' he said, 'I will sweep up. I am good at sweeping café floors. I did it in San Diego.' His grin almost matched Gonzales' as he reached out for the yellow broom standing in the corner.

'Hey, Martillo, that one can play,' said a smiling dark Mexican as Matthew passed by with the broom.

'He can,' agreed another, waving a piece of tortilla on his fork. 'Like crazy.'

'So now we feed him,' pronounced Gonzales, happily. 'You like lobster?'

'I like lobster,' agreed Matthew.

★ ★ ★

In the morning, true to his word, Gonzales found a fish-truck that was unloading and would be returning to a fish camp near Bahia Tortuga in the afternoon. Matthew was treated to another enormous meal, and escorted downtown to the fish-truck by two of Gonzales' *amigos* — since Gonzales himself had to stay and run his café He gave Matthew a hard hug round his shoulders and sent him on his way with a bag of tortillas and some oranges to keep him going, and the comforting Mexican farewell: Go with God.

Matthew climbed on board the truck among the fish-crates and boxes of stores, and settled down for a long, dusty ride.

The country they went through was extraordinary — desolate and harsh, with strange man-shaped cactus growing among the rocks and sandstrewn *arroyos*. Once or twice the truck stopped to put down some stores and a few empty crates by some pre-

arranged spot on the dirt road — and here a can of coke or a
bottle of beer would be passed round before the bone-shaking
journey continued. It seemed to go on and on through this
dried-up, featureless land, and Matthew began to wonder if it
would ever end. But at last the truck pulled up again, and this
time the driver climbed down and said to Matthew: 'We go to
the fish camp from here. The road to Tortuga is that way.'

'How far?' asked Matthew, also climbing down and looking
round at the empty landscape with some misgiving.

'About six kilometres,' said the Mexican, smiling. 'Not far.
I am sorry we do not go all the way — we have to get the
crates to the fish camp.'

'Of course,' agreed Matthew. 'It was very kind of you to
bring me all this way.' He began to fumble with his precious
moneybag, but the friendly Mexican quietly shook his head
and said:

'It was a pleasure — for a friend of Martillo's!' Then, before
Matthew could protest, he had climbed back into his truck and
begun to drive away. Hands waved, voices called, and a cloud
of dust rose in the air. When it had settled, Matthew was alone
in the desert with nothing but the lizards for company. At least,
he hoped it was only the lizards. But it was certainly rattlesnake
country, and he felt sure there were tarantulas and scorpions
or, worse still, black widows behind every stone. He kept to
the main track for this reason, and did not dare to wander into
the scrub and cactus terrain on either side, but even so he was
not vigilant enough. The rattler was lying in the middle of the
road, perfectly camouflaged, and when Matthew came within
striking range, it reared up in the midst of its own neat coils
and began hissing and spitting a furious challenge to Matthew's
approaching feet. He side-stepped very smartly, making a swift
detour through the nearby scrub and stringy grass, leaving the
rattler to hiss and rattle on its own. But as he hurried to get
past, he felt a sharp sting in his right leg, and looked down to
find a large yellow scorpion clinging to his calf. He brushed it
off in angry haste and put his foot on it. But the damage was
done.

A scorpion sting, he thought. How bad is it likely to be?
Some of them are lethal. But some aren't. I must just hope I'm
lucky — and get to Petra's place fast.

He went on walking, but his leg was beginning to swell in
an ominous fashion, and the pain was getting steadily worse
and shooting further and further up his leg. It was his bad leg

anyway. It had never quite mended straight and he still had a very slight limp when he walked, and running fast was always a bit uneven though it didn't bother him a lot. But this did bother him. The leg seemed to be going numb, and he had to drag himself along the road, forcing himself to keep going until the first little houses came in sight.

By the time he got to the little town, he was lurching and weaving on his feet and beginning to see double. He was also beginning to talk to himself, since there was no one else to tell him to keep going. He swayed blearily up to the first person he saw and held out the piece of paper, which said: 'Casa Davison, Bahia Tortuga'. He was answered with a flood of incomprehensible Spanish, and when he still looked totally bewildered (and probably very sick), he was seized by the arm and led unprotesting down the road. He scarcely saw the Mexican who was leading him — just a vague brown blur and a white hat and an equally white smile. But at the end of the street, the hand was withdrawn from his arm and the brown blur retreated, saying: 'Ahí — La Casa Davison.'

Matthew took a couple of blundering steps forward and saw a pinkish wall, a dusty courtyard and an open door. 'Petra?' he croaked. 'Petra? Are you there?' And before anyone could answer, he passed out cold on the courtyard floor.

★ ★ ★

When Harvey, the solicitor, reported back the news that Matthew had gone missing, the old Captain was very angry. But, characteristically, he did not waste time on recriminations. Instead, he went into swift and decisive action.

First of all, he rang Skip in Cornwall. 'Have you any idea,' he said, 'what or who this friend in Baja California might be?'

There was a slight pause at the other end, and then Skip's voice answered cautiously: 'Yes. I think it is probably Petra — Petra Davison, the marine biologist. I gave him her address.'

'Davison?' barked the Captain. 'Did you say Davison?'

There was another pause, and then Skip said mildly: 'It's a common enough name — but she's pretty well known in her own field.'

'Yes. Of course.' The sharp note disappeared from his voice. 'And she lives in Baja California?'

'Her work takes her all over the world. But she has a base there.'

'I see. How did Matthew come to know her?'

'Through me. She was — very kind to him when he was here last summer.'

'What was *she* doing here?' The sharp note was back in his voice.

'A survey on the seal colonies. And she got interested in Matthew's dolphin.'

'I see,' said the Captain again — and then there was an electric silence while he indulged in swift and furious thought. 'Skip,' he said at last, 'how busy are you?'

'Fairly,' Skip answered, not knowing what was coming. 'Nothing that won't keep, though,' he added, wanting to sound helpful.

'Could you go out there?'

'Out where?'

'To Baja California. To this address, wherever it is.'

Skip's unruly heart did a double flip of hope. *Go and see Petra?* You bet he would. 'I could,' he said cautiously.

'All expenses paid,' pursued the Captain, pressing it home.

'I'd have to make a few arrangements first.'

'How long would that take you?'

'Couple of days.'

'Heathrow, three days from now?'

'All right.' Skip tried to control his excited breathing and sound as cool as the Captain.

'I'll get Harvey on to it. He'll be in touch.'

'Right.'

'And Skip —'

'Yes?'

'Bring him back safe.'

'Of course.'

'I don't know why,' grumbled the Captain, suddenly sounding human, 'but I find I've got mysteriously fond of the boy.'

'Yes,' agreed Skip, smiling over the phone. 'So have I.'

★　★　★

When Matthew woke, he was lying in a hammock on someone's verandah, and a woman's face was looking down at him. But it wasn't Petra's.

'Who?' he whispered, finding his throat dry and fiery and his voice gone.

The face smiled. It was dark and plumpish and rather

pretty — especially with the smile lighting it and the long dark hair surrounding it in a black and lustrous frame. 'I am Mariana,' she said. 'The Flying Sams will be here soon.'

'Flying —?'

'Sams. They are doctors. They will make you well.' Her English was easy enough, he thought, but heavily accented, and she seemed determined to keep things simple and direct. 'Was it a snake?' asked the gentle voice, sounding a little more insistent now in spite of its lilting cadence.

'No,' he muttered. 'Scorpion.'

There was silence for a moment, and a quiet hand came out and brushed the hair off his forehead. 'Do not worry,' she said. 'They will know what to do.'

'Will they?' It all seemed a bit too much for Matthew and he shut his eyes and tried to marshal his drifting thoughts.

'Go back to sleep,' she said.

Matthew did.

★ ★ ★

The next time he woke, there were voices near him, and a tall, bearded man was leaning against a pink brick pillar, watching him. He reminded Matthew vaguely of someone, but he couldn't think who. There was another, younger man standing beside Matthew's hammock and holding a syringe in his hand.

'Just a little prick,' he said. 'Soon have you right.'

Matthew submitted, hoping it was true. He didn't feel right at all at the moment, he had to admit. He tried to smile his thanks, but his face felt all stiff and swollen, so it came out rather crooked. 'Sorry —' he murmured.

'What for?' said the young doctor, smiling back. 'I don't suppose you got stung by a scorpion on purpose.'

'No,' agreed Matthew, and failed to say any more.

The young Flying Sam turned to the bearded man and said cheerfully: 'That'll fix him. Swelling will go down by tomorrow or next day.'

'Any ill effects?'

'No. He'll be fine. He's got the resilience of youth on his side.'

'I wish I had,' said the bearded man, and the young doctor laughed.

The voices receded then, and Matthew fell into a dark hole of sleep.

269

After that there were several other times when Mariana's face swam into focus, but Matthew couldn't keep track of them. He swallowed cold drinks obediently, and drifted off again while deft hands did soothing things with cool sponges and soft, enveloping towels . . . His leg didn't seem to hurt any more. He could scarcely feel it at all. But he was hot. Terribly hot, and terribly thirsty.

'Just a little,' said Mariana's gentle voice. 'Sip it slowly . . . Now you can sleep again.'

Fiery oblivion claimed him. But in the night it was suddenly cool, and he woke briefly to see stars in a dark sky beyond the verandah pillars. There was a small night breeze on his face, and it felt wonderful. Then he sank into dream again.

★ ★ ★

In the morning — he knew it must be morning because the sun was just rising — he woke with a clear head and a thousand questions waiting to be answered.

He tried sitting up in the hammock, and found himself looking at the same bearded man, now spread out in a basket chair on the verandah and watching him with observant, tired grey eyes.

'Ah,' he said. 'You're awake.'

'Just about,' admitted Matthew, and then added somewhat shyly: 'Sorry to cause so much trouble.'

The man smiled. It was a sudden transformation, lifting the harsh outlines of his face to a curious sweetness, and it made Matthew blink. 'No trouble,' he said. '*De nada*. But perhaps you can tell me why you asked for Petra?'

'D-doesn't she live here?'

'No. I live here.'

Matthew looked confused. 'And you are —'

'Martin Davison — Petra's father.'

'Oh, I see,' breathed Matthew, though he was even more confused than before. 'But — doesn't she come here?'

'Not very often these days,' sighed Davison. Then, seeing Matthew's disappointment, he added quickly: 'But as a matter of fact, we are expecting her soon.' The intelligent grey eyes were regarding him steadily. 'How did you come to know my daughter?'

Matthew rubbed a bewildered hand over his face before replying: 'It's a long story —'

'We've got all day,' said Davison, smiling. He stretched out his long legs in a lazy sprawl and prepared to listen.

But Matthew seemed to find it hard to begin, so he prompted him gently, getting down to essentials. 'First of all, shouldn't we contact your family?'

'I haven't any family,' said Matthew coldly.

Martin Davison blinked. 'No parents?'

'No.'

'How come?'

'They . . . died in a fire.' And I failed to save them, he thought. It still hurt him when he remembered it.

Martin made no comment on this. But he did not miss the sudden look of stress in Matthew's eyes. Instead, he pursued essentials. 'Relations?'

Matthew hesitated. 'One — in San Diego. That's why I came out here.'

'And?'

'It didn't work out.'

'Wouldn't they want to know you were safe?'

'No.' Matthew's tone was so uncompromising that Martin decided to leave it.

'OK,' he said mildly. 'Now, about Petra — where does she come into it?'

'Well, after the accident —'

'What accident?'

'The fire — I told you.'

'No, you didn't.' Martin was patient. 'But you can tell me now — from the beginning.'

So Matthew told him most of it, including his marvellous friendship with Flite the dolphin, and Petra's concern that he shouldn't get too attached to him.

'We have dolphins here,' said Martin. 'Lots of them. You can go swimming in a day or two.' But somehow, he understood that however friendly the Pacific dolphins were, they would not be the same as Flite.

'What was the name of this place in Cornwall?' he asked, almost idly.

'It's only a small place along the coast — but it has a wide sandy bay and wonderful surf. That's why there's an Aqua Club there. It's called Porthgwillick.'

271

There was a moment's stunned silence, and then Martin repeated in a shock-ridden voice: '*Porthgwillick Strand*?'

'Yes. D'you know it?' Matthew looked at Martin Davison in surprise. It seemed to him that the friendly, bearded man at his side had gone visibly pale beneath his Mexican tan.

But he did not answer Matthew's question directly. Instead, he went on in a bemused voice: 'And — this old Captain who befriended you — what was his name?'

'St George. Verney St George.'

This time the silence was so long that Matthew was almost scared. 'It can't be,' murmured Martin. He seemed to be in the grip of something like anger, and he turned on Matthew with sudden violence. 'You come here out of the blue, asking for Petra, and you're all mixed up with that — that wicked old man.'

'What is it?' said Matthew. 'What have I said? The old Captain isn't wicked. He was very kind to me.'

Martin's mouth was set in a hard, thin line. 'He must have changed a lot then.' He still seemed to be seething with anger, but at the sight of Matthew's bewilderment, he softened a little and ran a distracted hand across his face. 'I'm sorry, Matthew. It's an old story. Not your fault.'

'Maybe not,' said Matthew slowly, 'but I think you'd better tell me. It was one of the things I wanted to ask Petra — what to do about the Captain.'

'Why Petra?' he asked swiftly. 'Did she know him?'

'No, I don't think so.'

'Didn't they — run across each other in such a small place?' His voice was curiously insistent, still laced with inexplicable anger.

'No,' repeated Matthew slowly. 'He did come down to the Club the night I was playing . . . but Petra and Skip stayed at the back. I remember thinking they were being a bit — unapproachable. And then they went out and walked off down the beach.'

Martin was staring at him. 'Close, were they? Petra and this Skip fellow?'

'You could say that,' agreed Matthew, smiling a little.

But Martin was not smiling. 'So they didn't meet?' he persisted.

'Who?'

'Petra and your Captain.'

'No.' Matthew shifted uneasily in his restricting hammock,

and then got out on rather shaky legs and squatted down on the floor beside Martin's basket chair. 'Please,' he said. 'I've upset you somehow. Tell me what it's all about.'

There was a long pause, and then Martin made up his mind. 'All right.' He gave Matthew a crooked, pain-washed smile, and then added, almost to himself: 'I don't suppose Petra gave you this address for nothing . . .'

Matthew looked startled, but he only prompted gently: 'So what happened?'

Martin took a deep breath. 'When I was young, I was a struggling painter. Well, I still am now, come to that. But now I do a few other things as well.' He took another breath, obviously finding it hard to recount this story. 'I went down to Porthgwillick to paint seascapes for the tourists. I did quite well in the summer — though it was a precarious living. Still, I loved the sea, and I was quite happy to be poor. Then I met this girl.' For a moment he was silent again, a flood of memory transforming that painfilled smile into one of extraordinary tenderness. 'She was very young, very beautiful — and very headstrong. Needless to say, we fell in love.' He glanced at Matthew half-humorously. 'She was a bit of a mystery, young Klytie. Staying at the hotel with her father, but she would never let me meet him. We used to meet on the beach and wander off for miles along the sands — and then she would slip off back to the hotel without a word. Almost as if she was afraid of being discovered.' He sighed again. 'She was, of course.'

'Was what?'

'Afraid. It turned out that her father was a shipping magnate — very rich and very possessive. He sent all her boyfriends packing, in case they were fortune hunters.'

Matthew grinned. 'So she kept you secret?'

'As long as she could, yes. She told me he used to come to Porthgwillick with her mother when she was alive, and it was a sort of annual pilgrimage. Also, he had wanted a boy to inherit his shipping empire, and she was a girl, which was a big disappointment to him.'

'Couldn't she go into the business?'

'Oh yes. She was under a lot of pressure to do so. But she hated the wheeling and dealing. She wanted to escape.'

Matthew looked at him sympathetically. 'With you?'

'Just so.' Martin's smile had faded now, and there was a grim slant to the line of his mouth. 'I was romantic enough to want

273

to see him and ask to marry her. She refused to let me. In the end, of course, he found out, and then I saw him with a vengeance. He bawled me out — forbade me to see her — locked Klytie in her hotel room and booked a flight to Paris.'

Matthew whistled. He recognized the autocratic hand of his old Captain now — and he could just see him barking orders and over-riding other people's objections.

'What did you do?'

'Eloped,' said Martin, half-smiling again. 'The real, traditional McCoy. She climbed out of her window and we fled. We got married and went to America, where I had an offer of a lectureship at a minor university. It was a living — though not what she was used to. But she never complained.'

'And — and Captain St George?'

'He never forgave her. She wrote to him several times. He never answered. When Petra was born, she wrote again. Still no answer.' Anger had crept back into his voice. 'And when she got ill — terminally ill, I mean — I wrote to him, begging him to send her a word, anything, to put her mind at rest. But there was no reply.'

Matthew gave a soft exclamation of disbelief. 'Are you sure it ever reached him? It doesn't sound like the Captain — well, not like he is now.'

Martin shrugged. 'How can I tell? He never forgave her. And I'll never forgive him.'

Matthew swore to himself, inwardly cursing these proud, angry grown-up people who wrecked each other's happiness and behaved like obstinate children. Like Jampy in a tantrum . . . Tiny tantrums again, he thought, remembering Tracey and the grey whales of Guerrero Negro. 'It's not like him,' he repeated. 'He's old now, and lonely and sad . . . I should think he probably regrets what happened as much as you do.'

'Maybe.' The grimness did not leave Martin's voice. 'But it's too late now.'

'Not for Petra,' said Matthew. 'She's his grand-daughter, isn't she?'

Martin frowned. 'I can't understand what she was doing in Porthgwillick. It can't have been by chance.'

'There was the seal colony,' Matthew reminded him. 'She was under orders, I think. And maybe she just wanted to see for herself.'

'But you say she didn't meet him.'

274

'No.' He was looking at Martin rather hard. 'Perhaps she thought you'd disapprove?'

'Possibly.' He was giving nothing away.

'Feuds are stupid,' muttered Matthew, only half aware that he had spoken aloud. He got to his feet and stood looking out at the sea beyond the pink-washed stones of the little courtyard. There are dolphins out there, he thought. Dolphins — laughing and diving. They don't have feuds.

'Where does Mariana come in?' he asked suddenly. 'She's been wonderful to me.'

'My second wife? She's been wonderful to me, too,' smiled Martin, seeming thankful to lighten the mood. 'I came down here to Baja when Klytie died. Petra was away at college, so I was pretty damn lonely . . . I do a bit of painting, and a bit of boat-building. I'm what they call "*Presidente*" of the inshore fishermen's collective here, which means I argue a bit for them about pirate factory ships, and quotas and so on . . . ' He paused, glancing at Matthew almost apologetically somehow. 'And Mariana runs the only *tortilleria* hereabouts. She's famous for her lobster *burritos*.'

Matthew looked hopeful. 'I'd like to try one of those.'

'So you shall,' said Martin, easing himself out of his chair in one supple movement and coming to stand beside Matthew. 'Right now. We've talked long enough. *Mariana?*'

There was an answering cheerful shout from the kitchen, and Martin turned with an arm round Matthew's shoulders and led him into the house.

★　★　★

Petra laid down her clipboard on the gunnel of the small boat, and signalled to the smiling Mexican to head back to shore. She had almost finished the Guerrero Negro whale count — but this time she had found it curiously disturbing. The great, placid creatures swimming with such calmness and patience beside their growing calves somehow seemed to shame her. They were both a reproach and a challenge.

She had made this journey down the Pacific coast of Baja to pursue her researches on whale populations several times before — both in Guerrero Negro and in Magdalena Bay. And each time she had been filled with wonder and admiration by the gentle, majestic cetaceans. But somehow this year she felt even closer to them than usual, and their bright, observant eyes

275

seemed to consider her incuriously and find her of no particular importance or significance in their long saga of birth and growth and death and endless journeying across the watery wastes of the world. She felt humbled by their vast indifference — humbled and rather small, her own preoccupations trivial and somewhat foolish in the face of their untiring strength and endurance.

I must put my life in order, she thought, and make a few decisions. It is time I stopped being so inadequate . . .

She put her notes away in her duffel bag, together with her precious camera, and went off to borrow a jeep from the whale research team. There was time to drive out through the Viscaino peninsula and visit her father before going on to Magdalena Bay. But a family visit brought its own hazards, and her thoughts drifted to a certain small bay in Cornwall, and that lonely old man she could not talk to — and another man, not nearly so old but just as lonely, who looked at her out of blue, blue eyes and said no word of reproach when she went away.

Cursing a little at her own weakness, she let in the gear and bumped away down the desert road to Baya Tortuga. It was a spine-jolting journey, as usual, and she parked the jeep near the pink wall of the villa and climbed out stiffly. But when she walked into the little courtyard, she found herself staring at a thin brown boy who was sitting on the verandah steps and smiling at her in extraordinary relief and gladness.

'*Matthew*?' she said, astonished.

'I knew you'd come,' he answered, and came down the steps to meet her in a rush of welcome.

'What are you doing here?' She laid down her bag and returned his impulsive hug.

'Waiting for you, of course.'

She looked at him and smiled. 'I see. Is my father here?'

'Yes.' His expression changed and became hesitant and apologetic. 'And I think I should tell you — I've rather spilt the beans about the Captain — and Skip.'

Petra's expression changed too, but Matthew thought it seemed to reflect relief rather than anger. 'It's about time —' she murmured. 'I should've done it long ago . . . ' She rubbed a dusty hand over her face and sat down on the step. 'Come on. Tell me what's been happening. Better know the worst before I see him.'

So Matthew sat down beside her and did his best to explain what had been happening. It occurred to him then that he had been telling his story rather too often, to various interested

276

parties, and he wondered if he was becoming far too self-centred, and possibly a bit of a whinger? . . .

But before he could finish recounting his adventures since leaving San Diego, Mariana rushed out of the house and embraced Petra with enormous enthusiasm, and then went running back to fetch Martino, who was in his studio painting, but he wouldn't mind being interrupted for this!

Petra and Matthew looked at one another in some doubt.

'Will he be angry?' asked Matthew.

Petra shrugged. 'He may. But I'm a big girl now, Matthew. He can't tell me what to do any more.'

Matthew nodded agreement, but he saw trouble ahead. 'Shall I go?' he asked.

'No!' Her answer was swift. 'Stay there. I may need you.'

Almost at once, Martin came striding out of the house, wiping his hands on a paintstreaked rag smelling of turpentine. 'Petra!' He gave her a swift, affectionate hug, and then held her back to look at her. 'You've been holding out on me.'

She sighed and shook her head, so that the blonde, sun-gilded hair swung and glinted in the light. 'Not intentionally, Pa. It just — kind of happened.'

'*Happened*? You couldn't have gone to Porthgwillick by accident.'

'No. Of course not. Though, actually, it came up on my schedule — several years ago.'

'*Several years ago?*' He sounded downright dangerous.

'Yes. We do a seal colony count every few years, around the coast . . . But when I saw the name, naturally I wanted to go and have a look.' She was still looking straight at her father, appeal in her glance, and Matthew suddenly realized how alike they were, father and daughter. The same straight, determined mouth with a hidden quirk of tenderness at the edges, and the same wide, far-seeing eyes . . .

But she was speaking again, softly, directly to her father. 'You've talked about it so much — the place where you and Ma first met. Of course I was curious.' She paused, and then added: 'I didn't know the old man still went back there — every year. Not till Skip told me.'

Her father's eyes seemed to change a little, and flecks of light began to dance in them deep down. 'Ah yes, Skip. Where does he come into the picture?'

'Quite a lot,' said Petra, with a smiling, sidelong glance at

Matthew. 'Since I've been back to Porthgwillick each year —
he's become fairly important.'

'I see I'm way behind the times,' grumbled Martin, ruffling
his own hair up the wrong way because he badly wanted to
ruffle his daughter's. 'You didn't actually meet the old man?'
he suddenly shot at her.

She stared at him, startled. 'No. No, I didn't.'

'Why not?'

She hesitated and then said mildly: 'Because I didn't know
what to say to him. And because I knew you'd disapprove.'
She sighed again. 'But now —'

'Yes? Now?' His voice was harsh.

Again, appeal was in her glance, and in her voice. 'He's old,
Pa. Old and ill — and lonely.' She turned suddenly to Matthew.
'Isn't he? You told me he was lonely.'

'Yes,' agreed Matthew slowly. 'A lonely, sad old man.' He
glanced at Martin. 'I told your father, too.'

Martin swore softly. 'You can't sentimentalize over that —
that monster.'

'Why not?' Petra's head went up in a kind of challenge. 'It's
all so long ago, Pa. The past is past. Can't you see that?'

'No!' snapped Martin. 'I can only see how much he hurt
your mother.'

Petra laid a slim brown hand on his arm. 'She'd forgiven
him — years ago. I know, because she used to talk about him
to me. She never held grudges.'

Martin was silent, arrested by her words. Had he, indeed,
gone on too long in his mind with the old feud, the old pattern
of bitterness and pain and useless pride?

'Well,' he said awkwardly. 'I can't tell you what to do. But
I want no part of it. Understand?' And he went back into his
studio at the far end of the house, and slammed the door.

Petra looked after him sadly.

But Mariana came back, smiling, and said: 'He will come
round. I am making lobster soufflé this time.'

'Anyone would come round for that,' grinned Matthew.

And Petra laughed.

★   ★   ★

In the morning, Matthew went down to the beach for a swim.
He wanted to get his mind clear before he talked to Petra —

though it wasn't too easy with her being so golden and so friendly.

There was quite a swell on the sea, since there had been a storm in the night, and the surf was pounding in and breaking against the rocks in vast, creamy cascades.

I mustn't go out too far, he thought. Not in that sea. And anyway, there are probably sharks. But I want to see whether the dolphins are there.

He stood for a moment looking out across the tumbling waters of the bay, and sure enough there were the dolphins, leaping and diving round the fishing boats clustered not far out round a shoal of fish that seemed to have been driven inshore by the storm. There was a cloud of sea-birds wheeling over-head, and the sea seemed to be alive with glinting fish and the silvery undersides of airborne dolphins.

I wish they'd come here, thought Matthew, plunging into the sea and promptly getting knocked down by a towering wave . . . But they are too busy chasing fish to bother with me . . .

He got beyond the line of surf and swam quietly about in the shallows. And presently, two blue-black shapes did leave the teeming fishing grounds and cut through the water to inspect this new intruder in their territory. They swam round Matthew in close, inquisitive circles, and then — deciding he was harmless — leapt in the air and laughed at him in the sun.

'Oh,' he murmured aloud in a watery voice: 'Aren't you beautiful! . . . And, yes, I know the world is beautiful, too, and I am alive, like you — today!'

Today — today, echoed the dolphins, diving deep and coming up in smiling arabesques right beside him. Watch us leap! Watch us fly! Watch us flash like swordblades in the sound-ing seas! Watch us dance with joy!

I'm watching, said Matthew, enchanted. I suppose you haven't seen Flite anywhere about?

But the dolphins did not answer. Joy, joy! they repeated to him in silent ecstasy, and leapt in shining arcs out of the water — a shimmer of gold and blue. Then they turned in one fluid movement and headed away out to sea.

Sighing a little, Matthew turned for the shore — but some of their brilliant, unquenchable joy seemed to cling to him as he swam, and would not be denied. When he emerged from the surf and stumbled up the sand, he found Petra waiting for him.

279

'Did you see them?' He was breathless and glowing.

Petra was smiling, her eyes crinkled against the morning sun. 'I did. Aren't you lucky?'

'What were they, could you tell?'

'Spinners, I think — though there are quite a lot of bottle-nose round this coast, too.'

'Like Flite?' He was staring out at the sunlit Pacific, his expression wistful.

Petra's smile grew gentle. 'D'you still miss him?'

Matthew nodded, sighing. 'Daft, isn't it? . . . I don't suppose I'll ever see him again.'

She was looking at him thoughtfully now, perhaps finding the opening she had been waiting for. 'They do sometimes come back to old haunts.'

Matthew was still staring at the sea. 'I met a fisherman — near Tijuana. He said that.'

'Said what?'

'I might find Flite if I went back.' ('*If he loves you, he will come.*')

'Will you go back?'

He turned his head and met her challenging glance. This was the crunch, he thought. And he didn't know the answer. 'I don't know . . . As a matter of fact, I came down here to ask you what to do.' His smile was shy.

'Why me?' She sounded genuinely surprised.

'Well, I was coming down to see the whales, and Skip had given me your address.' He was floundering a little. 'And I — you always seemed so cool, so certain of your direction . . .'

'Oh, *Matthew*!' She was laughing at him. 'If you only knew!'

He laughed too, still sounding shy and breathless. 'Aren't you certain?'

'Not any more.'

'That makes two of us.'

They looked at each other in friendly sympathy. Then Petra pursued it further. 'What exactly do you want to know?'

'As a matter of fact,' he was a bit wary now, 'I wanted to know what to do about the Captain.'

She sighed. 'Ironic, isn't it? I don't know what to do about him either.' She paused, and then added: 'But why are you hesitating?'

'Because he's been very good to me,' Matthew explained, 'and I owe him a lot. I think he'd like me to go and work for him — he as good as said so. I understand his computer system now — and I could probably get to be quite useful to him. It's a wonderful opportunity, I know. But —'

'But?'

'I don't really want to.'

Petra was regarding him with a kind of attentive sadness. 'History repeating itself.' Then she gave another gentle prod. 'So what *do* you want to do?'

He seemed to flush under his tan and then go rather pale, the shyness more pronounced than ever. 'I want to be a marine biologist — like you.'

She looked at him very straight. 'Why?'

He did not know how to explain to her that it wasn't just a whim, born out of a schoolboy crush, but something real and serious that he had been thinking about ever since he left Cornwall. So he just gazed back at her helplessly and said: 'Because it's the only way.'

'The only way for what?'

'To save them. The dolphins — and the whales. All of them. It isn't any good just going on demos and shouting. I've tried it . . . You've got to have —' He was floundering again, shaken by her clear, probing gaze.

'Knowledge?' she said gently. 'Authority?'

'Exactly. Then people will listen to you.'

She laughed. 'That's what *you* think!' Then she saw that he was serious, and was moved to warn him. 'It will take a long time.'

'I don't care how long it takes.'

Her smile came out again like the sun. 'Good. Well then, let's be practical. It'll mean A-levels — university — post-grad research and so on. How will you live?'

Matthew shrugged. 'I haven't a clue. I suppose the State would keep me — just. I'd get a full grant, wouldn't I?' He looked rather hesitantly at Petra. 'The old Captain would probably stake me — he's like that. But I — I'd have to work for him in between to pay it off.'

Petra nodded. 'You don't like charity much, do you?'

'Not much. I've had rather a lot of it lately.'

Her smile was almost tender now. 'I wouldn't say that. You seem pretty independent to me.' Then she went on more slowly: 'But as to the Captain — do you realize I have the same problem?'

'Why?' Matthew failed to follow.

'If I tell him I'm his grand-daughter, it looks as if I'm claiming

281

to be his heir. And he's very rich.' She paused, and then added half under her breath: 'And Skip hates money.'

Matthew opened his eyes very wide, but he did not dare to comment. Did that mean that she and Skip —? He didn't know — and he supposed it wasn't his business. But all the same, he was fond of Skip. He would like to see him happy. And the old Captain too, come to that.

'You've got to tell him,' he said suddenly.

'Who?'

'The Captain.'

'Have I?'

'You know you have.' He looked quite fierce. 'You can't let him die not knowing.'

She shook her head, and the sun made sparks in her hair. 'I don't know . . . It's all so complicated.'

'No, it isn't,' snapped Matthew. 'It's dead simple. You're his family. He needs you.'

He did not say: I wish to God I had some family that needed me. But it was somehow clear to Petra in his bleak, accusing glance, and she felt ashamed. This boy, she thought, with no roots and no support from anyone, coming to me for guidance when I can't even guide myself. He's already got his priorities right. Why can't I? Oh Skip, I wish you were here to tell me what to do.

A movement on the empty beach caught her eye and she looked up, startled. As if in answer to her thoughts, she saw a tall, sun-bronzed figure coming towards her over the sand. 'I don't believe it,' she murmured. 'It can't be.'

But Matthew had seen it too, and he was on his feet and running. 'Skip! What on earth are you doing here?'

'I might ask you the same question,' growled Skip, returning Matthew's wild hug with enthusiasm. But his blue eyes, above Matthew's head, went straight to Petra. She had risen too, and was coming more slowly towards him, but there was such a radiance of welcome in her face that he could not mistake its meaning. And then, all of a sudden, she was running too, and they were all embracing and laughing together.

It's all right, thought Skip thankfully. Matthew's safe, and Petra's glad to see me. Mission accomplished.

'I was just thinking of you,' murmured Petra into a brown shoulder.

'Hoped I'd find you here,' countered Skip, into a dazzle of sungilded hair.

Matthew, seeing how things were, thought it was time he sloped off somewhere. He disentangled himself from the general embrace and began to stroll off up the beach.

'Hey!' called Skip. 'Don't you dare disappear just when I've found you. The Captain will kill me.'

Matthew paused in his stride. 'The Captain?'

'Of course.' Skip kept an arm round Petra while he spoke. 'He sent me after you. Who else?'

The Captain again, thought Petra. He comes into everything. I've got to make up my mind. But Skip's here now. It will be all right.

Matthew saw the doubt flash into her eyes, and knew the cause. He turned away again and called over his shoulder: 'I'll be up at the house.' Better give them time to sort things out. Skip would know what to do.

Behind him, the two pairs of eyes met, and Skip said softly: 'Lots to tell you.'

'So have I,' murmured Petra.

★   ★   ★

'I don't know how it is,' grumbled Martin Davison, glaring cheerfully around at everyone as they all sat over a late breakfast on the verandah, 'but I seem to have gone wrong somewhere in my calculations.'

'Why, Pa?' asked Petra, passing a dish of mouthwatering *chilaquiles* to Matthew.

'She asks me why!' he groaned, casting a despairing glance to heaven. 'I come down here for peace and quiet, and buy the smallest house I could find on the remotest piece of coastline in the whole of Baja — and what happens? People descend on me from every side. It's like Piccadilly Circus.'

'Sorry,' said Matthew and Skip at the same time, and both with their mouths full. And both smiling.

'I hate to add to your tally of uninvited guests,' said a new voice from below the verandah, 'especially as I haven't come from anything like so far as they have. But you're right about it being remote!'

Matthew got swiftly to his feet. He knew that voice — soft-spoken and quietly humorous, but somehow steel-strong underneath, and with a faint hint of menace if pushed. 'Commander Morris,' he said, and looked from him to Skip and Petra, and then to Martin and Mariana in dismay. What would

283

they think, with him being pursued all the way to Bahia Tortuga by Security? He turned back to Morris, disbelief clear in his face. 'I can't be that important.'

'Of course not,' agreed Morris smoothly. 'I am on leave at present. Purely unofficial.'

'You can hardly say you were just passing,' retorted Matthew.

'Scarcely,' Morris agreed, smiling. 'Let us say, I had time to spare.'

'I'm glad somebody has,' growled Martin, not sure where this new guest fitted into the picture.

Morris climbed the verandah steps and held out a friendly hand, exerting all his considerable charm. 'I'm sorry to intrude. I was just a bit anxious about our friend, Matthew.'

'Why?' Martin was melting under the charm, but trying not to show it. Mariana was melting even more, and trying to show it for all she was worth.

Morris grinned, and lifted his hands in a curiously Mexican gesture of mock despair. 'Well, look at it from my point of view. After the dolphin demo — no doubt Matthew has told you about that — I go to see his aunt Della, and she doesn't know where he is, or even that he has taken off on a moped with his friend, Tracey. She only knows he has "gone to see a friend in Baja California". Then I hear that the girl, Tracey, has abandoned him in Guerrero Negro and gone off on a yacht with a man called Mitchell Anstey — who we also know quite a lot about.'

Matthew looked at him sharply. 'But she didn't abandon me,' he protested, all loyal indignation. 'He was her boyfriend. I told her to go.'

The shrewd grey eyes fixed on Matthew's face seemed to soften a little. But Morris made no comment about that. Instead, he went on quietly: 'The next thing I hear, he's got mixed up in a fight in a café somewhere, and then he's gone off with a crowd of Mexicans in a fish-lorry to the Viscaino desert, and last of all, the Flying Sams report they've just treated a very sick English boy out there for a scorpion sting.' There was a stunned silence round the table. 'You must admit it sounded a bit alarming,' he said mildly, 'so I decided to come and have a look for myself — in case he was still in trouble.'

'It was very good of you,' began Matthew, wishing not for the first time that they would all leave him alone to manage his own life and make his own mistakes. 'But I —'

'Oh, I can see you are all right now,' admitted Morris, smiling again. There was more than a spark of mischief in his glance this time. 'Let me guess. (I know most of Matthew's story, you see,' he confided to Martin by way of aside.) 'This must be your friend Petra, the marine biologist?'

'It is.' Petra couldn't help smiling this morning anyway, and she turned the full light of her present happiness on him.

Morris blinked. 'And — am I right in thinking this is Skip, the swimming therapist from Cornwall?'

'You are,' answered Skip, who seemed to be just as unable to stop smiling as Petra. The joy that burned between these two was almost palpable, and it made Morris feel old.

He blinked again. 'But you —?' he turned back courteously to Martin and Mariana.

'Davison. Petra's father,' said Martin. 'And my wife, Mariana, who, I am sure, is dying to offer you coffee and some fresh tortillas.'

It became quite a party then, with everyone explaining things to everyone else, and Mariana in her element dispensing food to anyone who would eat it, and more and more coffee to all the talkers before they went hoarse.

Finally, Skip said: 'I must telephone England. Can I do that here?'

Martin gave a rather Mexican shrug. 'You'll be lucky. There is a *caseta de teléfono* in the village, but international calls are rather beyond it, I fear. The delays are frightful.' He shrugged again. 'I don't bother any more.'

Morris looked at Martin Davison thoughtfully, and wondered why he was being obstructive. 'Maybe the salt works people in Guerrero Negro would have a decent exchange,' he suggested. 'I'm sure they'd oblige. They were very helpful to me.'

'In what way?' asked Martin, still sounding faintly belligerent.

'Lent me a four-wheel drive,' said Morris. He lifted a humorous eyebrow at Skip and added: 'How did you get out here?'

'Jeep-taxi,' answered Skip, blushing a bit at such extravagance. He still didn't like wasting the Captain's money, but somehow time had seemed important.

'I could drive you back to Guerrero Negro,' offered Morris.

'No.' It was Petra who sounded belligerent this time. 'I've got a borrowed jeep too. But we'll try the local *caseta* first.' She turned to go, with Skip beside her, and called over her shoulder: 'You coming, Matthew?'

He hesitated, but seeing the summer lightning glancing between those two, he shook his head. 'No. You go. I'll wait here.'

'No more taking off,' growled Skip, his deep voice somehow vibrant with unquenchable happiness.

'As if I would,' protested Matthew, all injured innocence, and everyone laughed.

When they had gone, he turned back to the others and said, almost crossly: 'I can't understand why everyone is so bothered about me.'

'Nor can I,' smiled Morris. 'But it seems, we are.' His eyes met Martin's, and he went on, with elaborate courtesy: 'Do you mind if I hang on a bit? I fancy I might be able to be of some assistance. After all, communications are my specialty.'

Martin smiled back and shrugged yet again, using the old Mexican phrase: 'My house is yours', but with rather less grace than most hospitable Mexicans.

Matthew was a little embarrassed by all these hidden tensions, and said to distract them: 'Can someone please tell me about the Flying Sams? Everyone keeps talking about them, and I know they more-or-less saved my life — but who are they?'

It was Martin who answered. 'They are a group of mobile doctors —'

'And nurses, and dentists,' interrupted Mariana in her lilting English. 'They cured my toothache.'

Martin smiled at her affectionately. 'So they did.' He turned back to Matthew. 'They fly about Baja dealing with emergencies in remote places, and they've started up clinics in various out-of-the-way communities. Very useful, very dedicated. Much needed out here.'

'How do they finance it?'

'Donations. Sharing expenses. They are all volunteers who give one weekend a month to the people of Baja — mostly based on San Quintin and El Rosario, but they will fly to almost anywhere so long as there is a landing strip. You were lucky there's one out here.'

'Very lucky,' breathed Matthew.

Mariana got up then to clear away the meal, and as usual Matthew offered to help. But — as usual — Mariana laughingly refused. 'You are still — how do you say? — *convaleciente*,' she told him, in smiling reproof, and went off carrying a pile of dishes.

Matthew sighed with frustration. 'No one lets me do anything round here.'

'What's the matter?' smiled Martin, lazily stretching out his long legs under the table, and reaching for the coffee pot. He also reached for the bottle of tequila and poured a generous tot for himself and one for Morris. 'Can't you sit in the sun and dream, like the rest of Mexico?'

Morris laughed and picked up his drink. But Matthew answered rather jerkily: 'I owe you all such a lot — and I hate being idle.' He looked at Martin Davison with a kind of desperate challenge. 'There must be *something* I could do.'

Martin could see the boy was troubled about something, and he responded with careless ease. 'I suppose you could sweep out my studio. By all accounts you are good with a broom.'

Mariana, who had returned for more plates, was scandalized. 'But you never let me touch it!'

Martin reached up a lazy hand and tugged gently at the lustrous black fall of her hair. 'You are too efficient, my darling. You would sweep everything away, including me! As for Matthew, I will give him strict instructions to leave well alone — and he will obey me, which you would not!'

He got up then, laughing, and laid a caressing finger on Mariana's pouting mouth, before leading the way to his studio. Matthew followed, and so did Morris without being asked.

The studio was at one end of a long, low outbuilding which stood at right angles to the house. It was painted white, and its new tall windows looked out at the blue Pacific beyond the dusty brown slope of beaten earth that called itself a street. Martin had also let a big skylight into the roof, and the whole area seemed to swim in light, awash with sungilded, vibrant colour. There were canvases all round the walls, stacked in heaps on the floor, hanging from nails, propped up against cans of paint and varnish, drying in corners, lying abandoned one on top of another. Brushes stood soaking in tins of turpentine, or lay forgotten on tables and chairs. There was a sturdy workbench at one end, with a pile of woodshavings all round it, for Martin made his own frames when he bothered to frame things at all. Also, his boat-building business, which really took place on the beach or in the little boatyard further down the shore, seemed to spill over into the studio as well, and there were

287

shaped planks and bits of unused deck–cladding stacked among the general clutter.

But it was the riot of colour from the paintings that held Matthew spellbound. Great sunbursts of red and orange, spirals of singing yellows, fierce blues and startling greens exploded round the walls. White houses in sunlight and sharp shadow, cloudless, burning skies, stark manlike cactus plants and blue, blue seas shouted at him from every side. They were mostly Mexican scenes — street markets, a man with his laden *burro* crossing a dried-up *arroyo*, a small boy herding goats on a stony hillside, an even smaller girl bathing a baby in a painted tin tub, an old man, seamed and toothless, smiling into the sun at a café table, a group of fishermen hauling in nets, or cutting up shark meat, or tossing their catch of lobsters into baskets on the quayside, and bright-skirted women haggling over the new-caught fish. And the sea — everywhere, the sea in all its moods from storm-dark to guileless Pacific calm, with the little boats of the Mexican fishermen afloat on its endlessly changing surface.

'Oh!' breathed Matthew, enchanted. 'Aren't they smashing!'

'Beautiful,' agreed Morris, behind him.

Martin laughed, but he was clearly pleased.

'But what are they all doing here?' pursued Matthew, sounding indignant and awestruck both at once. 'Buried in dust! They ought to be seen. Can't you have an exhibition?'

'Where?' said Martin baldly. And then, as if softening it, he added: 'I do sell quite a few. On market stalls and places like San Ignacio where the tourists go.'

'Is that enough for you?' Matthew turned round to look at him in outraged protest. 'Don't you want — recognition?'

Martin shrugged. 'Not much. I had some of that in the States. Private views and inane chitchat. My dear, how deeply moving. How truly magnificent. How primitive. How true.' He waved a careless hand at his exuberant paintings. 'I paint what I like — when I like — and make enough to live on. What more do I want?'

The other two were silent in the face of this simple philosophy, but Matthew was still a little shocked that all this richness and brilliance should remain unseen.

'Like your guitar,' said Morris suddenly.

Matthew looked startled. 'What?'

'When I heard you playing in that downtown café, I felt the same.'

'Same as what?' growled Martin, mystified.

288

'All that talent going to waste.' Morris spelt it out for him. 'When it could stir the hearts of men.'

Martin was looking from Morris to Matthew with startled attention. 'He can play like that?'

'Like that,' stated Morris, waving an expressive hand at the glowing canvases. 'With passion.'

'This I must hear,' said Martin, and seemed about to rush out of the studio forthwith.

'But you wanted me to tidy up in here,' protested Matthew. It somehow seemed to him to be the right order. It was a sequence he was used to, after all, and it reminded him of Mosky and his abrasive kindness. Serve the customers, sweep the floors, and then sit down to play . . .

'Oh, very well,' grumbled Martin. 'Have it your own way. Don't touch those. You can re-stack those. Leave the easels on pain of death.' He glanced at Matthew with cheerful arrogance. 'And when you've done that,' he added over his shoulder, 'you can come and stir the hearts of men.'

'All right,' agreed Matthew meekly. 'I will.'

★ ★ ★

It was while he was re-stacking a pile of old canvases against the wall that he came across the two small paintings. The colours were so different from the shouting reds and yellows and hot blue skies of Mexico that they caught his eye, and he paused to have a closer look. Cool green sward on top of grey-brown granite cliffs, pale washed sand and black lumps of rock, and beyond them a dark, dark sea . . . He caught his breath in wonder, for he knew that sea — those rocks at the end of the curving stretch of flawless sand . . . That was where he used to dive into the deep Atlantic swell and swim out to meet the blue-black shadow of a dolphin who came joyously to meet him . . .

Yes, he confirmed to himself, turning the little painting towards the light, it was Porthgwillick all right. There was the shallow cliff sloping down to the rocks at the far end, and there was even a hint of Skip's clubhouse roof set among the tangled gorse and seagrass beyond the point . . . There was the little row of fishermen's cottages above the ancient harbour wall next to the old lifeboat station with its broken ramp, and at the other end of the single village street the shabby, salt-stained walls of the old hotel. Somewhere between those two points was the

289

bench where the old Captain used to sit in the sun and watch the sea. But there was no dark-coated figure set there among those sun-washed spaces. There was a small figure further away, though — far out along the pale, smooth sands. Lovingly and delicately sketched in with almost transparent brush-strokes, so that it seemed to shimmer like a mirage — the figure of a girl dancing alone on the shore. A nimbus of blonde hair tossing in sunlight, two arms outflung in careless grace, a slender pliant back and white feet poised in a leap of joyous abandon . . . It reminded him of Flite, somehow — there was so much joy in that leaping, dancing figure — and he was ashamed to find tears in his eyes.

'Oh, you found those,' said Martin's voice behind him. 'I'd forgotten they were there.'

Matthew looked up, startled, and saw that the harsh lines of Martin's face seemed to have softened into an expression of extraordinary tenderness — a wash of radiant memory lightening his sombre mood and bringing a curious sheen to his eyes that was suspiciously like tears.

That makes two of us, thought Matthew, and yes, that man Morris is right about stirring hearts.

'That's how I first saw her,' murmured Martin in a slow voice of dream. 'Dancing all by herself on the sands . . . ' He paused, and then laughed a little. 'Escaping, she called it.'

'What from?'

'Oh — her father, and the shackles of wealth, I suppose . . . She was always a bit of a rebel, my Klytie.' His voice was still gentle and indulgent — only faintly saddened with regret. Clearly, the remembrance of things past conjured up by these small paintings were more filled with happiness than sorrow . . . Matthew was glad about that. It made what he wanted to do much easier.

He sighed, looking down at the little paintings with a loving recognition that almost matched Martin's. 'I wish I could afford to buy one.'

Martin withdrew from his dream. 'Buy one? But you're going back there — aren't you?'

Am I? thought Matthew. With no Flite there to greet me? Do I dare? But aloud he said carelessly: 'Oh, it's not for me. I wanted to give one of them to the old Captain.'

There was a long, taut silence. Then Martin spoke in a quite different voice: 'No. Out of the question.'

'Why?' Matthew knew he was issuing a challenge, and in any

case it was none of his business. But there was Petra to think of, and he had to try.

'You know why,' growled Martin, and turned away sharply from the little paintings that had so enchanted him.

'It would be a — a kind of —'

'Peace-offering? No!' He was already striding out of the studio.

'A kind of *end*, I was going to say.'

Martin paused in his stride, arrested. 'End?'

'Isn't it time?' Matthew looked down at the lightly-sketched-in ecstatic figure dancing away across the sea-swept sands. 'She looks so happy,' he murmured, not to anyone in particular.

'She was,' said Martin starkly. He did not turn round, but Matthew could tell from the set of his shoulders that his immediate anger was cooling. 'Come on,' he said at last, with rough kindness returning. 'Your turn for heart-stirring, remember?' And he left his newly swept and garnished studio — and all its disturbing memories — without a backward glance.

Obediently, Matthew followed him and went to fetch his guitar. He reflected that in one of the little paintings, the girl was dancing away from the viewer, still untouched by any pull of emotion save joy. But in the second one, she had been running towards the painter, her face alight with love . . . Which one, he wondered, would be most likely to melt the old Captain's stubborn heart?

But then there was no more time to worry about the Captain or anyone else, for music took him away to another place. He was still playing — having reached the beguiling voice of melancholy Granados — when Skip and Petra returned. For a moment he did not look up, his fingers occupied with rounding off a phrase, but when he did, he could see by Skip's face that there was something wrong.

'What is it?' he said quickly. 'Couldn't you get through?'

'Oh yes, we got through all right.' Skip's voice was curiously hesitant. 'It's the Captain. He's had another heart attack.'

'Is he —?'

'Hanging on, they say. And asking about you.' Skip was regarding him with some urgency, his blue eyes dark with concern. 'They think we ought to come home at once.'

'Of course.' Matthew laid down his guitar and got to his feet as if they were going to leave that minute. He looked at Petra then, and she responded at once as he hoped she would.

'I'm coming too.' She turned to her father and added simply: 'I'm sorry, Pa. I've made up my mind.'

Martin shrugged. 'You must do what you think best.' He turned away then, as if distancing himself from the whole situation, and Matthew felt Petra's disappointment that even in this final crisis he would not relent.

But here Morris stepped in briskly and reduced the tension. 'If you will allow me, I can probably get you all on an early flight.'

Matthew turned to him, half-laughing. 'Are you that keen to get rid of me?'

Morris pretended to be deeply offended. 'Matthew!' But then he went on lightly enough, but with an underlying seriousness which Matthew somehow knew to be genuine. 'You may not believe it, but my concern all along has been for your welfare.'

Matthew was instantly contrite. 'I do believe it.'

'Good.' Morris smiled at him briefly, and then became practical. 'Now we must make plans.'

★ ★ ★

They finally got off in a flurry of Viscaino dust, all crammed into Morris's borrowed Land-Rover. At the last moment, Martin became co-operative and offered to deal with Petra's jeep. He also thrust a small package into Matthew's hands. 'Here,' he said gruffly. 'Better have this — if it's not too late.'

Matthew did not need to open it to know it was one of the small paintings of Porthgwillick. (But which one, he wondered?) He smiled at Martin and murmured 'Thanks', but did not try to say any more.

Then Mariana flung her arms round his neck and cried '*Vaya con Dios*' to them all, and they were away.

'Sorry about the bumps,' said Morris, driving as fast as he dared on the dirt road towards the local airstrip. 'It'll get worse before it gets better.'

PART V

SUNSET?

In San Diego they had a couple of hours before their main flight home, and Matthew insisted on making three hasty visits. Since Skip, mindful of the Captain's commission, refused to let Matthew out of his sight, and Petra seemed to feel the same about Skip, they all three went in a taxi and squandered some more of the Captain's money. Skip approved of tidying things up with Della Grant — it seemed to him only right and proper — but the other two stop-overs mystified him.

'Why, Matt?' he asked, as the taxi wove its way through the traffic towards Tracey's apartment block.

'I owe them money.'

'Not a lot, is it? They probably don't expect to get it back.' He looked at Matthew's obstinate face and sighed. 'Anyway, we could send it on.'

'No,' growled Matthew. 'My mother owed money all over the place.' He gave a bleak, explanatory shrug. 'I never knew who I dared talk to —'

'So you talked to no one,' stated Petra, who was beginning to understand Matthew.

'That's about it.'

Skip was about to protest again, but the taxi arrived outside Tracey's tall, shabby apartment building. All three of them climbed the stairs and stood outside Tracey's door while Matthew rang the bell.

After a pause, footsteps came near and a tousled Tracey put her head round the door. 'Yeah?' Then she saw Matthew and her face lit up. 'Matt! You made it. Come on in.'

'No,' said Matthew, smiling. 'No time. Sorry. I brought back your sleeping bag, and the rest of your money.'

She looked incredulous. 'You *what*?' Then, unexpectedly, she came forward and hugged him. 'You're nuts, you know that?'

He laughed, returning the hug with enthusiasm. 'How's Mitch?'

'OK.' Mitch's voice spoke behind Tracey. 'We're both fine.'

He stood there, looking big and handsome and protective, but his smile was entirely friendly.

'That's good news.' Matthew smiled back, noting that he and Tracey looked almost as absurdly happy as Skip and Petra.

Skip and Petra. Hastily, he introduced them and explained why they were in such a hurry. 'Thanks for everything, Trace,' he added, thrusting some crumpled dollar bills into her hand. 'It was a great trip. Especially the whales.'

'They were great, all right,' agreed Tracey.

'Best thing that ever happened to me,' he stated firmly. (Except Flite, of course.)

'Was it?' Her smile was decidedly impish. 'Now he tells me!' But she moved back into the doorway and Mitch's encircling arm as she spoke. 'You take care now, Matt, you hear me? And don't get picked up by any more lonely women.'

Matthew grinned. But his mind seemed to give a small jolt of recognition. Lonely? He supposed she had been — before Mitch came back. And Della? Yes, she was lonely too — in spite of the breezy bonhomie of her husband, Des . . . He shuddered a little, dreading the next painful interview. But maybe Tracey's words had made him a shade less reluctant to face it.

'Write me sometime,' Tracey was adding, her smile somewhat sadder now.

'I will,' promised Matthew, and plunged rather recklessly down the stairs.

Behind him, Skip said softly to Tracey before she closed the door: 'Thanks for looking after him,' and did not wait for any reply.

Matthew knew Della wouldn't be at home in the daytime, so he took Skip and Petra downtown to the boutique where she worked, and begged them not to leave him alone with her for a single moment. It was going to be difficult enough anyway.

When she saw Matthew, she dropped the elegant black silk dress she was holding and burst into tears. Then she flung her arms round his neck, still sobbing wildly — much to the amazement of the customers in her shop.

'You're safe!' she cried.

'No thanks to you,' growled Skip, not too inaudibly, and sounding surprisingly angry and surprisingly out of character.

Matthew saw Della wince a little, and then rally and fix Skip with a bright, ridiculously roguish eye. 'And you are —?'

'Skip. David Alexander to you. Captain St George sent me to bring Matthew home.'

'Oh.'

There was not much more to say after that, but Matthew had rehearsed a polite speech, and now he made use of it to cover the awkward silence. He found himself oddly sorry for Della, who was, after all, only affectionate and lonely, floundering in a sea of nostalgia from which she could not extricate herself.

'I have to go home, Aunt Della,' he said, consciously using the hated word 'aunt' and watching her wince again slightly as he spoke. 'The Captain is ill, you see.' He paused, and then added more gently: 'But thanks for everything you've done for me.' (He was a bit reluctant about that statement, since what she had mostly done for him was ruin the last vestige of innocence about family ties — the last small fragment of adolescent illusion about his long-dead father, the last hope of ever being wanted for himself alone.) 'Maybe I'll be able to come back and see you — sometime,' he went on, and saw the certain knowledge that he never would come back become clear in her frightened eyes. 'I'm sorry,' he said suddenly, and went forward and hugged her, unable to bear the reproach in that stricken face.

Skip took over then, and bundled them off with the crisp apology: 'Plane to catch. Not much time.'

So then it was Mosky's turn, and this Matthew did not dread at all, even though he'd had to scrape up the last few dollars and sell his watch (refusing a loan from Skip) to pay back his debt. This time he insisted on walking into the diner alone, and the others stood in a smiling group near the doorway to watch the fun.

Mosky was, as usual, wildly busy and moving from table to table collecting dirty dishes on to an overloaded tray. Matthew went forward and took it from him without a word and carried it out to the kitchens. At first Mosky didn't even notice who it was, but then the light of recognition dawned and a huge smile nearly split his face in two.

'Matt!' he yelled. 'Come back here, you lazy son-of-a-bitch. You've left some cups behind.'

'Coming!' said Matthew, laughing, and ran straight into Mosky's outstretched arms.

The others came forward then and joined in the general rejoicing, and Matthew handed over the borrowed hundred dollars.

'You're crazy,' protested Mosky, scandalized. 'I don't want your crappy dough.'

'Please,' Matthew insisted. 'I can't stay to work it off like I promised.'

'No one wants you to work it off!' Mosky's indignant voice rose in outrage. But then something in Matthew's face seemed to reach him, and he paused in mid-spate. 'OK, OK,' he said, and stuck the dollar bills straight back in the till. 'Square now,' he grinned. 'No obligations. So welcome back!' and he gave Matthew another enormous hug.

Matthew knew then that he understood without being told.

When Skip and Petra were introduced, Mosky insisted on giving them all a cup of coffee, smiling his approval at their care for Matthew, and summing it up in the words: 'Worth it. Magic in those fingers.' He glared happily at Matthew. 'You keep it up, you hear?'

'I hear,' agreed Matthew, smiling.

'You still got that book? Joy as it flies?'

Matthew nodded.

'Not only dolphins, kid. Fingers have it, too.'

Matthew spread out his hands and looked at them reflectively. Joy? Did they? But not the wild, ecstatic leap of the heart that Flite brought to him . . . *Stir the hearts of men* came Morris's dry voice into his mind. Could I? wondered Matthew. Could I be like Flite? Me? A grounded, clumsy, two-legged dolphin? Struggling to reach the heights? . . . He looked up and found Mosky's bright, shrewd gaze fixed on him.

'Well?' The challenge was unmistakable.

'I — I'll try,' said Matthew humbly, and looked down again at his hands, finding his eyes unaccountably misted with tears. But then, suddenly, he remembered those other dolphins crying in the awful, suffocating nets of the deep sea trawlers, and he said unexpectedly: 'But it isn't joy or sunrise for them — not any more. More like sunset, really . . . '

They all looked at him in silence. Perhaps Petra was the one who understood him best, but Mosky shook his head and murmured obstinately: 'No. It's still there.'

'Come on,' urged Skip. 'We'll miss that plane,' and laid a friendly hand on Matthew's arm.

He got up to go then, and Mosky stood beside him with an

arm round his shoulders for a moment in a brief extra hug. 'So long then, kid. Keep flying!' he said, and rushed away to look after his customers, so that he did not have to watch Matthew go.

'Keep flying,' muttered Skip, trying to lighten the situation with a despairing grin. 'How right he is.'

★　★　★

They got back to Heathrow in a cold grey drizzle, whipped into their faces by a blustery March wind. After the warmth and colour of Mexico, England had never seemed more drab or less inviting.

But there was nothing uninviting about the welcome that met them on arrival. Madge and the entire family were there to greet them, and Jampy was jumping up and down and shouting: 'There he is! That's my Matt. Why were you so long, why were you?'

Even Jim was there, steady and rocklike amid the confusion, and explaining gravely to Skip that the Captain had insisted on them meeting Matthew, and had even arranged to pay them for the lost day's work.

'How is the Captain?' asked Matthew urgently, trying to contain with one hand Jampy's excited leaps and jigs of joy.

'Holding on,' said Madge, dutifully quoting the bulletin at the private clinic. 'Wants to see you tomorrow morning.'

'Not tonight?'

'No. Too late. He'll be asleep.'

'But if —?' Matthew did not dare put it into words.

'Tomorrow,' said Madge firmly. 'You're staying with us tonight. Captain's orders. Isn't that right, Jim?'

Jim nodded slowly. 'Bullies everyone. Best do as he says.' A faint glimmer of a smile touched his mouth.

'Come on,' urged Jampy, tugging at Matthew's hand. 'Come on. I gotta tanker lorry, an' I made a Lego bridge.'

'All right,' smiled Matthew. 'Give us a chance.' He fished in his rucksack and produced a small rolled-up sombrero decorated with vivid red braid. 'Here,' he said, clamping it on Jampy's head. 'Try this for size, and dry up.'

The whole party moved off then, though Jampy still didn't know how to dry up. Skip and Petra decided to stay the night in a nearby hotel. It had been agreed between them that Matthew (somewhat reluctantly) should prepare the way for Petra by showing the Captain her father's picture and telling him the whole story — that is, if he would listen. He might, of course, refuse to hear any of it. But if he did listen, and was willing to see Petra, then she would come over with Skip to meet him. It sounded a reasonable enough scheme, but Matthew was very doubtful of its success.

★ ★ ★

He arrived at the private clinic the next morning to find the place in an uproar. The Captain's sleek grey Rolls stood at the door. The Captain's chauffeur, Mackie, stood in the foyer, looking uncomfortable while an irate doctor harangued him about it being 'impossible'. Nurses rushed in and out of the Captain's room, looking harassed and disapproving, and from inside came the sound of the Captain's voice raised in anger, and another, less forthright voice arguing back.

Matthew's heart sank. He knew that voice. It was the awful Conrad, once again trying to persuade the Captain to do something he did not like. And it was clearly not the time or the place to cross the Captain and get him all worked up.

As he hesitated, wondering what to do, the Ward Sister caught sight of him and came across to say crisply: 'Are you Matthew? For God's sake see if you can talk some sense into him — and get rid of that nephew of his before he does any more harm.'

'Can't you?' asked Matthew, but he saw her despairing expression and allowed himself to be propelled with great speed into the Captain's small, white room. There, Matthew found the old Captain sitting up in a chair in his dressing gown, looking frail, belligerent and at bay. Beside him, almost leaning over him in a slightly threatening attitude, stood Conrad, red-faced and bellicose.

'It's madness,' he was saying — almost shouting. 'You can't go off on a silly jaunt when you're too ill to stand! Not without making proper arrangements.'

'I *have* made proper arrangements,' barked the Captain. 'There is a perfectly good board of trustees. The firm's interests are all taken care of.'

'But you haven't appointed a successor.'

'You mean, I haven't appointed *you* as my successor.' The Captain's old eyes snapped fire. 'There is safety in numbers, Conrad. You have your place on the board, like everyone else.'

'But —'

'Excuse me,' said Matthew, trying to sound as crisp and formidable as the Ward Sister behind him. 'I think you are tiring the Captain.'

'Visiting has to be strictly limited,' added the Sister, sounding equally determined. '*Very* strictly.'

'Is your car downstairs?' asked Matthew sweetly, taking Conrad by the arm and leading him swiftly away. 'You wouldn't want to cause another heart attack, would you?' (It was just like last time, in Cornwall. But he was tougher these days.)

'Of course not,' spluttered Conrad, outraged at the thought, though it had occurred to him that it might be easier to sway the board if the old Captain was no longer with them.

'Come back later,' suggested Matthew. 'When he's rested.' He stood there, four-square and uncompromising, and watched Conrad go away down the stairs.

When he returned to the small white room, the Captain looked up at him out of faded, angry eyes and growled: 'You led us a pretty dance.'

'Sorry,' said Matthew coming to stand beside him. 'I didn't mean to.' Without shyness, he took the old man's transparent hand in his, and added honestly: 'It never occurred to me that anyone would worry where I was.'

The Captain snorted. 'Never did have much opinion of your own worth, stupid boy.'

Matthew laughed. 'Anyway, I thought you were supposed to be at death's door.'

'Shall be if I stay in this place any longer!' He snorted again. 'And if that scheming bastard, Conrad, gets in here again.' Another young nurse came in, looking frightened, and he instantly barked at her: 'I thought I told you to bring me my clothes.'

She glanced despairingly at Matthew, murmured: 'Just a minute,' and hurried out again.

'What are you trying to do?' asked Matthew, finding himself still holding the old man's hand which was clutching him rather hard.

'Get out of here,' the Captain snarled.

'Where to?'

'Porthgwillick, where else?'

Matthew was startled. 'But — Skip's waiting to see you.'

'See me down there. Going home, isn't he?'

'Ye-es.' Matthew failed to put all his doubts and tangled requests into words.

'Well, so am I.'

There was a moment's silence while Matthew thought furiously. It figured, he told himself. Of course the Captain would want to go back to Porthgwillick . . . But how did that fit in with him seeing Petra?

'If I'm going to die,' rasped the obstinate old voice, 'I'll die where I like!'

Matthew nodded slowly. Then he took a calculated risk. 'In that case,' he said, 'it's hardly worth me giving you this.' And he unwrapped the small painting of Porthgwillick and held it out for the Captain to see.

There was a long, tense pause, during which Matthew wondered desperately whether the revelation would kill the old man.

'*Where did you get this?*' The sharp voice was curiously muted and softened.

'It's a long story —' began Matthew.

'So it *was* that Davison,' murmured the Captain, more to himself than to Matthew. 'I thought as much.' He seemed to ponder for a moment, still in that strange mood of unexpected gentleness. Then he peered more closely at the painting through misted eyes.

'She's there,' said Matthew, thinking with terror of the long journey to Cornwall and the risks it would involve for the old man. 'Your daughter, Klytie. Dancing alone on the sand . . . ' He put out a finger to trace the small, ecstatic figure poised against the pale, empty shore. 'Shall I tell you about it?' (At least it would delay things.)

'No,' said the Captain.

Matthew's hopes fell. It was no use after all. He wasn't going to listen.

'Come with me.' It was a plea, not an order.

'What?'

'In the car. Tell me on the way.' The old eyes looked into Matthew's with sudden urgency. 'Not much time,' he added, stating bleak truth without self-pity.

Matthew capitulated. 'All right.' He was still thinking furiously. 'But I must phone Skip first.'

The old man nodded. 'Get Mackie up here. I want to get dressed.'

302

Matthew made one last attempt. 'Are you sure you're up to it?'

'No,' growled the Captain. 'Not sure of anything. But I'm going.' He looked up at Matthew again, and a dim echo of his old, impish grin touched his face. 'Escape,' he said. 'Understand?'

Matthew understood.

★ ★ ★

During the long car drive down to Cornwall, the old man's heart gave him two small scares and he had to use his angina spray. But he insisted on continuing the journey, and insisted on Matthew continuing his story.

Bit by bit, Matthew told him all of it — his own discovery about Della's motives for offering him a home, his flight to Baja California with Tracey, and his meeting with Martin Davison. He told him about the studio full of vivid paintings, and Martin's unwillingness to sell them or display them, and he went on to tell him everything that Martin had said about the past, not leaving out the gentleness of his voice when he spoke of his young wife, Klytie, dancing on the sands.

He did not try to make any judgement on the story as he told it — his role was simply that of the neutral narrator, he knew. So he did not allow reproach to creep into his voice, even when he spoke of the many letters written, and the desperate final attempt at reconciliation when Klytie was dying. But there was a vital question to be asked here, and for Petra's sake he knew he must ask it. And besides, he loved the old Captain, and he could not believe in such unforgiving harshness.

'Why didn't you answer?' he said, turning to look into the tired blue eyes beside him.

The old man sighed and shook his head. 'Never got the letters. My own fault.'

'Why?'

'Gave orders. In the heat of the moment when I was still angry. Told my staff not to forward anything. No communication whatsoever. They obeyed me.' He sighed again, and rubbed a shaky hand over his eyes, as if to ward off his own reproach. 'Never rescinded the order — forgot I'd made it, really. In the endless ruckus of big business, got bogged down.' His voice was shaky too, now, and Matthew looked at him anxiously. 'But I did wonder — convinced myself *they* were the ones who wouldn't communicate.' He shrugged helplessly. 'How stupid can you get?'

And proud, thought Matthew. Stupid and proud. And probably ashamed to write and say: 'Where are you?' . . . His heart ached for all those years of empty silence. 'Will you see her?' he asked, abruptly coming to essentials.

'Of course,' sighed the Captain. 'Of course I will.'

Matthew glanced at him again, trying to assess his exhaustion. There was one more thing to be said, and it was important. 'Before you do,' he began, and this time he sounded shy and awkward again, 'Petra wanted me to tell you something.'

'Yes?'

'She doesn't want your money.'

'What?'

'She has her own career. She's independent. It's you she wants — her grandfather — not the St George empire.'

He watched the Captain's face as he spoke, afraid to see disappointment and shock make it even paler. But to his surprise, the Captain laughed.

'Another of 'em!' he said, the spark of mischief back in his weary eyes. 'Takes after her mother.'

There was silence in the quiet limousine as they purred on through the tors and cloud shadows of Bodmin moor. Matthew thought he'd better leave it there, and anyway, the Captain needed to rest. That paper-thin, transparent face looked even more fragile now.

'What about you?' the Captain shot at him suddenly.

'Me?' Matthew was bewildered.

'Do you want it?'

'Want what?'

'Bless the boy, he's thick as a plank! My money, Matthew. The St George empire. Do you want it?'

Matthew was not shocked. He had known this was coming. And he hated to disappoint the old man yet again. But he had to — even though he knew it was an enormous honour and a whole powerful future laid before him, something he had no right to expect let alone turn down in so ungrateful a manner. But he had to. He turned his head again, and looked at his old friend out of honest, troubled eyes.

'No,' he said gently.

The Captain did not seem surprised. He grunted: 'Thought as much!' and the old gleam of humour was back in his glance.

304

'What *do* you want?' he asked, the quirky eyebrows raised in half-mocking interest.

Matthew drew in a slow breath of resolve, and tried to set out his plans in coherent form. 'I want to be a marine biologist — like Petra. That means going back for A-levels. And getting into university. And specializing after that.'

'How do you propose to live — and where?'

'I'll get a grant — and I can have a room with Madge.' He looked seriously at the Captain, and added, with sudden reckless daring: 'I thought — if you'd stake me a little, I could work for you in the vacations.'

'Free?'

'Of course.'

'Done!' The Captain's smile was positively alight with mischief now.

Matthew wondered vaguely why the old man was so amused and did not seem to be annoyed at being turned down. In fact, he almost seemed to be pleased with him.

'Mackie!' commanded the Captain. 'Stop here a moment. This calls for a drink.'

The kindly face of Mackie, the chauffeur, turned round, looking concerned. 'Are you sure, sir?'

'Sure I'm sure,' grinned the Captain, and watched cheerfully while a small panel was opened in the car, revealing a neat array of drinks and glasses in a tiny bar. 'Champagne,' he demanded. 'Is there any? With a dash of brandy. Good for heart trouble.' His grin grew wider. And when the brimming glass was in his hand, he winked at Matthew and said: 'Warm and all shook up, but it'll do. What did you say about your dolphins? Today, today?'

Matthew nodded dumbly, and lifted his own glass to match that flawless courage. The old eyes and the young ones met in perfect understanding. Then they spoke in unison.

'Today, today!' they said.

★   ★   ★

When Petra came the next morning, she found the old Captain upright in his chair by the window, blue blazer brushed and neat with brass buttons shining, hair also brushed and neat but still rather bristly — and those faded blue eyes alert and watchful.

He looked at her in silence for a while, taking in the smooth, gilded cap of hair and the tawny gold-brown eyes, and not missing the proud, faintly challenging set of her head on its slender neck.

'You are very like your mother,' he said at last.

'So they tell me.' Petra smiled at him a little shyly, not sure if this was praise or blame.

'And do you dance on the sand, too?'

To his surprise, she blushed a deep, betraying scarlet, and murmured: 'It has been known to happen!'

He continued to gaze at her, and then spoke with crisp asperity: 'You are a marine biologist, they tell me. In what field?'

'Sea mammals. Cetaceans, mostly.'

His eyes were suddenly piercing. 'And what do they tell you?'

She looked at him very straight. 'That family life is important.'

A flicker of surprise crossed his face, and he was silent again for a few seconds. Then he jerked out abruptly: 'What do you want of me?'

Petra came forward, instinctive warmth making her reach out to take his frail, dry hand in hers. 'Only you, grandfather. Didn't Matthew tell you?'

The old man nodded, and did not withdraw his hand. '*Family life?*' he repeated, trying out the phrase as if it were strange to him.

'Something young Matthew has never really had,' she reminded him.

'He doesn't want my money, either,' he grumbled, sounding a little aggrieved.

Petra laughed. 'Independent, that boy is.'

'What's to become of him?' There was real anxiety in the old voice.

'He'll be all right,' Petra told him. 'He's a survivor.'

'He'll need to be,' barked the Captain grimly, 'in this cut-throat world.'

'He's got it all worked out.' She flashed an encouraging grin at him. 'And he wants to work for your company in between.' Just like the son you never had, she thought. But she did not say it. 'And you know very well we'll keep an eye on him.'

'We?'

'Skip and I.' The blush was back, but fainter this time.

The old Captain looked at her sharply. 'Like that, is it?'

Her smile was so radiant and full of certainty that he blinked. 'He's waiting outside,' she added. 'We'd — er — kind of like your blessing.'

The Captain snorted. 'I don't know anything about blessings.' But then he paused and thought: Yes, I do. That boy's a blessing. And so is this golden girl who looks so like my Klytie . . . I must be getting soft.

'What shall I do with my money, then?' he shot at her. 'Give it away?'

'Why not?'

He seemed to consider, but in truth he had already made up his mind what to do. 'How about a Marine Biology Research Centre?' he asked, casually tossing it to her over his shoulder.

'Where?'

'Anywhere you like.' He hesitated, and then went on more tentatively: 'Maybe, one day, Matthew could work there, too? And save those beleagured dolphins of his.'

It was on the tip of her tongue to say: it will take more than one research centre to save them! But of course, every step in the right direction helped. It would certainly give people a chance to do more . . . And she was most ungrateful not to be wildly enthusiastic about the plan. But then, she had had so many setbacks and disappointments, and she knew how hard it was to convince an uncaring world that the creatures she cared for had as much right to exist as they had . . . She was just stumbling into belated thanks when he interrupted her briskly.

'Fix it with John Harvey. I've given instructions. Might as well do something useful with my money.' An impish grin crossed his face. 'And it'll keep it out of Conrad's hands!' He looked into his grand-daughter's face and added, with an even more wicked grin: 'Deathbed scenes leave me cold.'

He began to laugh then, and Petra joined in. Then Skip, who was waiting patiently and in some trepidation outside, heard their laughter and put his head round the door. 'Can I share the joke?' He was relieved to see that the old man was not angry or overwrought. In fact he seemed to be enjoying himself.

'Skip, my boy,' he commanded. 'I want you to fix one of your music nights.'

Skip looked astounded. 'What, now?'

'Now. And get that boy to play, if he will.'

Skip nodded. 'Oh, he'll play all right.' He looked at the old Captain affectionately. 'Especially if you are coming.'

The Captain smiled. 'Whether I come or not,' he barked. 'The boy needs encouraging.' And when he saw the hesitation in Skip's eyes, he added sharply: 'That's an order, mind.'

'Ay, ay, Captain,' said Skip, saluting smartly with one brown hand.

The old man looked out at the bay, seeing a figure alone on the pale, tide-washed sands . . . It might have been his young daughter, Klytie, down there — or even his wife who had also had her dancing days on that golden shore . . . But when he shook off the tears of a foolish old man, he saw that it was only Matthew, standing below his window and looking up.

He lifted a hand in greeting, and Matthew waved back and smiled.

'As for "Joy as it flies",' he growled, to no one in particular, 'I've had my moments, too.'

★   ★   ★

Skip had his music night. The various local groups he knew, hastily summoned, descended on the clubhouse with mikes and strobe lights and earsplitting amplifiers. The pop groups and rock groups and folk groups from near and far did their utmost to outclass each other, and even the small jazz group that Matthew had liked before showed up and insisted on bringing Matthew and his guitar into the fun. Vocalists wailed and wiggled, trombones moaned, and drumkits fizzed with frenetic activity. And in between the items, Matthew played quietly by himself and everyone listened. He played everything he knew, both sorrowful and joyous. But the Captain did not come.

'Maybe if we play loud enough, he'll hear us at the hotel,' said one helpfully.

Skip cast him a baleful look. 'I should think he'd hear you at the Pearly Gates,' he snapped, and then fell silent, realizing what he had said.

Matthew intervened then. 'Let's sing,' he suggested. 'The old yelling songs. He liked those.'

He struck a chord or two, and soon the room was filled with the sound of young voices following familiar patterns, until they reached the 'Rio Grande' again.

'Then away, boys, away —' they sang, and Matthew knew they were singing the old man home, and found himself scarcely able to see the strings of his own guitar.

In the general noise, he did not hear the phone ring in Skip's office, or notice Skip slip away to answer it. But when he came back and stood looking across at Petra, Matthew knew.

His fingers faltered for a moment, but then they went on as strongly as before. Sing him home, he thought. Sing with all your might. Oh good old man, we'll make it as loud as we can. As proud as we can.

'So fare you well, my pretty young girl —' (and Matthew glanced up at Petra then, and smiled) 'For I'm bound for the Rio Grande . . . '

★   ★   ★

Much later, when all the shouting and the tumult had died, Matthew went alone to the far end of the shore and stood on the rocks, looking out at the night-dark sea.

Flite? he said. Are you there, somewhere in this shadowy ocean? The old Captain loved the sea, too — though he didn't know you like I did. Will you see him home?

He did not expect an answer. But as he stood there, suddenly there was a swirl of water close to his feet, and a dark, remembered head raised itself above the surface and looked at him.

'Flite?' he whispered, incredulously. '*Flite*? Is it you?'

The head drew closer, and a long thin tail-fluke beat the water with an answering slap of recognition.

Unbelieving, almost beside himself with joy, Matthew threw off his clothes and plunged into the sea. 'Flite!' he called, breasting the deep Atlantic swell in the blue-black night. 'You came back! You came when I needed you! Oh Flite, you came!' And he flung out his arms to embrace the warm, sinuous flank of the beautiful creature coming to meet him.

Come back? said Flite, curling round him slowly in a delicate curve, and coming up close with his smiling face near to Matthew's. Of course I came back. It's spring, isn't it? The seas are getting warmer. Time for rejoicing. Today!

But something about that slow, curving turn troubled Matthew, and he swam closer to have another look. The movement seemed heavy, somehow, and unlike the effortless glides and swoops he used to know. The dolphin turned again as he came near, and he saw with horror that it had suffered terrible injuries. One of its pectoral fins had been almost torn off, and hung useless in the water, upsetting the perfect balance of that long, slender body. There was a half-healed gash across the pale belly, and a thin line of strangling net-cord entangled in

309

its dorsal fin and round its neck. The crippled dolphin could still swim, but its movements were slow and somehow weighed down with pain.

'Oh!' cried Matthew, clasping the slim body in his arms for a moment. 'What have they done to you?' For it was clear that Flite had blundered into a net or some other horrific manmade means of destruction.

Flite did not seem entirely defeated, though. In spite of his injuries, he still gamely tried to play with Matthew. I can still dive, he said. And even fly, if I try. There is still joy in the sea. Watch me fly!

He lifted himself out of the water in the old, joyous way, but he came down with a dull, heavy splash instead of his usual running dive.

Matthew watched for a moment, riven by the dolphin's attempts at gaiety, and then turned wildly for the shore and his clothes. There was a penknife in his pocket. At least he could cut that wretched piece of netting away from that vulnerable throat. He collected the knife and swam back, waiting for Flite to circle round him once more. The dolphin seemed to know that he was trying to help, and submitted quite docilely while Matthew sawed away at the tangled netting embedded in the silvery skin. At last Matthew cut through the final thread and the fine green netting fell away and drifted off on the next wave. Flite gave an extra pirouette in grateful relief, but it was a bit lopsided, and he turned over on to his back and rested quietly in the water beside Matthew, as if to say: I would rejoice if I could. But it's harder nowadays . . .

Matthew's heart ached for him. What could he do? He supposed Petra would say there was nothing to be done, and Flite would just have to take his chance of mending or dying. You could not splint a wild dolphin . . . You just had to let him go.

But the dolphin seemed to sense his sadness and came close again, resting tranquilly in the dark sea-swell beside him, and nudging him gently from time to time with his beak.

'I don't know how to help you,' groaned Matthew, speaking aloud into the breaking waves. He felt like weeping with frustration because there was nothing practical left to do. The dolphin's pain seemed to communicate itself to him, and he rocked with Flite in the lift and fall of the ocean and cried inside. 'But I'm going to try to save all of you,' he said, crooning into Flite's ear. 'One day. Somehow. *I've got to.* Even if I can't save you, I'll save the others.' And he clasped the dolphin again in a sudden rush of love and terror.

But Flite would have none of it. Grief he had met before, and he had heard the voices of his own kind crying for help in the nets. But he did not remember it now. It was not in his nature to be sad. He turned in a lazy circle, with Matthew's arms still around him, and began to tow his friend gently out to sea.

Come on, he said. I am still alive. You are still alive. Life is for living. Now! No time for sadness. I can still rejoice. The sea still holds me. See? I am safe in its arms. So rejoice!

And he turned again, releasing himself from Matthew's embrace, and circled, and sank and rose in the best display he could manage with his broken fin. But he could not quite fly. After the night, the day! he said, whistling and clicking confidingly in Matthew's ear. The sun is coming — today! Beyond the dark is the sunrise! I can feel it coming. I can feel its warmth from the end of my bottle nose to the tip of my tail . . . Never mind the pain — I can still swim . . . There is still joy to catch — if I can fly!

And he wove one final, loving circle round Matthew — lop-sided and slow though he was, he was still a magnificent swimmer — and then headed out to sea towards the pale horizon.

Matthew watched him go, his heart lurching with pity. Pity and misgiving. For that brave, joyous fin cutting through the water was heading westwards towards the sunset, not towards the sunrise at all.

But as Matthew gazed out to sea after him, he became aware that Flite was not alone. There were other dark fins cutting the waves, other heads bobbing, other joyous bodies leaping in the air. A whole school of dolphins had come to meet Flite. They swam towards him, surrounding him in welcoming circles, dancing beside him in plumes of sungilded spray.

We are here! they sang to Flite. We have come to take you home! Dance with us, Flite. The sea is wide, and its gentle arms will heal your pain. Come with us, Flite, and rejoice in being alive. Now! Today! Sunrise or sunset is all one to us, we can still dance!

Matthew saw Flite reach them, and how they all curled round him protectively, even slowing their ecstatic sea-surge to keep pace with him . . . They will help him, he thought. They will care for him, and guard him from further hurt. They will see

311

him through, if he survives at all. Oh Flite, I hope you survive! Try to survive. Life is still sweet. They are trying to tell you so. Please try to survive!

For a long time he stood there, staring out towards the horizon, though his eyes were too misted with tears to see very clearly. Goodbye Flite, he said, and lifted his hand in a last farewell salute. Goodbye, and God speed to you and all your companions. May the wide seas never be empty of you and your kind.

Then he turned and walked away.

NOTE ON DOLPHIN MORTALITY

Since 1959 when 'counting' began, it is estimated that over six million dolphins have died in the tuna-nets. Netting a single school of tuna can kill 1,000 dolphins. The US Marine Protection Act of 1972 tried to enforce quotas and brought numbers down from 78,000 in 1976 to 20,500 in 1981. But it is still too high to avoid 'depletion' of stocks, and hard to enforce. Between 80,000 and 120,000 dolphins a year are killed by international purse-seine fleets, but observers report that mortality leapt from 57,000 in 1985 to 130,000 in 1986. Spotted dolphin and spinner stock are now depleted below optimum sustainable levels of population. Over-fishing of herring and mackerel have also caused bottle-nose dolphin depletion. Driftnets, with 50,000 to 60,000 sets made by these skipjack tuna fisheries (with one marine mammal killed for every ten tuna), has probably brought the mortality rate as high as six figures. In 1989 the UN passed a resolution prohibiting further expansion of drift net fishing. Dolphins are also caught in large numbers and used for bait, and also for food (as a delicacy) in Japan and the Pacific. The increase in demand for the food resources of the oceans will continue. Unless much greater legal protection is given, many dolphin species will not survive.